BOOMERANG

a novel

S. JENNIFER PAULSON

Book cover design by Sky Diary Productions and SJP Media

Content editing by Sky Diary Productions

Proofreading by C.E. McClung

Author photo by Bobby Ampezzan

Cover image: Girl swimming underwater, photo by asysoev (Asset #80765338), licensing purchased from Adobe Stock

First edition, 2024

Hardcover ISBN: 979-8-9901722-0-3

DEDICATION

This book is dedicated to my parents,
Karen and Ron Paulson.

"The greatest glory in living lies not in never falling, but in rising every time we fall."

— Nelson Mandela

A NOTE FROM THE AUTHOR

This novel includes depictions of sexual violence. Please proceed with caution if this is a trigger.

For anyone needing help, I encourage you to contact a national or local sexual assault crisis line or other resources available to assist survivors. RAINN (the Rape, Abuse & Incest National Network) offers resources twenty-four hours a day. Call 1-800-656-HOPE or visit rainn.org.

CHAPTER ONE

Taryn floored it on the Dan Ryan Expressway, the highway's light poles illuminating the neon-orange and white construction horses and cones framing the pothole-stricken pavement before her. Thanks to the late hour, there was barely any traffic to contend with—which was perfect, because Taryn couldn't get home fast enough.

Her thirty-minute trip had given her plenty of time to plot her grand entrance. Taryn could see herself bursting through her front door, her heart still thumping intensely, then running to find Graham to tell him what she'd learned just forty-five minutes ago. That Taryn, his new wife, had just scored the Investigative Reporter of the Year by the Illinois News Association.

But there was no Graham.

A stout, stern-faced police officer was waiting for her on her porch, sitting on the rocking chair closest to the double front door.

Taryn could tell from the man's stern expression, his difficulty bringing his eyes to hers, that her life was about to change.

And not for the better.

***

Less than an hour later, Taryn was whisked into room 703 at Woodlawn Memorial Hospital. It was there that time froze. Taryn listened to the beeps beating into the depths of her eardrums, the machine commanding her husband's chest to slowly rise up and down. They were interspersed with the buzzing of her phone—a slew of colleagues' congratulatory texts were pushing through every twenty minutes or so. Not that Taryn looked at them. She silenced her cell and tucked it into the side of her classic black Coach handbag—Graham's last birthday gift to her.

Taryn could barely recognize the mangled face. Even Graham's knees. Still knobby, protruding and tattooed with scars from a lifetime of exploits, they were torn up, bruised and bloodied. Especially that one deep gouge in his left knee from a lawnmowing accident as a teen that she lovingly called The Hook.

She knew the worst was inevitable from several hours sitting at his bedside, watching the clock tick, the monitors track his pulse.

Officer Anderson, who had met Taryn at her front door, had given her the lowdown in matter-of-fact, cold terminology. Something Taryn was familiar with from being on the media side of a story. But Taryn was not the journalist in this one. She was the collateral damage.

According to the police, Graham had been helmetless, riding his Harley-Davidson from Bottoms Up bar, a mere ten-minute drive from their home. At some point, he veered into the mighty oak tree in the middle of a roundabout. The skid marks confirmed he'd tried to avoid a collision. While the other driver, a female vacationer in a rental SUV, had avoided directly hitting Graham, she ended up careening her vehicle into the retention pond about one hundred feet from the roundabout. The female driver had survived—but police told Taryn the woman had been airlifted to the ICU at Midwest Medical Center. Anderson explained the woman was hanging on by a thread in a medically-induced coma.

Graham, weeks away from celebrating his thirteenth sobriety anniversary, had plowed into that tree with a blood-alcohol level nearly twice the legal limit—point-fifteen percent.

"What?" Taryn had pleaded with the officer. "He's been sober for almost thirteen years. Are you certain?"

Officer Anderson had said, yes, he was quite sure. And the bloodwork drawn at the hospital confirmed it. Graham's sobriety run had ended tragically, based on one bad decision. One bad night.

The doctors at least had a bedside manner. They had tried to explain to Taryn that her husband would never recover. He was brain dead. A shell of what he once was.

And she knew the choice she had to make. It just wasn't one she'd been expecting less than a year into marriage.

Taryn sat there for fifteen minutes, though her body and mind told her it was fifteen hours. Her mind replayed her last night out with Graham. Before this.

"I think it's time," Graham had told her, the first hint of nervousness about the subject evident in his eyes.

Taryn had been mid-slurp with her top shelf margarita, her mind preoccupied with the INA awards announcement, which was expected the next day.

Taryn had been thwarting The Baby Talk for months now, pushing it into the hollows of her brain as she'd seen Graham ogle Kendra and Tom's baby. Taryn sometimes felt like she could barely get her own shit together. How was she supposed to make a life for a baby, be responsible for a helpless little human life form? It was something she wanted someday, but not now.

A family would be later. Taryn had her plan, and Graham had agreed—and understood her stance before they married. But that didn't stop him from feeling her out every few months. He'd test her casually at dinner or during a walk around the neighborhood, just to see if Taryn had started to hear the clicks of her biological clock.

But the response was always the same.

"I'm not ready," Taryn would say. "You know that."

A crestfallen Graham would offer a meek smile, nod and embrace her firmly. She loved that she always felt safe in his arms.

"I know," he said.

But last night, Graham seemed off. There was almost desperation in his voice. *Did Graham really want to be a father now that badly? Why the urgency?*

Taryn thought Graham had been acting out of the norm lately. She had seen his eyes get locked in a gaze at times, as he would silently stand at their back bay window, just looking.

Every time Taryn asked Graham if he was okay, he'd snap to, look her way and say, "Yeah. Just a lot going on at work. My mind's just racing. All is well."

Taryn wasn't convinced. But whatever it was, Graham would tell her when he was ready. She wasn't worried. There were no secrets between the two. Graham was her best friend. At least, her closest confidante since Sam, almost two decades ago.

Taryn was determined. She would prove she was not only a seasoned journalist, but a damn good one. And someone who didn't just write about the community she called home, but fought for it, too. Her INA award was another one for her trophy shelf, which she'd planned to proudly display in her home office. She scored it for her reporting on a Chicago homeless nonprofit that had been using the bulk of their donations, grants and other funding for the CEO's weekend trips to the Caribbean and late nights with the C-suite at strip clubs. And the occasional eight-ball of cocaine. Her digging led to these revelations, and her series of reports led to the eventual ouster of the CEO, then the shuttering of the entire sham nonprofit.

Her work had made a real difference. And it made Taryn's heart swell each and every time.

Taryn's next step in her plan, which she'd crafted into a Vision Board as a constant visual reminder and inspiration, was to get her Master's degree in journalism. She'd snag her dream job as a syndicated columnist at *The Chicago Gazette*.

Now, none of that mattered. Her husband was dying, right before her eyes. He was already dead, she knew. Removing all the tubes and wires was all that was standing between Graham and the brilliant light that was likely beckoning him to the other side right at this moment.

Taryn had called Graham's parents and her sister, Lynn, barely able to choke out the words. Then, she'd frantically called Graham's sobriety sponsor, an older man who simply went by "Scoot," and begged him to come to them.

"Please," she said. "Help me. Help him. Help *us*."

Graham was her love. The man she'd married on that crisp autumn day last year at St. Francis' Catholic Church in Hampton Park, the golden and maroon leaves crackling under each step of her Jimmy Choo pumps.

Taryn had never felt more connected to another human being in her life as she did Graham that day.

Now, she looked at him, a heap of hurt in an impersonal, unloving bed flanked by cold aluminum rails on each side. His chiseled, handsome face was unrecognizable, the blue, black and yellowed bruises everywhere. His eyes were shut. Taryn could no longer see the piercing crystal blue eyes that had immediately drawn Taryn to him.

And now. Their three-thousand-square-foot home, sexual passion, future dreams. None of that made a heap of difference in this hospital room. She'd never feel him sigh deeply and gently kiss the crook of her neck post-orgasm again. By day's break, she would be a widow. A widow with a $300,000 mortgage, $17,437 in credit card bills and an empty life ahead of her.

As she continued to breathe almost in sync with the hospital machinery beeps, she thought about the Harley, the joint Christmas gift they'd bought together in December—the one that Taryn loved to ride with him, her arms wrapped tightly around his taut abs. And Graham's reluctance to wear a helmet.

It made no sense. He'd been sober for over a decade. Why, when there was so much promise, so much to look forward to, would a recovering alcoholic go to a bar and get so shitbombed? And then attempt to ride home? She'd never seen him drink anything except a zero-alcohol beer anytime they'd gone to a bar together.

"What was in your head?" Taryn wept to him during their few moments alone. "Why didn't you call me? Or Scoot?"

Taryn realized she might never know.

Once Scoot texted he was in the lobby, Taryn shot down to the elevators to meet him, bursting into shaking sobs and collapsing into his arms as he approached to hug her. After a quick embrace and bountiful tears shared by the two, Taryn grasped his hand and led him down the corridor to Graham's room.

When Scoot entered the room, his face drained white. Clearing his throat to compose himself, Scoot cautiously approached Graham, leaning his hands and weight on the metal bed rails as he hung his head and wept for a few moments.

When Scoot began to recite The Lord's Prayer, Taryn's insides felt as if they suddenly coagulated. She froze as she listened to Scoot asking to "deliver us from evil." *Had it really come to this?*

Taryn signed the DNR, intent to donate his organs. Graham had signed up to do so last time he'd renewed his license. Taryn wondered if any were even viable as the medical staff surrounded the bed alongside the family, right before the go-ahead was given to disconnect life support.

It wasn't supposed to happen this way. Despite her being five years younger than him, she'd hoped they'd grow old together, her dying first. Like that one comic strip, saying something like, "If you lived to be so many days old, I'd want to live one less day so it wouldn't be without you."

Graham was her soulmate. She was certain of it. Her soulmate who was about to depart her life.

Taryn wept as the beeps morphed into the screeching sound of a flatline. Lynn and the medical staff sniffled as their tears dribbled down their faces. Taryn sobbed uncontrollably, in tandem with his parents and Scoot.

And then Taryn just stood and stared. She never heard the "I'm so sorrys," "My condolences," and whatever else the medical staff around her said. She just listened as he gasped for a last time with one final facial twitch before he flatlined. Taryn's knees buckled as soon as she heard the screeching BEEEEEEEEEP. She grabbed Scoot's arm, her final thoughts battering her brain as she hit the floor, a painful blow to her right knee.

Now I have a hook knee, too.

***

Taryn had barely been able to dress herself for the funeral, asking Lynn to scour her closet for a black dress and pumps. She buried herself under the mountain of blankets and the comforter on her and Graham's California King-size bed. The one he'd said was too large for their needs but agreed to anyway, because that's what Taryn wanted.

"The kids will want to sneak in and sleep with us when they're scared," she'd teased him, pinching his left arm.

Once Taryn had slipped on the black sheath dress, she shuffled her way to the master bathroom. She brushed through her long blond hair—the hair Graham loved to run his hands through—and secured it into a low ponytail. The simpler, the better, she thought, sweeping a minimal amount of makeup over her face—just a little bit of eyeliner, waterproof mascara and powder foundation. She slid cherry-flavored Chapstick, her standby, over her lips and slipped the tube into her tiny black handbag. She'd last used the bag at Jimbo and Patti's wedding before stuffing it into the box labeled "purses," nestled on the top shelf of her walk-in closet.

As Taryn gave herself one last look, her tired, swollen, bloodshot and puffy eyes and pale, dulled skin, she noticed the hollowness of her neck. She slipped her hand over her jewelry tree and clasped the silver half-moon necklace Graham had given her last Christmas. She loved how it sparkled with its tiny diamond trim—and the card he'd written alongside it, declaring, "T—I love you to the moon and back. G."

Taryn picked it up and drew it over her neck, connecting the clasp at the back of her neck. Lynn sat on the bed, watching her.

"You look nice," Lynn offered as Taryn looked at the zombie staring back at her in the mirror. She nodded, grabbed her purse, and the two headed down the spiral staircase before Taryn paused at the front door, resting her hand on the knob to open it. It felt like a thousand pounds as she pulled it toward her, slipping out the door to head to her husband's funeral.

***

Less than six months ago, Taryn and Graham had stood at the front of St. Francis' Catholic Church in Hampton Park, exchanging vows for life. Now, instead of being up at the pulpit in a white, flowing dress and gazing into Graham's striking blue eyes, she slumped in the front pew.

Taryn's gaze was fixated on a 24-by-36 professional wedding portrait of Graham. He had been so strikingly handsome, the photo looked like something out of a bridal magazine. To the right of it, on a small table with a crisp white tablecloth, sat the urn with Graham's cremains—something he'd been clear about in his will. A slideshow of Graham's life played across the giant TV screens—snippets of his childhood, teenage years, family vacations, and his time with Taryn.

But all Taryn could focus on was that urn. And the portrait. As the pastor spoke, her eyes and brain darted back and forth between the two.

Nothing the pastor said got through to Taryn. Her body, her brain. Everything was numb.

The sniffles and weeping of Graham's mother, Greta, and others barely registered. It was nothing more than muffled background noise in her mind.

At the funeral luncheon, Taryn brought the urn, setting it in front of the seat next to her. She ignored the occasional odd stares, touching the coolness of the container every few minutes.

"Oh, Tare Bear," a deep voice said from behind Taryn as a hand rested on her left shoulder. She instinctively turned but knew from the deep voice and nickname she always secretly despised that it was Jim Paxton.

Jim, or Jimbo as he went by, had been Graham's frat buddy at Midsouthern Florida University. She'd heard all the crude "boys will be boys" stories of Graham's buddies and their sexual conquests. Like how Jimbo, junior year, had hooked up with a slightly high, redheaded freshman they'd only referred to as "Big Red"—she was a tall woman, about five feet ten with the bulk to back it up, explained Graham, who had an affinity for blondes. The big laugh was that Jimbo had told her he needed to check if the carpeting matched the drapes (groan) and she'd told him sure, check it out—"but only with your mouth." He did, getting nothing in return, except for a tawdry tale that would seem to come up at least every six months when his wife wasn't within earshot, ending with the clincher—Jimbo was never able to confirm the matching body hair hues because Big Red was hairless. At least, in the nether regions.

Every time Jimbo leaned in to greet Taryn with a kiss, she couldn't erase the visual of him going to town on Big Red.

Today was no exception. Even as she sat with her husband's cremains. Taryn stood up and turned to face Jimbo.

"I'm so sorry, honey," Jimbo whispered as he wrapped his arms around Taryn. She felt his firm, heartfelt hug as she stood there, but she felt cold—unable to reciprocate any kind of emotion but deadness. Cold and total deadness.

Jimbo was a screwup of sorts, but he'd recently seemed to finally get his shit together. He was newly married with an even newer baby. She couldn't help the hot jealousy that surged through her veins as she saw Jimbo and Patti, his wife, living the life she'd eventually foreseen for her and Graham. Which now would never exist.

"I'm so sorry," Jimbo said, tears spilling down his olive-skinned face as Patti, a blazing redhead herself, wrestled with their gurgling baby girl, Joy, as she stirred and bucked in her arms.

"Also," Jimbo said as he dug his right hand into the left breast pocket of his suit, pulling out Graham's iPhone, "I thought you might want this. I have the rest of his stuff from the scene at home. But I figured this was the most important."

Taryn took the phone, in its Chicago Bears case, twisting her wrist to look it over on both sides. As if it would undo the past ninety-six hours. It was surprisingly intact, considering the trauma it had silently witnessed. Taryn hadn't had the energy or the will to collect Graham's belongings the cops had scooped up at the scene, so she'd asked Jimbo to handle it. She completely forgot about his phone until Jimbo slipped it into her right palm.

"Sorry, it's dead," Jimbo said.

"Like Graham," Taryn said dully, her eyes remaining fixated on her husband's phone. She felt Jimbo and Patti wince, even though her eyes never left the phone.

"Let me know what we can do," Jimbo choked out. He was hurting, too, Taryn reminded herself.

She nodded as Jimbo and Patti moved on, leaving Taryn to do her stunned widow routine with the next funeral guest. She felt like she was floating above the funeral home, looking down at a surreal scene that surely would end soon.

But it didn't. Because here she was again. It was her mom all over again. And Sam.

Taryn needed her childhood best friend right now. Sam would have helped her through this hurt.

But that would never be possible. No matter how hard she prayed.

CHAPTER TWO

Taryn's curiosity broke her that night. It was three in the morning, and it wasn't like she could sleep anyway. She liked holding Graham's phone. She felt like he was still here. That he'd walk into the room and she'd hand the device over to him. Maybe even toss it at him, even though he always scolded her for slinging her own phone onto a couch cushion now and then. The thought made her smile. For the first time in days.

Why Taryn felt the need to charge the phone, she didn't know. Maybe seeing email or text alerts come in would make it feel like he was still alive, if only for a displaced moment or two.

As soon as she connected it to the charger, the screen blew up. Everything from "I love you" messages from his mom and sister to notifications he'd been tagged what seemed like three hundred times on Facebook. She even saw an alert for her last message to him—"I have some great news. SO good. Can't wait to get home to tell you! xoxo"—sent less than an hour before she found Officer Anderson at her front door.

But Taryn didn't know Graham's iPhone passcode. So, the best she could get was a general roundup of notifications. When she tapped a notification to learn more, it was a brick wall.

It felt like too much. She left it plugged in, shut it off and meandered down to the kitchen to pour herself a hearty glass of Pinot Grigio.

Another day. Another time.

That time was ten days later, when her official Illinois News Association award arrived in the mail. Her legs felt like one-hundred-pound logs as she slowly lumbered into the house with the urn's cardboard box. She climbed the spiral staircase to their bedroom, her heart aching with the heaviness of grief. To Taryn, that award would always be tied to the day she became a widow.

Her belly gurgling, Taryn sat on her white down comforter, setting Graham's urn to her left. It rested at a forty-five-degree angle on the pillow. Sick, she knew. But she liked that he was there, no matter the form.

Taryn needed to still feel him. And his contained ashes, settled on his side of the bed, weren't enough. Taryn walked over to Graham's nightstand, where she'd left his phone. She plugged it in to charge and powered it on.

The notifications flooded in again. *Bing bing bing. Whoosh whoosh whoosh.* They never seemed to stop. She scrolled through a few—more of the same, with tributes, social media tags and a tidal wave of too much to wade through—when a calendar notification popped up.

"Lobster tatts," the Google alert popped up as a two-day warning. "Three o'clock, Lion Face Ink."

That's right! Taryn started thinking about how just two months before, when they'd gone to that all-inclusive swanky resort in Cancun, they had decided they would get matching tattoos. They'd had surf and turf for dinner one night, and as Graham sipped from his Heineken Zero and Taryn downed one too many agave nectar margaritas, Taryn declared they would be get matching lobster tattoos.

"You're my fucking lobster!" she'd screeched, unaware her volume level was disproportionate to the conversations taking place in the seaside restaurant. "We're getting lobster tattoos, and they're gonna hold hands!

"I mean claws." She'd giggled as Graham slightly shook his head before nodding at the other guests who'd been drawn away from their snapper, steak and coconut basmati rice dishes.

They'd spent the next day intermittently scrolling the internet for the perfect design. Blue lobsters, in fact, since they signified something even more rare—the likelihood of catching one was one in two hundred million. Like their love, she pointed out.

The urge overwhelmed her. She needed to see it. That perfect design they'd picked out together. Because she was still going to do it. Maybe even with his ashes. She'd heard of that. People who have their loved one's cremains filtered into the ink. That would be perfect. That way, they'd both still get the tattoos they'd decided on. Just not exactly in the way they'd planned.

Suddenly, Taryn felt alive again. The thought of stitching Graham into her skin for eternity elated her. It was the best she'd felt since he died.

Now, she just had to find that design. Graham had saved it to his phone. He'd said he'd put it in a desktop folder and would share it with her, but he'd forgotten.

Taryn knew him though, inside and out. She could crack his iPhone code and find the design he'd squirreled away. She knew it. In every ounce of her being.

His passcode would be easy to unearth. Taryn began plunking in various number combos—their anniversary, his birthday, her birthday. The anniversary of their first date. The day they'd gotten engaged. Even the day he'd quit drinking, though she really had to dig deeply into her memories for that one.

None of them worked.

Increasingly aggravated, Taryn stood up and sauntered into the kitchen. She needed vodka on the rocks to calm her nerves. She poured herself a hearty glass over ice and swirled it before taking a sip. She looked up at the framed photos set on the entertainment center, just above the TV. Their wedding photo. Graham's family reunion in the southwest suburbs of Chicago a few years ago. And the photo of Graham and his mom, her right arm hooked under his neck, cheek to cheek. She scrambled back into the bedroom and furiously tapped the numbers into his iPhone passcode.

In.

His mother's birthday.

Of course.

"Maybe his tattoo should've been 'Mama,' " she grumbled.

But Taryn's annoyance was brief. She was in now. She'd find that design, text it to herself and have it permanently sketched into her skin in 48 hours.

She found it all right. And she found an untapped resource.

A Graham brain bank.

In a folder marked "personal" was a treasure trove. Subfolders of everything she needed to re-live him, whenever she wanted. Files upon files. Online account info, his will, his mother's, family photos. But no tattoo design.

But there was the code to get into his laptop in his Notes app, which Taryn had completely forgotten about. It had been sitting in the trunk of Graham's car. Taryn hadn't had the courage to drive it, even touch it, since his death. Taryn ran to the garage, retrieved it, and came back to the bedroom. She settled in on the bed, plugged it in and fired it up.

It's probably on his desktop. She tapped in the passcode for access.

Taryn felt slightly guilty going through his laptop and email. But, she reasoned, she also needed access, as Graham had managed the household finances, all from his computer. Taryn found the master file with passwords, accounts and due dates, then emailed them to herself. That lobster tattoo design was nowhere to be found.

But then something in Taryn's gut stirred when she noticed Graham's desktop had another cloud-based drive. Not just the Google one. She opened it. And started digging through hundreds of files.

None looked familiar to Taryn. She'd known about the Google Drive, as Graham would send her links to items she needed to review or sign. But in this cloud file, there were things she'd never seen. She entered "tattoo" into the search bar.

Bingo! Sure enough, there was the blue lobster. Taryn might not have her love, but she'd have the markings of him. A tear dribbled down her right cheek. Pure elation. She'd found it. She opened his email to send it to herself.

Seeing an email notification push through her phone from Graham both warmed and decimated her heart.

Yet Taryn was pumped, feeling a real connection to Graham again. She backtracked in his cloud drive to the main folder and stumbled as she spied a subfolder that caught her attention. One she'd missed before.

"Forgiveness."

Her heart skyrocketed into her throat.

There were two documents in the folder. One document was marked "Taryn." The other, "Evelyn."

Both had been written in mid-January, about two months before Graham died. And both instantly commanded goosebumps to spread across the flesh of Taryn's arms and legs. She felt as though she'd been socked in the chest. A tightness seized her heart.

Who the hell is Evelyn? she muttered as her heart thumped like bass drums in her chest.

Taryn opened the file bearing her own name first. Catatonic, she didn't know whether to believe what spilled out in front of her. She didn't want to. But she believed enough to scream "Motherfucker!" before her right palm slapped the urn that sat atop her bed, sending it ricocheting across the room before it settled in a metallic twang on the floor.

This couldn't be real. The words typed into the document surely were made up. A farce. A sick fucking joke in the cruelest of times.

But Taryn knew. They were his sayings, his words. His prose, his rhythm of writing. And his desires, which sickened her to her core. The document did, indeed, list him as the "author." There was no mistaking it.

This letter was legit.

She ran to the toilet and vomited the bile that gurgled in her belly. It was all over. Her love, her dreams, her hopes.

Her memories of a man who was supposed to be everything she wanted.

Dead. Done. With about eleven-hundred words.

The man Taryn fell in love with never really existed.

But the one she married? He was gone. His life was over.

And now, she thought, so was hers.

Chapter Three

Taryn sat in the corner of her walk-in closet, her five-days-unwashed hair pulled back in a clear elastic band, dirtier than her typical dirty blond hue. She wondered when she last showered. She really didn't remember. Maybe five, six days after the funeral?

That was the last time she had been out in public. Who cared now as she sat in solitude on the floor, her back against the beige wall as she blankly stared at Graham's favorite shirt—a ridiculous pink flamingo Charlie Sheen shirt, as she called it, from one of their jaunts to Florida.

I should've buried him in it, Taryn thought to herself. But just for a moment.

Fuck him, she reconsidered. *I should burn it. That worthless piece of shit.*

Taryn found herself sitting in silence for what was likely hours, holding the tattered corner of a postcard Graham had sent her from the early days of their courtship. Taryn had torn through boxes of their belongings and memories, looking for mementos that would erase from her mind the terrible thing her husband had done. To remind her of why she had loved him. Even if it was only temporarily.

Graham had been traveling a lot for work in the medical device field, his job sending him all over the Southwest. As the vice president of the Coronary Clinical Specialist Team at CoroMed, he'd be gone several days a week, guiding his team on how to educate clients on how to use the company's vascular devices. Because CoroMed was based in London, sometimes,

Graham headed overseas—and always offered Taryn the opportunity to join him and explore the sights as he worked during the day.

Taryn didn't like his frequent absences, but she'd be lying if she didn't admit she *loved* the financial stability his six-figure salary brought. It was just part of the deal, and they made it work as best they could. To be honest, she loved the traveling. Growing up, she'd never really gone on family vacations, unless the Wisconsin Dells or the Indiana Dunes counted as "vacation." Dirty beaches and campgrounds had been the extent of her childhood adventures, so getting to jet-set around the country and globe thrilled her. When she and Graham had first gotten together, she was still on a general assignment reporter's salary—and the only thing she could pop for on her own was a weekend excursion to Six Flags Great America.

Graham had taken Taryn to Seattle, San Diego, Aruba, New York City, San Francisco, London, Paris and Cork, Ireland, to, of course, kiss the Blarney Stone. Those were just a few of their travels. She always hated saying goodbye. But she knew his hard work and their sacrifices as a couple would make life a lot easier than it was for many of the struggling single journalists she worked with at the *Chicago Gazette*. His income was far beyond what she'd ever seen her dad bring in as a child. Suddenly, the newspaper she'd proudly toiled at for several years was no longer her own source of income. With Graham's gig, she felt emboldened, knowing she could be okay financially should she lose her job—she could always freelance. It was especially comforting, considering the bloodbath the newspaper industry had been subjected to over the past decade or so.

But it was a pride and passion thing for Taryn. From the moment she could put pencil to paper, she knew it. She was a writer. Even before she could write, really. Taryn would draw books from the moment she learned to draw.

Initially, Taryn had envisioned herself as a novelist. Her eyes would eagerly devour books in her spare moments, one right after the next. She knew in her heart she had it. The Gift. Her mom and her teachers saw it, too, marking up her papers with compliments of her thoroughness in the subject, as well as the prose she put to paper. The accolades—along with some encouragement from Mrs. Frank, her high school English honors teacher—helped her decision to try her hand as a staff writer for Hampton High's monthly school newspaper.

Having that outlet proved invaluable to Taryn—especially during her toughest times. It kept her grounded, her head in another place. It was a hobby that consumed her, so she momentarily didn't have to think about the life-altering incident that had torn her heart to shreds, never fully mending.

And writing was cathartic, too. When Taryn pitched the idea of doing a school newspaper story on teenage mental health—and how to get youth the support they needed—she ran with it. A local suburban newspaper, *The Hampton Park Herald*, caught wind and asked to rerun it in their publication.

That had been the moment. Being able to express her thoughts on paper—and the positive response she received from readers and peers—solidified it for Taryn. She wanted to be a newspaper reporter. For a daily publication in a big city.

And that's what Taryn did. She took a general assignment reporter role at *The Herald*, starting the Monday after her graduation from Edgewood University, a public college in Northwest Indiana, where she earned her Bachelor of Arts in journalism. Even though the newspapers overall were on the decline in both staffers and content, it spoke to her. Taryn wanted on this ship, even though she suspected it was headed for an iceberg. The decision was based not on her mind, but her heart.

Within two years, Taryn snagged a spot on *The Chicago Gazette* team. While being a general assignment reporter wasn't the most coveted reporter role, it was an in to a major metropolitan newspaper—just what Taryn was angling for. So, she accepted, her hands shaking as she ended her call with Gabe, the metro editor who offered her the job, and wept happy, proud tears.

She did it. Taryn climbed the next step of her career ladder. *And, perhaps, someday, I'll get my chance to take over the features beat,* Taryn thought.

As a journalist, Taryn felt like somebody. Whenever she told people what she did for a living, they would react the same—"Oh, wow. What a cool job!" Despite the fact the industry was in a freefall, she thrived on people's admiration of her work.

But Taryn did have her own emotional demons to conquer. Her experiences with men prior to Graham had been sketchy. Taryn had been an awkward teen, not exactly popular but also not one of the so-called outcasts. Until the night she and Sam had hung out with Les Bean and his crew. And high school went from palatable to unbearable.

When Taryn had morphed into a beauty at nineteen, her mind still hung on to what she'd seen herself as for much of her teen years—a nobody. She couldn't kick her own perception of her persona. That she was ho-hum, not worth a damn to anyone worthwhile, as far as she was concerned. Especially after the harassment that stemmed from the Les Bean visit. That was one of the only times—the last time—she drank in high school.

After what had happened to Sam, Taryn steered clear of alcohol.

But college changed the game. After initially resisting, Taryn met a group of classmates at a party one night. And her love-hate relationship with booze truly began. Taryn would drink hard and often during her college years, trying to block the memories of her childhood friend. She didn't just drink. She drank to get drunk. She drank to forget.

It helped. For a little bit.

But Taryn's penchant for drinking herself into false self-confidence came with its own pitfalls. Like not remembering how she'd gotten home from numerous parties and bars. With one, her last recollection of the evening was of being splayed out in the bathtub on a lawn chair, laughing as one of the school's star football players, their quarterback, doused her, fully clothed, with Jungle Juice. The sweet taste of the juice sliding down her throat as she thrust her head back was the last thing she recalled before waking up in her flimsy twin bed the next morning, reeking of the dampness left over from Everclear and sugar. Her panties and a condom wrapper were wadded into a ball in her purse. She couldn't recall having sex with the quarterback, but the remnants in her clutch suggested otherwise. "Touchdown!" her roommate, Jasmine, said as she high-fived a bleary-eyed Taryn the next day, when she stirred from her bed around noon.

Taryn brushed off her college behavior as a rite of passage. It was part of her own journey, her right to experiment and experience college life. Even though she'd really like to not remember those college trysts most of the time.

The revelation of Graham's sobriety had been refreshing. In time, Taryn accepted—and appreciated—that he didn't drink anymore. Initially, the disclosure had shocked her. But then she realized she would always have a designated driver, so yay her! Taryn knew he wouldn't, and couldn't, judge her. They'd both made mistakes. And those mistakes eventually brought them together.

The right place at the right time.

As the days, weeks, months and years ticked on, Graham's sobriety—and the benefits she saw from it—inspired her to cut back some herself. Yet Taryn could never fully commit to removing it from her life. It was something for later, when they started a family, she'd tell herself.

Someday.

With Graham usually scattered across the Southwest during his work cases, Taryn filled the void of his absence by joining her newspaper friends, sister, and even some old high school pals for dinners and happy hours. She also loved to nurse two or three dirty martinis from the comfort of her couch, Netflix turning off the noise in her brain, if only for the duration of the buzz.

Thank God for iPhones. During the days Graham was working remotely, Taryn would tap his location every so often to see where he was. Only a few times had she spied a locale that raised Taryn's eyebrows. Why was he at a place called Dick's Dugout Bar? Just joining the guys to kick back—with a nonalcoholic beer, he'd demonstrate, sending a selfie of him taking a sip with the zero-alcohol content prominently displayed on the label. His voice and the prose of his texts seemed to verify his sobriety. He was always crisp-clear in his communications, so she had no reason to doubt him. Plus, on the occasional instances the paper hosted a happy hour—celebrating someone's promotion, birthday or farewell to their next big gig—Graham would willingly join her, sipping from a rocks glass filled with Coke and a lime. Graham exquisitely played the part of supportive husband, never questioning how much Taryn herself consumed.

Whenever Graham was not traveling for business, he had become a regular churchgoer at St. Francis' Catholic Church in Hampton Park. He went, in part, because of their recovery program for alcoholics and addicts, dubbed "Get Sober with God," which participants referred to as GSWG. Hampton Park was a Chicago suburb, about thirty miles southwest of downtown. She personally didn't want to file into a pew every week to be preached at and handed a donation basket into which to drop her dollars. But Graham did without fail every week, at least when he wasn't away on business. He also routinely stuck around to share his recovery struggles with others.

But the letter Graham had written her but never given her, the one that had clearly sat inside his cloud drive for days as she mourned ... it twisted her now-tortured soul into a mess she wasn't sure she'd ever be able to untangle. She pulled it up on his laptop for what was probably the twentieth time and read it, the piercing pain just as agonizing as the first time.

My Dearest Taryn,

Words cannot express the sorrow, regret and remorse I have for what I am about to tell you. It is something I've kept locked inside my heart and soul for more than a decade, never speaking a word of it to you, despite thinking of it every single day. I've done something unforgivable, and I thought good deeds would make it easier to bear—and fade in time. But they haven't. The hole in my heart has just gotten bigger, and I can no longer carry this burden. I can no longer live a lie, especially a lie I've hidden from my love all this time. It's also an important part of my recovery, to acknowledge my mistakes, ask for forgiveness and become a better person. The man I want to be—and should be for you.

I made a terrible decision the summer after I graduated college. After the summertime wedding of one of my frat brothers, I went to a post-reception hotel party. And I did something awful.

I sexually assaulted a woman.

That line made Taryn choke and stop reading for a minute, every time. She lowered the top of the laptop for a moment as her throat swelled and the tears spilled, her days-old mascara dribbling into a tiny hint of black gunk on her jeans. She sniffled, wiped her nose with her sleeve like she did when she was six, and continued.

This sounds terrible, but it wasn't forceful. But I know that doesn't matter. She was an undergrad I'd known on campus, and we'd been flirting for months. She'd make sure to seek me out when walking through campus, lightly touching my arm as we spoke in the student bookstore, giving me a shoulder massage at the Lucky Charm bar, giving me all the signals she was interested. She had an engagement ring on, but when we both showed up at Bob and Jessica's wedding without significant others, the drinks were flowing and the flirting ensued. We danced some together—taking turns with other partners, too—and all the signs were there that she wanted to hook up that night. I figured she wanted a last fling before she tied the knot. We were both hammered when the reception wrapped up and climbed into the elevator to head to the afterparty in the bridal party staging room. We joined the rest of the partiers who weren't ready for the celebration to stop. Her drunkenness only worsened as the evening progressed. A couple of joints and Xanax later, she was facedown on the couch.

The groomsmen and I were tasked with moving her into a bedroom to sleep it off. I was pissed, honestly, because she'd given me every indication she wanted to hook up that night. So I pounded. Shots of tequila, a couple of lines of coke. And I just became unglued, not myself. The party began to dissipate, with everyone returning to their hotel rooms to sleep it off. The two-bedroom suite had emptied out, two of the bridesmaids claiming the one room to sleep in. And there I was, sitting on the couch, surveying the empty beer cans and rings of red staining the white coffee table from sloppy wine drinkers.

After the woman was in there for a while, I stumbled into the bedroom to see if she'd sobered up and was ready to do what we'd been dancing around all evening.

I rubbed her arm to wake her and she barely moved, except for a grunt and flop of her hand over her face. So, I did something that's haunted me ever since.

I had sex with her. And she never even knew it.

I don't know what possessed me to climb on top of her. It was like an out-of-body experience—I could see myself doing things I found utterly deplorable. Yet I couldn't stop. It lasted maybe only three minutes, but deep down, I knew it was wrong.

It breaks my heart to confess this to you, especially after keeping it from you all these years. I had realized immediately what a terrible thing I had done and vowed from that day forward to be a better man. And being a better man brought me to you. Had I not followed that path, despite my deplorable actions, I never would have joined the church and found my second chance through sobriety. I never would have been at the volunteering event I supported through GSWG. I never would have paired up with you at that table, where the connection between us was electric and clear. I knew that morning that you would be my wife. I just knew.

God had a plan for me. Somehow, my terrible deeds led me to something good. And that good was you.

I chose not to tell you outright because I was terrified I'd lose you. Deep down, I knew I should have been honest from Day One. But by the time we'd met, a decade had passed. A decade that had never led this girl to seek me out and ask why, or even press charges. As far as I know, she never reported it. I never heard rumors about what happened that night, so I believed I was really the only one who knew what I had done. If she didn't remember it, it couldn't hurt her, right? And by the time we had met and gotten serious, I knew that I couldn't be prosecuted.

That line made Taryn's stomach lurch every single time.

Why tell you now, you ask? Why in this fashion? And why would I choose to do what I've done to myself?

Part of it is considering what's become so evident in the last few years in our society. Survivors and the news media have stood up for women being abused. And it was a stark realization of mine, some real soul-searching, that made me admit that I was part of the problem. I recognize now, more than ever, what a terrible, egregious thing I'd done.

I write this now because I am seeking forgiveness. I have asked The Lord to do so, and I know He has. I have counseled with Father Tim and Scoot, and I know they, too, forgive me. So now, I must make peace with the love of my life. I ask you to forgive me for what I have done—both fifteen years ago and today.

I beg you to grant me at least that, in the name of the love we have shared for the past few years.

I ask you, because I know you have the heart, courage and love to grant me mercy. And mercy is what I need to make the rest of my life one that makes up for the misdeeds of the first part of my existence.

I love you with all my heart and soul, no matter what you choose.

Forever your love,

Graham

Taryn flung the laptop at the dingy closet wall. She pulled at her stringy hair as she screamed and wept. At least this time, she didn't act on the urge to go scrub the shit out of her hands, mouth, crotch—anywhere that Graham had shoved that disgusting dick of his.

Twenty-four hours ago, she loved him. Now, she hated that dead prick. Her whole life felt like a farce.

"I've had sex with a rapist!" she screamed, no one but the walls of her empty home to absorb her angst. "I married, lived with and slept next to a goddamn sexual offender!"

Taryn's body shook and her back ached from sitting on the gray wide-plank wood flooring they'd just installed in the entire house six months ago. And her mind wandered into the deep depths of her memory. And the horrible things she'd seen way too early in life.

Not again, she thought.

Even though what had happened to Sam, her teenage best friend, had been some time ago, Taryn found her mind drifting back to The Night. The Night that had smacked Taryn in the face with the brutal reality of life.

The Night that taught her there were rotten, deplorable people out there. And the people who'd fallen prey to what appeared the best intentions, only to quickly realize something. That one simple choice, one single bad decision, can transform into something terrible.

Even beyond terrible.

Taryn was sickened by the irony of it all. How she'd met Graham at a nonprofit event. An organization that was in stark contrast to what was painfully detailed in Graham's letter. A service meant to help those in desperate need of support. An organization created to demonstrate to the hopeless that there was, in fact, hope for them.

Yet hope was something that no longer lived in Taryn's heart. It was replaced by anguish.

"I should be dead, too," Taryn said.

But no. That would put her right there with that shitty excuse for a man she wished she'd never met. There had to be more to her now-mess of a life.

There had to. Or she was going to end up even worse.

Just like Sam.

Chapter Four

The ache in Taryn's brain met her with the glare of the blazing orange sun. She hadn't bothered closing the blinds the night before. A 1.75-liter of vodka was nudged in between the couch cushions, which she didn't discover until she rolled onto her belly, the mouth of the bottle poking her stomach, which jostled with liquid.

Her unsettled mind and belly seemed to work in tandem.

"Who is she?" Taryn mumbled, bringing her right palm to her forehead to massage the piercing headache she'd grown accustomed to daily. While Taryn blamed the bottle, as it had become her crutch in recent days, she knew the stress didn't help, either. Her mind constantly raced. Even in her dreams, she conjured up her own sickeningly deplorable images of Graham's assault on a continuous loop.

Maybe Taryn had been his reckoning. His new start, making amends for the girl he'd homed in on during his own #metoo moment of non-glory.

Taryn rolled off the couch like an athlete with a rib injury. As she caught herself with her left hand, the shrill pain shot through her wrist.

"Shit!" she screamed. She looked down and saw her knuckles were bloodied and bruised, her wrist swollen like dough after it's risen.

Taryn couldn't recall what she did. *Did I ride my bike down to the 7-Eleven for more booze while I was shitbombed? Maybe took a spill in a bush off a sidewalk?*

Nope. It all came back as she made her way to the kitchen for a glass of ice-cold water. The glass encasing Taryn and Graham's wedding invitation was shattered, the pattern like a tie-dyed shirt. Tie-dyed with only crusty brown reddishness.

Taryn checked her phone, filled with sixty-seven messages.

"Hugs," read the one from her sister last night. "Thinking of u."

"Hi honey," the one from her Aunt Dee said. "Uncle Eddie and I are going to the Rooster Roof for an early bird dinner. Do you want us to pick you up? It would be good for you to get out of the house."

Taryn declined. As she did with every other offer of comfort and companionship.

The same went for Taryn's boss at *The Gazette*. She saw Gabe's name come up on the caller ID. She let out a heavy sigh, not wanting to talk to him, allowing the call to go to voicemail. After thirty seconds, the ping came from her iPhone and the red button indicating a voicemail was awaiting gnawed at her. Taryn wasn't in a place to deal with this. Or anyone. But then a text appeared on her phone, with Gabe's message: *Please call me. There's some news here. And I think it may be what you need right now.*

Taryn sighed again. What could be so important, right after her husband's death, as she wallowed in grief and self-pity?

And then some texts began popping up from her co-workers, including, "Sorry to bother you so soon. But did you hear? Think you're going to go for it?"

Oh God, Taryn thought. *Was there finally an opening in the features department, after all these years covering the cops beat?* Anne, who had held the coveted beat for so long, a good eight years, had been talking about applying to *The New Yorker, The New York Times,* anything in the Big Apple, because she was certain she belonged in Manhattan, living her own *Sex and the City* dreams. Not that Anne was any Carrie Bradshaw.

But the thought of even considering vying for a new role, one she surely didn't have the headspace for at this point, wasn't even on her radar. She simply existed right now, struggling to get through each dreary day. But she knew she couldn't ignore him for long, if she wanted to go back to her job.

Then came a third text that popped onto her phone's screen from Gabe, simply saying, *Please call me. I think I have something you may want to hear, given your new situation.* She opened the missed calls log and tapped on Gabe's name.

"Taryn," Gabe said softly, forgoing a "hello" as Taryn gently breathed into her receiver. "I know this is a terrible time, but there have been some developments at *The Gazette*. Some that may affect you. And they might not be a bad thing for you right now, given your recent loss."

Taryn was silent, but her sniffles let Gabe know she was still there.

"Hear me out," Gabe said.

Taryn had worked under Gabe for two years. He was the best metro editor she'd reported to during her journalism career. He was funny, in a sarcastic, biting kind of raw way, but she loved that about him. She liked to hang with her own kind, and working for someone with a similar outlook on life and humor had been a highlight of her career in the newsroom. He didn't just tear up her stories and submit them to the copy desk. He taught her, walking her through his changes to each of her pieces, explaining the reasoning for every edit. That back-and-forth had helped her writing considerably—to the point that by now, the edits were minimal and her knowledge even greater.

Taryn knew what it took to write a great story. And quickly, given the push in an industry that was becoming increasingly digital. It was all about metrics, with large computer screens hung up in the newsroom, monitoring the top ten stories on the website, watching as they danced up and down, each desperately competing to be on top. Taryn's stories had increasingly risen to the top, which she attributed to the subject matter. Because when headlines such as "Disgruntled neighbor kills 'junk man' with meat cleaver, police say," or "Report: Chicago Health Alliance chief used company card to pay for sex" ran across the breaking news banner on the *Gazette's* home page, readers clicked.

"Did Anne put in her notice?" Taryn asked. She'd previously felt free to share her career aspirations with Gabe, who'd been her biggest cheerleader since coming aboard. "Because I don't even know what to do in the next five minutes. Not to mention the rest of my life."

Gabe grew silent, then expressed a deep exhale.

"She possibly could soon," Gabe said, pausing for about ten seconds before continuing. "News Associates Inc. made an announcement this morning. They're reducing staff across the board by twenty percent."

Taryn's heart stopped. *Oh Jesus. Is he calling to tell me I'm being laid off?* NAI, the parent company of *The Gazette*, had more than one hundred newsrooms across the country. This had become a cyclical activity since the mid-2000s. With print readership drastically dipping downward every quarter, Taryn and the rest of her colleagues had grown accustomed to such gloom-and-doom announcements at least every year, if not biannually. So far, she'd survived but had seen plenty of her cohorts pecking away at their computers, wrapping up their latest story, only to be stunned when they got the tap on the shoulder and were led down to Human Resources for their exit package.

Taryn bit the right side of her lower lip before breaking the awkward silence.

"Let me guess," Taryn said quietly. "I'm on the chopping block."

"Not necessarily," Gabe said. "But you could be if you wanted to."

Taryn's left eyebrow arched upward as she held her breath for about five seconds before exhaling.

"Are you saying I can toss my name into the ring for a layoff?" she mused. "Why?"

"They're offering voluntary buyouts first," Gabe said. "If they can't get enough, then they'll have to cut. But I think you may want to consider it."

Taryn paused before saying, "Go on."

Gabe explained that NAI was offering a year's pay to those who accepted, in addition to an extension of the employee health plan through the severance package life. So as long as she was getting a paycheck, whether she was working there or not, she'd be covered. Not that health insurance was even on the radar now. She was young, barely going to the doctor except for her annual gynecological checkup.

Taryn let the information swirl around in her head. The thought of heading back to work after Graham's death was incomprehensible at this moment. And the idea of being able to take a year off work to figure out what to do with herself? It could be just what she needed. She could find another job by then. Gabe would surely be a great reference for her. And her portfolio had plenty to entice another news organization, when the time came.

"You don't have to do this," Gabe said. "But I just wanted you to know that this is an option for you. If they don't get enough takers, they may be forced to turn to layoffs. And I'm not so sure those severance packages will be as generous as this one."

Taryn let this new development ricochet around in her boggled brain. She promised Gabe she'd think about it.

"Take the time you need," Gabe said. "At least until the end of the week. That's how long they're giving people to snap up the buyout offering."

Taryn promised she'd give him an answer by the week's end and hung up. She meandered to her home office, where the stories she'd been most proud of hung on the walls, tacked onto a corkboard that she couldn't even see anymore. It was a collection of newsprint and thumbtacks now, shrouded on each side by the two awards she'd scored during her newspapering years. Both were first place, both for her breaking news coverage for the *Gazette*. Taryn hoped for more to line the walls, like the one she scored the day Graham died. While Gabe had sent the award in the mail, Taryn couldn't bring herself to hang up the thing she was so very proud of. All she could think of when she looked at it was Graham slamming into that tree. And dying.

Taryn couldn't even think about filing into that newsroom right now.

Grabbing a bag of tortilla chips, she shuffled back into the living room and plopped on the couch. And sat. Even moving toward the TV remote didn't seem worth it.

Taryn heard the metal clink of the mailbox top shutting and knew the postman had just delivered probably a stack of sympathy cards, still flowing in to console her for her loss. She wondered if Hallmark had a market for widows of sex offenders.

Despite her pounding headache, she reached for the bottle of vodka on her coffee table, pouring it into the coffee mug that still had the stench of two-days-old brew. She took a swig. Then another. Then enough until she felt nothing.

Taryn drifted off into a drunken stupor, pleading with whatever god there was to hit the reset button on her life. Maybe a miracle would happen.

CHAPTER FIVE

Taryn woke up to the blaring car horn of her teenage neighbor's impatient and ill-tempered boyfriend. At first, she didn't move. It wasn't worth it to exert energy. But as the *beep-beep-beeps* grew into *beeeeeeeeeeeep*, she couldn't stomach it any longer. Taryn flung herself from the couch, stormed to the door and tore it open.

"The fuck?!" she screamed, not caring if old lady Glenda across the street—or anyone else—took in her tirade. "Be a goddamn man and get out of the car and ring that fucking doorbell!"

By then, the object of his affection had scurried outside and climbed into the passenger's seat, giving Taryn a meek "I'm sorry" wave as her jackass squeeze offered Taryn a double middle finger salute before peeling out and hauling ass down the road.

Taryn stood there, completely disheveled and not giving a fuck that Glenda, on her front porch, was eyeing her in her ripped yoga pants and crappy, braless camisole. Glenda gave Taryn a perfunctory nod. Taryn dully waved back, expressionless.

Taryn turned to shuffle back into the house and tipped open the top of the mailbox, clasping the stack of cards and advertising mailers that had built up over the last three days. As she meandered back into her living room, she tossed them onto the ottoman, half of the items spilling onto the throw rug, tissues and a few pretzels that were strewn about.

The mail piece with Universal Life Insurance in the return address said SENSITIVE: OPEN IMMEDIATELY.

Taryn knew what it was. But she couldn't bring herself to open it until she'd plowed through a dirty martini. Who cared if it was eleven in the morning. She'd graduated to the stiffest drink she could get her hands on. Because Taryn knew when she opened it, there was no more denying it.

Her husband was dead. Really, really dead.

And a rapist.

Seeing it printed out was a culmination of it all. Graham insisted on a decent policy that would ensure Taryn could get by in the event of his untimely death. The reality was that she was now a widow. And she could be a widow who wasn't forced back into the reality of work. At least, if she chose that.

Seven hundred and fifty thousand dollars.

That was Taryn's consolation prize for having a dead husband. A horrible, piece-of-shit dead husband.

With this money, I could make it my full-time job to drink myself into liver failure by Easter, she mused.

But she could do better than that.

Within an hour, Taryn had shot off an email to Gabe.

"I'll take the buyout," Taryn typed. "Let me know the next steps."

She was at peace, at least, with this decision. She needed a sabbatical. A chance to figure out who she had become and where she was going.

And Taryn needed to know.

About her.

CHAPTER SIX

"It's not going to bring him back," Lynn blurted out, a look of annoyance across her face.

The girl never had any sense of compassion, Taryn thought, tossing back her long, blond strands of stringy and unkempt hair past her shoulders. Both women peered at their reflections in the master bedroom mirror, catching glances of irritation with the other.

Lynn sat, arms and legs crossed, in the vanity alcove chair, watching her sister's every move. Like a cat waiting for the perfect moment to pounce on its prey. Taryn ignored it, reaching into the bathroom drawer to the right of her sink, fishing out an elastic fabric ponytail holder and pulling her oily hair into a messy bun.

It seemed to be Taryn's look since becoming a widow. Disheveled. Unkempt. Dull. Drab. She'd been wearing the same gray tank top and black yoga pants for at least two days. She'd lost count. Taryn looked over her sister, her senior by three years, wearing her go-to outfit of skinny jeans and a baggy black T-shirt. Lynn's efforts to camouflage her extra fifty pounds with super tight pants didn't do her any favors, Taryn thought, despite her own sloppy appearance.

I'm a recent widow. I get a pass.

But Taryn knew better than to tell her to wear better-fitting clothing. Lynn seemed to think if she hid under oversize shirts, her wide hips and apple ass wouldn't be so evident. But Taryn wasn't telling her that her efforts didn't suffice. Or that her pixie cut didn't look right with her rounded face. Taryn had encouraged Lynn to grow it out into a trendy bob, but her sister argued that was too much work. Sure, they were sisters. But their blood bond didn't mean they were automatic best friends. Or even friends.

Ever since their mother, Nancy, had died, things drastically changed. Instead of the shared grief bonding them together, the two had drifted apart. Lynn's aggravation with Taryn's propensity to overdrink had been a source of contention between them for some time. After Nancy's funeral eight years ago, things took a nosedive at the celebration of life held at Lynn's home after their mother was laid to rest. Taryn, who considered her mom her closest confidante—a role she'd happily accepted after Taryn's trauma over Sam—had pre-gamed the service with a couple of glasses of wine in the morning. Plus, a flask of vodka that was tucked into her clutch for intermittent sips during her restroom breaks.

But once the mourners caravanned to the house, Taryn, in her grief, downed the rest of her flask in the bathroom before stumbling into the kitchen. Lynn had been prepping a plate of food for Aunt Mo, when Taryn, fresh glass of merlot in her hand, stumbled on a wet spot on the kitchen tile.

And it was then that Taryn spilled the red wine all over Lynn's brand-new, bright yellow dress. Lynn had insisted on a vibrant color, saying the service should be focused on the light and joy their mom had brought into the lives of all she touched. Now stained with blobs of deep red, Lynn ended up stomping upstairs and putting on a black dress after all. After changing, Lynn had journeyed down to the living room, whispering in her sister's ear as she sauntered past, "YOU are a pathetic fucking DRUNK. Get your shit together. *Please.*"

"At least I don't have to shop at Lane Bryant," a wounded Taryn had retorted. Her eyelids bobbed as she glared at her sister before bringing the lip of her wineglass to her own. Taryn never broke eye contact until Lynn's face lit up in fury and she stormed away.

Their relationship hadn't been the same since. Sure, there were obligatory biweekly calls to touch base. An occasional dinner. And Taryn even asked Lynn to be her maid of honor years later. While she accepted, she certainly didn't seem pleased to play the part. Taryn did it for Nancy's sake, as well as Lynn's. It was an olive branch. Hopefully, Lynn could see that—and her mom, too, from above.

But here they were again. Two sisters, bound by nothing but familial ties. Digging through the shrapnel of another loved one's untimely death. The cloak of unease and disdain still hung in the air.

Taryn marched over to the oak dresser she'd always hated, grabbing items from her "skinny clothes" drawer—things that hadn't fit her in years. Until Taryn had begun her journey to widowhood. Now, they hung from her limbs, like papier-mâché on a skeleton.

"Taryn," Lynn said, a little more softly this time. "Are you sure you really need this now? I think you're better off being around a support system. Not all alone, wandering the beaches of Central Florida."

"I know," Taryn snapped. "I just need a fresh start."

Lynn plopped down on the bed, letting out a sigh as she rolled her eyes. *She was probably jealous she really wasn't the skinny sister now,* Taryn thought.

"And a fresh start is running away to Florida?" Lynn argued. "Where your dead husband used to live? That seems *torturous* to me."

Taryn stopped to scowl for only a few seconds before slamming a drawer hard enough to knock the ugly brass handle off. She didn't bother picking it up before moving on to the drawer beneath. She just kicked it hard and heard it hit the baseboard of the wall as it gouged the wood. Lynn shuddered.

"I'm not trying to be a bitch," Lynn said faintly, running her pudgy fingers through her brunette hair before touching her little sister's arm. "Just realistic. Going there will only make it that much harder."

Taryn kept focused, moving on to each subsequent drawer as she inched closer to the ground. She didn't care what Lynn thought. Because Lynn didn't know. She didn't know Taryn was on her own covert mission. She didn't know about *her*.

"I just need to escape." She aggressively zipped up her duffel bag. "I can't be here right now. End of story. Now I've got to finish packing and get some rest. My flight is at six-fifteen in the morning. That's less than twelve hours."

Lynn shot up from her perch on the bed, loudly sighing and grabbing her purse. She curtly hugged Taryn goodbye and turned to look over her right shoulder as she crossed over the threshold into the night.

"Just text me when you get there," Lynn said. "Let me know you're okay."

Taryn forced a fake smile, nodded and gently shut the door. She shot up the stairs, taking them two at a time. There wasn't much time.

Taryn headed back to the master bathroom, pulling a plastic bag she'd shoved in her bottom cabinets. She grabbed the drugstore box of permanent hair color, quickly read the directions and set up her different mixing stations. Taryn thought the deep auburn shade displayed on the packaging was fitting—"Risqué Red."

By the time Taryn rested her head on the pillow for a few hours' sleep, there was no hint of greasy blond hair. Instead, Taryn was a blazingly bright redhead. Like Sam had been.

***

Samantha Freedman was a typical girl from a model middle-class home. At age twelve, she and her family had relocated to Hampton Park from Dallas, Texas. Her dad had a management opportunity with one of the Chicago-based department store chains that was too good to resist.

Lucky for Taryn, the randomly chosen seating assignments in Mrs. Tulley's sixth period English class had set the stage for the two girls to sit next to one another—and morph into best friends.

It began with Sam's request to borrow a pencil, soon blossoming into snickering and note-passing about Mrs. Tulley and her class pets, building from there. After years of daily phone calls, trips to the mall, the movies and countless sleepovers anchored by pizza and campy horror movies, the two girls were inseparable. They might not have been related by blood, but their bond was strong. If you took away each girl's distinct appearance, they could easily be mistaken for sisters, the two were so in sync.

When Taryn experienced her first kiss at fourteen, Sam was the first phone call to spill the details. When Sam's parents separated when she was fifteen, it was Taryn who rushed to comfort her—and offer her the opportunity to sleep over whenever she needed it—which turned out to be half the summer nights that year.

Sam was the first person she went to pick up after getting her driver's license on her sixteenth birthday, the girls giddy with excitement. The girls' close bond grew stronger as each day passed. They'd snuggle up in their sleeping bags in front of the TV, swapping their innermost thoughts about whomever they were crushing on, the annoyances of having siblings, and now, the commonality of coming from a broken home.

Both girls had each other. And that was fine with them. While they weren't necessarily in the popular crowd, they weren't outcasts. They were just two additional cast members in the theatrical production of high school.

The two had their routine. At first, they'd say, "Let's go stalking," and giggle as if they were mad. But once Sam coined it the "Hampton Park Hustle," it was on. And a daily occurrence.

Each day, after school or volleyball practice, they'd spill into Sam's car—a fourteen-year-old Honda Civic with a nail shoved into the radio's power button to keep it on. It wasn't a luxury ride but reliable enough for a teenager.

Taryn and Sam would talk and drive. First, through the McDonald's drive-through for a hot fudge sundae with nuts. Then, they'd drive by the homes of their objects of affection—or attention, really. Up first was the home of Todd Ferguson—the senior quarterback on the football team. Then, they'd move on to the others, like Taryn's crush, Billy Moran. They'd add or remove different stops into the rotation. Some days, they'd scoot by the popular Les Bean's house, who Sam was crushing hard for. Everyone called Les "Lesbian"—and he went with it.

"I love lesbians!" he'd yell out when someone called him by the moniker. His confident cockiness negated any attempted insult.

Most days, Taryn and Sam prayed no one would be outside during their Hampton Park Hustle and catch them. Which they never did.

Until that one Saturday night junior year.

That became The Night that changed everything.

CHAPTER SEVEN

It was April when Taryn left Illinois, and spring hadn't yet made up its mind on whether it had sprung. But that was typical Chicago. One day, it would be overcast and frozen. The next, the sun shone brightly as the dirty, salt-crusted snow melted. Taryn always loved the sound of the trickle of liquid snowflakes filtering into the storm drains.

But now, she couldn't stomach the thought of being in the Prairie State.

Starting today, Taryn was in the Sunshine State—which Lynn had always referred to as "the wang of the United States"—with no real plan.

From Graham's unsent confession and utilizing her journalistic knack for digital sleuthing, Taryn was able to piece together enough to have a starting point. She'd checked his email to see if he'd sent the "Evelyn" document to this woman or to anyone. It appeared he hadn't. Though she also realized he could have deleted it and emptied his recycle bin. Taryn knew she was no IT expert. But Graham's email recycle bin hadn't been emptied in the past sixty days, so Taryn was doubtful.

Evelyn, it turned out, was Evelyn Witmer. Formerly Evelyn Sanders. Thanks to his Google document with all his usernames and passwords, Taryn was able to access Graham's college alumni accounts to begin her research.

But it wasn't as simple as Taryn had hoped. Evelyn had absolutely no social media presence, except for pictures and videos of her shared by her employer.

Taryn knew it was a no-no, but she'd tapped into one of the online background check websites to unearth whatever she could about Evelyn. And that's where she struck gold.

Evelyn was 36, divorced and living in Gardenia Beach, a city on the east-central coast of Florida. It turned out she hadn't needed the bachelor of arts in social work degree she'd earned after all. From what Taryn could unearth from the background check report and a little bit of googling, Evelyn was now a bartender at the Wayside Watering Hole. It was the latest in one of many hospitality industry stints.

Looking at her research, Taryn could see Evelyn hadn't stayed at one job for long. Four months here, nine months there. There definitely was a pattern, not that it was anything out of the norm in the bar and restaurant business. A DUI charge and plea deal popped up in her criminal records, as well as a couple of disorderly intoxication charges. Taryn's heart sank as she scrolled through the rest, sickened by this snapshot of Evelyn's existence.

Taryn's breath had caught when she saw beyond the data. Wayside's social media accounts had unearthed the face of the woman who Graham had assaulted—a pretty but prematurely aging, deeply tanned, long-haired brunette with sparkling hazel eyes. "Enjoy 2-for-1 Happy Hour with our stellar Thursday night bartenders, Evelyn and Sheila!" one Instagram post beckoned, the two women hoisting up bottles of well liquor and smiling for social media. And then there was her ex-husband, who was on Face-book, his profile photo a photo of ... Evelyn? Fortunately, his news feed was public, and in it were picture after picture of not him, but just Evelyn. It befuddled her, given county records had shown they had, in fact, divorced three years ago.

Around the time Taryn exchanged vows with Graham.

That's when simply knowing who Evelyn was exploded into much more.

Right then, Taryn needed to know what Evelyn had become.

And if it was because of her husband.

CHAPTER EIGHT

The Tiki Torch Inn was exactly as it sounded—a "resort" that was just a dumpy old motel. A variety of colorful, big-toothed tiki heads adorned the sliding glass doors, some smiling, some scowling. Some even looking stupid. Taryn took note of their brightly painted, wooden horse-like chompers as she shuffled in at seven thirty at night, thankfully avoiding the backlog of tired tourists anxious to get into their rooms at the three o'clock check-in time.

"Aloha," the chubby, bearded registration clerk proclaimed as Taryn strolled toward the front desk. "Welcome to the Tiki Torch Inn."

His royal blue Hawaiian shirt was adorned with palm trees and hula dancers—and looked a size too small for the thirtysomething man, sporting a name tag reading "Rick." *Way to sell this place,* Taryn thought as she observed Rick's slovenly appearance when he greeted her.

"Thank you," Taryn said, feigning a smile.

Please don't let him be chatty, she thought.

"And who are we checking in this evening?" Rick asked with a grin, like a teenage boy who had just spied his first glimpse of internet porn. Taryn wondered what poor woman had said "I do," noting the cheap, tarnished knockoff silver wedding band.

"Metcalf," she said, a hint of exhaustion in her voice. "T.R. Metcalf."

Rick pecked away at the 2010-era keyboard, the keys making a pronounced *tap, tap, tap* with each stroke. He studied the screen, clicked on the mouse and said, with drawn-out fashion, "Ahhhh, yesss. Checking in for one."

His brow furrowed.

"I see you are staying with us for a full month," he said.

Taryn's heart picked up the pace. She offered a weak smile.

"Yes. But I'm not sure how long I'll be staying. Can I keep it kind of open-ended?"

Rick offered a grin that reminded Taryn of the Cheshire Cat.

"As long as we have the space," he said. "And we usually do. We do have guests here who stay while they're in between places."

"Wonderful," Taryn responded, immediately pirouetting into a lie. "I'm here to help my mom out for a bit with her health issues, so I'm not sure how long she'll need me."

"Can't stay with her?" Rick asked with a hint of concern.

Taryn's pulse continued to quicken. She didn't need anyone, least of all the Tiki Torch Inn desk clerk, to know her business. But she needed to act with grace. She certainly didn't need any bad juju on Day One.

"Sometimes it's best to have your own space, especially during a longer visit," she explained with a tender smile, her eyes pleading for empathy. "You know what they say about fish and relatives—after three days, they start to stink."

Rick chortled.

"Ah, yes," he said. "I understand all too well."

He finished checking her in, handing her a vintage motel-style keychain with the number 106 on it. *No wonder the rooms were so dirt-cheap*, she thought. *Almost every other place has a digital plastic room keycard. There'd better not be bedbugs.*

The thought made her quiver.

"Enjoy your stay," Rick said, the middle two buttons of his shirt fighting to break free from his pasty flesh underneath the fabric. He handed her a parking permit, which expired in a week. "Just make sure to come back every week you remain with us to make sure your pass is current, or you might get towed. We keep a close eye on them. You know, locals who want to go to the beach and don't want to feed the meters."

"Absolutely," Taryn replied, eager to get to her room.

"The pool is open from eight to eight each day," Rick said, running through the perfunctory check-in details. "There is no room service, but there are vending machines near the ice machines. The Wi-Fi password is on a leaflet in the room. Let us know if you need anything."

"Thank you," Taryn said, grabbing her purse and key and heading to the exit. "I will."

Taryn pulled her Ford Fiesta into a parking space as close as she could get to Room 106. The concrete parking block was cracked, with rusty rebar snaking out from the top. She grabbed her duffel bag and backpack, wheeling the former to the door with a matching number. The room was tucked into the back corner of the motel, closer to the beach than the pool, which pleased her. She didn't need to hear the screeches of small children and teenagers splashing into the water. The more privacy and sounds of the ocean waves, the better.

Taryn's hands were still chapped from the dryness of Chicago, which she noticed as she slid the metal key into its slot, deeply breathing in as she turned it clockwise, hearing the click.

The beige-walled room was what she'd expected for a cheap, three-star-rated motel that clearly hadn't been renovated since the 1990s. The queen-size bed's comforter was teal and pink, with whitewashed nightstands and a matching dresser to boot. The lamps were mauve and ceramic, the lampshades a dingy white—something that reminded her of her Aunt Mo's apartment some twenty-five years ago. All the hardware, including the hanging light above the small, two-person table in the corner of the room, was an ugly, weathered brass.

After bringing in the rest of her belongings, Taryn walked down to the corner liquor store, grabbing a bottle of vodka and a six-pack of club soda, which she plunked down on the countertop for the clerk to ring up. Tomorrow would be Thursday, the day she knew the Wayside Inn would be touting the top-notch bartending services of Evelyn, if the norm of social media posts she'd been studying followed its typical pattern. She spied the cornucopia of cigarette choices behind the clerk, recalling how aged beyond her years Evelyn appeared in the photos. She had to be a smoker. And Taryn needed to hedge her bets.

"Can I have a pack of Marlboro Light Menthols?" she asked the blond, surfer-looking guy at the counter.

He smirked.

"That's not what they call them anymore," he said, grabbing the white and green pack with hints of gold, tossing it in the plastic shopping bag. "But sure. Need a lighter?"

"That or two sticks I can rub together," Taryn said with a friendly-enough smile.

The clerk grabbed a Bic adorned with a surfboard illustration. He slapped it into the sack. Taryn handed him a fifty-dollar bill. He popped open the register and handed her the change.

"Surf's up," he said.

Taryn grabbed her bags and headed to the door before offering him a nod.

"Peace out, man," she said, heading into the night, back to her temporary seaside home.

***

When Taryn returned to Room 106, she was beat. She lifted her bags onto the table, setting them down with a thunk, and spied and grabbed the ice bucket. There was no plastic liner for it, not that she cared or had time to call down to Rick. Hopefully, it was washed, but she figured the alcohol in her drink would kill any germs teeming in it.

She shuffled down to the ice machine, her white and brown-soled flip-flops smacking as she walked, overfilling the bucket to the point she'd be unable to secure the lid on top. Her mind was preoccupied with tomorrow's quest.

When Taryn got back to the room, she spread out the tattered bathmat on the floor before running the shower as hot as she could get it. The tub tile was dingy, fitting for the room, and she hoped she wouldn't pick anything up from her bare feet's exposure to it.

After standing underneath the weak stream of water for ten minutes or so, Taryn emerged feeling somewhat relaxed but ready for a nightcap. She put on her usual bed clothes—a black camisole and yoga pants. The faded fabric hung from her ass, like a toddler with a urine-soaked diaper. Not that anyone was going to see. And not that she even cared.

Her bright, freshly dyed red hair tucked into a bath towel, Taryn grabbed one of the plastic water cups from the vanity, scooping it into the ice bucket. She'd have to ask for a glass tomorrow. Or maybe buy a tumbler at the drugstore. She'd probably need a to-go cup for the beach, anyway.

Taryn could taste the vodka as she poured it an inch from the lip of the cup, its scent wafting into her nostrils. Since Graham's death, her usual shot per drink didn't suffice. She needed a healthy pour to numb her reality and help her drift off to sleep. She topped it off with a splash of club soda, sat on her bed and sipped. She could go for a lime wedge. Not that she had a knife to cut one with anyway. She rested the cheap cup on the leaflet containing the Wi-Fi password, picked up her phone and texted Lynn.

"Made it. I'll be in touch. Just need time to recalibrate. XOXO," she typed before putting her phone on "do not disturb" mode, tossing it to the side on the comforter.

Within five minutes, Taryn downed a sleeping pill with a few glugs of her drink before shuffling back to the table to make another. Taryn flipped on the TV, watching a rerun of *The Golden Girls* as the pill and booze slowly muddied her thoughts. As she finished off her fourth drink, she leaned to put the cup on the nightstand and missed, the plastic and its cubes of ice tumbling onto the brown motel carpeting. She didn't bother to clean it up, figuring there had been worse things that had seeped into the carpeting.

Taryn turned off the TV and rested her head on the pillow, which felt about as thin as a buttermilk pancake. As she began to drift off, she stared above at the tobacco-tinged popcorn ceiling.

But all she really saw was Evelyn's face.

CHAPTER NINE

A knock at the door jostled Taryn out of her late-morning slumber. She groggily opened her eyes, scanning the room, and wondered where the hell she was.

"Housekeeping." The thick accent of an older woman was muffled through the door. *Knock, knock, knock.*

Ah, yes, she remembered. Florida.

"I'm good today," Taryn forced out from her raspy vocal cords. She heard the housekeeper's feet shuffle, the wheels of the cart squeaking by her window.

The familiar pounding of a hangover pulsed in her temple. She reached over on the nightstand for a cup of water, deflated when she discovered she'd forgotten to put one out. Taryn knew better. Hydrate, no hangover. No hydration, massive hangover.

Taryn flung her legs, which felt like they weighed fifty pounds each, over the side of the bed. As she stood up, her feet squished into the motel carpeting, a plastic cup crunching beneath her toes as she brought her body weight to the ground.

"Fuck," she said, remembering when she knocked over her late-night libation the evening before. Maybe sending the housekeeper away wasn't a good idea. Not that the woman had a steam cleaner in tow.

Taryn shuffled to the bathroom, looking at her reflection in the mottled motel mirror. Seeing the reflection, with bright auburn hair, peering back at her still surprised her each time, but the shock value lessened with every glance in the mirror. She looked like she'd aged five years in the five weeks since Graham's death. *Did widowhood do this to everyone?* she thought. *Or just widows of sex offenders?*

The memory made her stomach wretch.

Momentarily sickened and dizzy, Taryn headed to her bathroom. She lowered her bottom to the cold, small white tiles of the floor, peering up at the countertop and spying a bottle of ibuprofen. At least she remembered that. She grasped the floor, pushed herself up and steadied herself at the sink before opening the bottle and dispensing four gel caps into her palm. She tossed them back, ran the water from the tap and cupped her hand, taking several swigs before getting it all down.

After the ache in her head began to subside, Taryn knew some greasy food was in order. The perfect cure for a hangover. She'd spied The Pancake Place, a Southeastern diner chain, on the drive over, just a few blocks from the Tiki Torch Inn. A brisk walk, some sunshine and a greasy breakfast might be just the remedy.

Taryn brushed through her hair, assembling it into a messy bun. She splashed her face with water and a little of the hotel soap, brushed her teeth and slapped on some sunscreen. She slipped out of her camisole and yoga pants, slipping on her bra, Nirvana T-shirt and jean cutoffs before sliding her feet into her flip-flops. She grabbed her phone, purse and sunglasses and quickly glanced at her appearance in the dingy vertical mirror as she headed out the door.

She liked her new hue. *It suits me,* Taryn thought. She also liked that Graham was averse to redheads ever since Jimbo's Big Red college feat.

"I'm a sucker for blondes," he'd told Taryn early in their courtship. "Red doesn't do it for me."

The glaring sun struck her with full force as she headed down the tiki torch path to the sidewalk lining A1A. She made a mental note to buy a beach hat when she went to the store, feeling the sun's intense rays on her forehead as the traffic scuttled by.

The walk down to the Pancake Place reminded her of being in Vegas—the destination appeared to be just next door but was a little bit more of a jaunt. Within ten minutes, Taryn slid into a darkened wood-colored booth, her shoulders resting against the red cushion attached. She grabbed the plastic-coated picture menu and ordered her gluttonous indulgence—hash browns, fully loaded. And it hit the spot. All the grease, meat, cheese, potatoes, paired with a regular fountain Coke, seemed to instantly cure last night's overindulgence aftermath.

"Mmpfh," Taryn grunted as the waitress, an older woman with silver-coiffed hair, came to take her almost-clean plate away.

"Quite an appetite for such a skinny little thing," the server said with a Southern twang and a smile.

Taryn blushed bright red, pushing her plate away from her. Why she smarted at the comment of a woman who looked like she had a perm straight out of 1983 was beyond her, but it irked her.

"It'll be the only thing I eat today," she said. "Intermittent fasting."

"You don't need to explain nothin' to me, honey," the waitress said, winking so that her blue eyeshadow shone. "Whatever you're doin' works."

"It's called the dead husband diet," she said. The waitress's color drained her face to pale and her smile dissipated, and Taryn immediately felt like shit.

"I'm sorry, sweetie," she said, scurrying away before looking back. "I'll get you your check."

Taryn immediately felt horrible. *Why do I always get so defensive?* she thought. *Poor woman was just being friendly.*

The waitress came back and set the bill facedown.

"Have a good day, sweetheart," she said with a meek smile. "I'm sorry for your loss."

"Thank you," Taryn said sheepishly, wanting to duck out of there as quickly as possible.

When she righted the check, she was shocked. There was no total. Just a note.

To the beautiful redhead with a broken heart,

From one widow to another, this one's on me.

May you find peace and healing. If you need support, please reach out. God bless,

Dottie

Taryn felt even more awful. Dottie even left her number. Taryn looked over at the woman, who was reading out her next table's order to the line cook. Taryn dug into her purse, pulled out a ten-dollar bill, nestled it under the check and crept out the front door.

Enough of this bellyaching, Taryn thought. *It's time for an attitude adjustment. And time to focus on the reason you're here.*

Her stomach full, Taryn shuffled back a little more slowly to the Tiki Torch Inn and crawled right back into bed. A full three hours later, she awakened to the sound of teenage boy feet clomping past the outside corridor lining her room. At first she was annoyed, but when she saw it was already two fifteen in the afternoon, she knew she needed to begin her sleuthing for the evening's outing.

Taryn stripped out of her clothes and slipped into the black one-piece bathing suit with the sheer striping across the belly. Taryn had never been comfortable in a bikini, whether she weighed 148 pounds or her all-time low of 124, which she suspected was no longer the case. Just looking at herself in the mirror told her she was likely in the 110s. She grabbed a bath towel and beach bag, into which she crammed sunblock and a trashy celebrity magazine she'd grabbed at Chicago Midway International Airport while waiting to board her flight. Normally, a day outside lounging by the water would call for a Stephen King, chick-lit or domestic thriller novel, but she hadn't been able to focus on anything of substance since Graham's death. Taryn flipped her beach hat onto her head, grabbed her phone and headed to the ocean.

As Taryn's feet sank into the sand off the boardwalk, she was struck with the sense of peace the blue-green water brought her. She sauntered over to an open space with the least number of toddlers and teenagers around, flattened her towel out on the ground and let out a sigh of relief as her behind touched the fabric. Taryn gazed at the horizon, noting a cargo ship and what looked like a tiny cruise ship out in the distance. For a brief moment, she wished Graham was next to her. And, almost on cue, she heard the hum of a small plane. As it came into her field of vision, she saw the banner flapping behind it:

"HAPPY HOUR 4-7: WET UR WHISTLE AT THE WAYSIDE"

Taryn's stomach sank. She wished she'd had a few more minutes to forget about her derailed track to happily ever after. But the banner also compelled her to slide her hand into her beach bag, pull out her phone and start scrolling.

"Come see us for Happy Hour from 4-7! Early bird gets the tequila worm!" read the Facebook post of the Wayside Watering Hole. A tan woman's hand held up a bottle of tequila thrust into the foreground. She couldn't see the face behind the bartender holding it, the photo seemingly shot in iPhone portrait mode, blurring most of what was beyond the bottle. The post didn't tout who was bartending that evening, but Taryn wasn't worried. It was time to enmesh herself as a local. And step one was perching atop one of the Wayside Watering Hole's barstools. She scooped up her belongings and headed back to the Tiki Torch Inn.

"Time to get to work," Taryn muttered to herself.

Chapter Ten

T he walk from the Tiki Torch was less than ten minutes. It was a reasonable distance for Taryn, given her penchant for alcohol—and her purpose for being there in the first place.

When Taryn first soaked in the Wayside Watering Hole, she fully felt for the first time that she was in Florida, the warm, pleasurable breeze welcoming her. As she approached the gravel parking lot, she could see it certainly fell under the moniker of a typical Florida dive bar. The rickety deck was salt-worn and in need of a fresh paint job. The tropical foliage ensconced it and needed a trim. The picnic tables and the empty outside bar were likely reserved for busier time periods and overflow crowds. Maybe even outdoor music festivals. With each step closer to the bar, her heart's tempo grew faster. *Am I seriously doing this, whatever this is?* Beads of sweat from the walk and anticipation dotted her forehead. Taryn grasped the handle of the door of the turquoise-painted building and pulled it toward her.

As she stepped onto the terra-cotta tile, the sounds of classic rock—"Slow Ride" by Foghat—met her ears. She slowed her gait as she entered, wondering if she was moments away from meeting *her*.

It was only five thirty. Early enough for locals and snowbirds to be boozing but maybe not most of their customers. After all, it was only a Wednesday night.

As Taryn approached the bar, she saw only a few people, staggered almost purposefully, throughout its U-shape. A skinny, curly-haired brunette bartender stood on the other side, wearing a fitted black tank top, which read Wayside Watering Hole, and jean cutoffs. She looked to be in her mid-forties or perhaps even younger, Taryn thought, if years of hard living had taken their toll. A bottle opener protruded from her back left pocket.

"Hey there, honey," the bartender said with a warm smile. "Welcome to the Wayside. What can I do you for?"

Taryn glanced from side to side as the trio of other patrons all seemed to look up at the same time, looking her over. Two were older men, likely in their sixties and weather-worn, like they'd spent a lifetime outside mowing lawns or fixing air conditioners. The third, a fiftysomething bleached-blond woman gussied up in rhinestones and other accouterments, pulled a Virginia Slim from her cigarette pack before standing up to head to the door. She peered at Taryn under an arched, overplucked brow. A couple, likely in their thirties, sat at a table at the windows, overlooking the water, their backs to Taryn. She saw the man whisper in the woman's right ear, making her giggle.

"A Tito's and soda with a splash of cran," Taryn said as she rested her purse on the bar. She noticed it was clear, with sand nestling seashells, a variety of fish and even a seahorse between the plexiglass and the base.

"You got it, hon," she said, grasping a bottle, scooping out ice cubes with a translucent plastic cup, eyeballing a hefty serving of the liquor into it and finishing it off with a soda gun. "Want a lime?"

"Yes, please," Taryn said with a smile.

"I'm Sheila," the waitress said as she hoisted the drink toward Taryn, bending at the hip so her customer didn't have to exert much energy. "You startin' a tab?"

Taryn didn't want to use plastic. No last names needed to be seen in this establishment.

"Nah, I've got cash," Taryn said, opening the flap of her beige purse and fishing through it for a loose twenty-dollar bill. She found it nestled beneath the unopened pack of cigarettes and planted it on the bar.

"Good move," Sheila said, adding as she motioned toward a scribbled Post-it note taped onto the front of the cash register, "since we add a three-percent fee for credit cards."

Sheila scooped up the bill, traipsed over to the cash register and rang her up. She returned with the change. Taryn noticed the folds of her cleavage, mottled by years of sunbathing, cigarettes and probably too much booze.

"Thank you, dear," Sheila said, pushing the loose dollar bills and change onto the bar top. Taryn left a three-dollar tip and funneled the rest into her purse.

She held the drink with her right hand, fingered the plastic straw with her left thumb and index finger and sipped. It was stiff—just how she liked it. And it went down way too smoothly.

Taryn tried to slow herself down, though her nerves made it a challenge. Her eyes scanned the bar. Sheila appeared to be the only bartender on duty. A twentysomething dark-haired busboy came in through the north-side door, delivering a steaming plate of buffalo wings to the countertop.

"Thank you, Mike," Sheila said, scooping up the plate, walking it over to one of the older men—wearing a blue Salt Life T-shirt and a diamond stud in his left earlobe—and offered the patron a smile. "Here you go."

"Thanks, darlin'," he said with a grin. Steam rose from the wings, and Taryn could smell the spicy sauce from across the bar, shooting straight into her sinuses. She thought of how she and Graham would destroy two dozen of them easily.

Back when life was good.

Taryn could tell Sheila had her game down. She noticed her drink was three-quarters gone and came back over.

"Another?" she said with a non-judgmental twinkle.

"Absolutely," Taryn replied. "And a water, too, please."

"Sure thing."

Taryn laid another seven dollars out—four dollars for the drink, the rest the tip. She needed to gather information. So it was time to make small talk.

"So, is this the typical weeknight crowd?" she asked.

Sheila wrinkled her nose.

"Actually, this is kind of dead. It's been a little slow lately. Not sure why," she said, furrowing her eyebrows. "It depends on what's going on locally. Bigger crowds during spring break, summers, whenever we have festivals going on. Thursdays through Sundays are pretty hoppin'. It's really the off-season now. Our spring breakers have already come and gone."

Sheila wiped the countertop with a bar rag, then set it back down out of sight.

"I actually usually have another bartender here with me," she said. Taryn's heart jostled a bit. "But I told her to take the night off, since the last few Wednesdays have been uneventful. Not worth her time.

"And more money for me," she added, a smirk surfacing. "Besides, I know she was tearing it up last night pretty hard anyway. She could probably use a day to detox."

Taryn forced a laugh but thought she passed it off as genuine. "Well, couldn't we all?" she said.

"That would be true," Sheila said. "Do you want to see a menu?"

Taryn briefly thought about the buffalo wings, but after eyeing Mr. Salt Life gnawing on one across the bar like a gremlin, she decided to pass.

"Maybe a little later," she said.

"Okay, hon," Sheila said. "You just holler. I'm gonna see if anyone else needs a refill and then sneak out for a smoke."

"Sounds good," Taryn said. "I could use one myself."

"There's a bunch of ashtrays out on the north deck," Sheila said before turning to check on the other customers. "I'll see ya out there."

Taryn nodded and took another swig. As she began to hoist herself off the barstool, an olive-skinned, blue-eyed man with a generous head of thick brown hair appeared at her left. She breathed in the salt and sweat that clung to him as she tried to secretly peer to her side. Normally, that kind of smell would disgust her. But she found it oddly appealing.

Taryn quickly corrected her gaze straight ahead, zeroing in on a bottle of gin as she sipped on her water before taking another swig of her drink. She scooped up her purse, leaving her water and sunglasses behind as a placeholder.

Taryn hadn't smoked a cigarette in a good five years. She swung the door open and stepped outside, where she saw Sheila bring a lighter up to the smoke pursed between her lips.

Following suit, Taryn dug into her purse, pulled out the pack of menthol cigarettes and instinctively smacked the box against the palm of her hand. She grabbed the plastic tab, unraveled the top of the wrapper, flipped the top and swiftly tore the foil off. She pinched the top of a cigarette filter to slide it out of the pack.

Taryn brought it to her lips, the lighter to her mouth and inhaled. Immediately, it went to her head. Sheila giggled.

"Your first time?" she said. Now, Taryn felt judged. And ridiculous.

"I quit for a while," Taryn stammered, as the lightheadedness began to fade. "It's been a rough couple of months. Old habits. They die hard, as they say."

Sheila nodded.

"No worries," she said as she dragged. "There are so few of us left, I'm happy to have the company."

Taryn sucked on the cigarette, first wondering why she even bought a pack. But then she remembered. She had to fit in. If she wanted to get to know *her. And honestly—and with complete disgust—it kind of tasted good*, Taryn thought. It brought her to a simpler time. *One in which I didn't have a rapist husband*, she thought, as her face flushed at the thought.

"Are you okay?" Sheila asked. "You don't seem right. Not that I know you."

Taryn forced herself to smile weakly, nodding her head in reassurance.

"Yeah," she said. "Just getting used to my new digs and all."

"Oh?" Sheila asked with a sudden interest. "You just moved?"

Taryn's defenses kicked into high gear, not wanting to reveal too much or raise any red flags.

"Kinda," she said. "I'm visiting my mom. Just a change of pace."

"Ah," Sheila said. "You didn't seem local. Your twang ain't from around here. Wisconsin?"

"Chicago," she said, the booze acting as a truth serum. "South-sider."

"Ah," Sheila said, snubbing out her cigarette. "You Midwestern folks are good peeps. Explains the healthy tip," she said with genuine gratitude.

"We try," Taryn said, putting out her cigarette, too.

"Well, shall we?" Sheila said.

"Of course."

When they walked back into the bar, Taryn saw her sunglasses and water didn't do much good. In fact, her sunglasses were currently bridged on the nose of a brunette who had interlocked her left arm into the crook of the man who'd saddled up next to Taryn's seat just five minutes ago. The woman snorted as she giggled, playfully punching the man in the chest as she leaned into him. Taryn was immediately annoyed that someone would be so brazen as to put her Maui Jims on, but then, she remembered, she did leave them unattended in her quest to befriend the bartender.

"Oh, Everlast," Sheila huffed. "I thought you were taking a breather tonight."

Everlast looked up at Sheila, her right hand grasping the arm of Taryn's sunglasses, then tipping them down to reveal her hazel eyes.

"I am," she said.

And that's when Taryn realized Everlast was more than a pourhouse powerhouse.

She was Evelyn. She was *her*.

CHAPTER ELEVEN

Taryn froze as she looked over Evelyn. From the way Evelyn slyly returned her gaze, she knew she had to act fast.

Sheila butted in first.

"Everlast," she said. "Those ain't yours."

Evelyn's grin expanded.

"Oh, I know," she said, removing the nearly three-hundred-dollar, polarized, turquoise-tinted sunglasses and setting them on the bar. "I was just borrowing them. They suit me, though, don't you think?"

"Sure," Sheila said. "Maybe I've been a little heavy-handed with the tips if you can swing those and I'm wearing Walmart shades."

Evelyn brushed her hair back, tucking her brunette locks behind her ears. Her body was taut, evidenced by the skin-tight purple tank top she sported. Her olive skin was deeply tanned. Fine lines were beginning to set in around her mouth, a telltale sign of years of heavy smoking. Evelyn ran her right hand through her thick hair, and Taryn noted the cubic zirconia horseshoe ring nestled on her middle finger. Evelyn's hand slithered back to the sunglasses atop her head, removing them and then scrutinizing the polarized lenses.

"A girl can dream, right?" she said to the man saddled up next to her. "Don't you think these suit me, Austin?"

"They're very nice," the attractive man said. "And they definitely suit you. But they're not yours."

Evelyn looked at Taryn and cocked her head to the left.

"Sorry, sweets," she said as she curled the left side of her mouth. "I was just testing them out."

Taryn, not wanting to stammer or seem out of sorts, smiled.

"It's fine. Just be warned—you wear a pair of Maui Jim's, and you'll never go back to what you wore before," she said, attempting to defuse the tension so thick in the air. "Guaranteed."

Evelyn smiled as Austin leaned his head into her left shoulder. Then her gaze turned cold.

"Well, good," she said, snatching the tinted spectacles from the bar and popping them back onto the bridge of her celestial nose. "Looks like I have a new pair of sunglasses."

Taryn couldn't stop her mouth from falling agape. *Was this woman for real?*

"Ev," Austin said. "Don't be a dick."

Evelyn sneered at him, her head snapping quickly to face him, her eyelids bobbing with booze and rage.

"Why?" she barked. "*She* was a dick for thinking she could reserve a fucking spot at *my bar*. Who the *shit* is she?"

Evelyn turned back to Taryn, the pupils of her eyes dilated in an alcohol-induced haze. She began wagging her finger at the newcomer.

"Who *the fuck* do you think you are, anyway?" Evelyn slurred, suddenly standing up, the barstool's feet shrieking as she forcefully shoved it away with her butt. She tried to steady herself with her hands on the bar but tipped to the left a bit. Taryn, still unable to move or even speak, noticed the broken capillaries on the right side of Evelyn's nose. Clearly, this bender wasn't the first.

Sheila rounded the bar and, motherly, took to Evelyn's side.

"Okay, Everlast," she said, gently touching her arm. "Time to recharge your batteries. Or you're going to hate your two o'clock shift tomorrow. And we don't need a scene. Unless you want Jimmy to witness this shit show and send you packing."

"Okay, *Mom*," Evelyn retorted, her eyes rolling with annoyance.

Austin wrapped his arms around Evelyn and led her to face the door. As they neared the threshold, Evelyn abruptly stopped, turning back to look over her right shoulder to sneer at Taryn.

"Oh, here, Red," she said, yanking the sunglasses nestled atop her head and hastily tossing them at Taryn's feet. The metal frames hit the tile, and she could hear the crack.

"All yours," she snarked.

"*Enough*," Austin said sternly, guiding Evelyn past the doorframe to the front entrance. He quickly turned back to catch Taryn's attention, his eyes electric yet apologetic. He mouthed, "I'm so sorry," before continuing out the exit with a stumbling Evelyn, who spewed profanities with each step forward.

Taryn stood silently, unable to move. The static built so quickly in her brain, she felt as if she could barely keep her head lifted from where her chin shakily nestled onto her heaving chest.

Her mission hadn't begun how she'd hoped. Taryn's quest for peace, for the comfort and reassurance of knowing Graham's assault survivor was okay, was no longer on the table.

Evelyn was not okay.

As she stood in stunned silence, Taryn's mind ricocheted from Evelyn's meltdown to the disturbing details of what Graham had written, forever burned into her mind.

"I'm so incredibly sorry," Sheila said, ushering herself from behind the bar, bending over to pick up the mangled, cracked sunglasses.

"I … I …" Taryn trailed off, her eyes brimming with tears. *What the fuck have I done, thinking coming here was a good idea?*

"It's okay, honey," Sheila said, pulling out her phone. "What's your name and number? I'll make sure you get a new pair."

Taryn tried to fight the offer at first. She just wanted to forget this whole thing and crawl into bed back at the Tiki Torch. But Sheila persisted.

"I'm Rebecca," Taryn said, the first lie pouring from her lips with complete ease. "My phone is not working at the moment, and I'm due to get a new one, so I probably won't have the same number. But I'm in Room 106 at the Tiki Torch Inn."

"I'm so sorry this was your welcome party to Florida," Sheila said, outstretching her arm to touch Taryn's. "But really, did you expect any less from the wang of the U.S.?"

Taryn's tears trickled into laughter, thinking of how her sister's moniker was a common acknowledgment of the state of this state.

"I guess I just met Florida Woman," Taryn mused in between sniffles.

"Oh, honey." Sheila chuckled back. "She was just the opening act."

CHAPTER TWELVE

The searing sun woke Taryn the next morning, streaming in from the dingy white PVC vertical blinds she forgot to tightly shut.

"Ugh," she said, rolling to her side and burying her face into the pillow. She just wanted to forget last night.

What the hell was I thinking, coming down here? What did I expect I'd find?

Her hangover wasn't as bad as the night before. Still shaken from Evelyn's tirade, Taryn had stumbled home, popped an Ambien in her mouth and crunched down on the bitter pill, hoping to feel its effects as soon as possible. She slept like a log, which she hadn't in months. She knew she shouldn't mix booze with sleeping pills, but she really didn't care anymore. *Is this rock bottom?* she thought.

Once Taryn heard the scattered clomping footsteps of children running down the walkway, she flipped over and looked at the clock. Eleven o'clock. Her stomach almost instantaneously rumbled, and she immediately fantasized about scooping up a healthy serving of loaded hash browns and cramming their delicious greasiness into her mouth.

"Yes," Taryn said out loud. "Mama needs her some Pancake Place."

Taryn shuffled over to the bathroom, peed and turned to the mirror while washing her hands. She looked worse than she felt. She didn't bother washing her face last night. Remnants of her mascara and charcoal pencil eyeliner pooled into crusts at the corners of her eyes.

"Graham would certainly love you now," she said. But as she thought of the totality of that statement, the sickness and rage filled her innards. She spat at her reflection. The spittle stuck, then slowly sank in streaks, dripping in a tiny, nasty pool of liquid filth on the Formica countertop.

As she began to compose herself, Taryn thought about how she'd fibbed to Sheila the night before, saying her name was Rebecca.

It was more of a half-fib, really. Her full name was Taryn Rebecca Metcalf. And Taryn was incredibly grateful, especially now, that she'd hung on to her maiden name—something Graham had been okay with when they wed. Taryn had worked hard to build a professional reputation. And her mother, before her death, had been a proponent of women maintaining their identity. When Taryn and Lynn's father had abruptly abandoned the family to start a new one with his paralegal twenty years his junior, Nancy took back her maiden name of Metcalf. And she encouraged her girls to never lose sight of where they'd come from.

"You are who you are, and you should be proud," she'd told them on several occasions. "Embrace it."

Taryn followed, legally changing her last name to Nancy's about a year after the divorce. Her mom was her rock. Her father was dead to her. Not physically but mentally. He'd screwed over her mother. And her and her sister.

Shifting surnames mid-career wasn't something Taryn wanted to do. *Gazette* readers—as well as digital gloom-and-doom news consumers who clicked on her couple dozen viral stories that had stretched across the globe—had always known her as T.R. Metcalf. And she preferred to keep it that way. She didn't bust her ass in school and in the journalism world to abandon the name she'd worked so hard to boost.

So, it wasn't a complete lie. Taryn didn't want Sheila to know her real name. She wondered if that woman even existed anymore. The pre-widow Taryn was gone. And unlikely to ever come back. Taryn did tell Sheila where she was staying, though, specifying the room number and avoiding a cell number. She didn't want any confusion at the Tiki Torch front desk, now that she realized she'd backed herself into a corner.

Still fantasizing about a greasy, fat-laden breakfast, Taryn grabbed a bra and tank top out of the closet, tossed it on and eyed a pair of indigo jean shorts. She thought about all she planned to consume, knowing she didn't want her belly restricted, so she slipped into a pair of gray capri yoga pants. As she fed her feet into her flip-flops, she heard a light rap at the door.

"Hang on," she said, feeling guilty housekeeping would have to clean her saliva of shame from the vanity. "I was just heading to breakfast. I'll be out in a minute."

Taryn scurried back to the bathroom, grabbed a dirty towel and wiped the remnant of her meltdown from the mirror and counter. The house-keeper tapped on the door again.

Taryn huffed, grabbed her purse and beach hat and headed to the door.

"I'm leaving n—" She stopped mid-sentence as she swung open the door.

Taryn felt as the blood visibly drained from her face. She immediately saw the Sunglass Space plastic bag.

Held by Evelyn.

***

The two women stood there for what seemed like a full minute, communicating only with their eyes. Taryn's were filled with caution and apprehension. But Evelyn's spoke of sorrow and remorse.

"I was a total cunt," she said, sighing. "I am so sorry I acted like a complete asshole."

Taryn remained paralyzed. *Was this a ploy? Would this off-kilter hotbed of emotion pounce on her if given the chance?*

"Here," Evelyn said, holding out the white plastic bag for Taryn to take. She offered a genuine smile. "I'd write you an apology note, but I'm not into that shit."

Taryn meekly curled up the crevices of her mouth, still unsure of the woman before her. She took the hard sunglasses case out of the plastic bag and popped it open, revealing a beautiful, much more expensive pair of Maui Jims than she'd previously owned. They were crystal-colored with a hint of pink, large like a "Jackie O" pair of shades.

"They're called 'Siren's Sunset,' " Evelyn said, blushing. "The newest style at the shop. I thought they'd frame your face nicely. At least what I could remember of it."

"Oh," Taryn said, slipping the cat-eye shades on. They felt amazing, and from Evelyn's reaction, they must have looked it, too.

"Besides," Evelyn said, "being in Florida, you need a little more coverage for your eyes. The bigger, the better, I figured."

Taryn's heart began to beat heavily in her chest. She stammered, unsure of what to really say.

"Thank you so much," she said. "You really didn't have to. These are way more expensive than the old pair I had. They were probably on their way out, anyway."

"I did," Evelyn said, grinning as she ran her hands through her hair, gathering it into a high bun on the top of her head. "Now let's do this right."

Evelyn reached out her right hand to shake Taryn's. She slowly obliged.

"Hi, Rebecca," she began. "I'm Evelyn. And it's very nice to meet you."

Taryn pushed her new glasses to the top of her head and extended her hand.

"Hi, Evelyn," she said, clasping her hand in Evelyn's, shaking it. "It's great to meet you. With both of us sober."

Evelyn laughed, and the tension seemed to lift.

"True," she said. "But I suspect both of us are a little hung over."

"I think I'll plead the Fifth," Taryn said, attempting to lighten the conversation a little more.

"What do you say we grab something to eat?" Evelyn suggested. "Get last night's bad taste out of our mouths?"

Taryn nodded, her straight red hair bobbing as she agreed.

"I know the perfect place."

***

"I fucking love this shit," Evelyn said as she enthusiastically dug her fork into the heaping mess of gooey, cheesy hash browns piled on a plate in front of her. "I thought I was the only girl who would eat this crap on a plate."

Taryn nearly choked on the forkful of greasy food she'd shoveled in her own mouth.

"I know, right?" she said. "I'd never eat like this around people I know."

Evelyn took a swig of her Coke, which really looked quite delicious to Taryn, the fizzle of the carbonated bubbles rising to the surface.

"Well, it can be our little secret," Evelyn said. "I can't eat like this all the time or I'll look like ten pounds of shit in a five-pound bag in that tight little Wayside tank top."

Taryn giggled.

"I imagine you get plenty of exercise running back and forth in that bar on a Friday or Saturday night," she said.

Evelyn finished chewing, leaving half of her meal uneaten. She pushed the plate away.

"I'm done," she said, wiping the corners of her mouth with a napkin. "Yeah, it gets hopping, especially during touristy times. But I walk a lot, too. I only live about ten minutes up the road from the bar. It's convenient.

Especially considering I like to close the place down, even when I'm not pouring drinks. I don't need another DUI."

Taryn felt the unease rise from her throat, remembering her research revealing the arrest. But she had to act otherwise.

"Eeek," she said. "When did that happen?"

Evelyn sipped more of her Coke, completely unfazed by her own revelation.

"About a year ago," she said, pulling her phone from her purse. "I made the mistake of hitting another bar across the causeway on the mainland. Just dumb luck. My taillight was out, and a sheriff's deputy spotted me at the stoplight on State Road 520, right before the Banana River. Next thing you know, I was blowing a .09, handcuffed and sitting in a cell at the county jail, waiting for Austin to come bail my ass out."

"Oof," Taryn said, offering a glance of sympathy. "I'm so sorry."

"Don't be," she said. "I learned my lesson. Drink within walking distance."

"Ha," Taryn chuckled.

Deep down, it sickened her. A DUI wasn't enough to produce a wake-up call? Taryn wondered if Evelyn considered herself to be a problem drinker. But asking? There was no way. *Besides,* Taryn thought, *like I should be questioning anyone else's alcohol use.* Taryn shuddered, brought back to the realization of why she was here in the first place.

Evelyn rustled her shoulders back. She wiped her mouth with a napkin, placed it on her polished-off plate and pushed it toward the middle of the table.

"Enough about me," Evelyn said. "Tell me about you. I know nothing except that your current residence is at the Tiki Torch. What's your story?"

While Taryn had been expecting this question, it still took her off guard.

"Well," Taryn said, her mind immediately going to the fable she'd concocted in her head. "I am visiting my mom, whose health isn't well."

Evelyn looked intently at Taryn, swirling the plastic straw in her plastic glass to the left of her plate.

"I'm sorry to hear that," Evelyn said. "Can I ask what she's ill with?"

"Early-onset Alzheimer's," she said with poise, hoping to convince Evelyn of the tale she was spinning. "She's taken a turn for the worse in recent weeks, so I thought I'd come down to spend some time with her—before she completely forgets who I am."

Evelyn nodded, her eyes showing nothing but genuine interest. "I can understand why," she said, pausing to sip from her drink. "Where are you from?"

"Chicago," Taryn said, her heart fluttering a bit. *Please don't let her connect the dots,* she thought in between the story's pause. "I actually live downtown, close to Printer's Row."

"Wow." Evelyn listened with fascination. "What do you do for a living?"

"I'm in finance," she lied, her heart starting to pick up the beat. "It's a boring-ass job. I'll put you to sleep if I explain any further."

"Well, that sounds lucrative," Evelyn said. "Especially if you can afford a place downtown. I can't imagine the rent there."

"Thirty-one-hundred a month for a three-bedroom," Taryn said, immediately regretting she didn't say it was a one-bedroom studio. *Here it comes,* she shuddered.

"Holy crap," Evelyn said, picking up a napkin to wipe the corners of her mouth. "That's a lot. And a lot of space."

Evelyn looked at Taryn's hands before moving on to the next round of lies.

"I assume you aren't married, but in a relationship?" Evelyn asked. "That's a lot of space for a single person."

"Yes, it is," Taryn answered. "I'm actually divorced. It's somewhat recent, so I'll be looking for a new place once my lease is up. Maybe a one- or two-bedroom, depending on what's available. I'd love to stay at the same place and save a little on movers. But I also want a fresh start. I really don't want to live in the home where my marriage crumbled."

Taryn hoped her nerves, ramped up by her lies, weren't apparent to Evelyn, who took a moment before responding.

"You wanna talk about it?" she said, reaching out to touch Taryn's arm from across the table. "I know from experience that divorces are anything but enjoyable."

Taryn took a moment to compose herself. The tears streaming down her face weren't because of a failed marriage. But Evelyn didn't need to know.

"It's still a little raw," Taryn said, wiping her wet cheeks with a paper napkin, her eyes casually glancing over at Dottie, who was taking an order three tables down.

"I'll tell you another time. Just not here or now. I think I'd need a drink to delve into that whole mess."

Taryn saw Evelyn wince. She knew she convinced her. And maybe even upset her.

"Yeah," Evelyn responded, a hint of sadness on her face. "Another time."

Their waitress, wearing a name tag that said "Jenae," arrived as if on cue, scooping up their plates. As Taryn sat with the woman whom her husband had sexually assaulted years earlier, she wondered. *Had Jenae ever been subjected to such horrors? Had anyone else in the restaurant survived a sexual assault?* It was something she never gave much but a passing thought to prior to the letter. And now, through her internet research, she knew that one in five women are raped in their lifetime. She glanced around the room, silently tallying the ladies also patronizing the place. Ten, twelve, fifteen. So, statistically, about two or three people sitting here—eating their waffles, eggs and bacon and drinking steaming hot coffees—had been forced to have sex against their will at some point in their lives.

And one of them was sitting right across from her.

The thought made her want to regurgitate her breakfast on the table. She felt sick and weakened at the thought.

"You ladies need anything else?" Jenae asked when her rounds brought her back to Taryn and Evelyn's table, her eyebrow cocked.

"I think we've inhaled enough for the rest of the week," Evelyn said, leaning back and letting out a groan. "Just the check."

"Coming right up," Jenae said.

Evelyn finished off her soda as Taryn excused herself to go to the bathroom.

"That coffee's running right through my bladder," she said, standing up. "I'll be right back."

"Good luck," Evelyn said, peeking up briefly with a wry smile before noticing the ghastly, sick pallor that clung to Taryn's face. "Wait, you okay?"

Taryn nodded and bolted out of the booth, scurrying to the restroom. The women's single bathroom was locked.

"Oh shit," she said out loud.

She turned to the men's room as the door swung open and a tall, lanky, unshaven man in work boots, faded jeans and a "Make America Great Again" red hat emerged. Taryn dove in, quickly locking the door behind her before she skidded to the toilet and emptied the contents of her stomach into it. As she paused to breathe, she caught a whiff of the deodorant cake in the urinal that stood beside where she rested on her knees.

After five minutes of retching, she got up on her feet, wiping her mouth with the back of her hand. She flushed the toilet, walked over to the sink and splashed her face with cold water. She looked to her left. The paper towel dispenser was empty, so she lifted her shirt to dry off her face and hands.

For the second time today, there was a tap on the other side of the door.

What am I going to say to Evelyn? she thought. This conversation had been harder than she ever envisioned.

But when she opened the door, it was someone else. Dottie. The sweet waitress who had picked up her breakfast earlier in the week.

"Food's so good you couldn't wait to come back, I reckon?" she said with a concerned smile.

Taryn offered a meek grin. "I overdid it last night," she offered. "You'd think by my age, I'd have learned my lesson from my college days."

Dottie smiled. Her penciled-in eyebrows rose along with the edges of her mouth.

"Honey, you don't have to tell me. I was a slave to the bottle for years, especially after my husband died," she said, clearly recalling their earlier conversation. "Luckily, a dear friend talked me into getting help. And now, I'm eleven years sober. All in due time. You'll know if—and when—it's time."

Taryn smiled back, praying Evelyn would not overhear their conversation—because Dottie had a closer version of the truth than her current lunch mate. It didn't seem like a lecture, but a loving gesture to reach out to another hurting soul. *If only she knew what kind of an epiphany I'd recently had,* she thought.

"Be easy on you, my dear," Dottie said. "Because that's the best thing you can do for yourself. That, and helping others. If you ever have interest in the latter, give me a call sometime. I'm involved with a few local volunteer efforts. I'm sure one of them would be the perfect fit for you. Just let me know."

Taryn nodded and smiled at the sweet woman. And with that, Dottie adjusted the tie at the back of her apron and headed toward the kitchen.

Taryn lumbered back to the table, where Evelyn was scrolling through her phone. She looked up, and her expression turned to concern.

"Jesus," she said. "Looks like you won't be up for visiting me at the Wayside tonight."

Taryn's stomach gurgled again. Not so much at the thought of alcohol but of this oddly budding friendship.

"Yeah, I don't know," she said. "I think I need a serious nap."

Evelyn nodded. "Well, let's get you home. I'm due at the Wayside at two o'clock."

And with that, Evelyn pulled cash out of her purse, tucked it under the bill and rose to give it to Jenae.

"Oh, Evelyn," Taryn started. "You really don't need to. You've already given me those beautiful sunglasses."

Evelyn shook her head.

"Please, Becks," she said, a stark reminder that Taryn was not Taryn to Evelyn, but Rebecca. "That was my way of making amends. And this is my way of welcoming you to Gardenia Beach."

Taryn smiled and stood up, grateful but guilty for Evelyn's olive branch. As the two women approached the front door, Taryn heard a loud, "Wait, ladies!"

Taryn turned to see Dottie, who held out a small, folded piece of white receipt paper with her phone number scribbled on it. Again. Taryn took it as Dottie said with a sweet smile, "If you are interested, here's my number." And then Dottie slipped away to tend to her next customers, a family of five, which included a crying toddler.

"What's that about?" a befuddled Evelyn asked as Taryn marched out the door quickly. She made a mental note—no more Pancake Place meals unless she was alone.

"Oh, I told her about my divorce, last time I was here," Taryn quickly responded, leading the way to the sidewalk lining a bustling, tourist-packed A1A.

Evelyn looked confused. "I thought you didn't like talking about your divorce?"

Taryn looked at the cars whizzing by. "I don't," she said. "I just asked if there was a recent divorcee discount. I was a little fired up, just thinking about it all."

Evelyn's gaze appeared curious, but luckily, a text message popped up on her phone, drawing her instant attention.

"Looks like Wayside needs me as soon as possible," Evelyn groaned. "Mike, the morning shift, went home sick, so they're strapped. Duty calls."

Relief flushed through Taryn. Crisis averted.

For now.

CHAPTER THIRTEEN

While Taryn might have lied about her name to Evelyn, she didn't fib about her desire to climb back into bed. Once the ladies left the Pancake Place, they exchanged hugs, awkward for Taryn, yet Evelyn seemed unfazed. They said their goodbyes, and Evelyn told Taryn she should stop by the Wayside during her shift, if she started feeling better.

"I'll take care of you." She winked. "And I promise I won't fuck with *those* shades."

Taryn grinned, showing off her nearly perfect, broad smile, the product of her two years in braces. The whole situation still made her a bit unsettled.

"I have to go visit my mom today," she lied as her pulse quickened. Her mom's only visiting hours were from sunrise to sundown daily at Woodlawn Memorial up in Hampton Park, Illinois.

"Gotcha, gotcha," Evelyn said as she slipped a cigarette from her purse, bringing it to her lips and lighting it. "Well, you know where to find me. See ya later."

Evelyn turned, facing the breeze as she began her walk north on A1A. Taryn stopped only for a few moments to watch her stroll away, brown hair flapping in the breeze. She breathed in the remnants of the secondhand smoke. *A cigarette sounds good right about now,* she thought. She dug through her own bag for her smokes.

As Taryn headed to her motel, the traffic whirring by, she couldn't shake her troubled thoughts. Here, she'd come down to Florida to find the woman her dead husband had assaulted over a decade ago. And now, after a tumultuous start, Taryn was strangely drawn to her. Yes, it had started out horribly. But the woman had quickly made amends and tried to make things right—with a total stranger. The kind of thing Taryn's late mom had instilled in her.

"Always own up to when you're wrong," Nancy had often told her. "Say you're sorry as soon as you can. Because if you wait, you might not get the chance."

Her mom was a living example of that every day. Nancy was a truly happy, content woman who had moved on remarkably well after her husband, Taryn's father, Tom, had left for a handle of Jack Daniels one Sunday night and never came back. He'd simply sent Nancy and the girls an email, saying he needed to find his happiness.

Tom's definition of happiness was starting a brand-new family with his much-younger paralegal, Krystal, who quickly became his wife after his first marriage was legally dissolved. Nancy had been the rock her young girls needed as their family unit suddenly became a single-parent household. Taryn and Nancy were more than mother-daughter. They were almost like best friends. Taryn knew she could go to Nancy about anything. There was her pregnancy scare at seventeen—thank God it was just her teenage reproductive system figuring itself out. When her friend Julie had a sleepover, the girls snuck into the liquor cabinet and downed half a bottle of Beefeater, which ended in Julie's parents finding the girls drunk and sick—and calling Nancy to pick up her daughter. The time she got in a fight with her crazy boyfriend after her first year of college during a visit home. He'd falsely accused her of cheating, turned to her in a drunken haze behind the wheel on a winding road, his dark-as-death crazy eyes fueling her fear as he screamed at her, "You wanna meet your maker?" Taryn wept in pure terror as he accelerated to 120 miles per hour and begged him to stop. He eventually pulled over on the shoulder and Taryn scurried out, crying and running until a cop saw her and pulled over to assist. Again,

Nancy picked her up, never scolding her but being a source of comfort and strength—and making sure Crazy Eyes had a restraining order slapped on him.

Nancy was always there, unconditionally. She was Taryn's rock.

Until that January night, a week after New Year's, when the Mazda Miata she was driving during a brutal Chicago winter hit a patch of black ice, sending Nancy careening into a vacant strip mall. The doctor told Taryn and Lynn that Nancy never felt a thing.

How Taryn could use her mom's guidance right now. And her embrace.

***

Taryn woke up from her delicious two-hour nap and debated—did she go to the pool, beach or hit the grocery store so she wouldn't have to depend on vending machine snacks and restaurants for all her sustenance? She still didn't really have a plan in place.

Taryn needed to clear her head, maybe try that meditation bullshit her more earthy friends suggested. But for now, she felt the urge to shop. It had been ages since she'd gone to a supermarket, turning to delivery services in the days and weeks after Graham's death. Partly because she didn't have the stamina to push a cart through Jewel—and partly because she dreaded the thought of running into someone she knew and being the recipient of pitiful, sorrowful stares. She didn't need the widow treatment. She just needed the vodka treatment.

But here, in Gardenia Beach, it was different. No one knew her. No one would recognize Taryn as she pushed her cart down the frozen pizza aisle, accidentally locking eyes, awkwardly attempting small talk or suffocating her with inquiries about her well-being. Asking how she was doing and what they could do for her—even though that type of chatter always tended to be a pleasantry, not a sincere offer.

Taryn checked her phone and saw Publix was the closest place to stock up—and she really wasn't in the mood to hit another convenience store. Even though she really didn't care about money now, she wanted more variety. In two minutes, she was back behind the wheel of the Ford Fiesta and headed down A1A.

Taryn noted the huge neon, three-story surf shop on the east side of the road, just before the A1A intersected with Gardenia Causeway. Tourists flowed in and spilled out of the doors. Many more walked along the sidewalk, some headed for one of the cheaper beach stores hawking five-dollar T-shirts and beach towels, others filing into sandwich shops touting a quick bite or hand-spun milkshakes. Once she got north of the traffic light, past the Shark Bite Grill with the fake, chiseled predator jaws hanging from the marquee that advertised fish-kabobs and two-for-one Hurricanes, she spied the supermarket as her iPhone's GPS beeped at her to hang a left.

Taryn glided into the parking lot, gravitating toward the southern-most aisle from the front entrance—she didn't want to battle for the middle row, which seemed to be the way of the snowbirds down here. Her mom, who had loved that damn little car that ended up being her momentary coffin, had always parked it in the farthest spot possible in the lot of whatever shopping establishment or eatery she was patronizing. She didn't want her prized convertible to get dinged up by another errant car door, backed into by some jackass not paying attention. It had initially annoyed Taryn at first, but now she missed those quirks that used to irritate her. In her mom's absence, Taryn found herself adopting some of the behaviors that used to exasperate her.

The more walking, the better, Taryn told herself. Especially after that breakfast.

As she walked to the entrance, the doors parted and the shrill arctic breeze of the air conditioner swept into her face. Taryn shivered as she adjusted to the starkly different temperature inside the store.

Taryn grabbed a cart, even though she could probably get away with a handheld green plastic shopping basket. She wandered through the produce section, unable to remember the last time she ate a salad or some kind of vegetable. Even fruit had been shockingly absent from her diet lately. Back home, Lynn, who had been concerned with her sister's new widowhood diet of takeout and liquor delivery, had started showing up every few days with grocery staples—lunchmeat, cheese, bakery bread, pre-packaged salads and fruit. But, as did most of the food, it just sat there, either liquidizing or growing white or green-ish-black fuzz until Lynn came with the next supply. The first couple of times, she threw them out and balked at Taryn. After that, she only brought the items that would last longer, thanks to preservatives.

Taryn slowly pushed the cart past the apples and cherries, grabbing a small bunch of bananas. No washing, no refrigeration needed. There. That was her commitment to eating better for the week. She walked by the deli counter, thought about grabbing a half pound of turkey or cheese, but kept going. As she rounded the corner, the wine selection sat on her right. Her cart automatically began perusing the three short aisles of merlot, chardonnay, Riesling and more. While a vodka girl, she enjoyed her wine, too, often selecting a bottle from its name or label alone. She couldn't resist a libation with the moniker Fat Bastard or The Middle Sister. They were just fun.

It was the bottle of Gemma di Luna that made her heart and feet stop. As she spied the sleek, light pastel-blue bottle, she was brought back to her and Graham's honeymoon. They had splurged on one fancy dinner at a waterfront seafood restaurant in South Beach, eating surf and turf after Taryn downed that bottle of pinot grigio to Graham's three zero-alcohol beers. Taryn was too buzzed to really savor the food, as she giggled and even snorted at Graham as he tried to impersonate his softball league teammate George, who would jumble up sayings and have no clue he did so.

"Graham," George had told him once after he had hit a home run, even though it had been against a particularly shitty team. "You never seem to amaze me."

Taryn had been sitting on the metal bleachers and overheard it. Being a wordsmith and grammar whiz, the improper use of "seem" for "cease" cracked her up, and she had chuckled in the stands. When clueless George looked at her, puzzled, she simply said, "I tell him that all the time, too." Graham had tweaked his left eyebrow up in amusement in response.

It became their inside joke whenever one of them made a good choice with something. After Taryn had suggested the Ocean Waves Grille on a whim after seeing the Polynesian style ambience, the two had settled in and raised a glass. Graham smiled at her and said, "Taryn, you never seem to amaze me." They smiled their knowing smile, one shared between two people truly connected, and clinked their delicate wine glasses together, Graham's filled with sparkling water, before each taking a hearty sip.

Now, the bottle that used to bring her joy whenever she spied it on a grocery store shelf brought her a sensation of rage boiling up, first bubbling in her arms, making its way up her torso to her neck and flushed face. She could hear the blood whirring through her ears, pulsating as her temperature rose and her heart quickened.

"Can I help you with anything?" a sweet voice cut in, jarring her back into the brightly lit aisle of the Gardenia Beach supermarket. Taryn looked to her right, met by the kind eyes of a fair-skinned redhead with a green vest.

Taryn snapped out of her trance, wondering how long she had been numbly staring at the slick, pastel bottle of now-tainted memories. She feigned a smile.

"No, thank you," she said, grabbing two of the nondescript plain olive-shaded bottles next to it, not even looking at the labels. "I'm good."

She put them into her cart and pushed it right past the few-hours-old sushi selection she and Graham would snag from the seafood section during their jaunts to Florida, often late-night snacks if they had the mid-night munchies.

Instead of buying decent sustenance, Taryn piled snacks into her cart—Goldfish, teriyaki-pineapple beef jerky, electrolyte drinks for when the hangovers hit, a jar of peanut butter, Colby Jack cheese cubes and some artisan crackers. As she neared the checkout line, there was a display of hard seltzer beckoning her. She grabbed two twelve-packs and headed to the checkout line, grabbing a *People* magazine on impulse.

Taryn piled her cart of crap onto the conveyor belt and watched as an acne-faced teen named Erick rang it all up.

"How are you today, ma'am?" he robotically asked. "Did you find everything you were looking for?"

"Yes," Taryn said, "though I need a pack of Marlboro Light Menthols."

Erick turned around to grab the smokes, and she noticed the semicolon tattoo on the back of his neck. She wondered what he had to be depressed about.

"The green and gold pack, right?" he said, craning his neck back at her.

"Yes," she said. "It's been a while since I smoked."

"My dad used to smoke these," Erick said as he rang them up and gently placed them in the plastic bag.

"Did he quit?" she asked.

"Yeah," he said. "When he died."

Taryn felt her face heat.

"I'm sorry," she said, zipping her debit card through the machine, hurriedly grabbing her groceries and leaving as quickly as she could.

Taryn, a sinking feeling in her stomach, bolted to the car with her groceries, loaded them in and got ready to speed off toward the Tiki Torch. She didn't know why she was in a hurry, but she just wanted out of there. Once in the beige cloth driver's seat, she flipped open her pack of cigarettes, brought one to her lips and reached into her pocket for her lighter. A folded piece of white paper fell out as she retrieved her lighter. She noted the "no smoking" sticker affixed to the rental and sighed.

As she stepped out of the car for her nicotine fix, she dialed the number scribbled, her fingers trembling.

"Hi," she responded to the voice that answered. "I want to help."

CHAPTER FOURTEEN

After getting back from her grocery run and phone call, Taryn slipped into her one-piece black swimsuit with sheer striping across the belly. She slid the beige beach hat she'd picked up at the store atop her head before grabbing a beach towel from the Tiki Torch's pool. With her blue beach bag carrying her *People* magazine, cigarettes and a few of the hard seltzers, she headed down to the surf. She'd lain the towel some twenty feet from the shore, covered her eyes with her new specs and dozed off to the calming sounds of the ocean waves.

Taryn felt a sense of purpose after that call. A surprised Dottie had said, "Yes, absolutely! I have a few connections with local volunteerism."

Dottie went on to share three local nonprofits she spent her time with.

"We're always looking for help cleaning junk from the beaches through Save our Seas," she'd said excitedly. "And then there's the local Gardenia Beach Hospice House, which is always looking for people to help out."

Dottie explained the work could span from answering phones to sitting with patients as they neared the end, having no loved ones by their side. Taryn's heart sank at the thought of dying alone. *How could people have no one who cared they were about to die?*

"And then there's our local AA group," Dottie said. "But that's for recovering alcoholics only."

Taryn nodded as she said, "I know," even though Dottie could not see her.

After a quick conversation, Taryn had told Dottie she'd like to help Save our Seas, to Dottie's delight. While the hospice opportunity tugged at her heart, she'd seen enough death in her thirty-three years on this earth.

"I think beach cleanup is more my style," she'd said.

So, Dottie had explained the website where she needed to go to register. And she encouraged Taryn to stop by the Pancake Place on her next shift, where Dottie promised she'd bring a sack of cleanup bags, should Taryn feel compelled to do solo surf cleaning while soaking up the sun.

It sounds perfect, Taryn decided as she settled onto her towel on the sand. Sun, surf and helping the environment could help heal her tattered heart. Plus, it gave her a place to be. A place to be when she was visiting with her "mom."

A deep, booming voice startled Taryn awake from her oceanside snooze about a half hour later. "I see someone made right with you."

Taryn opened her eyes and saw the glistening, tanned muscles but was unable to make out the face. She knew, from the context of the question, it was Austin. Evelyn's Austin. She abruptly sat up, shielding her slightly exposed belly with her knees.

"Hi," she responded awkwardly, combing back her red hair with her fingers. "I must've fallen asleep."

As her eyes adjusted, Austin's chiseled jaw came into focus. His dark hair dripped, and beads of water dotted his suntanned skin. His right hand held a longboard steady in the sand. His smile was a dazzling white, a perfect set of teeth. *He must whiten them regularly,* she thought.

Austin was handsome, by every societal standard. As she sat staring at him, she could understand why Evelyn was drawn to him. The dark hair, piercing blue eyes, buffed bod. He was an exquisite specimen of a man.

"They look good on you," Austin said, offering a nod.

"Thanks," Taryn said, forcing a weak smile and suddenly feeling stupid. Her face flushed. She wasn't sure if it was his comment about her new eyewear or the fact she felt the blood rush over her body when she realized how attractive he really was. "The sunglasses. They are amazing. Evelyn really didn't have to do that. I can't imagine what they set her back."

Especially on a bartender's paycheck, she thought.

"Evvy can be a real piece of work when it's bottoms up," he said. "But deep down, she can be an old soul. It just gets buried sometimes."

Taryn felt the blood settle a bit, slowing down as it coursed through the veins in her ears.

"We all have our moments," she responded. "I guess it's how we follow up that counts."

Austin smiled at her, then surveyed the area around them.

"So, lazy beach day?" he asked, moving to her right side to avoid the sun's rays that shone directly on his face. "It's almost happy hour."

Taryn wrinkled her nose and peered at his through her polarized shades.

"Happy hour started a little bit ago for me," she confessed.

"Well, like with any sport," Austin said, "it's important to warm up. And I know the best personal trainer around."

Taryn didn't hesitate to jump at his barfly innuendo.

"Well then," she said. "We'd best get to our training center."

As Austin and Taryn walked along the perimeter of the Atlantic Ocean, their feet sinking into the wet sand with each step, she momentarily forgot the mess that was her life. Instead, she wondered how everyday people could live in paradise and function normally.

Being here, the sun shining and warming her skin, seemed like the ultimate reality deterrent. How could anyone sit in a work cubicle, filing papers away in desk folders, knowing that beyond the meat-locker coldness of an air-conditioned office was the joy of the outdoors? It seemed almost cruel for the working folk.

"Look," Austin said, snapping Taryn out of her daydreaming fog. "Got to be a foreigner."

Taryn peered to the left, watching a seventy-ish, wrinkly, leathery man as he squirted a healthy dollop of suntan oil into his grubby old palm. He rubbed it onto his arms, belly and then face, but Taryn didn't so much look at that as the skimpy Speedo that exposed his stretch-marked ass cheeks and thighs and, well, everything. The man turned to face them and caught Taryn staring, which prompted him to grin at her. His crooked, tar-stained teeth repulsed her, but she felt her face blush, regardless. She forced a smile and sped up her gait as Austin waved at the sunbather, adding, "Good afternoon." The glistening man returned a nod and began to back into his beach chair, as Austin nuzzled his nose toward Taryn's left ear and whispered, "Busted." Taryn shot him a dirty look.

"Only because of you." She giggled. "Now I really need a drink."

"Live here full-time and you'll need a lot more," Austin said. "Bodies on display that shouldn't be are the norm."

Taryn could see the Wayside Watering Hole in the distance on the left. She could hear the buzz of the bar grow louder with each step. Even though they were coming up to a building full of liquor, she felt the urge to slip her right hand into her beach bag and pull out a can of seltzer. She cracked it open and brought it to her lips, the raspberry fizz tickling her mouth as she gulped it. She noticed Austin's quizzical stare as he cocked an eyebrow.

"None for me?" he asked.

Taryn felt her face flush again and forced her hand into her bag. She darted her thin fingers around, only feeling a lighter, pack of cigarettes, a hair tie and her motel room key, nestled in a plastic bag with a wad of cash. She kept all her credit cards and other IDs in the safe at her motel room.

"Sorry," she said meekly, tipping her can toward Austin, who took it in his hand, then gulped the offering.

"Blech," he said. "This shit is for amateurs. I bet you drank wine coolers in high school."

"No," Taryn protested, her lips curling at the sides, because, yes, she had. "Sorry, I hadn't planned on sharing with a guest, you know."

Austin made a gagging face, sticking his tongue out. "Good thing I don't judge," he said, handing it back to her. As they closed in on the steps from the beach leading to the outdoor platform bar of the Wayside, Taryn tipped the aluminum can to her lips, guzzling the remaining tepid liquid into her mouth.

Austin stood at the first step, offering his hand to present the entrance to her.

"Ladies first," he said, "even if they have no taste in refreshments."

Taryn rolled her eyes, feeling somewhat comfortable with this man she'd known for less than a day. She scrambled up the steps, tasting her next drink. She anticipated the high of the drunk, knowing she'd be in her mellow place shortly. As she went to place her hand on the door handle, she paused, remembering she was clad only in a damp swimsuit.

"Wait," she said, turning to Austin. "Can I go in there like this?"

Austin chuckled as he grabbed the tank top he had slung over his left shoulder and slipped it over his head.

"It's a dive bar in Florida," he said, smiling. "We expect no less."

CHAPTER FIFTEEN

Taryn had wondered if Evelyn might be miffed if she saw her stride into the bar with Austin in tow. It was completely innocent, a happenstance he'd found her at the beach, but Taryn didn't know how to read her yet. Especially given their first meeting. And she knew from experience that some women are confident, unthreatened by another woman's presence. Others' radar goes up as soon as more estrogen enters the room.

Luckily, it was the former for Evelyn. She'd been pouring a Beefeater and tonic into a plastic bar cup, piercing a sliver of lime with a drink sword when her eyes met Taryn's and lit up. Her smile was instantaneous as she strode over to her tattooed, older female customer at the bar, resting the drink on a cocktail napkin. Taryn approached the bar, falling behind Austin, who went up to an empty stool and slid onto it.

"Hello, my dear," he said to Evelyn. "Look who I found down the beach, fighting off creepy old men in Speedos."

"Ah," Evelyn said, a genuine smile spreading from her lips as her gaze flowed from Taryn to Austin. "I see you're on the Gardenia Beach Welcoming Committee again."

She turned to Taryn, grabbed a plastic cup, scooped up some ice and asked, "What's first up for you, Becks?"

Taryn stood for a minute, letting Evelyn's question sink in as her pulse quickened, briefly forgetting her nom de plume for her Florida excursion.

"Hey, Evelyn," Taryn said, offering her own gentle smile. "Tito's and soda is calling my name. With a splash of cran."

Evelyn nodded and headed to the row of various vodkas lined up, wrapping her right hand around the neck of the bottle before pouring a healthy helping into the cup. Taryn's mouth watered, thinking about how much better she'd feel when the warmth of the alcohol seeped into her throat, finding its way into her belly. Soon, her heart wouldn't feel as if it were to burst out of her chest. Soon, maybe she'd be able to not think about how this beautiful, broken woman fixing her a drink had been violated by the man she'd promised to love until death—which, as it turned out, she had.

Good thing the vows said nothing about eternity, she thought.

Evelyn placed the stiff drink before Taryn on the tropically themed bar, flashing a smile as her ponytail bobbed behind her.

"Cheers," she said. "To new friends."

Taryn smiled, feeling the guilt as heavy as the sunglasses on her head.

"To new friends," she said, motioning her glass toward Evelyn.

She gulped the drink, which tasted of pure ethanol, and waited for the calm to wash over her.

***

Evelyn smirked as Austin leaned his head into her left shoulder. She shoved him away playfully. Her shift had ended an hour earlier, and she'd needled her way onto Austin's barstool, pushing him to stand to her right as Taryn, seated to her left, sipped from her third drink. Taryn's head had begun to spin, especially as Evelyn grew chattier with them both. She'd seen Evelyn steal a swig or two out of a Styrofoam cup with her name written in black ink on the side. She'd filled it with something from the soda gun but topped it off with a healthy pour from whatever bottles she was preparing drinks for customers from. Taryn could see Evelyn had a penchant for partying. Not that she was one to judge.

For now, Taryn sat and absorbed the frenzied pace at which Evelyn spoke, which became more frenetic with each sip of her drink.

"Go pick me a song," Evelyn ordered Austin, who seemed nonchalant as Evelyn's pace for both drinking and talking picked up. "I'm feeling nostalgic."

"Whatever the missus wants," Austin said, standing up and tipping his imaginary hat to her. "Got anything in mind?"

"I think some Aerosmith is on the menu," Evelyn said, directing her two index fingers toward the jukebox as her thumbs shot up. "And nothing sappy. I'm not falling for that shit tonight."

"Oh please," he said, backing up before turning and striding toward the jukebox. "It's not like I don't know what gets you in the mood."

As he walked away, Evelyn rolled her eyes and turned toward Sheila, now back behind the sea life bar top.

"Just because he's ridden the train before doesn't give him an unlimited pass," she huffed. "He's got to work for it."

"Well," Sheila said, "it's not like he's got a reason to think otherwise."

"Touché, bitch," she retorted. "Now, how about a warm-up round for me?"

Sheila chuckled.

"I think you've been warming up for a while now," she said, arching her eyebrow.

Evelyn nodded. "You know me, boss. But it's not like I'm on duty."

Sheila scoffed, grabbing a bottle of Jose Cuervo. "You know I hate it when you call me that." She poured it into a shot glass. "Makes me feel old."

Taryn still stood beside Evelyn, wondering if she should continue her awkward stance of waiting for her original barstool or move a couple seats down. Regardless, she couldn't stop looking. Wondering. Thinking about Graham forcing himself ...

Her heart raced a sickly, rapid beat.

Sheila pushed the shot glass in front of Evelyn and scooped some ice into a plastic cup, drowning it in well vodka and topping it off with a soda gun serving of tonic before squeezing a lemon and lime into it. She set it in front of Evelyn, ignoring the glazed look in her eyes.

"Thank you," Evelyn said, sucking the tequila down in one swallow, pushing the shot glass to the edge of the bar and grasping the plastic cup of vodka tonic, bringing it to her plump pink lips. She snorted and giggled. "I think I'm gonna need a bigger boat."

Sheila looked unamused, as if she'd grown accustomed to this routine.

"Or a bigger liver," she said under her breath.

"Hey!" Evelyn retorted as Steven Tyler's humming voice filled the room. "I'm not fucking deaf."

Sheila just rolled her eyes as the melody filled the air.

"Good choice, baby!" she screeched as she looked over her left shoulder to Austin, grinning and pleased as he pecked away at the buttons, searching for the next tune in the lineup.

"This is my new friend!" Evelyn screeched to Sheila, wrapping her left arm into the crook of Taryn's right.

"Oh, I remember," Sheila piped in with a smug glance. "Glad you made nice."

Sheila motioned toward Taryn's cup, her eyes inquiring if she was ready for another.

"Sure," Taryn said, trying to mask the slur of her speech. "I think I have one more in me."

Evelyn turned to Taryn with a giddy, drunken grin.

"This one's on me," she said. "So, make it count."

Taryn contemplated what to order. She always told herself to keep her faculties. Even though they were long gone.

The invisible pressure of the situation made her crave more.

"I'll do a margarita," she said, adding, "with an extra shot of Cointreau, please. And a splash of orange juice."

Evelyn's face lit up.

"Now we're talking." She giggled, motioning her thumb in Taryn's direction. "I like this one."

Don't be so sure, Taryn thought to herself as she offered a smile as genuinely as she could.

Two margaritas later, Evelyn had Taryn howling with legitimate laughter over the tale of Austin being stuck on the side of Interstate 75 early in their courtship, when a chorizo burrito hadn't agreed with him and he needed a place to, um, evacuate—quickly.

In the middle of a traffic jam.

"He just got really quiet." Evelyn snorted and giggled, regaling Taryn with the tale of how Austin had been sitting behind the wheel one minute, bemoaning the forty-five-minute wait, and then suddenly clammed up. "He looked straight ahead, and I could see the sweat start to trickle down his face."

Austin tossed his head back, rolling his eyes and bringing his hands to his hairline, running his chewed-up fingernails through his darkly coiffed head.

"Why?" he asked. "Why must you always—"

"And then he just threw the door open and bolted!" a glassy-eyed Evelyn screeched as she bellowed in uncontrollable laughter, leaning toward the bar to steady herself. "He was unbuckling his pants as he ran toward the shoulder!"

Taryn knew she shouldn't laugh, but several drinks in, she just couldn't help it. She began uncontrollably hiccupping in her giggles.

Austin just shook his head as Evelyn continued, recalling how the other drivers, also at a standstill, began honking at him as he tried to scramble behind a roadside bush.

"And then," Evelyn snorted intensely, "he just started shitting! Right there on the side of the road."

Both girls buckled over in roars as Austin sighed deeply, acting as if he'd been through this routine many times before. Evelyn's shimmering brown locks swooped forward as she smacked the bar top three times with her palms. Taryn threw her head back, mascara-stained tears dribbling down her cheeks. Sheila looked incredulous, resting her back on the opposite side of the bar, her arms crossed. The remaining few other patrons looked annoyed.

Austin let out a breath of defeat, pulling out a credit card and motioning at Sheila that he'd had enough of this literal shitshow. He signed the tab after Sheila returned, handed the receipt back to her and faced the girls.

"Ladies," he said, nodding before heading out the north door. "I'm glad I could provide the entertainment tonight. Try to stay out of trouble."

Evelyn barely turned, just holding up a hand to half-wave goodbye. She turned back to Taryn and smirked.

"Thanks," she said. "That story always gets rid of him. And I can only use it on someone new."

Taryn turned to Evelyn, slightly confused. "Aren't you leaving with him?" she asked.

Evelyn steadied herself. "I probably should head home," she said, finally maintaining composure. "But he's not my husband. At least, not anymore."

Taryn wasn't able to hide the shock from her face. While her social media research had indicated Evelyn was divorced, she'd nearly forgotten. In the short time she'd been in Gardenia Beach, just seeing the two interact, she'd assumed they were still a couple, divorced or not.

"Oh," she said.

Sheila meandered over. "That's what everyone thinks," she butted in. "Never know from the way these two carry on, would you?"

Taryn's mind, in the absolute fog she was shrouded in, began to wander. But Sheila's voice cut in and disrupted her train of thought.

"He got you ladies. Time to call it a night," she said, then wagged her index finger at Evelyn. "Especially you. You start at noon tomorrow. You need to sleep it off. Or go get some food and sober up."

Evelyn sighed, muttering under her breath to Taryn, "She thinks she's my fucking mother. But I am kinda hungry."

Taryn nodded quickly.

"I am, too," she said.

"Whatcha got a taste for?" Evelyn said.

"Sushi," Taryn blurted out. "Please tell me you love it, too."

Evelyn braced her hands against the bar and pushed her barstool back.

"I do," she said, "and it's right across the street."

CHAPTER SIXTEEN

Twenty minutes later, Taryn and Evelyn were settled at their table, diving into the spider roll, a "Gardenia Beach roll," and an appetizer of gyoza placed before them. They'd also ordered a serving of Pad Thai to split—and soak up some of the alcohol in their bellies.

"So, Becks," Evelyn began, "tell me about your divorce. If that's okay."

A lump formed in Taryn's throat. She was grateful they'd both ordered Cokes. More alcohol would make it hard to keep the lies straight. She cleared her throat.

"Okay," Taryn said, the wheels of fiction spinning in her brain. "We don't have enough time for the long version. So the short version is this. We were trying to get pregnant since we got married about three years ago. But nothing was happening. After a year, my ob-gyn prescribed Clomifine, which gave us a renewed sense of hope. But even with the ovulation stimulant, nothing."

Evelyn listened intently, the empathy flourishing in her eyes. Taryn took it as a good sign, though the guilt was beginning to brew.

"After another year with no positive pregnancy tests, we sought further help," Taryn said, secretly praying her fib didn't sound far-fetched. "We thought maybe his sperm count was low. But, no, that was just fine. So, we began looking at me. And that's when we learned I couldn't have children."

Evelyn audibly gasped, prompting the couple at the table next to their booth to glance at them before quickly diverting their eyes.

"Sorry," she mouthed to the couple before turning her attention back to Taryn. "Go on."

"So we were at a loss," Taryn lied, leaning over to pick up another piece of the roll. "I suggested maybe adopting, but Mark's face said it all."

Mark, Taryn thought, kicking herself for crafting yet another lie to keep in check. *I guess that's how I'll refer to Graham from now on.*

Evelyn's eyes begged for further detail.

"I could tell that wasn't really an option, especially since Mark had always talked about what our babies would look like," Taryn went on. "My soft skin, his sparkling blue eyes. He wanted his own lineage to carry on.

"And he found that in his administrative assistant," Taryn spilled out, her stomach silently churning out of shame. "He divorced me last year and married her within two months. By then, they were already expecting."

Evelyn's face grew ashen.

"Whoa," she said after about fifteen seconds of silence. "What a dick move."

Taryn nodded, just as the server arrived with the Pad Thai, placing it in the center of the table, along with two empty plates for each.

"Enjoy," he said before leaving the two to continue their conversation.

Evelyn fiddled with her chopsticks, then suddenly put them down.

"Well," Evelyn said, "I think you dodged a bullet. So much for 'in sickness and in health' and 'till death do us part.' "

Taryn offered a sad smile. She was done with this fake story and wanted it over.

Evelyn seemed to sense her unease and lifted her glass of soda.

"Cheers," Evelyn said, seemingly still stunned, "to taking out the trash and starting fresh. Fuck Mark."

Taryn lifted her glass and clinked it with Evelyn's.

"Fuck Mark," Taryn agreed, and both ladies took a swig of their Cokes. "To fresh starts."

Taryn wanted the subject changed. And fast.

"So," Taryn began, "tell me about you. You know I came down here to nurse my wounds. How'd you end up in Gardenia Beach?"

Evelyn bestowed a vague smile at the thought. She picked up a piece of the Gardenia Beach roll, dipping it into her tiny bowl of soy sauce mixed with some wasabi.

"Well," Evelyn said, glancing at Taryn before popping the piece of food into her mouth, "I came here because of Lucas."

Taryn's bewilderment was written across her face.

"He's my best friend's son," Evelyn explained. "He's two and the cutest little damn thing you'll ever see, I promise."

Taryn's confusion continued to grow. Evelyn paused, then explained further.

"Ashley is my best friend," Evelyn said, her face turning stoic. "Or was. She died of breast cancer when Lucas was only six months old."

"Oh, my God," Taryn said, shock in her voice. "I'm so sorry."

Evelyn nodded, accepting the sincere condolences.

"Thank you," she said, drawing in a deep breath as she briefly shut her eyes. "Ash was something special. She found out she had cancer when she was twelve weeks pregnant. Despite her doctors' pleas, Ash refused any kind of treatment during her pregnancy. She had wanted that baby so badly, she refused to do anything that didn't put his health first. Thankfully, Lucas was born healthy. Ash was anything but.

"The cancer was too far gone by then." Evelyn sighed. "Ash was given three months to live. She made it another three months before she took a nosedive and was rushed to the hospital's hospice unit.

"I was holding Lucas at her bedside when she died," Evelyn added. "She was only 36."

Now, it was Taryn's turn to gasp. She didn't know what to say.

"It was awful," Evelyn continued, her voice choking a bit. "Honestly, it still is. I miss her so, so much. But I promised her I would be there for Lucas. And Paul, her husband. Ash gave that little boy every chance she could to be born healthy, even knowing her decision was likely to be her death sentence.

"So," Evelyn continued, "that may not have been what drew me to Gardenia Beach several years ago, but it's definitely the biggest factor in why I've stayed. I can't let that little boy down."

Taryn didn't realize she was crying until Evelyn handed her an extra cloth napkin to dab her eyes with. She felt like a heaping pile of shit. Here, she'd concocted this bullshit story about a cheating, baby-hungry ex-husband, only to be met with a truly heartbreaking story. One that was real.

"Oh, Becks," Evelyn said. "Let's stop with our sob stories. Or we're going to have to switch back to booze."

Though Taryn wanted to know more, she also wanted the backstory of what brought her to Gardenia Beach buried, never to be disturbed again.

"*That* I can agree to," Taryn said. "Let's hang it up for tonight. Happy thoughts from here on out."

Evelyn appeared to be lost in thought for a moment, then gently rested her chopsticks on her plate. She looked intently at Taryn.

"One more thing, though," Evelyn said. "About Lucas."

Taryn nodded, and Evelyn continued.

"He's my little buddy," Evelyn said. "I usually visit him a few times a week. And we have a standing weekly 'date' at the Sunrise Park playground on Sunday afternoons. That's one thing I refuse to miss. I love the time with him. I can see a glimpse of Ash every so often. It makes me still feel connected to her. And it gives poor Paul a chance to breathe for a few hours. I don't know how he does it, working full-time and raising a toddler on his own."

Evelyn suddenly paused as her face lit up.

"I'd really love for you to meet Lucas," Evelyn said, sincerity shining in her eyes. "You should come with me tomorrow."

Taryn's response was truly genuine. "I would love that."

Evelyn didn't wait for the server to return. She lifted up her glass of soda, as did Taryn.

"To fresh starts," Taryn offered, clinking her glass to Evelyn's.

"To fresh starts," Evelyn said. "And new friends."

Chapter Seventeen

April 2018, Chicago, Illinois

When she woke up in the hospital bed, Adrienne felt like her body was broken. Everything ached. Sharp pains, almost in tandem with the beeps chronicling her heartbeat, seeped in and out of her body. And when she turned to look toward the door, the pain shot through her head like a knife.

It took her a moment to realize she wasn't alone. To her left, by the hospital's windowsill, her sister, Leanne, was curled up in a medical recliner, her chin resting on her chest as she slumbered. She snorted as she slept, her snores coming in rhythmic succession.

What am I doing here? she wondered, her mind temporarily blank, unable to recall what led to her lying upon a stiff mattress, wires seemingly attached all over her bruised, bloated body.

Then it hit Adrienne. The memory of parking her silver Chevy Malibu down Wildwood Street in the darkness, anxiously awaiting for The Rapist to fire up his Harley-Davidson and speed down the street. Her tailing him as the bike weaved unsteadily as it traversed the residential area before hitting the open road. How she observed the man pulling into the parking lot of the nondescript pub. She'd watched him briskly walk in as she sat in her vehicle for about five minutes to stagger her arrival time. She'd swept her fingers through her silky blond locks, checking her reflection in her visor mirror before heading in herself. Adrienne had casually meandered in, breathing in the plumes of cigarette smoke as she passed the smokers getting their fix in the chilly weather before hustling back inside to the Kelly-green walls and neon Guinness signs bolted throughout the darkened confines. There, they could warm their throats and bellies with whiskey and Irish dry stouts. She selected a stool at the northern edge of the bar, ordering her mocktails and sipping as she observed The Rapist, who sat exactly opposite her, at the southernmost edge of the bar.

To her, he had no name. Just the label. It made it easier for her to think of him that way. He didn't deserve anything more than the moniker. No one who used their dick as a weapon deserved one. She didn't care that he was someone's best friend. Or husband. That there were parents and nieces and nephews who loved him. Anything slightly linking him to humanity was null. What he had done swept all of that away. As did anyone else who had done the unthinkable to a woman, man, or worse, a little girl or boy.

Like Uncle Coop.

He lost that privilege, that title, after he insisted on taking her, his goddaughter and best friend's daughter for a fun "Uncle Coop's Camp," as he'd told her mom.

But it hadn't always been that way.

Adrienne's earliest memories of Coop were good ones. Great, actually. While he was technically not her uncle, she considered him one.

***

Cooper Canton and Lisa Snyder had been childhood friends whose bond continued beyond high school. While Coop and Lisa had never dated, they had a connection that began in middle school after Coop came to a bullied Lisa's defense.

It started in eighth grade. Oddly, over mean-girl stuff. It began brewing in her fifth-period English class with Mrs. Lightfoot. As Lisa had walked to the front of the classroom to submit a test her teacher had administered to the class, the snickering started. Lisa was perplexed why the gaggle of girls at the back of the class burst into guffaws and giggles as she, wearing her new pair of white jeans, strode to the front of the classroom. She'd been excited to wear them, a special treat from a weekend shopping spree with her dad, who'd promised her a choice of three new outfits for her hard work and straight A's in school last quarter.

It all made sense when she went to the restroom in between periods—and found herself smack-dab in the middle of just that. She scurried to a stall and pulled her pants down—only to find bright red blood had saturated not only her underwear, but straight through her pants. And it was visible to all. A mortified Lisa had gone to the school nurse and pleaded to go home.

The next day, as Mrs. Lightfoot had her back to the class as she wrote on the chalkboard, Lisa felt something light hit the back of her head. Then again. And again. To the thunderous laughter of most of the class.

When Lisa looked at the floor, she saw what had hit her—individually packaged tampons. Three of them. Lisa quickly scooped them up and shoved them under her bookbag. But it was too late. Clearly, everyone knew she had gotten her period the day before. And this was not the confirmation she needed.

Mrs. Lightfoot was clueless, telling the class to pipe down.

"Some of your classmates are still finishing their exams," Mrs. Lightfoot noted, a stern look on her face as she addressed the class with a pointed finger. "Another outburst, and you'll all get a detention. Just knock it off."

Lisa just wanted it all to go away. But when she got to her locker at the end of the day, the additional snickering and quiet laughter from those who passed her in the hallway made sense. Her locker had been decorated with maxi pads from top to bottom. As she hurriedly tried to remove them, much of the adhesive stripping had stuck to the metal of the door, which looked almost as bad as the sanitary napkins themselves.

Coop, who not only had a locker next to Lisa but had been in the English class where the tampon tossing had occurred, looked as sickened as Lisa did.

"Those fuckers," he said, shaking his head in disgust.

The next day, the lockers of Jenna Flatley, Cassidy Colson and Roxy Fenton were all covered in dog diapers for females in heat. The word "Bitch" was the centerpiece of each display, written in permanent marker at the top of each locker.

It was the first time Lisa had smiled in days. It landed Coop a week's suspension from school. But it was the start of a decades-long friendship between the two. He fought for the underdog. He didn't care about his own social status. And Lisa saw a true friend before her.

CHAPTER EIGHTEEN

Adrienne always knew she was her uncle's favorite honorary niece. Or nephew, when you counted the whole Landley crew, which Coop had been considered a part of, having been a staple in the family since he and Lisa bonded in middle school.

Adrienne's earliest recollections were those of Coop coming to visit her whenever he had the chance. He'd seem to find a reason once or twice a week to pop in with a treat in hand, be it a stuffed animal, coloring book and crayons, or a chocolate shake from the local dairy store, which she'd devour despite her mom, Lisa, telling her to save it for after dinner so she wouldn't spoil her appetite. But Coop, despite his sister's protests, would simply wink at Adrienne, giving her the go-ahead to slurp it down as soon as Lisa left the room. Coop would sit and do puzzles with her, her favorite being one of Fantasy Fun World's instantly recognizable Dragon's Detour rollercoaster. Mostly because she'd never been and he'd promise her that one day, they would indeed go. She'd squeal in delight every time she plugged in the last pieces of the depiction of the park's signature structure, with Coop whispering into her ear, "Someday soon, we'll see it in person. Together."

It gave her such hope, something to look forward to beyond the everyday doldrums of school, homework and half-assed meals of mac and cheese or Sloppy Joes prepared by Lisa, given she didn't have the time to do much more than quick meals, thanks to the two jobs she juggled to keep the lights on and the water running. It has been that way since Lisa's husband

and Adrienne's dad, Colton, had split after way too many years of a toxic relationship. Even though Adrienne was barely two.

While Lisa was a dedicated provider to her children, her maternal instincts were nearly nonexistent. There was a coldness to her. Not a motherly, loving vibe. Just the adult in charge at home. Adrienne recalled Lisa telling her she loved her only three times before. Hugs were seldom, as were other displays of affection. It was like something shut down in Lisa after her husband's abandonment. There was no emotionally nurturing parent. Just one who kept the lights on and the fridge semi-stocked.

That's why, when Coop paid attention to Adrienne, it filled the void of her mother's emotional absence.

In Colton's absenteeism, Coop's intense interest in his youngest "niece" had bloomed. Coop became the father figure in Adrienne's life. Not only was Adrienne thrilled, but so was Lisa. Coop's constant presence alleviated much of the guilt and pressure Lisa felt, being a busy, always-working single mom. She welcomed the help.

Adrienne had known nothing but what she'd experienced, so to her, the extra attention, which was not bestowed upon her sister or cousins, was normal to her. The fact Coop would take her and not the other kids to go grab a hot dog on a Saturday or experience the thrills of the closest cheap, knock-off theme park didn't register as odd. And Lisa didn't seem to be concerned. She knew Coop would look out for Adrienne, as he had Lisa all these years. He was a true friend, blood or not, through thick and thin.

But Adrienne's sister, Leanne, complained to her sister when Coop didn't extend any such offers to her.

"Why does Coop do all this stuff with you and not me?" Leanne would grumble as Adrienne scurried into her room to grab her sparkly, sequined pink purse before an outing. "Don't you think it's weird?"

"Uh, no," ten-year-old Adrienne would protest before leaving her sister standing in the doorframe of her purple and pink bedroom, clothes and napkins and other discarded items strewn about her floor. "And be-sides, I *am* his goddaughter."

Leanne, exasperated, would puff out a breath from her pursed lips, leering at her sister as she brushed by her to run to Coop, waiting at the front door for her.

Their good times continued on. Until they didn't.

Adrienne was fourteen, the transformation of teenagedom in full swing. Not yet a woman, but metamorphosing into a gangly but more mature version of herself. Leanne had been accepted to the University of Northwestern Florida, a whole eight hours away from their home in Coneflower Clove, a small town on the southern Gulf Coast of Florida. And Lisa would be driving Leanne up to Rockville, Florida, to get her oldest settled in.

Lisa was thrilled with Leanne's hard work. And, finally, there seemed to be a perk for the trio's tough times. Lisa and her girls had shuffled through life with extremely tight finances, the single mother working two jobs for much of her daughters' childhoods. She'd clean houses and office buildings during the day, then marched into a local pizza joint at four o'clock for a nighttime shift of dealing with overserved patrons and young families with whining toddlers. It wasn't the life of which Lisa had dreamed, but she and her girls made it work.

Except for phone calls and cards on holidays and birthdays, the girls really hadn't seen their father since he left. They'd lived on SpaghettiOs and hand-me-downs for more than a decade. But their lack of cash flow, coupled with Leanne's straight A's in school, had landed her a full ride, if she kept up the good work. And with every square inch of their rickety old red Toyota Celica crammed with all the things Leanne had insisted she needed, that left only the driver's and front passenger seats free for the ride up.

Adrienne watched in delight as the back seat's available room shrank with every box, stuffed animal or clothing item Lisa insisted she couldn't be without.

"You're going to have to stay with Uncle Coop for the night," Lisa told her after surveying the stuffed car.

Adrienne felt a twinge of excitement, knowing she'd not have to suffer through sitting in the backseat of a car stuffed like a sausage, Lisa's cigarette smoke wafting back into the rear seat, coursing through Adrienne's nostrils and lungs. Plus, it meant more one-on-one time with Coop, which surely meant delectable treats, fun outings and more.

When Coop pulled into their driveway, the weeds sprouting through the pavement's cracks and rust stains speckled on the gray, her heart pounded with excitement for the weekend ahead. Maybe he'd surprise her with a beach day or a trip to the springs to cool off. Or maybe even fishing. They'd gone a few times, with Adrienne accidentally reeling in a tiny hammerhead shark and taking photos of herself and her catch with her little Nikon camera, Coop's last birthday gift to her, before releasing it back into the sea. Surely, Coop had something fun planned.

"Hey, my favorite goddaughter!" Coop said as he flung open the passenger door of his red Acura Integra, a recent purchase following a promotion at work. Adrienne slid onto the taupe leather seat, leaning to embrace him in a hug before strapping on her seat belt and flipping the radio station to one that featured today's hits of 1997. White Town's "Your Woman" blasted from the speakers, slightly vibrating due to the high volume. But instead of insisting she turn it down (something her mom would always reprimand her for, out of fear of blown speakers), Coop let it be. And even cranked it up a little more when Chumbawamba's "Tubthumping" rolled into the rotation.

When he started heading toward I-75 and turned on it to head north, her belly bubbled with excitement.

"We're not headed toward your house," Adrienne said, trying to suppress the hopeful excitement building in her belly.

A sly smile began to appear on Coop's face, the corners of his mouth upturning slowly.

"No, we're not," he said, his hands on the steering wheel at nine and three as he kept his eyes focused on the road ahead.

Adrienne knew it. They were, in fact, finally going to Fantasy Fun World.

"Are we going to FFW?" she excitedly blurted, her hazel eyes pleading. Even though there was no reason to.

"We are," he said, keeping his eyes still straight ahead, fighting back a smile.

Adrienne screeched, Coop jumping in his seat from the unexpected shriek, then both of them suddenly startled—and burst into belly-deep laughter.

Adrienne felt like the luckiest girl in the world right then. Or at least, the luckiest out of her small social circle. Who else got a surprise trip to a killer theme park from their uncles? She guessed not many.

About an hour later, Coop's shiny red car came to rest in a sea of minivans and SUVs, parents unbuckling their little ones from car seats, holding their little hands as they walked to the tram that would whisk them into the Orlando theme park.

Just being here was a triumph. Despite living in a state fueled by tourism, Adrienne had never set foot in any Florida theme park. Over the years, she'd begged her mom to take her and Leanne, but, as Lisa explained, it simply wasn't in their budget. Money went to pay bills, sustain basic living. There just weren't enough funds to cover a day of frolic, even though it was about forty dollars then. The one hundred twenty dollars to get in the door didn't even cover gas, tolls, parking, lodging and, of course, food and merchandise.

But today, that didn't matter. She was going. Finally.

"And I have another surprise," Coop said as they neared the entrance. He pulled a folded piece of paper from his back right pocket, not catching eyes with Adrienne as she unfolded it and screeched in delight.

"We're spending the night here, too?" she shrieked.

Coop had scribbled the details and a confirmation code for the room he booked at a nearby motel, the Sun Vista Lodge. It wasn't on property, but she didn't care. It was next to a souvenir shop and an Olive Garden, two places she'd definitely want to patronize during their short stint here. Maybe in the morning, before they headed back to Coneflower Cove. Her mind was so full of possibilities, she could barely contain herself.

It truly felt magical. From sliding through the entrance turnstiles to soaking in the massiveness of the Dragon's Detour rollercoaster, the iconic structure settled at the front part of the park, Adrienne felt a rush of happiness she'd never experienced. She really felt loved. No one, not her mom and especially not her dad, had ever taken her on such an excursion. She felt such gratitude as they meandered toward the rest of the park, veering toward the left to begin the lap around the central pond as they explored each themed "land." Dragon's Detour beckoned them deeper into the park. Adrienne was in awe of the towering ride before them.

"Wow, that's super cool," Adrienne exclaimed as they made their way down the ramp inside the ride's main building, which billowed with tourists. She immediately made a beeline to the various carts, delicately picking up pieces of dragon-themed souvenirs and examining each her eyes spied. Coop told her she could pick out one—any souvenir she'd like. She thumbed through the various wares and settled on a tiny metal dragon statue with fierce teeth. It would be the perfect accessory to showcase in her bedroom, she decided. And a great item to gaze at and remember her first real theme park trip.

"Thank you so much, Uncle Coop," Adrienne said as she embraced him, tears trickling from her eyes as her heart swelled with appreciation. "This is the best weekend ever."

The two continued their trek around the park, stopping at each pavilion to ride whatever rides were there and soak in the ambience of each space. A few hours in, her belly began to rumble and her throat ached for hydration.

"Can we get something to eat and drink?" she asked as they neared a beverage cart.

"Absolutely," he said, motioning toward an empty bench by the lake. "You stay right here. I'll surprise you."

About five minutes later, Coop approached Adrienne with two drinks, one looking like a beer and the other, some kind of frothy concoction. He also carried a huge soft pretzel and empty paper cup along with it.

"Here you go," Coop said, handing Adrienne the hand-twisted bready treat. Then he poured the daiquiri-looking beverage into the empty spare cup before tossing the now-empty, dirty cup into a nearby trash can.

"What is this?" she asked, as she furrowed her eyebrows in confusion.

"It's a 'fun' drink for a special occasion," Coop said, his eyes shielded by his sunglasses, making it impossible for Adrienne to look at him directly. "I mean, I'm sure you've had a drink by now, being your age and in high school. You've been to parties, I presume?"

"Holy crap," a stunned Adrienne said.

She was both excited and perplexed. Her mom had made it quite clear that if there were any rules in her house, smoking, drinking alcohol and doing drugs were at the top of the barred-activities list. But Lisa smoked—"Believe me," she'd tell her daughters as she took a drag, "it's not worth it. Once you're hooked, you're hooked." Which made Adrienne a bit skeptical. *Why tell me not to do something—but do it right in front of me?*

But she'd known her friend Kara's parents had allowed her to try beer at home. In fact, they'd even allow it at her little sleepover parties, when a small group of four or five teenagers descended on an evening of binge-watching R-rated movies, like the "Friday the 13th" series or raunchy, old-school comedies like "Revenge of the Nerds." The rules? You can drink here, under our roof, as long as you spend the night and keep it quiet. Adrienne had imbibed before, loving the feeling the buzz brought her. She felt fun, confident. A totally different version of her awkward, acne-faced self.

Even though she felt in her gut that this probably wasn't something she should be doing, it titillated her. Especially since it was her adult uncle allowing it. That made it okay, right?

"Okay," she said before Coop outstretched his arm to touch hers.

"You just have to promise me one thing," he said, a stern look on his face. "This will be *our* little secret. *No one* needs to know. I could get in a *lot* of trouble. But I *trust* you. And I *know* we have a very special relationship."

Adrienne beamed. "Got it. It's our little secret."

She sipped from the cup, barely tasting the liquor in the frosty concoction. This was the best day ever.

An hour later, Adrienne was on her third "fun" drink and feeling on top of the world. No wonder people drank this stuff. She felt unbelievably joyous and confident.

She and Coop continued their lap around the park, stopping at each area to experience the shows and rides offered. And Coop continued to bring more drinks.

By the time they completed their journey, Adrienne felt tipsy but still able to navigate her surroundings. Coop observed as she stumbled a few times, then suggested maybe it was time to call it a night as the darkness began to fill the sky.

"I think it's time to head back to the motel," he said. "How about we grab a pizza on the way and eat in our beds as we watch some TV?"

Adrienne nodded, the thought of consuming greasy, cheesy pie incredibly appealing. He hooked his arm into hers as they exited the park and headed back to the car. He stopped at a strip mall, grabbing a cheese pizza from a hole-in-the-wall joint right next to a liquor store. Adrienne sat in the car, her head slightly spinning as she watched Coop go from the pizza place to the liquor store, from which he emerged with a brown paper bag before reentering the restaurant to retrieve their piping hot meal. She slumped into the seat further as the car headed to the motel, eager to get into the room and crawl into her bed.

Coop left her in the car as he went to the front desk for their room key. "Someone needs to guard the pizza," he said with a wink as Adrienne remained strapped into her seat.

When he returned, she stirred from her sleep as he shut the driver's side door and headed to the back of the building, to park near room 154. She wobbled as she walked to the door, secretly praying no one else was around and would notice her unsteady gait. Luckily, not another soul was seen as they slipped into their room for the night. Adrienne plopped onto the bed and exhaled loudly, the giddiness of the intoxicant coursing through her.

"How about a drink with dinner?" Coop asked as he removed the bottle cap from a wine cooler before handing it to her and cracking open a beer for himself. She accepted the bottle, chilled to the touch, and brought it to her dry, dehydrated lips. It was delicious, and she guzzled down the strawberry-flavored concoction, immediately warming her belly. Before long, she was on the last bottle of her four-pack and the room was spinning. She shut her eyes, quickly falling into a deep sleep.

***

When Adrienne awoke, her mouth was disgustingly dry, her stomach queasy, and her head was pounding. And she felt a throbbing between her legs, like nothing she'd ever experienced before. And there was wetness. *Oh God,* she thought. *I was so drunk I peed the bed!* She shot up and lunged toward the bathroom, closing the door as gingerly as she could before violently spilling the contents of her stomach into the toilet. Coop never stirred, snoring in the bed opposite hers.

Never again, she thought, the pain in her head excruciating.

Adrienne flushed the toilet and turned around to sit on it, pulling her shorts to her knees as she positioned her bottom on the seat. She peered at her panties and stopped abruptly. She was horrified to see bright red blood, and what appeared to be some kind of gel, soaked into her underwear. This couldn't be her period, she thought, remembering it had just finished a couple days ago. Why would she be bleeding now? And what was the gunky clear stuff mixed in?

But the pain in her crotch was not right. The only time she'd felt something even remotely like that was when she had tried riding a stationary bike, the firm seat bruising her pubic region for days after—and Adrienne vowing she'd never hop on the exercise equipment again. She was perplexed in the hangover fog that clouded her brain. What happened to her? This felt worse than the aftermath of a sturdy workout seat.

Adrienne turned to the toilet paper roll affixed to the wall opposite the commode, looping it around her hand several times before wiping herself and tossing it into the water. It had to be her period, maybe just still the remnants from the week before. It just didn't make sense.

She turned to her toiletries bag on the bathroom countertop, immensely grateful there was a leftover tampon among her lip gloss, mascara and other personal care items, like a small container of hand lotion and travel-size hairspray. She fumbled with the plastic wrap as she removed the cylinder from its casing, ripping it and turning back to sit on the toilet to insert it. But as Adrienne slipped the plastic tubing into her body, she abruptly retreated in agony. Her insides felt raw, torn. They burned. Like pouring rubbing alcohol into an open wound. She immediately tried removing the tampon, gingerly guiding it as each movement made her grimace in unbearable pain. With no pad in her bag, she turned back to the roll of toilet paper, winding several layers around her fingers before weaving it over her panties, again and again. It would have to do until she got home and was able to access a maxi pad.

She saw Coop's hunter green toiletries bag, stationed next to her floral one near the sink. Maybe he'd have some ibuprofen or acetaminophen for her raging headache and sore innards. Even though he was still sleeping, she quietly unzipped his bag, so as not to disturb him, despite her violently puking just a few moments earlier.

Adrienne suddenly stepped back in horror, the full realization hitting her as she took in the contents.

There was a tiny bottle of pain pills, but she couldn't bring herself to touch them. Nestled next to them was a small tube of lubricant and a three-pack of condoms. The security seals on both were broken. She couldn't help herself from flipping open the pack of condoms, seeing one was missing.

Maybe he used it before, she thought. *They could be old.*

But they weren't, she realized as she thumbed through the rest of his possessions in that tiny glum bag. Lubricant was caked onto the side of the tube, and from lifting it, she could tell it was nearly empty. But what made her accept reality was the crumpled-up wad of toilet paper nestled at the bottom. She couldn't help herself from unfolding the layers of toilet tissue, which uncovered its contents—a bloody, gloppy used condom filled with semen. She held it between her fingers, rubbing it between her thumb and first two fingers in complete disbelief. It still felt slightly warm. She dropped it in horror. There was no way this was old, from a secret fling or one-nighter. And Coop had no girlfriend, as far as Adrienne knew. In fact, she couldn't recall him ever dating anyone, in all the years she'd known him.

But it hit her with searing clarity.

This rubber was freshly used. By Coop.

On her.

In those few moments, the best weekend of her life had suddenly become her worst.

After carefully rewrapping the soiled, bloody condom and nestling it back into the position she'd found it, a stunned Adrienne rinsed her face with water and headed back to her bed. She couldn't even look at Coop as she made her way back to her bed and slipped beneath the covers. She spent the next several hours just lying there, at times, hot tears streaming down her cheeks.

How? And why? Why would someone Adrienne adored so dearly do something so violating to her, his self-professed niece and *goddaughter?* She couldn't wrap her head around it. But she just wanted to be home. Away from this.

Once dawn arrived, Coop stirred as Adrienne pretended to still be asleep. *What would she do once he knew she was awake?*

She smelled coffee brewing as Coop utilized the tiny coffee maker. Eventually, he positioned himself at the side of her bed and tapped her shoulder.

"Get up, sleepyhead," he said in a teasing tone. "It's time to get the day started."

Adrienne opened her eyes a crack and feigned a smile, trying not to think about the piercing pain in her head and between her legs.

"Sorry," she said. "I guess I was really tired."

"Well, we had a long day," Coop said, his eyes shifting toward the grungy beige carpeting. "All that walking can take a lot out of you."

Adrienne nodded, grasping the cup of water on the nightstand and guzzling it down.

"And we partied a little hard," he said, a wry smile spreading across his face. "Want a hair of the dog to get your day started?"

The thought of drinking again made her stomach churn and she quickly shook her head "no," from side to side.

"How about some Tylenol?" he asked.

Even though Adrienne knew where the pills were, tucked right next to a wadded up condom that was the aftermath of her sexual assault, she knew she needed it. And needed to act like nothing was wrong. Did he really think she didn't know what he had done to her?

"Sure," she said, maintaining the charade.

Coop offered to take her for breakfast, but Adrienne declined.

"I really don't feel well," she said, offering a weak smile. "I really just want to go home and crawl into bed."

Coop nodded, a look of concern across his face, and the two climbed into his Integra for the hourlong trip back to Coneflower Cove. It was a quiet car ride home. And it felt like the longest of her life. Adrienne peered out the windows on the ride back, observing the trees that lined the roadway, the fake prehistoric reptiles that lined Intersate-4 near Dinosaur World in Plant City, and well as the airplanes ascending and descending from Tampa International Airport. But Adrienne wasn't really seeing them. They were simple objects, her mind focused on how sore her body and brain were.

When Coop pulled into Adrienne's driveway, she could see her mom still wasn't home from dropping Leanne at her new life at college. How she so wished that could be her, away from this. Away from Coop, who had just decimated her sense of self. And life.

"Thank you," she said as she scrambled from the passenger's seat, grabbing her bag in the back seat and quickly heading toward the front door.

"Don't I get a hug?" she heard Coop ask from behind her. A lump formed in her throat. Adrienne took a deep breath, slowly turned to face Coop, and then vomited in the green, yellow and orange crotons to the right of her home's front door.

Coop looked on in horror.

"I'm so sorry," Adrienne said, wiping the sprinkles of vomit from her lips. "I really don't feel well."

Coop glanced between the puke, Adrienne and the ground as he retreated with backward steps, grabbing the handle of his car door.

"All good," he said. "You get in there and rest. Maybe a shower, a Sprite and some crackers will help."

Adrienne weakly nodded and shoved the key into the front door's lock.

"I'll do that," she said. "See you later."

Adrienne didn't even wait for a response before quickly closing the front door and deadbolting it. She stood with her back to the front door, waiting to hear the Integra's engine fire up, then the sound of his car growing more distant as it headed away from her home.

Once Adrienne knew Coop had turned down the street, she sank, her back to the door and her bottom hurting as she rested it on the tile flooring. And just sobbed.

CHAPTER NINETEEN

Adrienne no longer existed. At least, the version of her prior to the weekend that had changed her life—and outlook on it—forever.

She grew reclusive. Especially after her mom returned from taking Leanne to college that weekend. When Lisa had finally gotten home, she knew something was off with her youngest. And when she sat at the edge of her daughter's bed, stroking her leg as she asked what was wrong, Adrienne had recoiled at her touch. She never wanted to be touched by another human again.

"I think Coop raped me this weekend," she blurted out to her mother with an expressionless face.

Lisa had shot off the bed.

"What?" she said, fury in her face. "That's *not* possible."

Adrienne had diverted her gaze to the floor, littered with used tissues and dirty clothes.

"I hurt," she said. "I know he did."

"Why would you *say* such a thing?" Lisa snapped. "He adores you. Not to mention he just spent a *shit-ton* of cash on you this weekend, taking you to Fantasy Fun World. Why would you make up something so horrendous, Adrienne Marie? *Why?"*

The two sat in silence, Lisa looking at her daughter as her feet fiddled with each other as they dangled off the side of the bed.

"Is this because you didn't get to come along to see your sister off?" Lisa asked.

Adrienne's blood grew hot. She rolled to her right, her back to her doubting mother. How could she dispute the truth? Here she was, being completely vulnerable, turning to the now only trusted adult in her life. But now, it seemed, she could trust no one. Her sobs shook the bed as she tried to erase the images of the used condom in her mind, the burning feeling still throbbing between her legs. She had absolutely no doubt she'd been assaulted. *How could my mom accuse me of lying about something so serious?* Adrienne thought.

"Adrienne," Lisa said, as calmly as she could, "Uncle Coop loves you. You're the closest thing he has to a child of his own. He would NEVER hurt you. EVER."

"Fine," Adrienne shouted. "My sore, torn vagina must just be a figment of my imagination."

Lisa huffed and then gave an exasperated sigh.

"I don't know what's going on in that head of yours," Lisa said, her voice heightening with irritation. "But I know Coop. He's my brother, blood or not. And I know he'd never, ever do such a thing. He has gone above and beyond to not only support me for decades, but you and Leanne, too. His heart is pure gold."

With that, Lisa sharply stood up, walked toward the bedroom door, and turned as she reached the threshold. Coldness was written all over her face, a firm look of disappointment as her eyes met Adrienne's. Lisa pulled a cigarette from her pack of Marlboro Reds, resting one between her lips before bringing the lighter to it. She didn't even notice the one that had fallen from the pack onto the floor. Lisa took a deep breath in, exhaled with closed eyes, then fixed her gaze intently with Adrienne's eyes.

"I *never* want to hear about this nonsense again," she snapped. "*Ever.*"

With that, Lisa departed the room with the slam of the door, leaving her daughter alone.

In all the ways a person could be left alone.

That was the true moment that everything changed. Her one source of support had evaporated with a simple sentence. Adrienne knew then that the only person she could rely on was herself.

And she decided right then that Coop would pay for this.

Maybe not today. Or next week. Or next month. Or next year. But he'd pay.

Someday.

***

As Adrienne lay in her hospital bed, her childhood assault rang fresh in her mind. Despite the passage of time, it felt like it was just last week. Her mind was interwoven between her long-ago trauma and snippets of the memory of the accident that landed her in the hospital.

Well, it wasn't really an "accident." Though that's what she was going with.

Adrienne hadn't intended to survive. Living wasn't part of the bargain she'd silently made with herself, but she really didn't want to go on. Her intent was to eradicate a societal monster by taking out someone else's sexual assailant.

In return, someone else would take care of Uncle Coop.

That was the agreement.

Her chest felt heavy. Her entire body ached. She ran her hands, attached to IVs, down her arms and legs, bristling at the searing pain of the bloodied bruises.

"Adrienne!" Leanne suddenly shrieked, realizing her younger sister had finally opened her eyes, weeks after the crash that had nearly taken her life. She leapt from the hospital recliner, rushing to her sister's side, slowing as she approached her, gingerly leaning over to embrace her tattered body. She looked older than the Leanne she'd remembered. The Leanne she still saw as an eighteen-year-old headed to her new life at college, away from the broken home her sister had remained caged in until she fled. Adrienne had essentially shut Leanne out of her life after her departure, no explanation at all.

"You're awake!"

Tears gushed from Leanne's eyes as Adrienne's face remained expressionless.

"This isn't Heaven," Adrienne whispered slowly, a tear of her own trickling down her bruised and stitched-up face.

"Thank God it's not!" Leanne wept, her crystal blue eyes pleading with her younger sibling. "I don't know what I'd do without you. You're all I have left."

Adrienne hadn't thought of that. Not like she had anyone much left, either. Her relationship with her mother had drastically changed since she'd confided her assault to Lisa. After that initial blowup, they'd never spoken of it again. Adrienne spent most of her time in her room. She stopped going to family functions. And Lisa didn't push. She figured Adrienne had progressed into a spoiled, self-centered, fibbing brat who made up lies when things didn't go her way.

By seventeen, Adrienne had left her mom's home, choosing to live with a string of friends, boyfriends, wherever she could find refuge. She was done with this life, with this family who had hurt her in so many ways.

Adrienne had maintained some contact with Leanne, but it was scant. A text here and there for birthdays and holidays. A random phone call when Leanne, who worked as a sales rep for a medical device supplier, had big news—such as her engagement to Dr. Pete, the cardiac surgeon she'd met on the job when visiting a Tampa-area hospital. And the follow-up call about her engagement being called off—after Leanne discovered Dr. Pete in an empty OR, his surgery coordinator's legs wrapped around his waist, only her calves and nude pumps visible. But, except for Facebook and random FaceTime calls, which Adrienne rarely answered, they hadn't actually seen each other since that day Leanne and Lisa had left in the loaded-up Celica. Adrienne just hadn't been interested. Leanne had tried and tried, calling her sister, emailing, writing. Anything she could to maintain a connection.

Adrienne's responses were always curt and brief. She wanted nothing to do with her former life. Even if it meant cutting out her sister.

When Lisa died of lung cancer ten years ago, Adrienne couldn't bring herself to go to the service. She watched from afar, peering from behind a thick Winged elm tree, as mourners gathered as the casket was lowered into the grave. She'd once gone to visit the gravesite, some five years after her passing.

Instead of leaving flowers, she'd spat on her mother's final resting place.

"Adrienne," Leanne said, cupping her sister's bruised and battered hands into her own. "I don't know why you shut me out, but I don't want it this way. Not anymore. I *want* you in my life. I *need* you in my life."

Adrienne sniffled stoically. Did she want this? She was supposed to be dead, the moment her car had violently lurched, forcing the helmetless Rapist to veer off course and slam into that giant oak tree. She wanted to be dead, even though that wasn't part of the agreement. It was simply an eye for an eye.

"You don't want to be in my life," Adrienne said, shifting her gaze to the oak trees swaying in the breeze outside her window. "I'm broken. And I don't have anything to give. Just consider me dead. In my heart, I already am."

Leanne's eyes bulged.

"*Don't* talk like that," she insisted. "I don't *care* what's happened. I want to go back to what we once *were*."

Adrienne heaved an intense breath.

"That'll *never* happen," she said, already exasperated by the conversation.

"Adrienne," Leanne said sternly. "You are loved. I love you. Our family loves you. And Uncle Coop loves you."

Adrienne shot up in her bed, her sudden shift pulling painfully at the IVs inserted into her. Everything seared in pain. She gently lay back down in the bed, the medical cords irritating her every movement.

"NO," she spouted. "That, I know, he does not."

"Adrienne, come on," Leanne said. "He has always adored you, even though you shut him out during your terrible teens. I need to call him and let him know you're awake."

Adrienne's stomach sank. *Coop was still alive?*

That couldn't be. *Criss-cross. Criss-cross.*

"Alive?" Adrienne screeched, rage in her voice. "He's still *alive?*"

Leanne looked at her sister, astounded, nothing but perplexity in her eyes.

"What do you mean, 'He's *still* alive?' " Leanne asked, confused. "Why *wouldn't* he be?"

Adrienne looked at her bruised, battered hands. She wished that when she'd nearly plowed into the motorcyclist, two lives had ended. Now, she realized, she was likely to face manslaughter charges, but not a DUI. Her blood-alcohol content had been .00. At The Rapist's bar, she'd opted for a Coke in a rock glass with a lime. Adrienne needed to be clear-headed to carry out her plan, yet look like she was imbibing in an alcoholic drink to other patrons. She was still going to be under the microscope, though. Dealing with Coop herself wasn't an option.

Adrienne was enraged, her blood spicy. Coop was supposed to be dead by now. Even though she had no clue how long she'd been hospitalized, she knew it was long enough. The transaction was supposed to be completed within three days of hers. That was the deal.

She felt violated, all over again.

"Never mind. Just know he's dead to me," Adrienne cried, starting to choke on her tears. "And if you even think about contacting him because of me, you'll be dead to me as well."

Leanne stood up, beginning to pace in her frustration.

"I don't understand you. *Why* are you so *hateful?*" Leanne pressed. "You need family more than ever. Especially considering the legal battle that you're likely facing."

The silence echoed in the room among the beeps of the heart monitor.

"Adrienne, I am your sister. Your blood," she said, her voice cracking. "Whatever it is, whatever this demon is you're battling, we can face it together. I'm here for you. No matter how awful you think it is, I promise, it's not. And I vow, I will help you. Whatever it is."

Adrienne brought her gaze from her hands to sister's eyes. She felt the connection. The bond that sisters share. Sisters who would do anything for each other.

"*Whatever?*" Adrienne's inquiry trailed off. "I need your word. That no matter what I tell you, it is between us. And you're in. *No matter what.*"

Leanne's eyes reddened and clouded with tears.

"Yes," she whimpered. "Whatever it is. It'll be in the vault."

Adrienne blew out a deep breath.

"Okay then," she said quietly. "Let's go back to the weekend you moved to college. And how my life changed forever."

***

Leanne stood in complete silence amid the beeps of Adrienne's heart monitor, looking out the hospital room window as her mind absorbed all that her sister had just told her.

"You haven't spoken in ten minutes," Adrienne finally said, breaking the eerie silence in the room. "What are you thinking?"

Leanne slowly turned from the window, her eyes rimmed red and mascara streaks running down her face. She wiped them away as she drew in a deep breath and slowly sat in the hospital recliner she'd been glued to for days.

"I'm thinking..." Leanne trailed off, sniveling as she spoke, "that I don't know what to think. That I can't believe while I was off, living my college life, graduating and more, that I thought you were just a troubled, hateful soul. And how ignorant I was that there was something more. How stupid I was that I never found it strange that Uncle Coop never spoke of you, never asked about you. How it never dawned on me that his slipping away from the family didn't trigger something more in my mind. That I thought you were just bitter for Dad leaving and my success. I never imagined it was something more."

Adrienne shushed her.

"It's not your fault," Adrienne whispered, her voice cracking.

"But it *is*." Leanne wept. "If only I'd been less self-absorbed. I just wanted out of our old life. And into a new, better one. Which I got.

"But you didn't," she said, breaking into sobs.

Leanne leaned over Adrienne's hospital bed, holding her in a tight but gentle embrace, as Adrienne rubbed her sister's back in an attempt to comfort her. And she sighed as she thought about her life up until now. What could have been had Coop not raped her. Maybe she wouldn't have started hanging out with the bad crowd. The kind that always had cigarettes, alcohol, pot, cocaine, shrooms and whatever other drug that could momentarily mute her mind. How perhaps she would have graduated with honors, or at least good grades, like her sister. And gone on to college, earning a degree and a better shot at a life. One that was not like her mother's.

But instead, Adrienne had bounced from one low-income job to the next, never settling in for more than six months. She'd worked retail, been a gas station cashier, a grocery store stocker, a bartender. And bartending had been most natural to her, given her affinity for numbness, the mind-eraser that alcohol delivered, allowing her to just get through the day.

It wasn't until Adrienne had been watching one of those "Dateline"-type news magazine shows when the wheels in her garbled mind began errantly spinning. That episode was about a woman, Heidi, who had egged her boyfriend on to murder her stepfather, the man who'd raped her years earlier. He'd gotten caught—and both ended up in a prison cell for the man's murder.

To Adrienne, there were plenty of shades of gray when it came to justice. You just had to be smart about it. Plan it methodically. And make sure there were no ties back to you.

Because she got it. She understood why Heidi had taken justice into her own hands.

Heidi just hadn't been smart about it. But Adrienne would be.

That evening, she vowed to herself she would not abandon her mission to make Coop pay. And not get caught.

Or live.

But Leanne's revelation that Coop was alive and well enraged her further. Someone hadn't held up their end of the bargain.

And somebody needed to right that wrong. Adrienne would make sure of it.

Chapter Twenty

Taryn made sure her trash picker and bucket were in her rental car's trunk by the time Evelyn was expected to arrive at the parking lot of Seaside Shores Park. She'd woken up early this morning, before dawn, and after several minutes of trying to fall back asleep, she gave up and started her day. After grabbing a coffee from the gas station across the street from the Tiki Torch, Taryn had tossed on a tank top and capri leggings to head over to the park early to clean the beach it butted up to. She was relieved she'd picked up the cleanup supplies the day before from Dottie.

There was barely anyone on the beach, just a few joggers, walkers and sunrise-watchers. Again, a feeling of peace washed over her in these moments of solitude and service. Maybe it helped alleviate the guilt of tailing Evelyn—evening out her questionable decisions with ones that made her a better person. A selfless one, she hoped.

Once Evelyn texted she was five minutes out, Taryn trotted back to her car, dumping the garbage in a proper container before putting the container and picker back in the trunk. As soon as she closed it, she heard the tires on the gravel getting closer as Evelyn pulled her Toyota RAV4 into the spot next to Taryn's rental.

"Becks!" Evelyn said, flinging open her driver's side door and offering a quick hug. "I want you to meet my main squeeze."

Evelyn opened the back seat, where a tiny little towheaded boy sat, secured by the straps of his car seat. He had fallen asleep, and his eyes slowly opened as Evelyn gently woke him. His hazel eyes appeared startled initially, but as soon as Evelyn leaned over to unbuckle him, Lucas' face erupted in delight.

"Hey, my little love," Evelyn said as she delicately unbuckled the car seat straps, lifting him out by the crooks of his armpits.

Evelyn held Lucas on her hip for a few moments as he buried his face into her neck and nuzzled her. Taryn stood to Evelyn's right, out of view from the toddler. She didn't want to scare him as he awakened to see not just Evelyn, but a total stranger.

"I have a very special friend who just moved here," Evelyn continued, peering into Lucas' eyes as he rested on her hip.

Evelyn turned to her right to bring both into Taryn's line of vision.

"This," Evelyn said, "is my new friend, Rebecca. I told her all about you, and she's *super* excited to meet you."

Lucas, still groggy from his car seat nap, rubbed his eyes, then gazed at Taryn's face. His face remained stoic as he looked at her. He quickly buried his head onto Evelyn's neck again, playing the part of a shy toddler. Evelyn leaned closer to whisper into his ear.

"Can you say hi to Rebecca?" Evelyn cooed. "You can also call her by nickname. She has one, just like you. But only you can be my Little Butter Bean."

"Little Butter Bean?" Taryn asked as she looked at Lucas. "That is one cool nickname. And, did you know that only cool people get super special nicknames? Do you want to know what mine is?"

Lucas brought his head from the safety of Evelyn's clavicle and peered at Taryn. Taryn offered a huge smile to try to sway him to open up. Lucas looked up at Evelyn, who smiled and nodded.

"I am really Rebecca, but only special people can call me Becks," Taryn said, still hanging on to the smile to sway the boy. "And you're so awesome, I hope you call me that, too."

Lucas continued his intent gaze. *This is going to be a long outing,* Taryn thought.

But it wasn't. Evelyn gently rested Lucas to stand upright, anchored by his royal blue tiny Crocs. The boy immediately grasped Evelyn's hand, still cautiously observing Taryn.

As soon as the trio made it to the neighboring park, Lucas hightailed it directly to a spring rider modeled after a bumble bee. Evelyn kept up with him and lifted Lucas into the small plastic seat. As Lucas began to rock back and forth, he squealed in delight at the fake antennae, which wobbled in various directions as his small body swayed.

"Auntie Ev!" Lucas squealed. "Lookit da crazy bee ears!"

Evelyn's smile was infectious as she glanced over at Taryn.

"Wow!" Taryn interjected. "I've never seen anyone ride a bee so good, Lucas. Great job! Keep buzzing!"

With that, Lucas looked up at Taryn and broke into a gigantic smile.

"I a bee!" Lucas excitedly shrieked. "Buzz, buzz, buzz!"

Evelyn watched as Taryn attempted to bond with the little guy. Taryn pretended to fear Lucas' rocking yellow-and-black-striped ride, scurrying away dramatically to hide behind a tree, then a garbage can, and following up with heading over to the slide anchored to the playset, peering from behind it. Lucas erupted in laughter each time she snuck a look and pretended to hide again in fear.

"You are the coolest bee I've ever seen," Taryn said as she crept back toward Lucas, Evelyn with a firm grasp on the bee's backside to sturdy it. "Just don't sting me!"

Within two minutes, Lucas was bored of the bee life and begged Evelyn to "get me down." After she carefully eased him to the ground, Lucas took off as fast as his little plastic-shoe-covered feet would carry him. He scurried to the base of the standing playset structure and boosted himself onto it. Evelyn and Taryn trailed behind, watching as he changed his mind and skipped the playset for the swings he spied.

"Auntie Ev," he said, his tiny fingers grabbing her right hand. "I wanna swing with you."

Lucas paused, looking at Taryn. He was observing her carefully.

"Can I push?" Taryn asked excitedly. "I bet we can get you to swing higher than Auntie Evelyn."

Lucas yelled "okay!" and picked up speed again. There were two swings on this part of the mulch-covered ground. Lucas picked the one with the blue bucket seat, gesturing toward Taryn to help him. Both Evelyn and Taryn fought back the smiles that were beginning to brew. He was warming up.

Taryn gently lifted up the tiny boy by his armpits, nestling him in the plastic seat.

"You ready?" she asked, peering around the chains to catch eyes with Lucas. He smiled back at her, his few tiny teeth revealed in his grin.

Lucas nodded excitedly, and as Evelyn began swinging in her seat, Taryn pulled back the little seat, releasing Lucas with a push so he'd sway in tandem with Evelyn.

"Now I'm a bird!" Lucas screeched, his voice growing more excited as the swing extended a little bit higher with each push.

Evelyn slowed down a little, and Taryn followed her lead, reducing the intensity of her pushes.

"Down," Lucas demanded, turning his head to the left to look over his shoulder at Taryn. "Me want down."

"Please," Evelyn interjected. "Remember, we always use manners, especially around new friends."

"Pwease?" Lucas asked Taryn, a twinkle in his eye.

Taryn lifted the boy from his swing saddle bucket and set him on the ground. He grasped her hand and began pulling her toward the sandbox.

Taryn peered back at Evelyn as Lucas led her to the new play area. The grin on Evelyn's face was the biggest she'd seen on the woman so far.

Maybe there was hope, Taryn thought. *Just maybe.*

CHAPTER TWENTY-ONE

T aryn had lost track of time as she scoured the beach for trash. She'd used the trash picker provided by Save our Seas, scooping up every cigarette butt, chunk of plastic and other random garbage in her path.

It was so cathartic, it had become Taryn's almost daily morning ritual. She found herself frequently tending to the shores that butted up to the Tiki Torch, stretching farther north or south, depending on her mood. She'd plug in an audiobook or some current pop hits on Apple Music to mentally disengage. While she enjoyed volunteering like this, she needed to keep her circle tight. Taryn typically skipped group beach cleanups, telling Dottie she was busy tending to her mom—a tale she'd also spun for this good-hearted woman. She felt remorse as the lies poured from her mouth, but she also knew she had to maintain consistency in her story. God forbid she cross paths with Dottie while with Evelyn. She secretly prayed that would never happen, given Dottie had been provided with one truth—that Taryn, or Rebecca, was a somewhat recent widow.

"Please don't tell anyone else my husband just died," Taryn had told her when she stopped to pick up trash-bashing supplies. "I don't want any kind of pity."

Dottie had agreed, much to Taryn's relief.

Today, as most days, Taryn checked her cell phone to verify the date.

The second of May. Taryn had entered the fourth week of her new residence at the Tiki Torch and hadn't made any plans to leave.

Oddly, Taryn found solace in being here. Watching over Evelyn. And she found comfort in her presence. Like every moment she spent with her, she was helping, though unsure of exactly how, to heal this woman. To help her feel normal.

If there was such a thing.

Taryn had gotten into her own routine. In the mornings, after nursing her hangovers that seemed to plague her at least five days a week, she'd throw on her yoga clothes, a wide-brimmed hat, lather herself with sunscreen and just walk, her trash picker and bright blue bucket in tow. She'd scour the beach, letting the bubbling blue-greenish waves splash onto her feet, her toes sinking into the sand, as she sweat off last night's bender. And she'd just think. About what was. And what was now.

Taryn toyed with the idea of staying. Maybe selling her place up north and buying a condo on the beach with some of Graham's life insurance money. Starting fresh here. Perhaps she'd even change her name legally to Rebecca. And leave that old life behind.

But not here. Not now.

CHAPTER
TWENTY-TWO

"Hey, Becks?" Evelyn said at the end of another playdate with Lucas. This one was on a random Wednesday before Evelyn's Wayside shift. "Got any plans tomorrow? And maybe a hair?"

Taryn's innards recoiled, but she quickly told herself it could be something G-rated. Like taking Lucas to Busch Gardens for a weekend adventure. Lucas was toddling around in the mulch, underneath the playset with a fort up top. He liked looking through the fishbowl windows at the bottom portion of the playset. And Taryn had begun enjoying the time she spent bonding with the little boy.

Evelyn would have been a good mother, she thought. *She still could be.*

"Go ahead—shoot," Taryn said, wondering if she'd soon regret her agreeability to listen.

"Every so often, I like to wrangle up a girlfriend and head down for some South Florida fun," Evelyn began, cautiously watching Lucas from their not-so-comfortable royal blue metal park bench. "Like for Ladies' Night at the Lucky Phoenix Casino. BOGO drinks and twenty dollars in free slot money to play. If you're in the Lucky Phoenix members club. Which I am."

Hmm, Taryn thought. Last time she had been in a casino was when she and Graham hit the Joliet Riverboat for his work holiday party in December. She'd hit big on Moon Shot slots—enough that Christmas was paid for. Including the Harley.

"When is Ladies' Night?" Taryn cautiously asked.

Evelyn's smile spread from ear to ear.

"Every Thursday," Evelyn responded. "Which happens to be tomorrow."

Taryn looked surprised, though she had no reason to be. It's not like she was on any kind of schedule. Days were days. It didn't matter where they fell on the calendar.

"If it sweetens the deal, last time Austin and I went, I *might* have gambled enough to get me a free deluxe double-queen suite for a night," Evelyn tempted her. "And I haven't used it yet."

The whole mini-getaway sounded nice. But something, a feeling of dread, perhaps, swirled in Taryn's stomach.

"Come on, Becks," Evelyn pleaded. "I haven't had a girls' night out in years. I can't even recall when. Everything I do, Austin seems to follow. I just want a break from testosterone."

Taryn nodded, a knowing, forced smile on her face.

"Jeez, Ev, it sounds like fun but kinda last-minute," Taryn explained.

Evelyn's glance was one of annoyance as she turned to fully face Taryn. Enough with this talking while not even looking at each other.

"I'm going regardless," Evelyn pressed, her eyes narrowing as they locked with Taryn's. "Don't make me white-girl dance at a club on my own."

Taryn felt fiercely protective. The thought of Evelyn in South Florida while Taryn herself was nearly two hundred miles away? Her mind shuddered as her face faked delight.

"It also happens to come with two free tickets to the Casino Comedy Cellar," Evelyn said.

"I'm in," Taryn said, offering a fist bump despite her souring stomach. "But I don't have any 'going-out' clothes."

Evelyn jumped off the bench and did a happy dance, clapping her hands like a kindergartner. Lucas stopped fiddling with the sticks he'd been collecting, dropped them, and immediately mimicked Evelyn. She jogged over to him, grabbing his pudgy little palms and dancing them around in a circle.

"That's okay," Evelyn said. "Mi closet is *su* closet. So, we'll just stop by there first, pick you out an outfit and head out tomorrow around noon?"

"Sounds great," Taryn said.

But something gnawed at Taryn's gut. She wasn't convinced this was a good idea. But she couldn't let Evelyn head down there alone. *I owe it to her,* she told herself.

***

When Taryn arrived at Evelyn's apartment the next morning, she tried not to let her face reveal the thoughts trickling into her mind. The place was stuffy and hot, as if the air-conditioning hadn't even been on in days. From stepping into the front room, she could see it served as a holding pen for a lot of Evelyn's belongings. There were cups strewn throughout, empty potato chip bags crumpled up and left lying on countertops, the coffee table and side tables, among other trash and various belongings. A hairbrush sat on the top of the stove, a curling iron and its twisted, knotted cord encasing it at the breakfast bar. Clothes scattered the dingy, dirty beige contractor's carpeting. Taryn wondered if any were left in the actual closet.

"Sorry," Evelyn said, kicking a pile of clothes from the walkway. "I never have anyone over really, so I really don't keep up much. Well, except for Austin, but he knows I'm a slob."

Evelyn smiled with a twinge of embarrassment on her blushed face.

"I'm living in a motel," Taryn tried to reassure her. "Like I have room to talk."

Evelyn waved Taryn toward the bedroom.

"Come on," she said. "Let's find you a killer outfit for the show and some fuck-me pumps."

The bedroom carried the same vibe as the rest of the apartment. The crappy old white dresser that faced the queen-size bed was cluttered with more dirty clothes, various hair products and empty bottles of beer and wine, some tinged with the ashes and butts of lipstick-stained cigarettes. The place looked and smelled like a frat house room, an undeniable stench of cigarette smoke and spilled beer lingering. Like the frat houses Taryn would pass out in at college parties.

Evelyn sauntered over to the closet, shoving the stubborn closet door that had fallen out of its tracks, forcing it open with a loud screech. It was crammed with more clothes than Taryn believed could be in there, given the rest of the wardrobe scattered throughout the apartment. Plastic bins of shoes lined the closet floor; another held an array of clutches. Evelyn began moving hangers, searching for something for her friend to toss on.

"Ooh, here's a sexy red one," Evelyn said, removing the hanger from the closet rod and holding it up to Taryn. "You'd definitely look fuckable in this one."

Taryn took the dress from Evelyn, aligning it against her body and peering at her reflection in the mirror that rested at an angle against the wall. With its sharp V-neckline, fitted bodice and super-short hemline, Taryn wasn't so sure that it was her style. It was sexy, albeit borderline trashy.

Evelyn could see the apprehension in her friend's face as Taryn crinkled her nose as she surveyed it draped across her.

"Just try it and see," Evelyn persisted, scouring her closet for an equally tantalizing outfit for herself. She spied a black dress with mesh cutouts that wrapped around the waist in a triangular pattern and pulled it from the hanger, tossing it onto the unmade mess of a bed. Evelyn stripped her shirt and shorts off, standing there in only her lacy black bra and panties, which Taryn saw was a thong. There, in the middle of Evelyn's back, was a tattoo etched into her skin, right on her backbone. The face of the mythological figure Medusa, with sharp-toothed, venomous snakes sprouting from atop her head. However, unlike typical sketches of the Greek mythological feature, this Medusa face didn't look evil. It was beautiful, with kind, knowing eyes and a pouty lip. Like it was looking for a new lease on life—one that wasn't shrouded in anger and shame, but a renaissance of sorts.

Evelyn turned her back to her while tugging the garment over her head, yanking it downward. There was a deep V-cut on the back of the dress as well, leaving more of her back exposed than covered. Evelyn ran her hands over the polyester fabric. Her eyes caught Taryn's in the mirror, once Taryn's gaze on the tattoo drifted to Evelyn's eyes.

"Checking out my ink, eh?" Evelyn said with a hint of amusement before swiveling around to face the other woman.

Taryn's face blushed red. She offered a gentle smile and swept her right hand through the crown of her red hair.

"Yes, I was just admiring it," she lied, knowing damn well why Evelyn chose the snake-haired gorgon. "I'm always fascinated at the permanent art people want sketched into their skin."

"I put it along my spine," Evelyn began, slightly pausing, as if she was contemplating revealing more but hesitation won out. "Because no matter what shit life throws at me, I still need to remember I have a backbone."

"Ah," Taryn said, unsure of what to say, as her mind raced back to Graham's confession.

"I love it," Taryn forced herself to respond, making a heart symbol with her hands—even though she despised that move, a photo trend for a hot minute.

"I do, too," Evelyn said. "But I honestly forget I have it there most of the time. Only when I catch a glimpse of my backside in the mirror—or Austin runs his finger over it and says something."

Taryn lifted an eyebrow. *What was the deal with these two? Weren't they divorced for a reason?*

"I know," Evelyn said, as if she was reading Taryn's thoughts. "We have a long, complicated history. But I can't seem to quit him."

Taryn nodded, turning her attention back to the sleek red dress she now held at her side.

Evelyn looked at her friend from head to toe.

"So?" she said. "What are you waiting for? We gotta get you ready for the ball. Try that sucker on!"

Taryn giggled, relieved the conversation switched from the tattoo to her outfit for the evening. Evelyn beckoned her hands with a "come on" motion, egging Taryn on. Taryn let out a sigh before grasping the bottom of her shirt and guiding it over her head, tossing it onto the bed. She slid her thumbs under the waistband of her yoga pants and pulled them off as Evelyn turned to survey her jewelry, scattered in a wooden cigar box on her dresser. When she turned back to her friend, Taryn posed in her attire, showing off the form-fitting, deeply revealing cherry-red dress. It was way shorter than anything she'd ever worn before. Or felt comfortable in.

"Damn, girl," Evelyn said, feigning being overheated as she fanned her face and neck with her right hand. "You're definitely gonna turn some heads tonight."

Taryn blushed. How could she go out in such an outfit? Her ample cleavage spilled from the deep V-neck, and the hemline was a tad shorter than mid-thigh. Not to mention how tight it was. Like a second layer of skin. She felt like she was naked with only body paint covering her skin. She felt borderline obscene. Like a thirtysomething-year-old woman who was desperately trying to reclaim her youth by camouflaging herself in juniors attire.

"Well," Taryn stammered, thinking of how it had been months since she last had sex. And it had been with her now-dead husband. The Rapist. Getting laid was the last thing on her mind. "That's not my goal tonight."

"You never know," Evelyn said with a wink, sliding some large silver hoop earrings into her earlobes. "Get a few more drinks in you and you may change your mind."

CHAPTER TWENTY-THREE

W hen Evelyn pulled her car into the lot of Lucky Phoenix, Taryn was mesmerized by the gigantic seventy-five-foot sculpture of said bird. Anchored in the center of a roundabout as guests drove in, the monument was bright red and yellow, its wings thrust out as if about to fly off in a fury. As they drove past it, smoke belched from its mouth, causing both women to say a sudden, "Wow."

"Wonder how much that thing cost to make," Evelyn observed as they passed the statue.

"Or maintain," Taryn added. "But it's a casino. I'm sure there's plenty in their coffers for stuff like this."

Twenty seconds later, the pair pulled into a temporary parking spot for check-ins. Taryn let out a deep breath as she exited the passenger's side. Evelyn took note.

"You okay?" Evelyn said, a look of concern on her face.

Taryn snapped her head toward Evelyn and forced her best fake smile.

"Yep," she said. "I was just thinking about the last time I set foot in a casino. It's been a while."

"Well," Evelyn said, "I can feel it already. You're going to have some luck tonight. I just know it."

I sure hope not, Taryn thought.

***

The day had been quite lovely, Taryn silently told herself. After checking in to their room, Taryn and Evelyn had spent a couple of hours by the Lucky Phoenix's sprawling series of pools, enjoying frozen margaritas as they soaked up the sun. As they walked through the casino to head back to their room, Taryn saw a slot machine with the moniker, "Breaking News Bucks," and made a beeline to it.

But a brief lightning bolt of terror shot into Taryn's mind. The chances of winning were slim, of course. But on the off chance she did, Taryn realized she might have to hand over her ID. And there could be none of that. So, she told Evelyn she felt that slot was calling her name—but specifically for Evelyn.

"I think this one has your name on it," Taryn egged on Evelyn. "Just toss in twenty bucks and see what happens."

Taryn's hunch had been right. On her third spin of the slot's wheels, Evelyn hit the jackpot for twelve hundred dollars—the exact amount that required Evelyn to fill out a form for the IRS. Taryn had grown ghastly white at the sight, relieved that her gut averted that close call. Evelyn still insisted she'd split it with Taryn since she was the one who pushed her to play, but Taryn brushed it off.

"Looks like we're lucky together, Becks," Evelyn said. "We make a good team."

Taryn nodded, fighting off the sickening feeling in her stomach. No more close calls. Which meant no more gambling or anything else that might need an ID. That led them to take a delicious two-hour nap before the comedy show, which was not as great as advertised. Denny Donato didn't deliver on the laughs, except for a few random chuckles.

"Well, that was underwhelming," Evelyn said as she and Taryn exited with the throngs of people. She looked at Taryn, seemingly feeling guilty over dragging someone on a nearly three-hour car trip for maybe two genuine laughs.

Taryn rested her left arm on Evelyn's right. "At least the price was right," she said.

"I wonder if they'd refund our gas money if we bitched about it," Evelyn snorted, heading right to the bar outside the comedy club. "I need a stiff one after that."

As the women made their way to the smoky bar, with all the beeping and blaring of the slot machines' music, they noticed three spots suddenly open as a trio of men departed with their frosty mugs of beer. Taryn walked alongside Evelyn as they slithered onto two barstools.

Taryn felt eyes on them as they ordered their drinks from the bustling bartender. Not that she was surprised. The duo was dressed for attention, blinged out in hoops, chunky silver necklaces and clutches—Taryn's a bejeweled silver purse, Evelyn's a rose gold shade. Both women had gingerly walked in their three-inch nude strappy sandals across the casino's carpeting, hues of black, purple and aqua that sported rainbows, planets and shooting comets.

After ordering two vodka-tonics with a lime stabbed with plastic drink sword, the girls each raised their glasses and clinked to a "Cheers." Evelyn offered an "ahhhh" after she swallowed the first sip. She lit a cigarette, offering the pack to Taryn, who happily eked one out of the crammed pack with her right index finger, settling it between her lips and taking a deep first drag.

As Evelyn blew out a puff of smoke, a musclehead seated to her left turned his gaze to the two women. Taryn watched as his line of vision took in every inch of Evelyn's body, from the strappy shoes to the abundant cleavage peeking out from her dress V-neck. She didn't like how he eyeballed Evelyn—almost like a cat ready to pounce on an unsuspecting bird before sinking its sharp teeth and claws into its prey.

"Got an extra smoke to spare for someone who just lost his ass on roulette?" the man asked, an air of flirtation in his tone.

Despite the inverted visor perched upon his head, the guy was handsome, the muscles accentuated through his thin, long-sleeved white shirt. But when he offered a broad smile, showing off his teeth, one in the front overlapped the others, stained with tobacco.

Evelyn, loosened up by the evening's libations and her earlier jackpot, appeared generous, not annoyed, sliding out a cigarette and handing it to Muscle Man.

"Thank you, Punkin'," Muscle Man said, much to Evelyn's apparent annoyance.

"*Punkin*?" Evelyn scoffed. "What am I, your child?"

Muscle Man grinned.

"Well, no," he continued, "but you could be my baby tonight."

Evelyn swiveled slightly on her stool, her back to Muscle Man, looked at Taryn, and rolled her eyes.

"I saw that," Muscle Man cooed, motioning to the mirror behind the bottles of liquor lined up behind the bar. "You're a firecracker, aren't you? I figured that would fall more to Red."

Evelyn's visible annoyance was beginning to bubble.

"Her name is not Red," Evelyn flirtatiously argued with the man. "Don't go all pet names on us. We have real fucking names, you know?"

Muscle Man swiveled his barstool to directly face Evelyn's left side. She turned, her eyes electrified for a little entertainment.

"Okay," he said, extending a hand to Evelyn. "I'm Courtney. Nice to meet you."

Evelyn swiveled her chair to face Courtney.

"Isn't that a girl's name?" she teased, arching her eyebrows in mock perplexity.

"Let's have a few more drinks and maybe you'll find out for sure," Courtney said with a wink, then turning to Evelyn. "And you are?"

"Evelyn," she said confidently, twirling a strand of her hair before tucking it behind her left ear. "And this is my friend Rebecca."

"Becks," Taryn jumped in, offering her lie and own hand to shake Courtney's. "My friends call me Becks."

"Well, Evelyn and Becks," Courtney continued, motioning over the bartender, despite his hurried pace back and forth, "I think this calls for a celebratory toast."

"You buying?" Evelyn said, batting the fake eyelashes she'd glued on earlier in the hotel room's elongated mirror.

"Abso-fucking-lutely," Courtney grinned, leaning forward to pull his wallet from the back pocket of his pants.

Taryn's eyes bulged when the bartender brought over three shots of Fireball. She had purposely avoided the cinnamon whiskey ever since her night at the Pickled Bear, the downtown bar kitty-corner from *The Gazette's* offices. It was a happy hour work outing a few years back, which started out jovially—but ended in Taryn not remembering how she safely arrived back at her Hampton Park home. That bender ignited a bit of belief in Taryn—a strong feeling that a Higher Power was watching over her—considering her stupidity for downing four shots of the liquid fire in an hour. Taryn winced, thinking of all the times she got behind the wheel and shouldn't have. She'd covered enough fatal drunk-driving stories, interviewed more than her share of grieving families and quoted enough justice-seeking district attorneys to know better. The scenes. The pain. The time she covered the death of a pedestrian taken out by a drunk driver as he attempted to jaywalk across Lake Shore Drive. As Taryn interviewed the police and witnesses at the scene, she'd been tucking her tiny reporter's notebook into her back pocket when a blast of wind gusted from Lake Michigan, blowing the tarp from the top half of his body, exposing his bruised, bloodied, lifeless face.

It was a mere matter of seconds before an officer quickly re-tarped the body. But it was too late for Taryn. Especially after she learned that the motorist's blood-alcohol content had been three times over the legal limit. The image was burned into her brain, only to pop into her consciousness at various intervals. Like when she spied a wreck on her way home or heard the police scanner static report a 10-50.

Or when she drank a shot of Fireball. Which was what the Lake Shore Drive motorist had been sipping on for two hours before he plowed into the unsavvy tourist, effectively ending the man's vacation—and life—in an instant.

Taryn always remembered that. And avoided that brand of liquor.

But tonight was an exception. It had to be. The fewer questions, the better.

"Cheers," Courtney said as the trio clinked their shot glasses together. "To new friends. And two smokin' hot women."

Evelyn and Taryn groaned before downing their shots in one swoop.

"Cheers," Evelyn said as a look of amusement lit up her face. "To new friends. Even the douchebag."

Courtney chuckled. "Don't talk about Red that way," he chided.

"Tuh—" Taryn said, a look of horror on her face, then quickly bouncing back. It was damage control time. "Becks! You can call me Tootsie for all I care. Just not Red."

Fuck, Taryn thought. *Too close of a call.*

"Okay, Toots," Courtney snarked back. "Now, let's have some fun. And I know the perfect table."

***

Two hours later, Courtney had cleaned up at the roulette table, bringing his fistful of chips to the cashier to exchange for the $5,500 he'd won.

Betting on red.

"See, Red, I mean, Toots," Courtney said after filing his crisp hundred-dollar bills into his billfold. "You're my lucky charm tonight. Let's get another drink. And I'm treating, since your hair inspired my winning bets."

The three skipped the bar outside the Comedy Cellar, opting instead for Ozone, a nightclub nestled on the rooftop of the resort. Being May, the weather was perfect for enjoying the expansive views surrounding the property, even though the ocean was barely visible. But they did have a decent view of Fort Lauderdale International Airport and sipped their drinks as they watched the white lights align as a Boeing 747 began its descent for landing.

The bar was a totally different vibe than the casino-level ones. Waitresses were scantily clad, wearing tight-fitting black and gold cocktail leotards with tiny skirts that offered about three inches of ass coverage. Paired with fishnet tights and a push-up corset, the deep V-cut barely contained their full bosoms. Bass music thumped through the air as they weaved through the crowd past the dance floor. Neon lights strobed across the club, dancing on smiling and energetic faces swaying to the electronic dance music.

This was not Taryn's scene. At least not at thirty-three. Her mind zipped back to her college clubbing days. The bodies writhing against one another. The yelling in the ear of the person next to you because it was too damn loud—or you're both too damn drunk to comprehend anything.

As the trio approached the elegant bar, the bartenders looked more like showmen, juggling liquor bottles with a rehearsed elegance. Taryn observed the colorful cocktails being served, varying shades of blue, pink, even purple. Stationed throughout the club as an immersive visual experience, including the ends of each side of the thirty-foot-long bar, glittery-costumed go-go dancers gyrated in suspended cages. Their movements were synchronized to the melodies of Doja Cat, Dua Lipa, and a little Cardi B tossed in. The kaleidoscope of lights danced over their nubile bodies as they writhed, and Taryn took note of the assortment of men whose eyes were glued to the dancers' curves—much to the annoyance of many of their female companions. She watched as one slightly chunky woman, wearing leggings and a pink tunic shirt, smacked her beer-bellied husband's back with her left hand, only to have him turn back and throw up his hands in a "What do you expect me to do?" gesture.

Taryn didn't feel an ounce of jealousy. She just didn't care. Plus, she thought the go-go dancers added a hypnotic touch to the electrifying aura of Ozone. And it was a way to pass the time. People-watching. Even though she wanted to do nothing more than crawl into bed.

But Taryn knew she couldn't leave Evelyn with Courtney, who continued his efforts to romance her, plying her with more drinks and shots. After Courtney and Evelyn took a spin on the dance floor for a house mix of "Borderline" by Madonna, they returned to the polished mahogany and marble bar, where Taryn was guarding two additional plush velvet stools sitting on either side of her. Each spot was marked with a full drink set on a napkin, meant to hold Evelyn and Courtney's places. Taryn had watched as Tom, the bartender serving her end of the bar, meticulously crafted a cucumber-jalapeno margarita on the rocks, a spicy rim of cayenne pepper circling the crystal glassware. She felt like she was living the real-life version of the 1988 movie *Cocktail*.

"You put on a hell of a show, Tom Cruise," Taryn told the bartender, who smiled with a slight aura of irritation. She assumed he'd been called that many times before, given his dark hair, good looks, and slightly short stature.

Tom set her drink, a Smoked Maple Old Fashioned, smoldering from the top, before her right as Evelyn sat to her left, which led Courtney to move the barstool on Taryn's right side to the left of Evelyn.

Christ, Taryn thought. *This is going to be a long night.*

***

By the time it neared midnight, the cloudiness in Taryn's head was getting more intense. Her head began to ache, and she motioned over the bartender for a bottle of water. As she gulped it down, the loud conversations and the clinking of glasses intensified their pinging in her head. Taryn turned to Evelyn, who had rested her iPhone on the bar top.

"I think I'm about tapped out," she said loudly into Evelyn's ear. "The bed is calling my name. And maybe a pizza?"

Evelyn nodded, the back of her head to Courtney, as she rolled her eyes, indicating it was about time to tell him they were about to scram.

"Courtney," Evelyn said as she rose, Taryn following suit, "it was nice to meet you. We had fun. But these two girls gotta hit the hay."

The color drained from Courtney's face, apparently realizing that all the flirting, drink-buying, chatter and dancing was about to end with zilch. Except for a goodbye. Courtney stood up to face Evelyn, wrapping his arm around her waist, pulling her closer.

"Or we take this upstairs," Courtney said. "I've got some coke and other fun pills in my suite. And a pretty killer jacuzzi. You can even bring Red."

Evelyn looked unamused.

"Becks," Evelyn said, her annoyance growing. "Her name is Rebecca."

Sure, Evelyn had been toying with him all night. But she had no plans to bring anything with Muscle Man to the next level. Courtney peered at her as he brought his mouth to her ear.

"Maybe she likes to watch," he whispered as he boldly nibbled on her ear, "or join in."

Evelyn let out a guffaw, smacking her right hand on the bar in amusement as she dipped her head in laughter before tossing it back.

"That's *never* gonna happen," Evelyn said. "I told you earlier. We're both taken."

Courtney acted like he didn't hear a word Evelyn said, cupping her face in his hands and drawing her close for a kiss.

Taryn looked on, horrified, as Courtney's lips were about to touch Evelyn's—who, at the very last moment, dodged his mouth by turning her head to the right. Taryn could feel the eyes of the other patrons on the pair as a defeated Courtney began to redden with a mix of embarrassment and rage.

Courtney sneered, shoving the barstool into the bar with a loud thud, causing both women and others in the vicinity to startle. It was a face she'd seen before. An angry, horny, drunk man pissed off he'd just been denied what he wanted—right in front of a sea of people.

"Well," Courtney said, "I'd say you're welcome for the drinks. But I think I owe you a 'fuck you,' you disgusting tease of a whore."

Evelyn snapped her head back at him, getting right in his face.

"What the *fuck* did you just *say* to *me*?" Evelyn yelled, her chest rising in anger. "Which is it? Am I a tease or a whore?"

Evelyn didn't give Courtney the chance to reply, even as he began to open his mouth. She abruptly cut him off.

"I don't know who *the fuck* you think you are, but no one, not even a short little musclehead douchebag like you, fucking talks to *me* that way," she said, trembling with her own fierce fury. "*No one.*"

"Go choke on a dick," Courtney said, the veins bulging from beneath his thin cotton shirt. "Or maybe that's not your thing. Sure, you girls are taken. But I think it's more with each other."

Courtney ranted on as the women stood there, speechless at his seemingly uncontrollable outburst.

"You two are probably fucking bi anyway," he jeered, getting in Evelyn's face again. Taryn stepped in between the two, grasping at Evelyn's hand and pulling her in the direction of the exit. Her eyes pleaded with Evelyn, *Let's just get out of here.*

But Courtney wasn't done.

"You'll experiment, fuck whatever, I bet," he snapped. "Maybe even a woman. I'd put money on it that at least one of you has had a threesome, wearing those skank suits. Maybe even together. But you're not the hot shits you think you are. You're fucking past your prime, bitch. I know your kind. A power player and cocktease. So, fuck you. I'll have no fucking problem replacing your sorry-ass company with someone hotter. Who's not a *fucking cunt*."

Evelyn seemed to suddenly regain her composure. She folded her hands together, letting her elbows rest on the bar, looked directly at Courtney and smiled.

Which then turned into a sneer.

"Go for it, Man with a Girl's Name," Evelyn barked, looking directly into his eyes. "You look like a total douche in that fucking inverted visor and V-neck shirt. I mean, you can see your fucking nipples through it. Who are you? Jennifer Aniston on *Friends*? Because *she* can pull it off. *You* cannot. You just look like you've stepped out of a meat locker in your Hanes undershirt. If your vision isn't blinded by the wafting scent of that nasty-ass teenage boy cologne spray you've clearly bathed in. Is that really the best you can do on your pussy patrol?"

Courtney's face fired up with fury. He shook his head from side to side as he began to move to another section of the club. The girls breathed a sigh of relief. Message received.

"Evelyn," Taryn said. "Let's get out of here. Plus, that twenty-four-seven pizza place is down in the casino food court."

Evelyn nodded, and neither woman looked back as they headed to the elevators.

***

Thirty minutes later, the girls had polished off half a Margherita pie and sat back in their seats at the table positioned on the rim of the casino floor.

Stuffed with food and alcohol, and still unnerved by their debacle with Courtney, the two were tired yet still hadn't wound down.

They'd dissected the evening in between bites of fresh mozzarella, basil and tomato, and sips of a fountain Coca-Cola. Despite their sloshing bellies and tired eyes, Taryn could see Evelyn was still unsettled.

"My shift tomorrow starts at three," Evelyn began. "So, with checkout at eleven, that should give us enough time to sleep in a bit before we hit the road. So, how about we hit the slots one last time?"

Taryn hesitated. But she could see Evelyn had made up her mind. And the last thing she wanted to do was leave Evelyn alone in the casino.

"Okay," Taryn agreed. "But just for a little bit, all right? I'm beat and can barely keep my eyes open."

Evelyn wasted no time. She grabbed her purse and hopped up, ready to spring into the slots.

***

Evelyn's insistence on hitting the slots again proved profitable. After jumping onto a Wheel of Fortune machine one older, petite female gambler had been glued to since before the comedy show, Evelyn's third pull hit the mini-jackpot for five hundred dollars.

"Let's cash out and head to bed," Taryn suggested, her eyes fighting to stay open. "Don't put it all back in."

Evelyn hit the "cash out" button, grabbed her cash-out voucher and stood up. Taryn spied a ticket redemption machine about one hundred feet away and pointed.

"Come to mama," Evelyn cooed as she began to walk toward the machine.

The pair was three-quarters of the way to the machine when Evelyn abruptly stopped. She'd spied the mid-casino bar between where they stood and the redemption machine.

There, they saw Courtney. Hanging all over a woman. More like a girl—she looked like she was eighteen, wearing a one-piece black, form-fitting jumper, complete with wedge sandals, heavy makeup and wildly teased hair. She had to be at least twenty-one, given it was a casino. Taryn stood, motionless, watching as Courtney rubbed the girl's arm, wrapping his arm around her waist, and pulled her in for a kiss. The woman pulled from his embrace and smiled, whispering something in his ear. Courtney smiled his devilish grin and pointed toward the ladies' rooms. The girl, a sly smile on her face, grabbed her clutch before heading toward the restroom.

"What a piece of work," Evelyn muttered. "He doesn't waste much time."

Taryn felt sickened watching the whole scene. She just wanted out.

But then, she saw it.

At first, Taryn felt like she was in a trance, watching a movie unfold. She stood frozen. Taryn watched in complete horror as Courtney dipped his right hand into his front pants pocket, removing something minuscule with his fingers. He quickly surveyed his surroundings, glancing at the busy bartender, then the other patrons deep in inebriated conversation. It seemed no one had their eyes on Courtney. He turned back to the drinks in front of his and his new companion's seats.

Taryn's mouth fell agape. She watched as Courtney sprinkled a powdery substance into the drink the girl had been sipping. He surveyed his surroundings again before using the girl's drink stirrer to mix the substance in.

But Taryn wasn't the only one who noticed.

Evelyn was making a beeline straight to the bar. To Courtney. Taryn trailed behind her, stopping about three feet behind Evelyn as she saddled into the seat next to Courtney. Taryn's heart thumped. *No, no, no.*

Evelyn plopped onto the young woman's barstool, perplexity written all over Courtney's face.

"Well, if it isn't the past-her-prime cock tease," he sneered at her. "Change your mind? Because it's too late. You've been replaced with a newer, hotter model."

Evelyn twirled her hair as she grasped the girl's drink, sweating with condensation, holding it up as if she were to take a sip.

"Mind if I take a swig?" she asked, swirling the contents as she played with the glass.

"Get the fuck out of here," Courtney sharply retorted, protectively pulling the glass from Evelyn. "That's not yours. And your ship has sailed."

It was then the girl cautiously approached what had been her perch just minutes prior. Confusion covered her face as she observed Evelyn seated next to her bar mate. Her eyes, rimmed in heavy black eyeliner and a deep brown eyeshadow, began to well.

"Hey, Chloe," Courtney said as he noticed her presence, extending his arm to reassuringly touch hers. "This head case was just leaving. She's a little bitter I denied her advances earlier. Because I'm only into hot chicks, like you."

Evelyn leered at Courtney, Chloe's drink next to his, protectively.

"May I have my seat back?" Chloe meekly asked Evelyn. "Courtney and I were just having a great conversation."

"Absolutely," Evelyn said, starting to rise, looking intently at Courtney.

Suddenly, Evelyn quickly grasped Chloe's drink, lifted it up to her lips as if she was about to sip it. Taryn audibly gasped.

But Evelyn didn't drink it. Instead, she suddenly threw the contents in Courtney's face, who rocketed up in shock, his complexion a deep maroon as the drink dripped from his hair, cheeks and nose.

"What the fuck, lady!" he screamed at her, as the bartender and other patrons suddenly shifted their attention to the group.

"Get out," the bartender snapped to Evelyn. "Or I'll call security."

Evelyn just waved her acknowledgment at the bartender, indicating she knew she was no longer welcome.

"I'm going," she said.

Then Evelyn turned to Chloe.

"You're welcome," Evelyn said, approaching the woman, whose face was a pale white. Evelyn suddenly touched Chloe's arm tenderly. "Your fucking 'friend'? He roofied your drink when you were in the restroom. Don't accept any more drinks from him. *Please*."

Chloe's face grew even ghastlier. Her eyes darted between Courtney and Evelyn as Taryn looked on from a few feet back.

"Don't listen to her," Courtney butted in. "She's just jealous of you."

Chloe's eyes danced between Courtney and Evelyn again. *She doesn't know who to believe,* Taryn thought, wishing Evelyn hadn't tossed the drink. Any proof was now soaked into Courtney's clothes and seeped into the carpeted floor. Taryn left her bystander perch to approach the confused girl.

"She's not lying," Taryn told her, genuine concern in her eyes. "I saw it, too. *Please* be careful."

Courtney blew up.

"You two are such lying, bitter old hags," he growled. "Look at you. Dressed like you're still undergrads but clearly approaching middle age. Your shelf life is about to expire, ladies. Or ma'ams."

Courtney turned to reassure Chloe. But all he caught was a glimpse of her backside as she scurried away, her steps growing faster with each succession. He turned back to Evelyn and Taryn, who were leaving Courtney, all alone, to head back to their room. As they crossed the threshold of the bar, both women heard his voice. Right behind them.

"Oh, and by the way?" Courtney's hot breath whispered from behind the women, startling them. "You're safe. No one would bother spiking either of your drinks. You're not worth the waste of a good rubber."

Evelyn stopped suddenly, snapping her head around to look at Courtney. He brought his face within two inches of hers, seething, as Evelyn looked firmly into his eyes.

"It's bitches like you who deserve to get skull-fucked," he snarled.

With that, Evelyn cold-cocked him. Directly in the nose.

"Bitch!" Courtney screamed as blood poured from his nose, lunging for Evelyn as Taryn tried stepping between the two.

Suddenly, the bartender broke into the scene, forcing himself into the middle of the trio, pointing furiously at the exit.

"All three of you. Out! Now!" the bartender commanded. "Unless you want me to have security escort you from the premises. You are no longer welcome in this bar."

Taryn shuddered. *This can't happen.*

Please, please, no cops, she silently prayed. *No charges. No statements. No identification cards needed.*

"*Ev,*" Taryn said, grabbing Evelyn's hand firmly. "Let's *go.*"

As Courtney continued arguing with the bartender, Taryn firmly grasped Evelyn's hand and pulled her toward the elevators. *Please don't let security follow us,* she silently begged.

The two women, still in shock, stepped into the elevator and rode up to their floor. They said little to one another as they slipped into their pajamas and washed their faces.

When they were both lying in bed, Taryn willing sleep to come to her and end this unsettling night, she heard Evelyn quietly crying.

"Ev," Taryn whispered in the darkness from the double bed next to Evelyn's, "you did a good thing tonight. You probably saved that girl from something that could have ..."

Taryn trailed off. There was no need to connect the dots. Evelyn knew. And she remained silent, except for the sniffles in between deep breaths.

"It just *can't* keep happening," Evelyn said, her sniffles intensifying. "It's *got* to stop."

Within a matter of seconds, Evelyn began weeping. Taryn's heart sank with sickness, sorrow and pride for Evelyn's fierce intensity to protect someone she didn't even know from something surely sinister. Taryn stood up, slid next to Evelyn in the bed and motherly held her as both women cried themselves to sleep.

CHAPTER TWENTY-FOUR

"**G**et the fuck off of me!"

The scream of terror jolted Taryn out of sleep. She had fallen asleep next to Evelyn, and the piercing cries prompted her to sit up sharply, despite not being completely cognizant. Her heart raced as she scanned the room in total darkness, then turned to the lamp on the nightstand to illuminate the space. This wasn't the Tiki Torch Inn.

"Stop!" the yelling continued.

Taryn turned to her right, and she gasped as she watched Evelyn, her arms thrashing, swinging into the empty air, grazing Taryn's right cheek, causing her to wince with pain. Her eyes were closed, but the tears flooded her face as she continued to take swipes at someone who wasn't even there.

Taryn was frozen as she watched in horror. *Was it a night terror?* After about thirty more seconds of the guttural sounds, Taryn grasped Evelyn's shoulders with her hands. "Evelyn! Wake up! Wake up!"

Evelyn's red eyes popped wide open. Her cries softened as she recognized Taryn and shot up in the bed.

"It's okay," Taryn murmured in reassurance, embracing Evelyn as she fully awakened. "You're safe. I'm here."

Evelyn let out a deep breath, sighing in relief before her face turned beet red.

"Oh my God," Evelyn whispered, a hint of shame in her voice. "I'm so sorry. I didn't mean to scare you."

Taryn nodded, then wrapped her arms around her friend, holding her tightly. She swept her right hand over the crown of Evelyn's brunette hair, slowly caressing her from the top of her head to the nape of her neck. When they broke their embrace, Evelyn's eyes were fixated on the white down comforter she'd been covered under. She thrust the fabric from her body, pushing it to the foot of the bed before it dropped to the carpeted floor.

They sat there for a moment, neither woman saying a word.

"Let me get you some water," Taryn said, slowly making her way to the bathroom to grab a plastic cup, then filling it with the coldest water she could. Taryn's gait was still unsteady, the alcohol from just hours ago leaving her with a hint of intoxication. Water spilled from the cup as Taryn lumbered back to the bedroom, handing it to a still-shaken Evelyn.

Evelyn thrust her hands at the cup, grasping it with both hands as she poured the water down her throat, a *glug, glug, glug* sound loudly echoing each desperate gulp.

Once she'd downed the entire cup, she angrily tossed it onto the floor, then rested her face in both palms. Taryn didn't hear any sounds from Evelyn, but her shoulders shook for a good ten seconds before the tears resurfaced with a vengeance.

Taryn rested her bottom on the bed, next to Evelyn, continuing her embrace. Outside of their initial meeting, she'd never seen Evelyn come unglued like this before tonight. All she'd ever seen was a confident, head-strong, sure-of-herself woman. Intoxicated a lot, sure. But not this crumpled, emotional mess sitting in a heap of tears and terror, cowering in a hotel bed.

"Evelyn," Taryn began, "are you okay?"

Evelyn sniffled as she wiped her nose with the back of her deeply tanned hand. She let out a slight, sad laugh.

"Well," she began to choke out the words. "I guess not. But I'll be fine. Just another nightmare."

Taryn paused before carefully choosing her next words.

"Do you have them a lot?" she asked.

"Here and there," she said.

Taryn didn't want to ask. But she couldn't help herself. The words spilled from her mouth before she had a chance to think them through.

"Do you have any idea why?" Taryn asked. "Is there something that triggers them?"

Evelyn paused, wringing her hands before running them both through her gnarled locks, remnants of last night's look.

"Something happened to me a long time ago," Evelyn said. "And the funny thing is, I don't really remember the incident itself. But I knew what had happened the next morning. "That girl ... it almost happened to her, too. I just couldn't ..."

Taryn sat, frozen, as Evelyn broke down.

It was everything she'd feared. Her eyes fought the tears building, trying not to let them spill onto her cheeks. But her resistance was no match for her sorrow and deep guilt. Between Evelyn's nightmare and the events of the evening before, she finally had her answer.

And it wasn't the one for which she'd silently prayed.

Evelyn was not okay. She was far from it.

Graham had ruined her. Then. Now.

And quite possibly, for the rest of her life.

CHAPTER
TWENTY-FIVE

"**B**ecks! We gotta go. It's almost checkout time."

Taryn pretended not to hear Evelyn, her face buried into the luxuriously soft resort pillow as her head pounded. The thirst rising in her throat seemed unquenchable, but Taryn didn't want to move. She just wanted to stay right where she was, motionless, even though she wanted to guzzle a gallon of water.

Evelyn grasped Taryn's left arm, shaking it lightly and then more briskly as her friend didn't react.

"Becks," Evelyn urged. "We *have to* go. Housekeeping has already knocked on the door twice. You can sleep it off in the car."

Taryn rolled onto her back and let out a groan of aggravation. She slowly opened her eyes. Evelyn peered straight into her eyes with a bemused look. She'd already tossed on her Def Leppard T-shirt and short shorts, her brunette locks swept back into a high bun. Without makeup, she looked a little less worn. Foundation wasn't caked into the wrinkles that seemed too advanced for Evelyn's actual age.

Taryn raised an eyebrow and let out a sigh as she sat up and turned to the plastic cup of water on the nightstand. She slurped it down, the gulps in her throat audible with each swallow.

"Here," Evelyn said, thrusting four ibuprofen pills into Taryn's left palm. "If you don't need them yet, I'm sure you will pretty soon."

Taryn let out an *ughhh*, popping the tablets into her mouth and washing them down with the last of her tap water before heading into the bathroom, She refilled her cup, then relieved the irritating pressure in her bladder that had been building as she slept off last night's overindulgence. She swept the back of her palm under her runny nose as she observed herself in the mirror. Her eyes were swollen and bloodshot, and she felt like she could feel every beat of her heart in her head.

Taryn smiled weakly before letting out a huff. She guzzled down another cup of water from the sink, then refilled it and began drinking it again.

"I'll buy you water at the gas station next door," Evelyn said. "But seriously, we have to go. And I start work at three today."

Taryn shuffled back into the main room, pulling a spaghetti-strap gray cotton jumpsuit and black cropped tank top from her overnight bag. She tossed them on the bed before stripping off her pajamas, wishing the memories and hangover from the night could be cleared from her mind as easily. She slowly pulled the shirt over her head before sitting on the edge of the bed and guiding her jumpsuit over her feet, then pulling it up over her shoulders. Taryn slid on her flip-flops and stuffed last night's outfit into her bag, along with the fuck-me pumps and toiletries scattered across the bathroom vanity.

Within ten minutes, Taryn and Evelyn were on I-95, heading north toward Gardenia Beach. Luckily, Courtney was nowhere to be seen when they exited the elevators. The pair stopped at a ticket redemption machine to retrieve Evelyn's $500 winnings, then beelined it to the front door. They'd grabbed a couple of breakfast burritos from the gas station along the interstate entrance, plus two bottles of water and two extra-large coffees. Both women wolfed down their food, which seemed to help settle the nausea from the night before.

They sat in silence, Evelyn behind the wheel, fiddling with the radio to find a station with some light rock. Any kind of music that might have been pulsating at the club last night was the last thing either wanted to hear.

"Ev," Taryn gingerly began, "I'm worried about you. Especially after last night. Do you have episodes like that often? The nightmares?"

Evelyn pulled a cigarette from the pack nestled in her center console, slipping it between her dehydrated lips and bringing a flickering lighter to it. She paused before continuing, offering the pack to Taryn, who, despite her sickened belly and head, followed suit.

"Sometimes"—Evelyn reflected—"past experiences mold our current attitudes and outlook on things. And they stick with you. You can try to bury past traumas, but they always seem to resurface."

Evelyn paused as she blew smoke out to the left, aiming it to escape from the cracked window. Taryn noted she sounded almost like a social worker or therapist. Something she had originally been on the path to becoming. Something she'd planned to devote her life to.

Taryn's heart thudded as she thought of Graham and Evelyn. She began imagining that same man, the husband she'd vowed to love "till death do us part," climbing atop a passed-out Evelyn. She shuddered as the tears began to well in her eyes.

He did this, Taryn thought, the rage building in her body. *He put her on this path of self-destruction.*

"Becks," Evelyn suddenly interrupted her thought train. "Are you *crying*?"

Taryn snapped back to the present moment, wiping her eyes with the back of her fingers as she tried to compose herself.

"Why are *you* crying over *me* having a night terror?" Evelyn asked, confusion dancing across her face and in her voice as she quickly took her eyes off the road to glance at Taryn. "I'm *so* sorry if I scared the shit out of you."

Taryn took a long drag of her cigarette, flicking the ashes out the passenger's side window. She had so much she yearned to ask. But she knew she couldn't. She contemplated where to go with the conversation from here.

Evelyn drew in a hit of nicotine. Taryn watched as a long ash fell to the floor of the car, Evelyn not noticing or seeming to care.

But that was why she was here, after all. To see how Evelyn had recovered from that night Graham had taken her power away from her.

Taryn couldn't fight the urge any longer.

"What happened?" Taryn asked, touching Evelyn's arm. "What happened to you?"

Evelyn sighed before letting out a slight chuckle.

"That's a story for another time," Evelyn responded. "Another time with a few shots under our belts."

This wasn't healthy. For Taryn or Evelyn. For their minds, their livers ... everything. Something needed to change.

Taryn couldn't take it anymore.

She needed to confess why she was here.

"Evelyn," she said, a lump growing in her throat as her voice started to crack. "I think we need to talk."

"Okaayyy," Evelyn said, flicking ash out the window and then quickly taking her eyes off the road to look at Taryn. "What's up?"

"I need to tell you something," she drew out, her heart beating rapidly. "I came down here for a reason. I came down here after I found out something—"

But the shrill ring of Evelyn's phone, set to a Lady Gaga song, interrupted her. "Austin" appeared on the screen, announcing his call.

"Hang on," Evelyn said, letting out a heavy, defeated breath, her face hinting at her remorse. "Time for damage control. I *might* have used Austin's credit card for a few things on this trip."

Taryn's eyes bulged as Evelyn picked up the call, bringing the phone to her ear instead of using the car's Bluetooth speaker.

After a brief, curt conversation, in which Evelyn got in "maybe," "I know," "I'll pay you back," and "fine," she ended the call, shaking her head.

"Well, I'm going to get an ass-reaming when we get back to Gardenia Beach," Evelyn huffed. "Can't wait for that. But our winnings will cover it."

Evelyn tossed her cigarette into an empty Coke can nestled in the center console. She immediately lit another and turned her attention back to the road. After a deep drag and exhale, she glanced at Taryn for a moment before setting her eyes back on the road.

"So, what did you want to tell me?" she asked.

Evelyn's face, her eyes, the fact that she was driving eighty miles per hour on the interstate, jostled Taryn. *No, no, no,* she thought. *Bad idea. Now is not the time.*

"I just wanted to tell you how lucky I feel to have found a Floridian friend," Taryn said, giving her best fake-but-real smile.

"Ditto," Evelyn said. "I'm so sorry your mom is sick. But meeting each other was definitely a silver lining."

"It sure was," Taryn said, grabbing another cigarette and taking a deep drag.

They continued their journey, nothing but music to fill the void.

CHAPTER TWENTY-SIX

Taryn took the whole day to sleep off the night before, ordering Chinese food and a jug of Gatorade to replenish her fluids. She binge-watched old episodes of *Dateline* and fell asleep before eight o'clock.

The next morning, Taryn stirred before the sun even rose. Again, she woke up drenched with sweat and cold, the rest of the Lucky Phoenix escapade's remnants having been expelled through her pores.

Taryn slipped out of her toxin-soaked clothes and pulled on a tank top and capri yoga pants, then crept out of her room and headed to the boardwalk that led her to the beach.

Except for an occasional walker or two, the beach was barren. Taryn left her shoes at the bottom of the boardwalk and headed toward the surf. The cool waves lapped at her feet, her feet sinking farther into the sand.

There was such peace here, Taryn thought. The sounds of the sea, the squawking of seagulls, and nothing but her thoughts to fill her mind and heart.

Taryn retreated to the dry sand farther away from the shoreline, spread out a beach towel she'd had hanging in her bathroom for days, and gently sat down.

Sam would have loved it here, Taryn told herself, aching for the comfort of her best friend. The two had often fantasized about a high school graduation trip to South Florida, once they'd received their diplomas and had a couple of months to spare before heading off to college.

Taryn still blamed herself. Her actions set forward a series of events that meant no graduation trip. Or any trip for the two of them.

***

It was a Saturday night in October 1999, the time of year the leaves in the Midwest began morphing into their brilliant shades of orange and yellow. The air was cool and crisp—perfect sweater weather. Taryn and Sam were making their latest of dozens of Hampton Park Hustles, driving by all the popular boys' homes before scraping up enough change for a sub sandwich to split. One of their last "spots" was turning onto the street where Les Bean lived.

As the Honda Civic neared the property, they realized the jig was up. Les, along with fellow football players Tim Scully, Mark Franklin and Scott Randall, were in the front yard, playing a game of basketball. To throw a U-turn now wouldn't matter. Les and the others stopped for a moment to look directly into the car.

"Shit!" Sam yelped. "They saw us. What the hell do we do now?"

But Les took care of their conundrum. He tossed the basketball toward the girls' car, then motioned for them to roll down the windows.

"Hey ladies," Les said, looking at Sam and adding a wink. "Care to join us for a few brews?"

The girls were stunned. Was Les Bean *really* inviting them to hang out? Had he really just given Sam a wink? That had to be good.

The two girls looked at each other. Their eyes met in agreement, and Sam parked the Civic on the street.

Taryn's nerves were starting to rip at her stomach. Just being there felt, well, weird. Wrong. Even though she felt like they were on the cusp of attaining exactly what they'd been vying for.

Acceptance.

"Just play cool," Sam whispered to Taryn as they walked toward the boys. "Like hanging out with them is no biggie."

Taryn nodded. Les already had two beers for both girls, handing them off with a click of "Cheers."

But Les liked to fuck with people. Even though he had the beautifully blond, large-busted and impeccably stylish Jasmine Keating as an on-again, off-again girlfriend. The two had been an item for about six months, but rumors had been circulating that Les was about done with her high-maintenance attitude. And he liked to play the field. Thus, the on-again, off-again ongoing situation.

Taryn knew Les was unattainable. For her or Sam. But she couldn't crush her friend's hopes. Sam swooned over Les as he dunked the basketball into the hoop, then turned to her, flexing his muscles. And winking again.

"Holy fuck," Taryn said, having caught the exchange and realizing perhaps the game had changed. She whispered to Sam, "He is *so* flirting with you!"

"I know," Sam whispered. "Do you think he's done with Jasmine?"

"Sounds very possible," Taryn said, both hope and caution dancing in her eyes for her friend.

The girls continued to enjoy the outing, following the boys inside and munching on some pretzels and chips before switching from beer to vodka.

Sam and Taryn started to feel like maybe, somehow, they could finally belong. Here was their "in" with the popular crowd, if they played it right. They'd never been to a high school party before. Their names were never on the guest list for impromptu keg parties, nestled deep in Archer Woods.

But tonight, things changed. Finally, Taryn and Sam had arrived.

"Let's do this," a confident Sam said to Taryn. "It's show time."

Both girls called their moms, fibbing they were having a sleepover. Taryn told her mom she was staying at Sam's. Sam did the same, feigning a sleepover at Taryn's.

Les's parents were out of town—and both girls were confident he wouldn't make a stink if they needed to sleep off their inebriation.

Yet, Taryn was so shocked to see Sam's sudden confidence. She watched as Sam exited the back patio slider and strode right up to Les, Tim, Mark and Scott. They'd been passing a joint around, their feet dangling in the in-ground pool that was growing colder by the day, as fall crept closer to winter.

"Got some for us?" Sam asked as she approached the boys, Taryn trailing behind her nervously.

Les took a deep drag, held the smoke in his lungs for about fifteen seconds and blew forcefully into Sam's face. As if on cue, Sam breathed it in before taking the joint from Les, then taking a overzealous inhale herself—and breaking out into a minute-long succession of coughs.

As Les, Tim, Mark and Scott chided Sam—"Amateur!"—she began handing the joint to Taryn, who followed her friend's lead.

Within three minutes, the two joined their male counterparts—all were stoned out of their minds. It was a completely new experience, and Taryn loved how it made her feel. Happy. Giggly. Heavily in tune with every sensation in her body. And a little bad.

But Sam seemed to like it, too.

"Holy crap," she said. "Why am I just discovering this now?"

Sam touched the bricks on the side of the house to steady herself as the group made their way back inside. Windy City Pizza Pros had just delivered three pies, and everyone was ready to scarf them down.

By ten o'clock, both girls were heavily intoxicated. Despite her being equally inebriated, Taryn turned to look toward Sam, standing in the kitchen, picking at a cold piece of pizza. *How was Sam even standing?* she thought.

As the alcohol and drugs seeped further into their minds, party mode continued to progress between the two girls and their four counterparts.

First up, a game of truth or dare. And anyone who wouldn't follow through was ordered to suck down a shot of tequila.

It was around round three when Taryn could see the situation shifting. And she didn't like it.

In her drunkenness, Sam enthusiastically agreed to perform a lap dance on Tim, the school's star running back. While Sam seemed to be enjoying her debut as an amateur exotic dancer, Taryn grew worried. Les salivated over her moves, a wide, almost wicked grin on his face. His dark brown eyes focused intently on every hip shake and ass grind. Taryn tried to not notice that Les was now sporting an erection.

"Now, it's my turn. But I want a private viewing," Les said, motioning toward his parents' bedroom. "Follow me to the VIP room."

Taryn knew. This was Sam's moment to connect with Les, the boy she'd been pining over for months. But she was not in her right mind.

"Sam," Taryn said, quickly grasping her friend's dainty left wrist. "Maybe it's time to take a breather. Maybe we should make some coffee. Or eat a little more pizza."

Sam snapped her head back to look at Taryn, silently mouthing "no."

"This is my shot," Sam whispered into Taryn's ear. "This is our chance to finally fit in. So just let me have a little more fun. I'm dying to make out with Les."

Taryn hesitated, and as she was about to say more, Sam cut her off.

"This is my choice," she said. "Not yours. Just chill."

Taryn sighed and nodded. And then she watched as Les led her best friend upstairs, no one else trailing them. She tried to brush off her negative thoughts and concern. Sam was completely capable of handling herself. When she was sober. Taryn just wasn't so sure how capable she really was, given she'd never seen her best friend so drunk—or high.

Taryn tried. She tried to tell herself she was happy for Sam. That this was Sam's chance to connect—and hopefully pique Les's interest in exploring a relationship. And a chance for both girls to feel like they were finally accepted by their popular peers.

Wow, Taryn thought halfheartedly, trying to convince herself to be happy. *My bestie just might be having her own rom-com moment. Yay for her!*

But her gut didn't align with her mind's attempt at making the situation palatable. Taryn tried to ignore it as she made her way to the powder room on the first floor, freshening up as best she could in her stupor. She plunked down on a recliner, watching the rest of the guys sit down to play a few rounds of Super Mario Bros. to pass the time. She shut her eyes as she waited for Sam and Les to rejoin the gathering.

The last thing Taryn recalled was her concern for every moment her best friend was upstairs with Les. But the alcohol and pot were not her friend, and they beckoned Taryn to drift into sleep within minutes of settling into the recliner.

***

When Taryn sobered up, it was four in the morning. She was still sprawled out in the lounger. Her eyes danced around the room. It was empty.

Sam, her mind suddenly commanded. *Where is she?*

Taryn pushed the recliner to an upright position, steadied herself and stood up.

She surveyed her surroundings.

No Sam.

She quietly opened each bedroom door, trying to see if her best friend was sleeping off the libations of the night. Nothing. Just Tim, Mark and Scott sleeping off their buzz in various bedrooms. Les himself was sawing logs in his parents' bedroom. But no Sam.

Her last stop was the hall bathroom on the second floor. She held her breath as she grasped the doorknob, quietly pushing it open.

And that's when she found her.

Sam was coiled up, sleeping in a fetal position on the ivory bathroom mat. She was covered with two ratty beach towels. Taryn crept closer, gently touching Sam's shoulders to stir her.

The towel slipped onto the floor, exposing a completely naked Sam. Taryn felt remorseful as she observed her friend's nude body for the first time, like she was violating Sam's privacy.

Taryn stood in shocked silence once she saw it, her gasp audible as she brought her hands over her mouth.

"Sam!" Taryn cried out, shaking her friend at the shoulders. "Are you OK? Wake up!"

It took a sobbing, shaken Taryn about thirty seconds to rouse Sam into semi-consciousness, though she was still slightly buzzed. Bewilderment filled Sam's face as she realized where she was—and what she was wearing. Or not wearing.

"What the fuck?" Sam said as her eyes scanned the shredded towel draped over her exposed body. "What happened? Where are my clothes?"

Sam began weeping as Taryn tore through the bathroom hamper, wondering if Sam had accidentally tossed them into the household laundry, thinking it was her own. The pink tank top and black short shorts were nowhere.

"Let's get out of here," Taryn whispered, reaching for her friend's arm to lift her from the floor.

It was then that Sam buckled over in pain as she stood. She brought her hands to her crotch, visibly wincing, as she rose.

That's when Sam saw what Taryn had seen when the towel had slipped off her body—the trickle of a deep red between her thighs. Her face grew ashen as she observed the darkened, maroon-red stain left behind on the ivory rug as Sam rose. Sam recognized fright in Taryn's face and looked at the soiled mat beneath her naked feet.

When Sam brought her gaze back to Taryn's, tears were pouring down her face, trickling down her nude body and the ratty towels to which she desperately clung.

"Oh my God," Sam whimpered. "I think I was raped."

CHAPTER
TWENTY-SEVEN

January 2018, Coneflower Cove, Florida

Adrienne didn't know what overcame her when she finally decided this was the year Coop would pay for his transgressions.

She'd read a story about a woman being gang-raped at a college party, somewhere in the Northeast. It had been captured on video and shared, and it quickly grew its viral feet. Thousands of people's prying eyes couldn't resist—and many felt compelled to share it with their friends, mostly college kids. It enraged Adrienne that anyone could look at how that poor girl was denigrated and destroyed by one single night.

Adrienne withdrew several hundred in cash from her bank account and headed to a local superstore, wearing nondistinctive black clothes, a plain black baseball cap and sunglasses to buy a new laptop—one that was designed for a single purpose.

Once she made her purchase, Adrienne headed to a local coffee shop, where she could set up her new computer and be anonymous. She kept her hat and glasses on as she began her search, having mentioned to the barista when she ordered a latte that she'd just had her eyes dilated. Hopefully, the teenager wouldn't know that had she actually been to the eye doctor, her eyes wouldn't be able to fully focus for a while.

Adrienne set up the laptop and registered it to "Josie Parker," then downloaded a secure browser that concealed IP addresses. That would prevent anyone looking into her later from connecting her to her mission, since the browser blocked her true identity—and location. Though she fully intended to trash the thing once her plan was in place.

Adrienne wasn't sure what that plan was, so she started searching for "dark web duty swap." Several came up, but Adrienne was immediately drawn to one dubbed SOAT, named after *Strangers on a Train*, the classic Alfred Hitchcock movie. Adrienne stirred with hope as she created a profile, using the name JusticeSeeker908, and began poking around. She stumbled upon DojaFire2, whose profile indicated they were "seeking justice for the sexually assaulted."

Adrienne's heart pounded in her chest as she crafted a message to DojaFire2. She was careful at first to tiptoe. God forbid it was really a cop setting her up to get busted for vigilante justice.

"Hello," Adrienne began. "We may have some things in common. Wanna chat?"

She was shocked she received a response within five minutes.

"Hello," DojaFire2 responded. "I think you're right."

Adrienne quickly pecked at the keyboard with a response. DojaFire2 was online. And she wasn't letting him go just yet.

"What's your story?" she replied.

The bubbles in the chat lit up. DojaFire2 was responding.

"Someone I love was sexually assaulted," it read. "And the guy got away with it. He's living his happily-ever-after life with a new wife and no repercussions."

Adrienne's pulse quickened.

"Very similar, indeed. Except I was the one raped in this case—and that guy got away with it, too."

Adrienne shuddered for a moment, realizing her revelation likely clued him in to her sex. Not that men aren't sexually assaulted, but it's far less likely. But the bubbles continued.

"That's bullshit," DojaFire2 wrote. "He needs to be held accountable."

Adrienne's heart leapt into her throat as she composed her reply. She was being vulnerable, maybe revealing too much information. But she felt it. This guy was legit.

"He's a family friend. Or at least, used to be. And yes, I agree. He needs a stiff serving of justice. And so does the asshole who raped your loved one."

Adrienne clearly struck a chord. DojaFire2's reply was only four words long.

"It was my wife."

Adrienne felt the rage boil in her veins. Yes, she had come to the right place. She felt emboldened in her response.

"Are you a cop?" she typed in.

"Absolutely not," DojaFire2 replied. About ten seconds passed, then: "These motherfuckers need to pay for the lives they've ruined. No police needed."

His next words gave her the reassurance she desperately sought.

"If I have to take someone out, I will," it read.

Adrienne breathed a sigh of relief. She had no clue who this guy was—it had to be a guy, she reasoned, unless it was a woman with a wife. Possible. But not probable. From the profiles she'd scrolled so far, she thought most of the members were men.

"Ditto," she replied. "I think we can fix this. If we help each other out."

The response shot through immediately. "I agree. Want to hear my plan?"

CHAPTER
TWENTY-EIGHT

Normally self-conscious, Taryn had spent enough days in a Florida coastal beach town to realize anything goes. She'd seen obese women in G-string bikinis. European men with pot bellies walking the shoreline with no shame for the Speedos they sported. She knew could pull off a bikini now more than ever.

Taryn pulled her hair back into a sloppy braid before slathering sunscreen over every inch of skin exposed before topping it off with a straw, wide-brimmed beach hat. She grabbed a water, a pack of smokes and a lighter and tossed them into her insulated beach bag before heading out the door, sliding her flip-flops that sat under the front window onto her feet. Grabbing her blue trash bucket and picker, Taryn headed toward her car. She snagged a towel from the pool area, ignoring the sign that said they were to be kept in the pool area only and promptly returned after being used.

Taryn had been cleaning the shores fronting the Tiki Torch for weeks, so another spot was probably in need of some TLC. She knew Dottie and others with Save our Seas were doing a beach cleanup at Seagull Point Beach. She headed south on A1A until she found the parking lot. She grabbed her bucket and picker, leaving the cigarettes behind out of shame. As she began her descent to the wooden walkway, she could see a scattering of others, blue buckets and pickers in hand. She noted the rip current warning sign posted as beachgoers descended the walkway. The hot sand burned the sides of her feet that spilled from her sandals as she navigated the burning beige grit. She ambled along the surf, stealthily sliding into the group as if she'd been there all along.

"Rebecca!" said a voice behind her.

Taryn turned to see Dottie, clad in a sun shirt and shorts, smiling and waving at her.

"So nice to see you out here!" Dottie said, bringing Taryn in for an embrace. "What's good for the sea is good for the soul, too."

"You are right about that, Dottie," Taryn said.

She was grateful to see a familiar face that didn't stir up memories she wished didn't exist.

"I've really been enjoying my little solo beach cleanups," Taryn continued. "You were so right. It does feel good to just get out of my head for bit."

The women walked in tandem, making small talk about the rocket launch from two nights ago, the local gas prices that continued to tick upward, and the fatal accident on I-95 last weekend, which left a family of four without their patriarch. Hunter Smithson, who ran his own local construction business, had been driving his work truck southbound when another driver, a fifty-seven-year-old man, had a heart attack behind the wheel. He'd lost control and veered off the roadway, taking the husband and father of two with him to their fiery deaths.

"Such a shame," Dottie said, explaining she'd known Hunter. His company had financially supported Gardenia Beach Hospice House, in addition to spending some of his spare time by volunteering at the Hospice House alongside his wife and kids. "At first, I'd feared it was a drunk driver—not that it would change the end result."

After a couple of hours of traversing the beach for cigarette butts, plastic caps and other assorted trash tossed onto the sand or sea, Taryn and Dottie had filled their buckets and were ready to empty their collections into their rightful resting places. After she and Dottie exchanged their goodbyes and hugged, she watched the older woman walk toward her Kia Soul and climb in, waving as she pulled toward the exit.

Dottie, despite losing her husband of many decades, had found a renewed purpose in life. A way to move on and heal. And it seemed to be working a lot better than Taryn's pursuit for peace.

Regardless, Taryn didn't want to think about it right now. She walked to the convenience store next to the parking lot, bought an eight-pack of hard seltzers and headed back to the beach. She stopped to grab her beach bag from her rental car as she passed through the parking lot again. Taryn settled into a spot close to the shore, laying her stuff on the sand as she cracked open a can and dipped her feet into the wet sand. Taryn had come to love not only the sounds, but the sensations of the salt water splashing over her feet. It was cathartic, like reading a really good mystery novel. She watched a tiny school of fish scuttle by and wondered if they were trying to avoid a shark or something that threatened to gobble them up.

"Hair of the dog?" a voice bellowed from behind.

Taryn glanced in the direction the voice came from, the sun blocking her vision temporarily. She squinted as her eyes adjusted to the brilliance of the sun shining directly above her.

But she recognized the voice. Of course, it was Austin. That beautiful specimen of a man who suddenly plunged Taryn's thoughts into what it might feel like to be kissed by him. Or touched. Or more. Her face reddened at her immoral fantasy, and she forced a smile as she adjusted the brim of her hat.

"Hey," Taryn said, grateful he wasn't a mind reader. She grasped her braid with her left hand and fiddled with it in her nervousness. "I guess so. More like my endless vacation mode."

Austin chuckled, crouching down and resting his butt onto the sand just south of Taryn's towel. He settled in next to her, his gaze shifting to the brilliant sea in front of them. They sat for a few moments in silence, both soaking in the ocean breeze and soothing sounds of the waves lapping the shore. Taryn tried to sneak a glance at Austin, fighting the urge to touch his chiseled face, his arms, his chest. Everything that looked so appealing to her carnal thoughts. Luckily, Austin, still focused on the ocean waves, broke the silence.

"Any chance you could spare one for me?" he asked. "I didn't know this was a BYOB party. And since I recently picked up some of the Lucky Phoenix tab ..."

Taryn's face went pale, mortified she was an unknowing participant in his hijacked credit card.

"Of course," she stammered. "And is it considered the hair of the dog if it's a couple days later? Because I sure as hell didn't drink last night. I recovered."

Taryn leaned over to her bag, feeling around for another can, hoisting it from the insulation and handing it over to Austin.

"Hope you like mango." She smiled.

"I like whatever you have to offer," Austin said with a coy look on his face. Taryn's face heated again, and she prayed Austin mistook her reaction for too much sun exposure.

Whether he noticed her embarrassment or not, Austin didn't let on. He smiled at her, cracked open the can, lifted it toward her direction and said, "Cheers," as they clinked the aluminum together.

Taryn's mind buzzed with flashbacks from two nights prior. She felt guilty, almost worried that Austin could read directly into her mind. She had so much she wanted to ask him. She wanted to know more about their marriage and divorce. How two people who seemed so inherently drawn to one another and obviously in love couldn't make it work. It made her think of that Don Henley and Patty Smyth song from the '90s. About how love sometimes isn't enough.

Maybe they're their own versions of Don and Patty, Taryn thought.

But she was afraid. Not so much to open a still-healing wound for Austin but of what else she might learn. Her mind rocketed back to Austin's unexpected Lucky Phoenix bill. The guilt came roaring back.

"I'm so sorry about that night," she began, then turned her words into a fib. "I had no clue you were the one fronting the bill."

Austin stopped her. "It's fine. And I know you didn't know. Believe me, I'm used to it."

Taryn paused, carefully choosing her words before she spoke. "Can I ask something personal?"

Austin turned toward her, his right thumb and index finger grasping the arm of his sunglasses before he gently drew them down, exposing his sparkling blue eyes. Her stomach quivered, and she tried to quell it.

"Ask away," Austin said. "Though if you're going to ask me how many women I've slept with, you're not getting an answer."

Taryn let out a shocked cackle, not expecting his retort. "Um, no," she said, her body temperature heating up with embarrassment.

Austin let out a guffaw. "Becks, I'm just fucking with you. Gotta keep you on your toes."

Taryn took a moment to collect her thoughts, unsure if she should go on.

"Really," Austin said, reaching to touch her arm in reassurance. "I'm pretty much an open book."

"What's the deal with you and Evelyn?" Taryn began. "I don't get it."

Austin sat quietly for several moments, his gaze returning to the glistening sea. Taryn's thoughts recoiled, wondering if she'd asked something she shouldn't have. She shifted her bottom on the towel, trying to mask her discomfort. But then, after a deep sigh, the words came.

"Do you want the long version or the CliffsNotes one?" he said.

"Whichever you're willing to provide," Taryn said.

Austin continued to focus his eyes on the ocean for a few moments. Then, he began to speak.

"Well, we don't have all day," Austin began. "So here's the short of it all."

He paused, downing the rest of his High Noon before reaching for another, pulling the tab up, releasing the pressure from the sealed can. He brought it to his lips, took a swig and brought his knees up, resting his interlocked arms around them as he balanced the seltzer and began to share.

CHAPTER TWENTY-NINE

"Evelyn and I have known each other forever," Austin began. "We met in college, at Midsouthern Florida. From the moment I laid eyes on her, sitting there on a bench outside of the Student Union, I knew she was the one. There was something about her smile, her energy, as I approached her to ask some bullshit question, just to get her to talk to me."

Taryn took it in, listening intently.

"She was magnetic," Austin continued, his eyes sparkling and a smile slyly spreading across his face. "Before she even spoke to me for the first time, I knew I wanted her. Not just in a sexual way. But in every way possible. I wanted her mind. Her energy. Her companionship. I knew it, instantly. Yes, she was striking. Her hair was so sleek, her facial features so perfect. I loved her smile. And the more we got to know each other, the more I knew I couldn't live without her. Everyone seemed to be drawn to her. And she was overly friendly to everyone she met. There was just something so welcoming, so open, in who she was. I remember she was wearing this black, off-the-shoulder jumpsuit that showcased her chiseled shoulders and clung to her body in all the right places. And her olive skin was glowing. It sucked me in."

Austin took another sip of his drink, his glance fixated on the ocean waves in front of them.

"Evelyn felt it, too," he went on. "And after that, we were inseparable. And we were both so incredibly happy. On top of the world. She was killing it in school, getting pretty much straight A's as she worked on earning her bachelor's in social work, as I worked on my own degree in finance. Evelyn was a powerhouse. She was determined to make a difference with that degree, wanting to help others. Help others in the way she hadn't been able to get herself. She felt strongly she wanted to focus on helping people with mental health and substance abuse issues."

Taryn soaked it in, befuddlement growing on her face. *Evelyn's drinking wasn't an issue in college?* Austin noticed her perplexed expression and continued.

"Ev grew up with alcoholic parents. A dad who died when she was thirteen. He'd been driving drunk, heading home after a bachelor party, when he slammed his car into a light pole, just down the street from their apartment. And her mother dealt with it by drinking even more. That woman was never sober, except maybe first thing in the morning."

Taryn's breathing quickened, sickened at the thought of a young Evelyn learning her father's car—and body—was crumpled against the towering steel and concrete. It brought her back to the moment she learned her mother's life had ended in a similar way, though she hadn't gotten behind the wheel inebriated. But then Evelyn seeing her mother follow a path like the one that killed her father? Her throat began to tighten at the thought.

Austin's voice snapped her back into the present moment.

"Evelyn vowed she'd lead a different life," Austin continued. "And she was well on her way. Believe it or not, she wasn't a partier in college. Here and there, sure, she'd have a drink or two. But she never overdid it. School came first. She was determined to make the most out of her education, and she even planned to continue on with her master's degree after completing her undergrad studies."

Austin looked at Taryn's pack of cigarettes peeking out from her beach bag. Without exchanging words, Taryn picked up the pack, gave Austin a questioning look, and he pulled one from the pack. Taryn did the same, with both bringing the smokes to their lips. Austin held the lighter for

Taryn to fire hers up first, then did the same himself. He sucked in a puff, exhaled deeply and continued.

"We were so in love," he said, a twinge of melancholy in his tone. "She knew me inside and out. And I felt the same for her. I couldn't even fathom being with anyone else. Even the handful of times another co-ed would try to entice me to head back to their dorm room for some 'fun,' I never entertained the thought. I wouldn't do anything to risk what we had. She was my world. And that last year of school, I led her back to the place I'd first laid eyes on her, getting down on one knee, and asked her to marry me."

Taryn's heart fluttered at the scene she conjured in her mind. She loved love stories, and her heart thumped as she envisioned Austin proposing and the certain tears of joy that followed.

"She said yes," Austin said, beaming at the recollection. "I was the happiest man on Earth. I couldn't wait to officially start our lives together, and we planned to tie the knot on July 7, 2007. You know, on 7-7-7? It was the perfect date, it seemed. Since we both felt we hit the jackpot when it came to love.

"But then, some shit went down," Austin said, growing somber.

He downed the rest of his can of seltzer, prompting Taryn to grab two more to continue this tale. They both popped open their cans, swigging from them. Taryn put out her cigarette, immediately lighting another as she listened to Austin and Evelyn's love story. She so wanted it to end happily, but she knew the plot twist was coming.

The silence was killing Taryn. She wanted to hear what that "shit" was. She knew it, deep down, but needed someone else to verify it. She prayed that the shit was something else. Not Graham. But she knew.

"What happened?" she asked.

Austin drew in a deep breath, filling his lungs with as much air as he could suck in, then letting it all out with the saddest of sighs.

"She experienced a significant trauma," Austin said, taking a moment to collect himself. "I don't want to betray her confidence, because it really is her story to tell. And it's deeply personal and vulnerable. I don't think it's my place to reveal that to you."

Shame flooded Taryn's thoughts. She got it. If something horrible had happened to her, she certainly wouldn't want a friend or ex-lover to callously share that story with other people. That story was hers and hers alone to tell.

"Sorry," Austin said, drifting his gaze to Taryn. Their eyes locked, and she saw a tear trickle down his right cheek as it swept past the bottom rim of his sunglasses. "I'm not trying to be an asshole. Just respectful."

Taryn nodded.

"I'm so sorry I pried," she said. "I just haven't been able to piece together why you two aren't still together. It's clear there's still something there between you."

The corners of Austin's mouth lifted slightly as he attempted to smile.

"It's fine," he continued. "All I can say is that Evelyn had something terrible happen to her. And I wasn't there to stop it."

Austin lifted his palm to his forehead, whisking away the beads of salty sweat with his fingers.

"After that, things weren't the same," Austin continued. "I tried to help her deal with what happened to her. I told her that no matter what, I still loved her and that love would grow stronger every single day.

"We tried to get past it." He drank from his quickly disappearing seltzer. "We got into couples counseling to help us both. Not just to help her heal, but for me to know how to help her through that. We had our pockets of happiness. We went ahead with the wedding, which was the most amazing day of my life. And hers. But the glow of the big day couldn't sustain us long-term.

"I tried." His voice choked. "I did all I could to be supportive, to let her know I meant 'for better or worse.' But she was coming unglued as time went on. Evelyn, who had barely drank during our time at MFU, had done a one-eighty. First, it was just a few glasses of wine a night, to help her relax, be able to sleep. But by the time we'd been married a couple of years, I realized there was more to it. I found liquor bottles hidden throughout the house. They'd be in laundry bins, tucked behind hardbacks on the bookshelves, even stuffed in plastic holiday decoration bins in the garage. I didn't say anything at first. I knew she had a serious demon that wouldn't die. I figured she just needed to work her way through it.

"But then it got worse."

Taryn shifted her gaze from the sea and surf to Austin, who still stared ahead of him. She ran her hand over his left forearm, stroking it gently as a gesture of reassurance and compassion.

"Evelyn hadn't had the heart to use her degree," Austin continued. "In fact, she didn't even go to the commencement ceremony at MFU. That campus brought nothing but hurt, bad memories to her. After she barely graduated, since her grades sank into the gutter after the incident, she had no drive to go to work. I was able to score a decent job after graduation, one that covered our expenses and freed her up to deal with her trauma on her own time, in her own way. But she just had no desire to look. She was a shell of the bubbly, bright woman I'd fallen so hard for. I wanted the old Evelyn back. But I knew I wasn't being fair. I was being selfish, thinking more about what *I* had lost. Not what *she* had lost.

"After the first DUI she got, she was court-ordered to go to Alcoholics Anonymous," Austin said. "It gave me some hope, seeing her regularly go to meetings and get stuff off her chest. I thought it was helping. That she was healing, finally. That maybe, there was a sliver of hope that what we had been prior to the trauma would return."

Austin paused, then motioned toward Taryn as she lit another cigarette, taking one and doing the same. If any story needed chain-smoking to temper it, it was this one. He exhaled, then continued.

"Once her probation was up, as well as her required sobriety efforts, it was like a switch flipped," he said. "She was tipsy by the time I got home from work every night and full-fledged drunk by bedtime. The weekends were a blur, the majority of our time spent in bars and breweries. She was always drunk or hung over, no matter the day. I'd say I'm shocked she didn't get another DUI, but it was because she'd learned her drinking and driving lesson. She'd still pound, but she'd make sure she had a designated driver. Or she'd get an Uber. Or walk, even if it was a thirty-minute trek. She knew she couldn't get another DUI. But I guess she knew, or felt, like alcohol was the only bandage to fix her shattered soul.

"I tried to handle it," Austin went on. "I loved her, and I couldn't imagine my life without her. I gave her the grace she needed, but it wasn't enough. She'd jostle me from my sleep three or four nights a week, scream-ing and thrashing in terror as her sleep was shrouded in nightmares. She'd relive the incident regularly as she slept, coming to in a heated sweat, weeping, and crying, 'No! Stop it!' until I was able to reassure her that she was safe. She was home. She was with me. And I would never let anything happen to her again. But it didn't matter."

Taryn, still silent, grew sickened at the thought. Evelyn's night terror at the Lucky Phoenix rang vibrantly fresh in her mind.

"Things continued to go downhill," Austin continued. "I'd come home each night to an empty house. I'd track her phone to whatever bar she was at, only to find her completely drunk and hanging all over whichever warm body had bellied up next to her at the bar. Each time, I'd try to bring her home. And she'd refuse most nights, telling me she could damn well do whatever she pleased. That I didn't own her and no one else did, either. I'd watch over her until she could barely keep her eyes open, then lead her to the car to take her home. But it was taking its toll. I slept awful. I couldn't focus at work. All I could do all day was worry. Worry that she was already drunk even though it was ten in the morning. Worry that she might decide she no longer had the capacity to care about getting arrested. Worried that she might get behind the wheel of the car to make a booze run. And I was afraid that she might do something to harm herself, intentional or not.""

Taryn soaked it all in, continuing to stare at the ocean, watching a young redheaded, pale mother and her similarly red-haired, freckled toddler navigate the waves as they lapped at their feet.

"So why did you two divorce?" Taryn stammered, quickly adding, "if that's not too nosy."

"Funny story, but not," Austin replied. "I came home from work on May 5, 2015, and, like usual, she was not home. Not that it was a surprise. It was Cinco de Mayo. You know, another 'holiday' to celebrate with alcohol, so I figured she was somewhere getting her margarita fix. I checked her phone and was startled to see I couldn't find her location. She'd either turned it off, or her phone had died, but I knew I didn't want to wait for her to come home. So I started making the rounds of her various watering holes. I was able to track her down at Margarita Mama's, a local Tex-Mex place we'd hit up sometimes when we wanted a hardcore margarita. When I walked in, I saw Fred, the bartender. We locked eyes, and I could see a sheath of terror roll over his eyes. He knew something. And he didn't want *me* to know it. I could see the discomfort in his face. I asked if he'd seen Evelyn. He hesitated and then nodded. I asked him where. He said, 'I don't think you want to know.'

"My heart sank," Austin continued. "It was like I knew, right at that moment, that my marriage was over. I was afraid of where I'd find her, but I couldn't continue this life that had become complete insanity. Not the life I'd envisioned with her. Fred nodded toward the back door that led to the overflow parking lot. There was one vehicle there, a black Jeep Wrangler. I didn't recognize it and was at a loss. I didn't know why Fred had led me in this direction.

"But then I saw the Jeep rocking slightly. Like something out of a sex-crazed teen comedy movie," Austin proceeded. "And I knew. I didn't want to see what was in there. But I couldn't keep going on like this.

"As I approached the Jeep, I saw the fogged windows. It was like I was in a trance. I just kept walking toward the SUV, knowing I didn't want to see what was in there but also knowing I needed to.

"That's when I found her," he said. "I swung open the back passenger door, and a cloud of marijuana smoke wafted out into my face. And the rocking suddenly halted. Because I had interrupted her. Interrupted her fucking Doug.

"Doug, the twenty-five-year-old bar back, who had cleared our dirty glasses from the bar the night before. Doug, who I'd also bought a shot for less than twenty-four hours ago. Doug, who had told me how lucky I was to have such a hot wife on several occasions. Doug, who put the nail in the coffin of our marriage."

Taryn was silent. Her belly twisted and burned as she imagined the heartache Austin must have felt in that terrible moment. When you realize the person you love has hurt you in a way that's not repairable.

But it was a familiar hurt. Like her realization of what Graham had done. Who he was. No matter the fond memories, the good times they had shared, it had all shattered when she read that confession. But she couldn't share that with Austin. Instead, she touched the back side of his hand and let out a deep sigh.

"I'm so sorry," was all she could muster. "I'm so sorry for your hurt. And Evelyn's. Sometimes, we get handed a pile of shit we don't deserve."

Austin nodded, wiping the brimming tears with the back of his hand before clearing his throat.

"Thanks," he said. "I still carry immense guilt over not being there, the night of the incident. Which is probably why I let her slide with some of her bullshit. The drinking. The helping herself to my credit card. Making sure she gets home safely after she's gone on one of her many benders. Had I been there ..."

They sat there for a minute or two, not saying a word but just gazing at the sea and the people that spotted the shore. Surely, their hearts weren't as heavy as theirs at this moment. The curiosity was killing Taryn. She didn't want to pry further, but she wanted to know the rest.

But that wasn't happening now.

Austin stood up suddenly, brushing the sand from the back of his shorts and legs and rocketing toward the surf, his shortboard tucked beneath his right armpit.

"What the ..." Taryn thought as Austin jumped into the sea. *Did I go too far?* she thought.

Austin paused at the surf to scream back at Taryn. She saw, about fifty feet out, a woman's flailing hands before they were gobbled up by the surf.

"Call 9-1-1!" he yelled.

Taryn thrust her hands into her bag, fishing around for her phone, as Austin dove in.

By the time paramedics arrived, Austin was already performing CPR on the woman, whom he'd dragged ashore and lain on Taryn's beach towel with the assistance of three other beachgoers. They'd seen Austin rush into the angry waters and raced to the sea to assist him in bringing the woman to land.

As Austin continued chest compressions and breathing into the swimmer's mouth, Taryn couldn't make out the woman's face. She spied the spindly arms and legs sprouting from the body settled on the sand as Austin feverishly worked to save the woman. His rescue efforts carried on for what seemed like an hour, even though it was only a few minutes. At first, the woman hadn't responded at all. But after the second set of chest compressions, the gurgling began. A significant crowd had drawn around the scene, with several people whipping out their phones to record not only the rescue, but the CPR. It sickened Taryn. But then, she realized, had she been a reporter on the scene, she would have done the exact same. Or taken bystanders' video clips to feed into her breaking news story.

As the swimmer began to vomit, Austin rolled her to her left side, allowing her to empty the contents of her belly onto the sand instead of

aspirating the disgusting mess. She began coughing, choking and sputter-
ing, and a collective sigh of relief ricocheted through the bystanders.

"Thank God!" someone shrieked as the EMTs scrambled to the scene,
brushing back the crowd.

"Clear the way!" a young, buff and seemingly Sicilian paramedic barked,
prompting the crowd to slightly retreat. He swept in and took over efforts
from Austin.

Taryn stood, trembling from the shock of the situation. Which was
even more horrifying when she stepped back and saw the nearly drowned
woman being loaded onto a stretcher.

It was Dottie.

Taryn could barely recognize the sweet Pancake Place waitress. The
vibrant older warm-hearted woman looked nothing like herself after nearly
drowning.

"Oh my God," she said to Austin. "I know her."

Austin still intently looked on as Dottie was carried up to the beach
access to be loaded into an ambulance. It took a moment for it to sink in.

"What?" Austin said. "How?"

"She's served me," Taryn said, omitting the part about her volunteerism
with the woman. Nothing that could lead to questions.

"She's a bartender?" Austin said incredulously.

Taryn shook her head back and forth.

"No," Taryn said. "She's a waitress. At the Pancake Place."

"Oh my God," Austin said. "Come to think of it, she does look familiar."

The two stood in silence as they watched beachgoers start to disperse
back to their original posts—beach chairs under umbrellas, splayed out on
extra-long towels, or just walking the surf.

"I'm a little surprised," Austin said. "It's typically the vacationers who
get caught in a rip current. The locals usually know better."

Taryn looked at Austin. "I thought sharks are what you have to worry
about out here."

"They're pretty rare," he said. "Like winning the lottery. But rip currents? Those are just one of the rules of respecting the sea. Know your conditions. And if you ever get caught in one, go with it. Just swim parallel along the shore. You never want to fight it. The waves are more powerful than you. You must let them be. Or you'll end up like her. Or worse."

Taryn nodded, still shaken. "I don't think I'll ever swim alone again." She gulped.

"That's a good idea," he said. "For anyone."

The two stood there for a moment, their eyes locking and sharing the surge of adrenaline from the shock of the unexpected afternoon. Taryn felt even more attracted to Austin. Not only a hot guy but a good one. Who jumps into a rip current, risking his own life to save someone he didn't even know?

The kind of man she could fall for.

Taryn tried to disregard the thought, but it was nearly impossible as they stood within a foot of one another. Austin's eyes said something, too. She just wasn't sure what was swirling around behind them.

It was then that Austin pulled Taryn in for a hug.

The goosebumps spread across her flesh instantaneously, and her heart thumped so vigorously, Taryn prayed Austin couldn't feel or sense either.

Being attracted to the ex of her husband's assault victim wasn't part of the plan.

"Come on," he said as their embrace broke apart. "It's time for a real drink."

CHAPTER THIRTY

November 1999, Hampton Park

Sitting in the parking lot of a local coffee shop, Sam had tried to piece together her evening for Taryn. The last thing she recalled, she told Taryn, was Les handing her what he proclaimed was a "fun pill" as soon as they'd stepped in the bedroom.

"My mind just started to cloud," Sam said. "I honestly didn't know if I was awake or dreaming."

Sam hung her head as she explained what she could remember. Like when Les pushed her against the wall, kissing her feverishly while running his hands over her breasts, then dropping them to the waistband of her shorts. As he'd led his fingers down her thigh, she'd pushed him away, she explained to Taryn.

"I told him I was pretty fucked up," Sam recalled. "I said I didn't want to go any further. And I asked him, 'Don't you have a girlfriend?' "

Sam recounted how Les had huffed, coming in close, telling her, "Let's just pretend you're my girlfriend for a little bit."

"When he leaned in for another kiss, I tried to push him away," Sam said, tears trickling as she looked away from Taryn. "And things got hazy. It must have been that pill and everything else I took."

Sam told Taryn that she'd asked Les if she could sit down, since she didn't feel well.

"I just couldn't keep my eyes open as soon as I sat on the bed," Sam said, hanging her head. "The last thing I remember was Les standing next to me, then climbing on top of me for a kiss.

"That's all I recall," she said, sobbing.

Taryn begged Sam to report the assault. Or at least tell her parents.

"*Hell* no," she said. "Our moms will be *furious* we were sleeping at a guy's house. And drinking and doing drugs."

"But you were *assaulted*," Taryn insisted. "Nothing else matters. You were *raped*. And that fuckface needs to be held accountable."

"And be pitied or hated by our classmates?" an irritated Sam barked. "No thanks."

That was the moment. The line in the sand.

Sam's outlook on life had starkly, suddenly changed. And not for the better.

After days of pleading, Taryn finally was able to persuade Sam to go to her mom.

And that's when the bad became a whole lot worse.

Holly Freedman had been furious once Sam and Taryn spilled it all out. And she was going for the jugular.

Despite Sam's pleas, she marched her daughter down to the Hampton Park Police Department and demanded to speak to a detective. As soon as the report was filed—and Les was called in for questioning—everything took a nosedive.

Jasmine, the on-again, off-again girlfriend of Les, immediately launched her grassroots campaign to brand Sam a liar. She told anyone who'd listen that Les Bean was HERS—and would NEVER fuck a loser like Sam Freedman.

"I mean, *look* at her." Jasmine twisted her striking features into a sneer as Sam passed her in the hallways between classes. "Les has *me*. He doesn't need to hook up with the lower echelon of society. She's so, um, average. At best. And she has a dude's name."

It stung. So did the random notes shoved into her locker or the black marker on her locker door, which read, "Lying slut," "Loser" and "LIAR."

So did the anonymous calls to her cell phone, the caller hurling more insults through the phone.

"You're a fucking lying loser," the angry voice would bark. "Les Bean would NEVER stoop so low as to hook up with YOU. Fucking loser. Do us all a favor and just kill yourself already."

After a month of malignment, Sam started taking every word to heart. She grew more and more withdrawn, declining Taryn's company eight times out of ten. She just didn't want to do anything. She locked herself in her bedroom when she wasn't in school, mostly sleeping. And staring at the four purple walls that encased her bedroom.

Hours after a series of unanswered phone calls, Taryn's internal sirens started to go off. She hopped into her car, heading to Sam's, where she intended to beg Holly to let her in to pound on Sam's door. Sam was hurting, and Taryn just wanted to hold her. To make her feel safe and loved. If Sam would only open up, allow the people who loved her to support her through this devastatingly rough, unanticipated road in life. Taryn rehearsed her speech on the drive over. She planned to voice her worries and let Sam unleash her anger and pain. Taryn would vow to stand by her through anything.

But as she pulled in front of the Freedmans' house to park on the street, she knew.

There would be no talk. No healing. No helping her friend.

As Taryn walked toward the house, she heard Holly's howls of agony before she even set eyes on her. The woman, who'd been like a second mom to Taryn, screamed in anguish as her knees buckled and she fell to the asphalt.

Taryn understood why when she saw the Medical Examiner's Office roll out a body bag on a stretcher.

Taryn's gut instantly knew. Her best friend was gone. It was Sam who was wrapped in that body bag.

And, in that moment, Taryn wished she was in one, too.

CHAPTER THIRTY-ONE

2014, Hampton Park

S am's suicide might have happened more than a decade ago, but it always remained with Taryn. Sam would drift into her thoughts daily. As did the feelings of blame.

I shouldn't have insisted, a still-hurting Taryn would regularly berate herself. *She'd still be here today if I'd never pushed her to tell her mom.*

Les had been charged after the report had been filed. He was four months out from trial when Sam killed herself.

But the star witness was gone. That position had shifted to Taryn. She was the only one left to tell Sam's tale—and make sure that piece of shit paid.

Taryn shook and wept often as she was asked to share with the judge, jury and courtroom observers.

It had been a brutal, heart-wrenching experience. But Taryn's testimony, along with others', had landed Les a guilty verdict for the second-degree felony, with a ten-year prison sentence. Plus, he also earned his spot on the Sexual Offenders Registry. So, hopefully, he'd never wield his dick as a weapon again.

It was that experience that instilled in Taryn a desire to prevent others from thinking suicide was their best solution to an in-the-moment crisis. A desire to dig deeply into the criminal mind. *Why, in this day and age, do people still think they have a right to another person's body?* Taryn often wondered.

It was during a happy-hour discussion with her coworker Anne some years back that something sparked. Anne held the coveted features beat that Taryn hoped would one day be hers. Anne had written scores of stories on the Chicago area's different nonprofits and the people behind them.

"You should think about volunteering with a suicide prevention non-profit," she suggested, after Taryn had downed a good five glasses of wine and revealed her angst over Sam's suicide so many years ago. "You'd be amazed at how good it feels to be the sounding board others need. It's the perfect prescription to heal a hurting heart."

Later that night, several drinks in, Taryn searched "suicide prevention volunteers" and found just what she needed. "Sophie's Survivors" was a nonprofit based in Riverwood, a neighboring Chicago suburb, one town over from Hampton Park. It was started by the parents of Sophie Ambrose, a fifteen-year-old girl who had killed herself after a sexual assault.

It spoke to Taryn. The story paralleled Sam's so closely. Sophie had also been inebriated when she was assaulted at a high school party. The host's brother was home visiting from college and had a penchant for younger girls. He'd been charged, and a trial had ensued.

But the trial became a dumping ground to pull out Sophie's secrets. There were no boundaries. Everything was fodder for the defense, trying to paint a picture of Sophie being a "slut," a move meant to convince the jury to believe that the incident was not an assault but a mutually desired hookup. She was questioned under oath about the blowjob she'd given a basketball player in a janitor closet after they won the regional championship. She was asked to share about how she flashed her breasts in a hot tub filled with jocks. And the spotlight was shone on the fact she lost her virginity at thirteen to her seventeen-year-old next-door neighbor.

Like Sam, Sophie had committed suicide. It was Day Three of the as-sailant's trial, and Sophie's sexual experiences—and the intimate, embar-rassing assault—were all on the table. Sophie, after an intense cross-exami-nation by the defense, had broken down in tears, sobbing as she was forced to admit she'd been sexually active for years—and relayed her experiences as the defense continued to pounce, painting a picture of Sophie as nothing more than a promiscuous misfit. The judge excused her for the day, telling her she needed a night's rest and could continue her testimony the next day.

But Sophie hadn't shown. She'd downed a bottle of sleeping pills and a liter of vodka from her dad's liquor cabinet and never woke up.

***

Taryn was thirty when she filled out the volunteer paperwork. Sophie's Survivors was thrilled to have her. She'd take a night per week to field phone calls from hopeless people, giving them an ear to bend and a feeling that they were not alone. She'd write public relations copy to pitch to news organizations, and *The Gazette* had even let her write a column on her experience—and the impetus behind it.

And then there were booths at various local fairs. Taryn would be teamed up with another volunteer to provide pamphlets, business cards with the organization's crisis line number and to just be on hand to speak from the heart about her experience.

It was at a cool fall day, just a few months into her volunteerism, when Taryn was paired with another volunteer to work the booth.

The very handsome, career-driven Graham Sloan was her co-pilot for the day.

Taryn felt the electricity from the moment they locked eyes to say hello. As the two waited in their chairs as most people passed up the table, they began spilling their reasons for volunteering.

"My best friend committed suicide after she was raped at a little party," Taryn had said, watching Graham as he listened to every word. "The harassment after she pressed charges, the cross-examination on the stand was too much. I watched her get wheeled out of the house in a body bag."

Graham's face was stoic as he listened, his eyes growing moist as Taryn went on. She shared her guilt. Her sadness. Her desire to help the Sams of the world—before it was too late. And her efforts to educate the public as much as she could, through her journalism career.

"Wow," Graham said, running his fingers through his handsome blond hair, then turning back to Taryn. "I think you're the single-most thoughtful, kind person I've met this week. Maybe even this month. Or year."

Taryn's face flushed with heat. She hadn't been expecting *that*.

"You're something special," he said. "I'd love to get together for a coffee or dinner sometime."

Taryn had been startled by his boldness. And the fact that such a beautiful man seemed to be interested in *her*.

"I'd love that," she said, unsuccessfully trying to suppress her smile. "In fact, when we wrap up here, you want to hit The Drain for some drinks?"

Graham's face mimicked a sunburn. He took a minute to pause.

It freaked Taryn out. How could he ask her out one minute and reject her the next?

"Never mind," Taryn hurriedly barked. "It was just a spur-of-the-moment thought."

"No," Graham cut in. "It's not that. I'd *love* to get drinks, believe me. But I'd let my sponsor down. And myself."

Taryn let it sink in. Graham was sober? Should she consider dating a man who didn't drink? The mere thought of eliminating booze from her life made her heart twitter.

"How about this?" Graham said, a sparkle in his eyes. "After we save the world here, we'll hit Coffee Tawk for a cup of joe. And I'll tell you about how my sobriety led me to a recovery group—and this exact moment I'm thinking might just be fate."

It was bold and brazen, this man's self-confidence. Taryn liked it.

She accepted the offer, which went from a cup of coffee to dinner, then a movie. And just sitting and talking in the car. Neither wanted the evening to end. When Graham walked Taryn to her apartment's front door, he brought his hands to her face, gently cupped it and brought his soft lips to hers.

It was a kiss that romantic movies were made of. A mixture of passion, tenderness and sensuality.

And that's when Taryn knew. She had finally found her person.

Or so she thought.

CHAPTER
THIRTY-TWO

Present Day, Gardenia Beach

A half-hour after Dottie's rescue, Taryn was three drinks in at the Wayside and feeling more at ease. The mind demons were at rest. She and Austin had found their usual spots at the bar, with Sheila serving them. Though Sheila's eyebrows had briefly lifted when the two of them walked in together.

"Well, you two have been up to some good in the world, I see," Sheila had said as they settled into their spots.

Confusion danced across Taryn and Austin's faces. But they didn't get a chance to ask a thing—Sheila had already pointed to the TV anchored to the wall. The twenty-four-hour local news channel was on, and there they were—Austin diving into the ocean, scooping up Dottie from the rip current to bring to the shore, and, then, the paramedics taking her away.

All those smartphones snapping footage had already ended up in the local news cycle. Thankfully, the media had the decency to not broadcast the CPR footage. No one needed to see chest compressions on a nearly drowned senior citizen—nor did they need to see her gasp for breath.

"Unfuckingbelievable," Austin muttered in disgust. "Fucking vultures out there, just looking to go viral. Even if it's video of someone nearly dying."

Taryn felt a twinge of shame. Guilt by association. Had she not been intimately involved in the rescue, she knew she'd likely have been one of those seemingly feckless scavengers. Breaking news had been her beat. Even in her own mind, she'd written the headline and lede of the story.

But she kept that to herself.

Paranoid, Taryn pulled out her iPhone and searched "woman," "near drowning" and "Gardenia Beach." Bam! Several results, with video clips of Austin at work, Taryn sprinkled throughout background shots.

It chilled her. Taryn didn't want to be known or noticed here. Especially with Austin. What if someone, one of Graham's friends, spied it and connected the dots? Even Scoot, his sponsor.

The potential ramifications sickened her.

Austin was shoveling a handful of pub mix pretzels into his mouth when Evelyn, her sunglasses shielding her eyes, slowly sauntered in, a sweaty bottle of an electrolyte drink clutched in her left hand. She lifted the removable bar countertop long enough to pass through, then let it drop down with a crash. It startled Sheila, who'd had her back to Evelyn as she poured a hefty serving of well vodka into a plastic cup, topping it off with a splash of soda water and a lime.

"Christ, Everlast." Sheila scowled. "Don't be slamming shit."

Evelyn gave a short chuckle, removing the cap from the bottle of her drink and taking a long chug.

"Sorry, Mom," she retorted, prompting Sheila to let out a huff. Evelyn grinned, then turned to face Taryn and Austin.

Sheila broke the silence, pulling up her phone and shoving the screen in Evelyn's face.

"Your main squeeze is having his fifteen minutes of fame," she said, handing over the phone.

Evelyn used her right index finger to scroll through the local newspaper's online article titled, "Beachgoers pull woman from rip current after near drowning." Her eyes widened as she read on.

"Holy shit," Evelyn muttered. "I can't believe this is you. There's not only video but a photo gallery? Wow. The reporters will be knocking on your door soon."

The comment made Austin visibly uncomfortable. Beads of perspiration built above his eyebrows. He shifted in his seat and groaned. "That's the last thing I want."

The four grew silent amid the regular chatter of the bar, Evelyn still flicking through the digital news.

"Is that you, Becks?" she asked, incredulously. "Were you there, too?"

Taryn knew she hadn't technically done anything wrong. But her unease grew like a cumulonimbus cloud, a thunderous storm about to unleash.

"I'd been hanging at the beach," she assured her. "Austin was surfing or something and noticed me when he came back ashore. We were just chatting when he noticed Dottie was caught in a rip current."

"Dottie?" a perplexed Evelyn asked.

"She's a waitress at the Pancake Place," Austin chimed in. "She's served Becks before, I guess."

"Huh," was all Evelyn said as her eyes swung between Taryn and Austin.

Taryn's unease continued to bubble in her belly. Austin downed the rest of his drink and set it alongside the bar's edge.

"Cheers," he said, not breaking his gaze from Evelyn. She lifted her electrolyte drink and clinked it against his cup before turning to Taryn and doing the same with her glass of booze.

"Cheers," Evelyn said. "To a new day."

Taryn wanted to avoid the awkwardness oozing through her, so she shifted her eyes to observe the rest of the bar crowd. There were about a dozen or so patrons there. Some sat alone at the bar, sipping their beers and watching Sheila and Evelyn wipe countertops, fetch drinks and beckon the barback, Mike, to clear tables. A group of three women, seemingly fresh from a day at the office in their work dresses and closed-toed heels, sat at the U-shaped part of the wraparound bar, talking loudly and giggling. One was presented with a gift bag, with the text "Happy Birthday" and a giant party hat, balloons and confetti emblazoned among the words. Taryn watched as the girl pulled out a giant wineglass bubble-wrapped in the gift bag. It was fused with a bottle beneath, the glass itself atop the bottle that read, "Finally. A wineglass that fits my needs."

Taryn's eyes continued scanning the bar. The fat man with a beard, a beer belly and stained Bass Pro Shops T-shirt sat alone, sipping his beer and observing the crowd himself. He and Taryn caught eyes, and she nodded and immediately shifted her gaze elsewhere.

As dusk grew closer, additional patrons began filing in. Taryn took another swig of her drink before pushing the cup to the interior edge of the bar, signaling Evelyn to refill it.

Evelyn grabbed the cup with an expressionless face. Taryn suspected she was rerunning the Lucky Phoenix events, plus Dottie's near-drowning, through her mind as she topped off the vodka with a splash of soda and cranberry juice, pushing it toward her.

"I need a smoke," Evelyn told Sheila.

"You've been here ten minutes." Sheila sighed, her exasperation apparent. "Make it quick. I'm leaving soon."

Evelyn motioned to Taryn to follow. Taryn braced herself on the bar, steadying herself as she stood up. With all the hard seltzers at the beach and now drinks at the Wayside, her head was in a muted, happy place. She trailed Evelyn through the side door heading to the Smoker's Outpost alongside the patio block trail that led to the front door.

At the outpost, the two women paused, each pulling a cigarette from their respective packs, bringing them to their lips and lighting them. Evelyn sucked in a deep breath, blowing out the smoke as she sighed.

"I think he still loves you," Taryn suddenly blurted out, regretting the words as quickly as they left her lips.

Evelyn flicked the ash from her cigarette.

"Uh, s-s-sorry," Taryn stammered. "I shouldn't have said that."

Evelyn chuckled.

"You can say whatever you want," Evelyn said. "We're friends, aren't we?"

Taryn nodded, though her heart hurt for the declaration. Considering the two had spent several weeks getting to know one another and operating in a drunken haze, yes, in a normal situation, she'd consider her a friend. But was she really? Or was Taryn really a twisted, wronged widow/stalker?

"Becks?" Evelyn broke her train of thought. "You didn't piss me off with that statement, if you're wondering. Your silence is starting to make me think you're just hanging out with me for the perks of buddying up with a bartender."

Taryn came out of her daze.

"Of course," Taryn hurriedly responded. "Sorry, my mind was just wandering."

Both women continued to drag on their cigarettes in silence. Taryn wondered what Evelyn was thinking about and was about to ask when a voice quietly said behind them, "Excuse me, coming through."

The women broke apart to allow a baseball-capped woman, wearing a black T-shirt and ripped faded jeans, make her way through on the path. Her blond bob peeked out through the bottom of the plain black cap, and the oversize aviator sunglasses covered much of her face, which was fixated on the ground as she swept through, not looking up. The two watched as the woman made her way to the door, pulling it open and slipping inside without a further peep.

"She's going to be a fun one to serve," Evelyn scoffed, slipping her cigarette butt into the tiny opening of the huge beige ashtray, which reminded Taryn of a gigantic genie's bottle.

Taryn did the same with her cigarette, following behind Evelyn as she headed toward the door the baseball-capped woman had just entered. Evelyn gently lifted the countertop partition this time, delicately placing it back into its resting spot as Taryn crept back over to her seat. Austin didn't respond or acknowledge her as she slipped back atop her perch. He seemed like he was in a state of bewilderment, staring straight ahead, as if he was contemplating something heavy.

"Austin," Taryn said after a good thirty seconds of silence. "You okay?"

When he still didn't respond, she ran her fingers over his right wrist, noticing how deeply tanned they appeared. When Austin continued to stare ahead, Taryn's gaze lifted to his face. He looked pale, almost sickened. She saw beads of sweat forming on his forehead and above his lips and began to grow concerned.

"Austin," Taryn repeated, a sterner tone to her voice. "You don't look right. Are you sick?"

Without even shifting his line of vision to Taryn, Austin suddenly bolted up and brought his hand to the back pocket of his shorts, pulling out two twenty-dollar bills and dropping them on the countertop.

"Yeah, I need to lie down," Austin said, still not directing his vision to Taryn. "This should cover it. I'll see you later."

Taryn's face grew bewildered, and she glanced toward Evelyn, who was taking a drink order from Ballcap Girl. She wished Evelyn would glance back to see this sudden departure from Austin, but by the time she turned around and began fixing a rum and Coke, Austin was already gone.

"So much for saying goodbye," Taryn muttered to herself.

Was she crazy? Had they not had a moment—or two? Or was she imagining it? Surely she hadn't.

Taryn sat in her silence and confusion. Was the booze and sun combination catching up with him? She couldn't believe that, given she had consumed just as much alcohol and sunshine as him—and she was petite compared with his six-foot-two stance and hulking muscles. Maybe it was something he ate? The rush of adrenaline from the rescue? Or maybe he was just really sick, coming down with something.

"Where did our local hero go?" Evelyn snidely said, jarring Taryn from her thoughts. "Did he down some chorizo burritos in between beachgoing and lifesaving?"

Taryn shrugged with an obligatory laugh. She focused her attention back on her drink, running her right index finger over the condensation dribbling down the plastic. She listened to Bruno Mars's "Locked Out of Heaven" blaring on the jukebox speakers as her mind felt like a tornado, all the thoughts and images from the Lucky Phoenix night and today's unexpected beach rescue swirling in her head. With only Evelyn to talk to now, she continued her bar patron observation, trying not to make eye contact with the bearded man again. The birthday girl party had dropped down to two people, and an older couple, probably in their late 60s, had joined the collection of customers lined up around the bar. The woman was admonishing her husband for asking for a separate cup of ice, which he shoved his fist into and grabbed a handful before tossing it into his beer. She saw Taryn observing and rolled her eyes.

"You'd think I'd have him trained by now," she said to Taryn. "I can't take him anywhere, I swear."

"Mind your own business," the silver-haired husband squawked, clearly annoyed with being corrected by his wife in public. "Just let me be!"

Taryn gave a half-hearted smile, almost envious of the couple. She wondered if they had any significant secrets they kept from one another. But then she figured it was unlikely, if they'd been together for decades.

Taryn's eyes flitted around the rest of the bar's perimeter. She noticed the Ballcap Girl, still wearing her sunglasses and hat, stirring the straw in her drink. *How odd she was still wearing her sunglasses,* Taryn thought to herself, noticing a thickened purplish scar splashed across her left cheek. It was clearly somewhat new, and Taryn immediately felt guilty that her gaze had locked on the girl's face wound.

"Lots of balls going out like that, huh?" Evelyn whispered as she leaned close enough in so no one else could overhear her, her eyes darting in the woman's direction. "I give her credit, though. I don't think I'd leave the house with a fresh scar like that on my face. Poor thing."

Taryn couldn't stop staring at Ballcap Girl. She seemed out of place, nursing a drink as she sat alone. She wasn't speaking to anyone. Just sitting.

An odd feeling rose in Taryn's chest. She couldn't see Ballcap Girl's eyes beneath the shades, but she felt like she was staring directly at Evelyn. Her head didn't move. It just remained fixated in one spot. After a good fifteen seconds, Taryn couldn't help but shift her line of vision elsewhere. She felt incredibly uneasy. She picked up her iPhone and began scrolling through her email. Even though nothing really interested her, she couldn't continue looking toward the woman.

As the customers continued streaming in, Taryn felt a bit more at ease. Maybe Ballcap Girl was having a rough day. Clearly, she wasn't here to socialize. She was just there to get her drink on.

After having a quick chat with Ronan, the other bartender on duty, Evelyn held up a cigarette and pointed toward the door. Taryn nodded and rose, following Evelyn directly out the door. They retreated back to the Smoker's Outpost and lit up.

"What's that girl's deal?" Taryn asked in a hushed tone. "The one with the hat. She seems off."

Evelyn let out an exhausted breath.

"Who knows," she said. "We see all kinds in here. That one just doesn't want to talk. I haven't heard her speak any words except 'rum' and 'Coke.' Not even a thank-you. But I'm used to it by now. Some people are nice. Some aren't. Some are just fucking weird."

Taryn nodded. It made her think of some of the oddities she'd come across as a reporter, canvassing scenes to interview people. She'd experienced her own share of oddballs. People without their dentures in. Those who thought nothing of going out in public without a bra on. People with gnarly teeth and stenches of marijuana clinging to their clothes. The politician she once interviewed who'd insisted on hugging her after their sit-down discussion, which was weird enough, but even weirder when she noticed his erection pressing against her thigh during their embrace. She'd never told anyone about it. Not her editor. Not her husband. She'd just prefer to pretend the inappropriate advance never happened. It was easier than getting others involved. But it always ate at her. *If he did that to her, who else would he do it to?* It haunted her. Even now. She felt guilty for not doing the right thing and calling him out for his shit.

Both women stood there in their thoughts, silently. They finished their smokes and, like last time, Taryn followed Evelyn's lead into the bar.

Evelyn slipped behind the bar again, Taryn resuming her post on the outside. That's when she noticed.

Ballcap Girl was gone. She'd left a twenty-dollar bill on the bar top and a half-empty drink.

Who comes to a bar to drink half a drink and leaves an eighty-percent tip? She watched Evelyn shrug, head to the register to cash out, slipping the bill in its place, then pocketing the other sixteen dollars. She lifted her hands in an "I don't know" gesture.

Taryn's head began to spin. All the drinks—how many had there been? Six? Nine? Twelve? She couldn't remember. She just knew she needed to get herself into her pajamas and really get a full night's sleep.

Taryn pushed off the bar and stood up, her legs wobbly. It took a few seconds to fully steady herself.

"It's time to hang it up," she told Evelyn. "I'm gonna head out. What do I owe you?"

"Nada." Evelyn grinned. "Austin's contribution covered you, too."

The corners of Taryn's mouth fought back a smile. This guy was something. He seemed to want to take care of the women in his life, and her heart warmed at the thought she was one of those women. *If Evelyn hadn't once been married to him ...* She quickly brushed the thought from her mind. *Jesus, you're a new widow. Take a breather, Taryn.*

Taryn saluted Evelyn as she grabbed her bag, which had been slung over the back of her barstool.

"Till next time," she said. "Have a great night."

Evelyn gave her a quick thumbs-up.

"Till tomorrow." Evelyn snickered, waving as Taryn stumbled toward the door.

Chapter Thirty-Three

T aryn paused as she stood outside the hospital room door, balancing a bouquet of yellow roses in her left arm. She took a deep breath and knocked.

"Come in," a soft voice instructed, prompting Taryn to twist the knob and push the door in.

Taryn slowly entered the warm, sunny room, finding Dottie, whose face lit up as she saw her. Dottie didn't look like herself, her signature penciled-in eyebrows nowhere to be seen. Her vastly different appearance startled Taryn a bit.

"Hi there," Taryn said with a warmth, leaning in to embrace the frail-looking woman.

Taryn placed the bouquet and a gift basket of small get-well treats on the side table.

"I hope you're feeling better," Taryn said, adding, "and I wanted to brighten up your room a bit."

"Oh, sweetheart," Dottie said, her eyes beginning to mist. "How nice of you to visit. I guess you saw me on the news?"

Taryn's pulse quickened. For some reason, Taryn felt compelled to continue her string of lies.

"Yes," she said, taking in the sight of Dottie hooked up to various machines. "I was horrified to see you nearly—"

Taryn suddenly stopped, choosing more thoughtful words.

"I'm just glad you're okay," Taryn said, settling into the chair at Dottie's bedside and grasping the older woman's hand. She was struck by the beautiful sight of the river below. "I guess you didn't really need anything to brighten up this room. This view is better than any five-star hotel."

Dottie offered a faint smile. Taryn could tell she was tired.

"It sure is," she said. "It's just not worth the nightly rate."

Taryn nodded in agreement.

"Absolutely not," Taryn said. "I'm just happy this news story was a happy one."

Dottie looked toward the window, stoically taking in the natural beauty on the other side of the glass window.

"Thank the Lord that young man saw me struggling," she said. "I don't know what I was thinking, swimming alone despite rip current signs. Guess I'm stubborn like a mule, thinking I'm a few decades younger than I am."

Taryn's heart sank. She felt compelled to leave out the fact that she witnessed Dottie's rescue.

"We all make poor decisions at times," Taryn said. "Don't beat yourself up about it. I'm just grateful your rescuer was in the right place at the right time."

"Amen," Dottie said. "Though, if I had been reunited with my sweet Fred, I think that would have been okay, too. I miss him so much."

Taryn's eyes began to well herself.

"Honey, don't cry on me," Dottie said. "I'm okay. When it's my time, it's my time. And I'll be happy to be with my husband again. Someday. But I guess yesterday was not the day."

Taryn's mind immediately went to Graham. In the days after his death, she wanted nothing more than to be with him. Until the confession. Now, she hoped she'd never be reunited with him anywhere. Especially if there was a chance he was burning up in the depths of Hell. She shuddered for a moment, and Dottie took note.

"It gets easier in time," she said, squeezing Taryn's hand with reassurance. "You'll find your way. And yourself."

Taryn nodded before shifting her gaze to the window, watching a seagull zip by. How she hoped Dottie's words were true.

Even though she didn't believe them.

CHAPTER
THIRTY-FOUR

January 2018, Gardenia Beach

It was a lazy Sunday when the idea hit Austin. He was scanning streaming services when he came over an old favorite movie of his, *Throw Momma from the Train*. It was a comedic spinoff of sorts, inspired by *Strangers on a Train*, the classic Alfred Hitchcock film. The 1951 movie centered around two strangers who, yes, meet on a train. They commiserate over personal troubles when one suggests the perfect solution—to swap murders. Each would kill the other stranger's problematic person. Through this random meeting and no ties back to one another, their problems would be solved.

Sure, the Hitchcock version was a classic film noir. But the Billy Crystal-Danny DeVito matchup was the comedic relief he needed right then.

Austin watched, laughing at the same lines he had a dozen times before. But the storyline suddenly morphed into more. He'd watched to shut off his brain for a bit. Instead, it set his neurons on fire.

Criss-cross, criss-cross. An eye for an eye.

And that's when Austin decided.

He was going to figure out who'd raped his ex-wife. And since the law hadn't had the opportunity to sentence him, Austin was going to do it himself.

"I need to know something," Austin had immediately texted Kiersten after his epiphany. Kiersten was Evelyn's best friend in college. She was there *that night*. "And I need to keep this between us.

"Who raped Evelyn after that wedding?" he texted. "I need closure. And I don't want to upset Evelyn. But I need it for me."

It took three hours for the iPhone bubbles to appear on his phone, showing Kiersten was about to respond with an answer—or a "fuck off."

"I'd rather have this conversation in person," she wrote back.

An hour and change later, they met at Kate's Koffee Shop in Orlando, the midway point between both of their homes. Kiersten appeared unsettled, like she wasn't quite sure she'd made the right decision. But her and Evelyn's friendship had crumbled after the night of The Incident, never to be resuscitated. Evelyn just shut down and shut out everyone, except Austin.

"I didn't see anything at first," Kiersten explained in a hushed tone. "Just three groomsmen who'd helped me get her in a bedroom to sleep off her drunk. She couldn't even walk. I made sure she was in there, made the guys leave, sat with her for about five minutes, making sure she was resting and had a bottle of water next to the bed. I kept my eye on the door for much of the night, making sure no one was going in there to mess with her.

"But then I got distracted myself," she confessed, her face reddening. "I was outside smoking a cigarette when I struck up a conversation with this hot grad school student, Todd. I recognized him from campus. And I wanted to know him more. So, the two of us chatted as we smoked and toked."

Kiersten looked down at her dainty hands, nervously rotating her wedding ring around her finger, again and again. Austin could tell she was embarrassed. Maybe even a little remorseful. Austin reached his hand out to her wrist, prompting her to look up and connect eyes.

"It's okay," he said as he looked at her with compassion, which seemed to settle Kiersten some. She took a deep breath and continued.

"So as Todd and I made our way back into the area of partygoers, we plunked down on a loveseat and continued our conversation," Kiersten said, her eyes avoiding Austin's. "Within twenty minutes, a group began chanting, 'Get a room!' We giggled. He motioned toward the house, and I nodded. We slipped inside, and I noticed Evelyn's bedroom door was still closed. I assumed she was still sleeping it off.

"Todd and I found an empty bedroom and spent the next forty-five minutes in there," she continued, skipping the intimate details of what happened. "He quickly redressed, turned toward me as he reached the door, still buttoning his shirt in a frenzy. He said, 'This was fun. I'll see you around.'

"I was left alone to pull my own clothes back on and get back to the party," she said, seemingly still miffed about being a notch on this guy's belt. "I grabbed my purse and headed out the bedroom door. And that's when I saw him."

Kiersten sighed deeply, her facial expressions crinkling, as if she wasn't sure she wanted to divulge what she was about to.

After a minute of silence, Austin's tone turned desperate.

"Please," he begged. "I need to know who ruined her life. And mine."

"While I didn't see anything actually being done to Evelyn, I am pretty sure I know who did it," she continued.

More silence. Then a pleading look that compelled Kiersten to open her mouth.

"I opened the bedroom door just a bit, because I wanted to make sure no one saw me slip out of my room," Kiersten said. "As I peered through the crack, I noticed the door of Evelyn's room slowly open. And a guy walked out, quickly."

Austin's eyes implored her to continue.

"Please," he begged, his eyes brimming with tears.

"Graham Sloan," she said. "That was who walked out, shutting the door behind him. If I had any doubts, they were erased as I saw him zipping up his pants as he walked back to the kitchen."

"Are you absolutely certain that's who it was?" he asked.

"Yes," she confirmed. "I'd been in a couple of pre-reqs with him, even worked on a group project with him in Philosophy 101. While I didn't know him well, I knew enough to know that was, in fact, him.

"That's when I made a beeline into Evelyn's room. I didn't want him to see me," Kiersten said, then paused. "If I had any doubt in my mind about what happened, her crumpled-up panties and dress pulled up to her chest confirmed any suspicions I had. She was completely incoherent. It took me several minutes to stir her awake, even though she was groggy and barely able to function.

"I knew I needed to get her out of there. So I did. And you know the rest."

Austin's throat began to ache, his head spinning. He nodded, thanked her, and excused himself.

"Austin," Kiersten said from behind him. "I'm so sorry."

Austin closed his eyes and mouthed "thank you" before standing up abruptly, then turning around, zipping out the door. He had work to do.

He was going to find Graham Sloan. And that motherfucker was going to pay.

***

Austin had found his avenue of justice on SOAT, the dark web's one-stop shopping for finding a partner in taking out perpetrators walking free from their crimes. Apparently, others were inspired by Hitchcock's foresight and had scores to settle, aptly naming the site SOAT—an acronym of the movie.

It was about five days later that he'd found the perfect partner in Justice-Seeker908.

Austin agreed to take out the uncle who'd raped her. And she'd take out Graham Sloan.

Austin had fully intended to fulfill his end of the bargain. And once he'd seen the news coverage that Graham had been killed on his bike trying to avoid a collision, he felt an immense sense of relief. He hoped the alcohol that asshole had sucked down prior to his fatal ride hadn't numbed him from any pain when he plowed into the massive oak tree that stole his final breath. He wanted that fucker to feel every ounce of pain, which didn't even compare to the pain he'd put Evelyn through for the last several years.

Graham's pain was quick and instantaneous. Merciful.

Unlike Evelyn's, which coursed through her veins and mind every hour of every day, for the last decade or so of her life.

But when it was time for him to fulfill his promise within the three-day window of Graham's killing, he froze. He'd been stupid, doing all this research and plotting on his own personal computer. Sure, he used incognito mode, even tapped into the TOR browser, which promised anonymity, but his paranoia overtook him. What if he got caught?

After doing more internet sleuthing, it was starting to look like his virtual partner in vigilante justice might not even survive the wreck. He'd figured out that JusticeSeeker908 was Adrienne Snyder. Her Facebook page confirmed it. Her friends had posted all over her page after the "accident," which landed her in a coma following the crash. Online news stories quoted a hospital spokesperson confirming, "The patient is in critical condition with life-threatening injuries."

If JusticeSeeker908 was likely going to die, why should he risk his own future to right a wrong requested by someone who might not survive to see it had been done? His main concern was Evelyn. Making sure her attacker was punished. And making sure he continued to be there to help her heal.

What happened to Adrienne was unfortunate. She wasn't supposed to nearly kill herself in this agreement. But she'd taken it too far. Whether on purpose or not.

Austin tried to convince himself that two wrongs indeed did not make a right. And the right for him, as of now, was to continue to tend to Evelyn.

He'd meant his vows. And despite their divorce, he fully intended to carry through with his commitment to her.

But after seeing Adrienne at the Wayside Watering Hole, he knew he needed a new plan.

And really goddamn fast.

CHAPTER THIRTY-FIVE

Present Day, Gardenia Beach

Adrienne felt fury every time she thought of DojaFire2. Adrienne had known her SOAT cohort was somewhere along the east coast of Florida. He'd shared that before, when they were figuring out how converge on their criss-cross missions. It had worked perfectly. Her traveling to Illinois to find The Rapist she needed to take out, in exchange for Uncle Coop meeting his maker, which was the agreement she'd come to with DojaFire2.

She was angry at herself. Again, Adrienne trusted someone—only to have them betray her.

Adrienne felt a sense of accomplishment as she opened her motel room door and let it slam behind her. She leaned her back against the door and let out a sweet sigh of relief, despite her lingering body aches and pains.

She'd found him.

It had taken her some sleuthing, and it was research she had to make sure was off the grid. Leanne had soaked in her whole story that day at the hospital, and Adrienne wasn't sure if she was going to turn her in. Or help.

Once Adrienne had bared her secrets, her soul, to Leanne, her sister surprised her. She stood in solidarity, promising to make up for the time they'd lost. And vowed to help Adrienne finish what she'd started. When questions came about the accident, why Adrienne was even in Chicago to begin with, she and Leanne had a narrative ready to roll. After a quick discussion before the police came in to question her about the fatal "accident," the two had their story straight. Adrienne had never been to Chicago before. So, given her Irish roots, which was maybe a tenth of her lineage, she'd booked a flight to partake in the St. Patrick's Day festivities, including seeing the Chicago River dyed green for the holiday. Plus, all the food and museums she'd heard so much about. Adrienne had simply been staying in the southwest suburbs, given it was less costly than lodging downtown, when she "mistakenly" nearly slammed into Graham's motorcycle, sending him careening into the tree that ended his life, as Adrienne swerved and plowed into the brackish retention pond.

Leanne had retrieved Adrienne's off-the-grid laptop and done the research for her, following Adrienne's specific instructions for being as untraceable as possible. She tapped into a hotspot at a diner down the street from the hospital. She was determined to find DojaFire2 for her hurting sister.

And she did. Leanne, ironically, uncovered DojaFire2's true identity the day Adrienne was released from the hospital—the day they planned to fly back to Florida. And it was Austin Witmer. Former husband of Evelyn. The other woman who'd been assaulted. His east coast locale meant getting there and back quickly was doable.

Leanne had joined forces with her sister. They both wanted Coop taken care of. He needed to pay. And DojaFire2 was going to do it. Just like he'd promised. She'd make sure of it.

He just needed a not-so-gentle reminder.

As soon as her broken body felt usable, Adrienne had begun plotting for her trip to Gardenia Beach. If she was going to go down for one death, what difference would another make?

Especially since Adrienne planned to slit her own wrists, somewhere back near Coneflower Cove, once she was done.

That had been the initial plan, after all—but a significant detail she'd chosen not to share when plotting her revenge strategy with Leanne.

Adrienne had been careful to set herself up for success. She borrowed Leanne's car. She left her cell phone at home and picked up the cheapest phone she could find that wouldn't trace anything back to her. Again, Leanne picked one up incognito, paying with cash, and loaded minutes through cards also paid for in cash.

Adrienne had made Leanne promise to send occasional texts and emails from her real phone, back in Tampa. After her discharge from the hospital, Adrienne and Leanne headed to Florida, with the understanding that law enforcement would be in touch. Adrienne expected to hear law enforcement knock at the door and handcuff her any day. While there had been no alcohol in her system when she plowed into the pond, she knew that didn't mean she was off the hook. She winced at the thought of facing manslaughter charges before she finished her mission.

That was why she needed to act fast.

Once she felt able to move, Leanne also was to check in and compose emails on Adrienne's behalf. She bought random things on Amazon and Target, under Adrienne's accounts, hopefully an ironclad alibi that Adrienne wasn't in Gardenia Beach but nursing her wounds in Tampa. Some of the online purchases were of medical equipment. Arm and leg braces. Crutches. Scar-fading gel. Anything to bolster the theory that Adrienne still wasn't well after the accident.

Adrienne made Leanne promise to drop comments here and there when meeting up with friends, telling them she had to leave early to check in on her sister. She'd even post pre-taken photos of Adrienne, which she posted as Adrienne on Facebook. Photos where the properties had been stripped, so should someone want to try to peg down when they'd been taken, they couldn't. The posts were more about the long road to recovery, apologies for being quiet—Adrienne just needed time to continue healing and getting herself back to normal.

Leanne was methodical, too, buying a to-go meal to bring home to Adrienne when dining out with friends. It helped drive the narrative that her little sister, just sprung from the hospital, was still bedridden. And using Uber or Lyft to get around as Adrienne utilized her car to travel to Gardenia Beach and take care of this situation once and for all. When people asked where her car was, she'd simply say she didn't want to drink and drive.

"After what happened to my sister," Leanne would spin the tale to her friends, "I'm not taking any chances."

Luckily, Leanne's job as a sales rep was within walking distance of her apartment in downtown Tampa, and most of her jobs were within the metropolitan area. Not going around in a car wasn't too suspicious. A lot of young adults who lived in Tampa could flitter around without a vehicle. With ride-sharing services, taxis and public transportation readily available, it was plausible.

For once, both sisters were grateful, as sick as that sounded, that their mother had died. It spared Lisa from the shame of knowing her daughter was directly involved in an incident that ended a man's life. Though Adrienne wondered, with Leanne's newfound support, if Lisa would have finally accepted the reality that Coop had, in fact, sexually assaulted her teenage daughter so many years ago. Would she have apologized for turning her back on her child when she needed her most? Adrienne would never know—and preferred it that way.

With Lisa gone, there was one less complication. Adrienne felt no guilt, just reassurance, that her mother was dead.

DojaFire2 was a man in his late 30s. A financial analyst. The ex-husband of a bartender at a local dive bar. A bartender who had also been sexually assaulted. Adrienne had been able to find the man's name, his Facebook and Instagram profiles, his email address, phone number, address. She carefully studied his life on social media, the online archive of stories, such as his engagement announcement, wedding photos and more. She'd realized that DojaFire2 was still close to his ex, thanks to social media posts of them hanging out at bars and more.

And Adrienne was glad she'd taken screenshots all of the pertinent information. When she attempted to pull The Rapist's social media accounts up again after her hospital discharge, they were gone. Perhaps his widow had closed the account.

That was why Adrienne had shown up at the Wayside Watering Hole. She'd been trailing Austin on the beach, watching DojaFire2 deep in conversation with a redhead right before he dove into the sea to save a drowning swimmer. She almost kicked herself for spending the time and money to track him down. If she'd been patient, she would've seen him on the news. Even if it wasn't national news, it was sure to make the social media rounds and go viral. Shit like that always did. But it didn't matter.

Adrienne had found DojaFire2. And he knew it.

Now, it was time for Austin Witmer to do what he was supposed to. And she was going to make sure of it.

CHAPTER THIRTY-SIX

For the first time in his life, Austin was truly and utterly petrified.

He knew killing the man who had sexually assaulted the love of his life wouldn't fix things. Life with Evelyn was irretrievably broken, just like their divorce decree had stated. There was no time machine. No way to go back and prevent her from going to that night that changed her life—and his—forever. No way for him to have been there, ultimately changing the course of how things unraveled. No way for him to erase the trauma that Evelyn had experienced. The thing that changed so much about her, from her drive to her aspirations. And her ability to truly experience love without the scars that had fucked her up.

Austin had felt immense guilt for his moments of weakness. The anger that bubbled up in him over time. Initially, it began with a burst. Immediately after the assault, it had taken Evelyn three days to reveal to him why she'd been buried under the blankets of their bed, skipping school and work. She slept and cried as he begged her to tell him what was wrong. What had taken the bright, beautiful, bubbly soul he'd fallen so deeply in love with and transformed her into a heaping, inconsolable mess who would barely utter a word?

At first, he figured it was a falling out with her best friend, Kiersten. She was an ever-present being in Evelyn's life, always hanging out, sitting atop the barstool at their kitchen countertop as Evelyn puttered about, fixing them snacks or drinks to accompany their conversations. There'd been no Kiersten sightings since the night of that wedding Evelyn went to as Kiersten's plus-one, and Austin was beginning to wonder if they'd argued there. Kiersten had been blowing up Austin's phone, saying she was worried about Evelyn and needed to talk to her.

But it wasn't just Kiersten that Evelyn had been ignoring. It was every-one, Austin soon discovered.

After three days, when he'd knelt at the side of the bed, grasping her hands in between his own, he'd begged her to look at him and tell him the truth.

"If you've cheated on me," he began, divulging his innermost fears and feeling like a paranoid psycho fiancé, "I need to know."

It was then that Evelyn's bloodshot, swollen eyes had shifted to his. His heart dropped into his stomach, fearing the worst.

"I don't know if I did," she sniffled.

Confusion and anger had flooded his brain.

"I just don't know," Evelyn croaked. "I can't remember what happened. I'd had a lot to drink. I wanted to let loose. And somehow, after some point in the evening, I couldn't remember anything. I'd been helped to a back room to sleep it off. I passed out. And I woke up to Kiersten shaking me awake."

Evelyn began to sob deeply, her body shaking, yet no sounds came out. Austin cradled her in his arms and whispered, "Shhhhh," into her ear, stroking the sweaty hair back from her face.

Before she said more, Austin knew.

"I love you so much," he said, beginning to cry himself. "Do you think you were raped?"

The silent heaving tears suddenly spilled out of her audibly. Evelyn nodded her head as she nestled it into Austin's collarbone, her tears and mucus spilling onto his white polo shirt as he lovingly touched her hair. There was nothing more she needed to say.

"Who did it?" he asked, looking into her eyes as he broke their embrace apart, his hands on both of her shaking shoulders.

Evelyn shifted her gaze to the framed picture of their engagement photo shoot, sitting atop her nightstand, next to a cup of water and alarm clock. Her eyes remained locked on it, a moment in time where they both looked indescribably beautiful and happy. It was as if each of them knew that kind of happiness was a thing of the past. This cloud was a dark one that promised to hang above them for some time, if not forever. The chances of it dissipating were slim. They both knew that without uttering a word.

Evelyn just shook her head.

"I have my suspicions," she said. "But I can't say for certain. I don't remember anything between being led to the bedroom to rest by a few former frat boys and them lowering me onto the bed. Next thing I remember is Kiersten shaking me awake and asking if I was all right. I just told her I wanted to go home. So, she led me to her car, took me home, and I told her I needed some time."

After holding Evelyn for several minutes, Austin broke the embrace, resting his hands on both sides of her arms. He was furious.

"We need to report this to the police," he said, his tone shifting from consolatory to venomous. "Whoever did this to you ... he needs to pay."

Evelyn sat stoically, still looking at their engagement photo.

"I just want to forget it ever happened," she begged, fear rising in her eyes. "Can we just do that? I've seen enough *Law & Order: SVU* shows to know how assault victims are treated. I don't want to be picked apart. I just want to get on with my life."

"Our lives," Austin insisted. "We're in this together."

Austin tried for days to get her to reconsider. But Evelyn wouldn't budge.

As time went on, Evelyn gradually got back to everyday life. But she was constantly on edge. Any errant, sudden noise made her startle. She was brisk in her responses to anyone. Her focus on school shifted to a dedication to drinking. It was the only thing that quieted her mind.

When they eventually made it to the altar, Austin meant every word. For better and worse. He'd seen the worst already, he had convinced himself. And he still wanted to devote the rest of his life to bringing back the old Evelyn. One filled with hope, a zest for life and love, and a drive to make the world a better place. One where they'd have their hokey happily ever after.

Austin fought saying something about Evelyn's heavy drinking as long as he could. As Evelyn fell deeper into the tentacles of alcohol abuse, he vowed to be by her side. He'd help her through this trauma, and they'd emerge triumphant in time. They were a we. A *me*, as they'd crowned themselves the year before—Austin and Evelyn. They were a me, one person.

But that didn't happen. And once he caught her blowing that guy in the Jeep, he knew. There was no happily ever after for their *me*. Just picking up after the carnage brought on by one selfish man's desire to get his rocks off on an inebriated woman.

His woman. *His* fiancée. His *wife*.

While their marriage had crumbled, his love for Evelyn hadn't. Austin felt such guilt he hadn't joined her at that wedding that night. Not that he was invited. But the price to pay for Evelyn accepting that invitation? That decision changed the courses of both their lives in one single night.

Eventually, as Austin began trying to reassemble his broken heart and broken life, he began thinking about the best way to come to grips with his shattered dreams. No other woman would ever compare to Evelyn. The Evelyn he'd fallen so deeply in love with. The Evelyn he hoped would one day return.

At first, Austin had just wanted to scare The Rapist. Tossing some anxiety into the mix would certainly keep that asshole's sins at the forefront of his mind. He wanted that piece of shit to feel the remorse of what he'd done. Every single day.

After all, the love of his life lived with it. Every single day.

So, during his December social media scroll to see what Mr. Rapist was up to, the happy pictures and posts became a breeding ground for ever-building anger.

This guy had the perfect life. A gorgeous wife, with a hoity-toity wedding to boot. A successful career. A beautiful home. And all that sobriety and volunteerism that Mr. Rapist was involved with was probably his attempt to alleviate his guilt. If he even felt any.

But that didn't help Evelyn.

That's why Austin needed to. That fucker, The Rapist, needed to admit his wrongs and make amends. And given his somewhat newfound sobriety, it shouldn't be a far-fetched ask. After creating a spam email account and utilizing a Virtual Private Network on his computer, Austin drafted and shot off his email.

Graham Sloan,

Your day of reckoning is here.

It's time for you to take accountability. Embrace your sobriety program and right your wrongs.

You raped a woman. I know that for a fact. And while you've skirted the legal system, you're not off the hook.

It's time for you to do the right thing. Your victim continues to live with the ramifications of you and your selfish dick.

It's time for you to apologize. Do the right thing. Help put your victim on the path to healing—something she has struggled to find since you helped yourself to her vagina.

I expect this confession to be in my inbox in the next two weeks.

If you don't, I'll be back. With another option I'm certain you won't like.

The Vigilante

When the two-week deadline came and went, Austin was fired up. His second email to Graham immediately bounced back to him. He turned to Facebook, Instagram and Twitter. Somehow, he had to contact him again and raise the stakes.

But Graham had moved quickly. After the email, all his social media accounts went silent. Austin presumed he'd temporarily deactivated them—or completely deleted them.

Austin had his workarounds. But Graham made it easy. He'd forgotten his work email and cell number were right there, nestled under his picture on CoroMed's "About Us" website section.

Bam! Off went the text on the burner phone Austin had purchased in cash at a Daytona Beach superstore.

"Graham Sloan, you're playing with fire. You don't know who you're dealing with. DON'T piss me off. Make your amends. Very soon. Or I'll have to turn up the heat—and tell your wife. I wonder how she'd feel about being married to a rapist. And you just might find out very, very soon."

A day later, it was there. Right in Austin's inbox. The document was aptly named "Forgiveness" and came from an unknown email. *Of course,* Austin thought. *Trying to bury the evidence.* Graham did not sign his name. Nor did he address it to Evelyn. Any digital fingerprints connecting him to the confession had been stripped from the file. To Austin, this defeated the purpose.

Austin fired off a response.

"You need to sign this with your name," he commanded. "You need to take ownership and full responsibility for ruining a life. Actually, several lives."

When Graham's response came through, it was blunt and to the point.

"Fuck off," it read.

A fired-up Austin began feverishly pecking away his response.

"I will FUCK YOU," he said, "if you do NOT do as I say. I'm sure not only your wife, but your family, friends and employer would surely enjoy this steaming pile of past shit."

But the email bounced back immediately. A text from the burner phone to Graham's listed work mobile number came back "undelivered" as well.

Austin's face grew hot. It was time to reexamine this plan.

Evelyn would get that freedom, that apology she so rightly deserved. It was just going to require a different approach.

CHAPTER THIRTY-SEVEN

L iving in a beachside motel in permanent vacation mode wasn't something sustainable for Taryn long-term. She knew that.

Taryn still had plenty of money, so that wasn't an issue. But she knew her current pattern couldn't continue. It wasn't healthy. And keeping her lies straight proved challenging. She'd nearly slipped a couple of times.

Taryn had almost entirely shut herself out from her former life. When her sister texted or a friend emailed, she was short in her responses. Just enough to acknowledge that, yes, she was fine, just working on getting through Graham's death in her own way. She didn't answer phone calls, sending each to an overflowing voicemail box.

"You ever coming home?" Lynn had texted her several times over the weeks Taryn had been in Florida.

Taryn would take hours to respond. She just didn't want to deal with her sister.

"Eventually," Taryn would tap into her phone. "I just need a break."

"Your break has been two months," Lynn replied. "How much of a break do you need? We miss you and want to help you."

"I'm fine," Taryn responded, the annoyance building in her. "I just need some me time."

"Maybe I should come down there," Lynn responded. "Spend a long weekend with you. Make sure you're really okay."

When Taryn's eyes scanned that message, her pulse quickened. She envisioned her two personas clashing into one. The possibility of Lynn interacting with Evelyn and Austin. The fear that her fake name would expose her. And the thought of having to explain why she was holed up in a town, tracing the steps of a woman her late husband had sexually assaulted?

She'd be exposed.

"No," Taryn shot off in a text. "Please don't. I promise, I'll be home soon. I just need some time alone."

Lynn's only response was an "I don't know" emoji. Taryn responded with a "hug" one. Hopefully, this would keep her at bay. For now. But having no plan wasn't going to work long-term.

The thing was, as sick as it sounded to her, Taryn found comfort in being here. In the random moments her mind escaped the horror of this reality, she felt at home. She loved the weather. The flora and fauna. The beach, which she walked along every day. It brought her momentary, fleeting solace. She could understand why people moved here. It would be a nice place to call home.

Taryn thought about just leaving all her belongings up North and staying put. She had enough money to start over. She could rent a place, maybe even for the short term. Maybe eventually buy a condo, perhaps even on the beach. But her funds wouldn't stretch long enough should she turn to such pricey real estate. She could get a job down here, to supplement—and keep her busy. Permanent vacation mode wasn't a real option for her, unless she wanted to be in the red in a couple of years.

But once she thought about moving forward with such a plan, it hit her—everyone here knew her as Rebecca. There was no Rebecca. Could she legally change her name, avoiding having to answer why her driver's license identified her as Taryn? Would Evelyn or Austin ever feel the need to Google her and unearth the façade? What the hell would be her explanation? And what would she tell her family about her name change? Her mind began to go into overdrive at the thought. She'd already mired herself too deeply into this mess.

The thought of starting over, becoming another persona for real, was tempting. Perhaps it was the reboot she so desperately needed.

Before her mind could delve further into her plan, her phone vibrated with an incoming text.

Jesus, she thought. *Lynn should just let up already.*

But it wasn't Lynn. It was from an unknown number. And with eleven words, Taryn's outlook on everything toppled over. Her hands shook as she held the phone, looking over the message several times before it dropped from her hands and clanked on the tile floor beneath her.

One simple sentence. But a sentence that had the ability to unravel everything.

"Does your new BFF know your dead husband was her rapist?"

CHAPTER THIRTY-EIGHT

When Taryn's stomach stopped doing its aggressive somersaults, she still felt sick.

She'd been so careful.

But someone knew.

Clearly, it was someone who wanted to torture her. Someone who'd somehow been affected by this domino effect—or thought they were.

Whoever was on to her wanted to scare her.

Mission accomplished.

Taryn knew she needed to do something. And quickly.

Everyone here knew her as Rebecca. She'd been careful to pay in cash, not show her ID or anything else with her true identity. When they'd gone anywhere needing ID, Taryn always guided Evelyn toward the bouncer first, so she wouldn't be able to catch a glimpse of her name on her license. The only one who knew any different was Rick, the desk clerk at the Tiki Torch Inn. And it's not like he cared or would do anything with that. She was just another face, another number in the long list of guests who flowed in and out of the place. And the car rental place, where she'd turned in her car about a week ago—Taryn had realized that being on foot or using a ride-sharing service made more financial and logistical sense.

But what now? Taryn's mind raced. Should she just pack everything up now and floor it home, abruptly ending her two-month stint with no explanation? Change her number? Pretend she never saw the damn thing?

Her mind raced with the thought of whoever was behind that revelation. Yes, they'd figured out Taryn's past. But what was their next step, if any? And more importantly, what was hers?

She stood in the bathroom in silence, frozen.

Taryn's thoughts were interrupted by another buzz of her phone. Another text message. Her heart began racing again. She didn't want to look but forced herself to after several minutes.

"Hey, girl!" it read.

Taryn's insides relaxed. It was Evelyn.

"Wanna test out the luck of the Irish at The Wailin' Pig? It's ladies' night, so half-price drinks from five to seven!"

Taryn took a moment to settle herself down. Was every text notification going to terrify her from here on out?

She needed time to think. To figure out where the hell to go from here.

Taryn needed to plot.

"Hells yeah," Taryn tapped into her phone, not wanting to appear out of the norm.

"Sweet!" came the response. "Meet me at the end of my shift. I get off at five. We'll hoof it from there."

"Sounds like a plan," Taryn responded.

She tossed her phone onto her bed, surveying the mess of a room she'd called home for the past several weeks. The room was as unsettled as she was. Clothes strewn about. An empty pizza box from three days ago. Dirty, wet towels surely incubating bacteria with every minute that passed.

It was a mess. Just like its inhabitant.

Taryn tossed on a pair of gray capri leggings, a fitted navy tank top and slid into her flip-flops. She didn't feel much like putting makeup on but knew she'd look amiss if she didn't at least brush on some mascara and lip gloss. Taryn quickly applied the basics, ran a brush through her hair and secured it in a high bun.

Taryn hated walking around with a ticking time bomb on her. At any moment, another text could unravel her. *What else did they know? What would they say next? And whoever it was, would they clue in Evelyn?*

Had they already?

The notion made her shiver.

Maybe I should block the number, Taryn thought.

She felt a momentary sense of relief. Granted, blocking that number wouldn't guarantee the sender wouldn't try again with a different phone. And would her attempt to avert further communication send a signal she was threatened? Worried? Would it bring on even more, versus never responding?

It hit her. She should respond but pretend she was someone else. Like a wrong number.

It was worth a shot.

Her hands trembled as she walked back to her bed, lifting the phone and scrolling through her messages. She selected the awful one, not even wanting to read over the sentence again. Looking at it again filled her with a rainbow of emotions. Fear. Unease. Sickness. Shame. And rage.

"This is Scott," her fingertips typed into the phone. "Wrong number."

Within thirty seconds, bubbles popped up on her phone. Taryn audibly gasped.

The sender was responding.

A laugh emoji came first.

Then more bubbles.

"I don't think so, TR, I mean TARYN METCALF," it read, sending chills down her spine. "But nice try."

"Fuck!" she screamed aloud.

And then, more bubbles. Taryn was beginning to regret her attempt to defuse the situation. *I should've left it alone. Just ignored it,* she told herself.

"Your bestie will eventually find out," the latest text taunted her. "It's only a matter of time until Evelyn knows who you really are."

That was enough. Taryn couldn't bear any more. She selected the message, clicked "info," and then tapped on "block this caller" as the bubbles continued.

Done. Before the next burgeoning message could eek its way through.

Maybe there was a crisis averted now. But Taryn knew she was working on borrowed time.

She needed a plan. And fast.

CHAPTER THIRTY-NINE

By the time she meandered up the walkway to the Wayside's entrance, Taryn was able to regain her composure. As soon as she swung open the door, she felt more at ease.

Evelyn was wiping down the bar top when she eyed Taryn.

"Becks!" she shouted, leaving the rag resting on the counter as she beckoned her with both hands. "Come on down!"

Evelyn's welcoming settled her nerves considerably.

The Text Tormentor wasn't her, Taryn told herself. Not that she thought it was, but the thought had crossed her mind. But no way. Evelyn wouldn't be that conniving, would she?

Taryn slid onto the battered bar stool and gently set her purse onto the bar top. Without asking, Evelyn slid a vodka-soda with a splash of cranberry juice in front of her, then quickly turned back to Sheila, discussing what was ready to go, who had open tabs and other end-of-shift bar business. Taryn picked up the glass, the liquid courage sliding down her throat with its calming effect. She had half of it downed by the time Evelyn turned back to her.

Evelyn's eyes studied Taryn as she took another sip, emptying the glass's contents into her belly.

"Well, now that you have the warm-up out of the way," she mused, a sly smile growing across her face as she lifted the removable bar top and slithered to the customer side, "let's get down to business."

Fifteen minutes later, Taryn and Evelyn were nestled into the packed Wailin' Pig as the crowd cheered the latest rendition of "Danny Boy," many lifting their beer steins enthusiastically.

Evelyn had ordered two shots of Jameson, pushing one toward Taryn as she lifted her own to her mouth.

"To alcohol and happy hour," Evelyn proposed. "The only reason I can sit here and listen to this Irish jam session."

Taryn laughed and clinked her shot glass to Evelyn's, the taste igniting her reflexes as she took down its bitterness. She couldn't help but gag, the flavor was so disgusting.

"I think the 'Irish goodbye' might have been inspired by having to listen to Irish folk music," Evelyn pondered aloud. "The more I listen, the more I need to drink."

Taryn giggled as Evelyn beckoned the bartender to reload her with another shot and beer.

Despite the jubilance surrounding her, and no matter how many drinks she consumed, Taryn couldn't shake the unease. Where was the Text Tormentor? Was he or she following her? Maybe even in this bar?

The thought sent chills from her head to her toes. Was there a real threat, or was this simply a cruel game being played on her? She was beginning to regret this whole plan.

"I think Austin's still pissed about the casino tab," Evelyn huffed as she downed her shot. "He's really been off the past couple of days. I don't get it."

Taryn welcomed the distraction from her unease about the Text Tormentor.

"How long does it usually take him to shake something like this off?" she asked.

Evelyn sipped her beer, pushing her shot glass toward the inside of the bar. She shrugged.

"Usually a few hours," she admitted. "But never this long. I don't blame him. But it'll eventually blow over."

It was almost like the two summoned his presence by speaking of him. As the front door of the pub swung open, Austin walked in, as if on cue. He scanned the crowd, observing the middle-aged men congregated at a table near the stage as they spoke loudly above the roar of the crowd. His eyes danced to the packed bar, the women who were gathering in line, waiting for their Happy Hour specials, before landing on Taryn and Evelyn. A tiny smile grew on his face as he nodded and began working his way toward them.

"Speak of the devil," Evelyn muttered, shining her best smile.

Austin sidled up between the two.

"Good evening, ladies," he said, kissing Evelyn's left cheek. "What kind of trouble are the Dueling Drinkers up to this evening?"

"No more than usual," Evelyn said. She stood up and motioned toward the restroom. "Time for a potty break."

Taryn and Austin sat in silence for a moment, Austin ordering a Guinness as Taryn nursed her own beverage. She could feel the anxiety in the air. Not just about the Text Tormentor. She was nervous, given her last real conversation with Austin. She wondered if he regretted spilling his soul to her.

"I haven't said a word to her," Taryn blurted out.

Austin's eyes examined the Wailin' Pig patrons, as if he was giving it some deep thought before responding.

"I appreciate that," he said cautiously. "I didn't tell you to betray her. I just want you to know why she is like she is. Why we're like we are."

Taryn paused, the drink starting to go to her head. She couldn't think of a proper response. Just a simple one.

"You're a good man," Taryn said, locking her eyes with Austin's. "I wish I had that. Thought I'd had that."

Taryn's face flushed, regretting her last comment immediately. She stammered to come up with a response.

"My ex-husband," she said quietly. "I just didn't know he wasn't all he seemed to be."

Austin nodded, just as Evelyn emerged from the bathroom, wiping her wet hands on her yoga pants. She looked aggravated.

"Un-fucking-believable," she said, tossing her phone onto the bar in exasperation. "Not only are there no paper towels in the damn bathroom, but now I have to go back to work."

Taryn and Austin's heads turned to fully look at Evelyn.

"Sheila is sick," an irritated Evelyn said, picking up her phone to scroll through her call log. "They need someone to cover her. And I was the first fool to answer the phone."

Austin motioned toward the bar.

"I got this," he said, nodding toward the bar. "You get to work. Rebecca will help me finish this round."

A hint of jealousy seemed to flash across Evelyn's face, but just for a moment.

"Alrighty then," Evelyn said, picking her purse up from the bar and sliding the loop over her shoulder, hugging Taryn before turning to Austin to kiss him on his chiseled cheek. "See you two tomorrow."

Taryn and Austin watched as Evelyn promenaded through the crowd, slipping out the front door as another gaggle of girls slid in past her.

The two sat in silence for a couple of minutes, sipping their drinks and watching other patrons milling around. Taryn was too unsettled to leave and end the evening. She needed something to still her mind. To make her feel better.

From the looks of Austin, Taryn thought he was in search of much of the same. She observed him as he seemed to zone in on one woman, a blonde with a beach hat covering much of her face, who sat kitty-corner from them. She couldn't make out much of her face, the brim of the hat dipping beneath her line of vision. Austin's gaze wouldn't break. He seemed frozen.

"You all right?" she asked, her eyes moving from Austin to the girl and then back to him. "You know her?"

Austin's eyes darted away from the woman as he looked toward his beer stein.

"No," he said, avoiding eye contact. "Just people-watching."

Taryn didn't fully believe him. But with her own recent vague statement, she wasn't about to push.

"Let's get out of here," Austin suddenly said. "I feel like walking the beach."

CHAPTER FORTY

A half-hour later, Taryn and Austin were skirting the shore again, their bare feet seeping into the sand as the waves charged them, then receded back into the depths of the ocean. They walked in tandem, the silence not so deafening as the waves crashed.

"Did you ever see that movie *Sliding Doors,* back in the late '90s?" Austin asked, breaking the silence surrounding them. "Not the greatest flick in the world, but still?"

Taryn thought about it, despite her mind befuddled by the booze she'd sucked down in the past hour or so.

"It's not ringing a bell," she said. "Why?"

Austin let out a deep breath before continuing.

"I caught it a couple of years ago, just flipping through channels," Austin continued. "I normally wouldn't watch something like that, but the teaser intrigued me."

He paused, as if he was waiting for Taryn to prompt him for more details. Instead, she just listened, and he continued.

"It's about this woman and two parallel lives," he explained. "Basically, it gave two timelines for her life, based on whether she made it onto a train after losing her job that morning. That one decision determined the course of events in her life. Some good, some not so good.

"It was an interesting perspective. I know it was fiction, but it really made me think. About how one tiny decision can change everything," he said as the two continued their moonlit seaside stroll, looking ahead and around them but not at one another.

"Sometimes, I wish I had that option," he wistfully said. "What I wouldn't give to go back in time."

Taryn looked at him, offering a knowing smile. She, too, wished she could do the same.

"I wish life was like a boomerang," Austin mused. "That if you give someone all the love you can, it'll return to you."

"Like karma," Taryn said with a nod.

Austin had a stoic expression as he contemplated what to say next.

"Yeah," he said. "Like karma. But hopefully the good kind. Hmmph."

Taryn's guilt built along with the darkness. Graham's choice that night didn't just affect Evelyn. It affected Austin. And eventually, Taryn. Talk about a goddamn boomerang effect. And not a good one, either.

It made Taryn wonder who else got caught in this mess, all spanning from one night of poor choices. She was beginning to realize that she hadn't even scratched the surface.

Austin cut into her train of thought, gently extending his arm to grasp her right one. The pair stopped, their eyes connecting.

"Do you ever think about that?" he asked. "If you'd made one simple different decision, your life would be in a completely different place?"

Taryn's heart froze. Sure, she'd kind of had those one-off thoughts, but she'd never really thought about it. Had she not met Graham that fateful night. Had she chosen not to marry him. Or something even deeper.

The past several weeks, months and years zipped through Taryn's memory. What if she hadn't been volunteering that fateful day she met her future husband? What if Graham had never gone out that night or been killed?

Or what if she'd made a different choice when she busted into his digital files? What if she'd never even opened the confession? Could she have gone on and been able to eventually conjure up some sort of happiness, despite the tragic death of her husband?

What sank Taryn's gut even further was feeling as if her Gardenia Beach adventure had been a really bad idea. Did her quest to find Evelyn knock the poor girl off course for her own soul-searching? She began to panic at the thought that her journey for justice, if that was even what you could call it, did more damage than good.

"Rebecca?" Austin interrupted her brain drain. Her mind zapped back to the present as she stopped walking. "Do you?"

Taryn took a moment to think, her mind jumbled with Jameson's and Guinness.

"I need to sit down," she said.

The two settled their behinds, side by side, staring out into the roaring ocean just feet before them.

"Yes," she said, "I wish I could have a do-over or two."

"Do you miss your former life? As a married woman?" he inquired. "Do you miss *him*?"

Taryn pondered the question. Did she? Because what she thought she had with Graham, the foundation they'd built, was all a farce.

"I miss what I thought we were," she said. "If that makes any sense."

Austin turned to her. "It makes perfect sense," he said. "Sometimes, we don't even really know what we have. Until we don't."

Taryn looked over at him, his eyes meeting with hers. Both smiled slightly at one another. Two broken hearts, just desperately trying to figure out how to pick up the pieces.

Austin's right hand rested on Taryn's left forearm. It brought her comfort, which she truly appreciated. Within twenty seconds, he'd shifted to leaning on her, his right arm wrapped around her shoulder. His movement jostled her heart, which thumped quickly as the two sat silently.

Taryn felt the stirrings again. Just like she had at this same beach, right before the rescue. She felt something. Something for a man for the first time since Graham was killed. It made her feel excited, sickened and remorseful, all at once.

Her pulse shouldn't quicken for her acquaintance's ex-husband.

Taryn didn't know how to categorize Evelyn. Under normal circumstances, yes, she'd consider her a friend. But their whole relationship was based on a lie. Or at least a truth with way too many falsehoods. Was she a friend? A colleague?

A *stalker*?

Taryn fought to turn off her brain, trying to focus on the moment. The sounds, the sights, the feel of being on the shore. The sensation of being held by someone for the first time in so long. This was the first time in several months that a man's presence could make her melt into a puddle of nerves. She felt a sense of peace, oddly enough, in between her moments of anxiety and guilt. His touch, his embrace, made her feel calm. And maybe even a little loved. Or at least cared for. She sat there, continuing to soak it in, before her mind drifted.

Austin's embrace was welcome, but it felt so intimate. Taryn could smell the Gucci Guilt on him—the fragrance was one of her favorites. She'd bought a bottle for Graham on their last anniversary, which he wore regularly, given Taryn loved the scent so much. The smells brought her to a simpler time. She tried to disassociate her feelings about Graham and fully enjoy Austin's embrace. Taryn wasn't sure when she'd be held by a man again.

They continued to rest on the sand, staring at the darkening water ahead. It was getting harder to see as the minutes passed, the sun beginning to set behind them.

Taryn didn't feel exactly right about their current stance. What if Evelyn saw them interlaced like this? Surely, it wouldn't go over well. Despite their divorce, Taryn still felt that they were an item. An odd, misaligned item, but an item nonetheless.

But Taryn didn't want to break from him. This was the first time in months she'd felt safe. Protected. Her belly gurgled as her mind raced to thoughts of what it would be like to kiss him. She imagined he was one of those romantic types. The kind that would look deep into a woman's eyes, bringing his hands to her face to hold her before bringing his lips to hers.

Her thoughts were interrupted as Austin broke his embrace and stood up. He extended his palm to her, bringing her to her feet again.

"I think it's time for us to head out," Austin said. "I think you've got more Jameson and Guinness running through your veins than blood."

Taryn giggled as she brushed the sand off the backside of her pants.

"That's probably true," she said.

"I'll walk you home." Austin guided her south, toward the Tiki Torch Inn. "And maybe we should get you something to eat."

The thought of a pizza or chicken wings immediately delighted her.

"Yes!" she said. "Can we get Battista's? A Hawaiian pizza? I love the sweet and salty mix."

Austin paused for a moment, then said, "Sure." He took his phone out of his shorts pocket, tapping the order into the online form.

"Twenty minutes," he said. "It'll be there quickly after we are."

Taryn panicked for a moment. The name. There was no Rebecca at the Tiki Torch. Just Taryn.

"Did you tell them the room number?" she asked, attempting to cover her unease. "I didn't think you knew it."

"Nah," Austin said. "Put it under 'Bob' and instructed the driver to meet me in the lobby."

Taryn felt immediately relieved. Thank God Austin had opted for the lobby delivery. But "Bob?" *What the hell?*

"Why don't you go grab us a couple of sodas from the vending machine?" he said. "Grab a bucket of ice and we'll enjoy it on the rocks."

"Perfect," Taryn said, relieved that she wouldn't be hanging around in the lobby, where Rick the desk clerk might notice her. She didn't think he knew her name off the top of his head, but no way she was chancing it. She began her trek to retrieve their drinks and ice as Austin headed past the lit tiki torches lining the way to the lobby.

Once Taryn unlocked her room door, she hurried over to the restroom and ran her eyes over the length of her body. She quickly rinsed her face, brushed her teeth and slipped some gloss over her dehydrated lips. She was definitely not drinking enough water to temper the climate—and replenish her fluids. She ran her hairbrush through her hair and felt slightly more presentable.

What are you doing? Taryn asked herself. *Why are you trying to impress Austin?*

Before she could answer herself, there was a rap at the door.

"Special delivery," the muffled voice said.

Taryn opened the door to a beaming Austin. She felt both exhilarated and confused by the feelings swirling in her stomach.

Turn it off, Taryn thought to herself. *Just disassociate.*

As Austin entered, he rested the pizza box on the worn, chipped rattan table. It was flanked by equally dated chairs with faded pink cushions.

Austin took in the room.

"Welcome back to the '90s," he observed. "All you're missing is a Nirvana poster in here."

Taryn giggled, ran over to the dresser and pulled a smiley face Nirvana T-shirt from the middle-left drawer, holding it against her body and modeling it.

Austin chuckled.

"Well, that takes care of that," he said. "Why don't you try it on for me?"

Taryn did a double take. As her eyes met Austin's, there was no denying it.

There was electricity there. A deep hunger to explore every inch of this beautiful man's body. And Taryn was starting to realize the feeling just might be mutual.

Stop, stop, stop, Taryn thought. *Don't go there. It would be so wrong...*

Taryn immediately attempted to avert whatever this innuendo was. Austin couldn't really be hitting on her, especially given his profound professed love for Evelyn.

Taryn began nervously chattering, as if the Nirvana shirt request had never happened.

"Outside of Nirvana, I hated the '90s," Taryn said. "I hope I never see another pair of Z Cavaricci or Zubaz pants in my life."

She turned serious. "Please tell me you never owned a pair."

"Of what?" he asked, a coy smile spreading across his chiseled face.

"Either," Taryn responded, an eyebrow arched as she teased him.

"Well," he said, creeping closer to her, "if I did, I promise you, I rocked them better than anyone else. Especially with my mullet."

Taryn couldn't contain herself. She burst into laughter that was so hard, she got the hiccups. Austin looked both alarmed and amused.

"Is that normal?" he asked. "Am I going to have to scare you?"

"I've had enough scares for the day," she said.

Taryn's face grew ashen, immediately regretting the words. Austin arched an eyebrow as he came closer.

"What do you mean?" he asked, concern growing in his face.

"It's nothing," Taryn stammered. "Just some old family drama."

"You know," Austin said, his gaze intensifying, "you've listened to my share of personal issues. I'm happy to return the favor. Sometimes, it just feels good to get it out to a neutral person. Someone who can offer an unbiased opinion. Or just listen."

Momentarily, Taryn thought how nice it would be to share her nightmare with another person. But that person would not be someone directly involved *in* the nightmare. She shook her head.

"Thank you," she said. "I truly appreciate that. But honestly, I just want to forget about it. For as long as I can."

"There's plenty I want to forget, too," Austin began, drawing closer. "Like how much I want to kiss those supple, irresistible lips."

Taryn's hiccups immediately halted. Her breasts ached as her pulse intensified. The craving between her legs was immediate.

This was so, so very wrong. But Taryn couldn't deny it anymore. And, it seemed, neither could Austin.

She wanted him. Right now.

Austin and Taryn's eyes locked.

In the dimly lit Tiki Torch room, his gaze, just inches away, confirmed it. There was no going back.

Taryn fought her conflicting feelings of excitement and apprehension.

The two stood at the foot of the bed, facing one another, a mix of curiosity and conflict. As Austin reached for her hand, subtle tension filled the air. Tension of both desire and guilt.

It felt like a stare-down at first, as if Austin was contemplating his next move. If he had any reservations, he discarded them the moment he cupped Taryn's face in his hands and brought her lips to his. Just as she'd envisioned.

Taryn felt a fluttering in her heart and stomach. Austin's touch ignited something in her. Something she hadn't felt in some time.

Austin wrapped his arms around her waist, drawing Taryn against his firm body. His stunning blue eyes mesmerized her before he shut them, and their mouths began a passionate dance. Their tongues coupled with intense fervor. Taryn's yearning only increased as her leg brushed against his pelvis, where she felt his swollen, stiff erection as the two, in unison, backed up to the queen-size bed. Taryn rested her bottom on the edge of the bed. She and Austin continued their fevered kissing, never breaking apart. Austin gently eased her backward as his hands ran up the underside of her top, gently tracing his fingers around the perimeter of her nipples, first the right, then the left. Taryn moaned in pleasure, aching for Austin to explore more of her body.

The two broke apart for a moment and gazed intently into one another's eyes. Taryn grasped Austin's shirt, guiding it over his head.

This is wrong, Taryn thought. *This is so, so wrong.*

Austin brought his hands to the bottom of his shirt, lifting it over his head and tossing it to the floor, never breaking eye contact with Taryn. With that, Taryn cast aside her conflicted emotions and stood up, attempting to seductively pull her shirt over her head, then slipping her fingers into the waist of her capri yoga pants. She gently slid them past her knees, her ankles. Until she was in nothing but her bra and panties, standing before him.

Austin pulled a wrapped condom from his wallet and approached her, his eyes electrified in a way Taryn had never seen. He began deeply kissing her, then reached around her backside. He unhooked her lacy black bra with one hand, letting the lingerie fall to the floor. Austin brought his mouth to her breasts, sucking and kissing them so intensely, Taryn was almost on the brink of an orgasm. She unbuttoned his shorts. Austin let them fall to the floor, then kicked them aside.

Beads of sweat built on both Taryn and Austin's skin.

Her desires, Taryn discovered, did not die along with Graham.

"Tell me you want me," Austin whispered as he licked her right earlobe, his erection hardening as he writhed against her thighs. "Show me how much you want me."

Austin zealously kissed her again, and the wetness between her thighs intensified. Taryn playfully pushed him down on the bed before turning off the bedside lamp, nothing but the glow of the bathroom light providing a faded glimpse of the outline of their naked figures. Taryn crawled up from the foot of the bed, slipping her finger into his boxers, removing them slowly as she took in every inch of his physique. Austin's shaft was pulsating, and she knew he wanted it. As Taryn slid his cock between her lips, Austin let out a groan of pleasure, tossing his head back as he moaned.

"Yes. Deeper," he whispered.

Taryn obliged. The ecstasy was electric, especially as she backed off, licking the tip of his shaft.

Austin clasped her head between his hands, prompting her to look into his eyes while she continued sliding her tongue up and down. She wanted him to want her *so* bad. Even more than he did.

"Rebecca ..." Austin groaned in pleasure. "I want you. Right now. Tell me you want the same. Tell me."

Taryn slowly slid her lips from the base of Austin's dick to the tip, keeping her eyes solidly glued to his. His utterly delighted face fed her desire even more.

She stood up, crawling toward Austin, sprawled across the bed. She straddled his body as she kneeled above him. Taryn scanned his muscled, taut body, then looked into his eyes. *Damn, he has some broad, chiseled shoulders and arms,* she thought. Austin's chest was even more alluring in the dimly lit room. Taryn ran her hands up and down his torso to his abs, feeling every ripple of molded physique. The narrowed waist, each muscle hard and defined.

Austin handed her the condom after ripping the package open with his teeth. Taryn carefully rolled it onto him. His biceps flexed as he pulled her atop him.

"Tell me," Austin begged again. "Tell me how bad you want it."

Taryn looked directly at Austin as she slowly lowered herself onto him. Austin groaned as she slipped him inside of her.

Taryn arched her back, her supple breasts on full display for Austin as he watched.

"Oh fuck," Austin groaned. He flipped Taryn onto her stomach, pulling her up in a doggy-style position.

Austin clutched her hips, thrusting into her with a feverish fury. It jarred Taryn, the fervor with which he pushed into her. As Austin continued to slide in and out, he sped up the tempo, fucking Taryn hard. Maybe a little too hard. He reached his hand around to grasp her breast, pinching her nipple. It hurt, but Taryn didn't want to audibly object, trying to keep the pain confined to her mind.

This lovemaking, this hot sex—whatever it was now—felt unsettling. Austin held on to her hip with his left hand, bringing his index and middle fingers to finger her clit, pinching her nub at random intervals, an odd mix of pleasure and pain.

The tip of Austin's dick plunged into her again, hitting her G-spot over and over. Taryn teetered right on the edge. Taryn let out a deep cry, one of pain and pleasure.

That was all it took for them both to come in quick succession. Once Austin felt Taryn orgasm, it was like a switch had flipped. As he began his guttural moans, Austin pulled out, flipping Taryn onto her backside. He ripped off the condom before moaning aloud, "Oh God."

And then, much to Taryn's horror, he came.

Right on her face.

Austin collapsed on top of Taryn, then rolled onto his back. Both lay there for a few moments in silence.

Taryn remained frozen as the semen dripped down her cheek. Her mind shot back to the horror movie *Carrie*, and the scene where the poor outcast girl was doused in pig's blood, much to her fright and humiliation. She stood up, walking to the bathroom vanity to moisten a washrag, wiping Austin's remnants of ecstasy from her face.

After Taryn washed and rinsed her face, she braced her arms against the counter, leaning forward. Her head hung to her chin for a few moments, before she brought her gaze to meet her mirrored reflection.

Taryn felt disgusting. Ashamed. Violated. Austin had ejaculated on her *face. Who does that the first time they sleep with someone?* she thought. *Especially without asking.* People had boundaries. And Austin just crossed one of hers. That act ... it wasn't about love or affection. It was something straight out of porn. Subordination. A power play intended to humiliate and degrade a partner.

And right now, Taryn felt like trash. Whatever afterglow she had quickly dissipated into humiliation and degradation. She felt completely disregarded and disrespected. Her stomach burbled with a sickening feeling.

This had been a complete mistake. Not just sleeping with Austin—but her whole purpose for being in Gardenia Beach. Taryn's remorse smacked her, and it was swift and heavy. She looked at the woman peering back at her in the mirror with complete disgust, flipping off the light switch and covering herself with a towel that had been tossed onto the floor.

Who are you? she thought as she crept back to the bed, slipping beneath the covers, then removing the towel and letting it drop to the ground. *What have you become?*

"Wow," Austin said, breaking Taryn's train of thought. "Full confession. I've been dying to sleep with you for weeks."

Taryn pulled the covers higher over her naked body.

"Me, too," she responded.

Because she felt that was what she should say in this awkward, disgusting moment in her life.

The sex had been astonishing to a point, yet a little rougher than Taryn anticipated. She'd envisioned fucking Austin plenty of times, and, in her mind, his touch would be tender. Loving. Beautiful. Not aggressive. She hadn't expected the nipple-pinching. Or when he twisted her nub with his thumb and index finger.

Or him blowing his wad on her face.

She shuddered. And then, the undeniable thought.

Evelyn can't find out.

But Taryn's exhaustion from the past few days, paired with the unexpected tryst with Austin, was more powerful than the guilt and befuddlement. Taryn's eyelids slipped closed as she drifted into a deep sleep. She had momentarily forgotten. About Graham. About Evelyn. About what she'd just done.

About the Text Tormentor.

About everything. If just for a bit.

CHAPTER FORTY-ONE

The knock of the housekeeper rattled Taryn out of her slumber the next morning.

"Come back later," she groaned as she pulled the covers over her head. It wasn't loud enough, and Taryn was jostled to full consciousness when the housekeeper opened the door and saw her sitting in the bed, naked except for the linens that covered her from the bust down.

"So sorry," the woman apologized as she quickly stepped back from the door, letting it slam shut.

Why the hell didn't I lock the door with the security chain? she asked herself.

But then she remembered.

Austin had been here.

His side of the bed was vacant. He left at some point.

After they had betrayed Evelyn.

Taryn felt sick as she turned to grab a swig of the cup of water that rested on her nightstand. She saw a note scribbled on the Tiki Torch-branded notepad that sat next to the phone.

"Early meeting," it read. "You are amazing."

Austin's handwritten note stirred a sense of melancholy in Taryn. She felt cheap, remembering her college trysts. The few guys who'd spent the night with her after a frat party, only to leave in the middle of the night, without the courtesy of a goodbye. She remembered how awful it felt to be awakened to the sound of her front door creaking open and her bedmate escaping into the night.

But this. This was different.

She was starting to feel something for Austin, as wrong as that was. But didn't he seem to be into her, too? He'd unearthed a hell of a lot of baggage on her, and she suspected, by his stoic nature, that Austin wasn't the type to share such a private demon with casual acquaintances. There was something there. She just wasn't sure what that exactly was. Especially with his sexual proclivities. Their recent tryst began to gnaw at her conscience. *Who ejaculates on someone's face the first time they have sex?* she wondered. It seemed more like something for later in a relationship, maybe a way to spice things up as time eked on—that is, if both parties were into it. Which Taryn was not.

It would have been nice if Austin had asked first, she thought, her disdain for him blossoming by the second. *And it's never, ever happening again. Not with him.*

Taryn shuddered at the thought of Evelyn and the next time she'd see her. How could she look at her? The fact she'd slept with Austin would be all over her face. She quickly grasped the note and tore it to tiny shreds before tossing it in the toilet and flushing the remnants.

Things were starting to get too intertwined. Taryn's charade of being a divorcee finding herself by spending a couple months in Florida. The Text Tormentor who was on to her identity and determined to make her squirm—or maybe something more sinister.

And the fact she'd just had sex with the ex-husband of Graham's assault victim.

There was too much at risk. The further entrenched she became, the higher the prospects blossomed for this, whatever this was, not ending well.

It was time to wrap up her time in Gardenia Beach. As quickly as possible.

CHAPTER FORTY-TWO

Taryn's plan was to keep it short and sweet. She'd feign a family emergency. Even though she'd told Evelyn and Austin she'd been staying in Gardenia Beach to spend time with her ailing mother, she needed a hefty crisis as a reasonable explanation for her sudden need to depart.

The reason would be her sister. Yes, her sister was just diagnosed with Stage Four ovarian cancer. And she, Rebecca, was heading home to Illinois to tend to her, offer her emotional support and provide transportation to chemotherapy sessions, doctor visits, whatever. She would explain that she was the only option, given how sick and incapacitated her "mom" was.

Taryn had already told the Tiki Torch she'd be departing in two days. She'd booked a flight to Chicago on Friday morning, leaving her enough time to assemble her stuff. And say goodbye to her two new friends.

Did Taryn even earn the right to think of them as "friends?" Evelyn and Austin didn't even know her real name. Or story. Everything she'd told them, or most everything, was a heaping pile of bullshit.

Just like me, Taryn thought.

Taryn walked down to the beach, a couple of hard seltzers in her beach bag, along with her phone, a towel, pack of smokes and a lighter. As she spread out her towel, sat on it and brought a cigarette to her lips, she thought about the fact that she was now a full-fledged smoker again. Part of it disgusted her. She knew better. She'd quit. She saw the eyes when she'd light up in public. The judgment and disgust. The coughing. The heavy sighs when her cloud of smoke wafted their way. But she also didn't care.

She was in survival mode. Even though it was in the mental and emotional sense.

The discomfort rose in Taryn as she thought about the exchange she'd have with Evelyn and Austin. She knew she had to make it quick or her face would give her away. They'd suspect something wasn't right. She was going to have to play the part of distraught sister. And finesse it pretty quickly.

As the sun shone down on her, Taryn slurped down the last of her first can and felt a momentary sense of calm. Though she didn't know why. Her whole purpose of coming down here was to find out how Evelyn had fared in life despite the trauma unearthed by Graham. And she'd seen, it was not so well. There really wasn't much for her to do. She couldn't make right the misdeeds of another. Staying wouldn't change anything. And the longer she stayed, the longer she'd have to keep her lies aligned.

Taryn plotted out her plan. She'd go to the Wayside, put on her best acting skills and say her goodbyes. And then she'd leave this experience behind her. Change her phone number. Keep her social media accounts permanently closed. And somehow, try to rebuild whatever ruins of her life were left.

The ping of her iPhone snapped her out of her thoughts. She felt a sense of panic. How would she respond to Evelyn after sleeping with Austin? The guilt consumed her. She brought the phone to her line of vision.

It wasn't Evelyn.

"Was stalking Graham's conquest not enough for you? It takes a lot of balls to fuck her ex-husband. I can't wait to see what you do next."

Taryn's hands trembled as she navigated the number to block it. But one more message came through. A quote she recognized as the wisdom of Buddha.

"Three things cannot be long hidden: the sun, the moon, and the truth."

Taryn had seen plenty of the sun and moon. And she needed to get the hell out of here before the truth came out.

CHAPTER FORTY-THREE

As Taryn traipsed up the walkway to the Wayside for what she knew would be the last time, her nerves were shattered. She wanted out of this town—and fast. With every step she took, she wondered if the Text Tormentor was in her midst. Were they trailing her? Did they follow her everywhere she went?

Note to self, she thought. *Change your fucking number when you get home. And keep it private.*

Taryn grabbed the wooden door handle and opened it. As she entered the bar, she could see them. Evelyn was behind the bar, leaning on it. And talking to Austin.

Shit, she thought. *This is fucking perfect.*

Taryn knew it was likely Austin would be bellied up to the bar, but she'd prayed he'd have something else to do tonight before she skipped town. *Why couldn't he be chained to the toilet with profuse diarrhea or something?*

She meandered around the horseshoe-shaped bar, her eyes set on the seat next to Austin. Taryn hesitated. She really didn't want to sit next to him. Especially after not having a chance to talk to him and ensure their dalliance would be their secret. A one-time thing. But sitting as far away from Austin would tip off Evelyn that something wasn't right. She'd have to sit next to him, as she almost always did.

Austin saw her first. His eyes darted to hers, then quickly diverted. His face was stoic. From the way he responded to her entry, she suspected there'd been no confession to Evelyn. By the time Taryn had made it around to the seat next to his, Austin forced a smile and nodded to acknowledge her presence.

When Evelyn saw Taryn, her face lit up.

"Becks!" she screeched. "You can help settle this argument for us."

Taryn slid onto the barstool and rested her purse on the bar. *Whew,* she thought. *If she knew, she'd have thrown a drink in my face by now.* She made it a point to seem genuinely intrigued by whatever the hell they were squabbling about.

"If a divorced couple were to remarry, is it in bad taste to wear the same dress?" Evelyn asked, a smile spreading across her face.

Taryn's eyes bulged as she looked from Evelyn to Austin, then back to Evelyn. This wasn't really happening, was it?

"What?" Taryn blurted out. "Are you two ..."

Evelyn broke out in a beaming grin as she slowly lifted up her left hand, her palm situated toward her face as she revealed the glittering diamond ring on her left ring finger.

Taryn's stomach dropped, and she feared she might vomit.

A mere night prior, Austin had shared her bed. So, he topped it off by proposing to his ex-wife? This was too much to decipher.

Austin gave her a pleading look as Evelyn kept her attention on Taryn's face.

"Becks," a disappointed Evelyn said, tilting her head to the side. "I was expecting a little more excitement than this."

Taryn put on the fakest "genuine smile" she could and began clapping. Evelyn ran from the back of the bar to hug Taryn, who then offered a perfunctory embrace to Austin.

"Congratulations," she said, trying to feign happiness amid her utter confusion. "I'm sorry. I'm a little discombobulated. I just got some upsetting news from back home."

Evelyn's face grew confused as the two broke apart.

"Oh," she said. "What kind of news?"

Taryn immediately felt like an asshole, hijacking Evelyn's happy moment to share her bad news. Even if it was fake bad news.

"My sister," Taryn replied, which prompted Austin to shift his gaze from Evelyn to Taryn. "She just found out she has Stage 4 ovarian cancer. I need to get home immediately. I'm leaving first thing tomorrow."

The color drained from Evelyn's face.

"Oh my God!" Evelyn said, rushing to hold Taryn again.

It was one of the most sincere, heartfelt hugs she'd felt in quite some time. Taryn found comfort in Evelyn's arms, despite her heavy sense of shame. For her lies. For coming to Gardenia Beach in the first place. For the line she crossed last night. But still, it was the first time she felt it.

Evelyn truly cared about her. Taryn could feel it by her touch. See it in her eyes.

Remorse sickened Taryn's heart and mind. *I am a complete piece of shit,* she thought, fighting her own urge to cry.

Evelyn drew away from Taryn, clasping their hands together as she looked straight into her eyes. Taryn saw Evelyn's eyes moisten as she smiled sweetly and brushed a loose strand from Taryn's face, tucking it delicately behind her ear.

She could be a good mother, Taryn thought.

"I'm truly so very sorry," Evelyn said in hushed seriousness. "What can I do to help?"

Taryn shook her head.

"Nothing," she said. "I just need to get back to Illinois and be there for her. Take her to chemo and doctor appointments. She's got no one else. Especially with my mom being so sick, too."

Taryn felt like an asshole, all the attention shifted to her. When it should all be on Evelyn's re-engagement, as awkward as that felt—considering Taryn bedded the future groom less than twenty-four hours ago.

"Enough about me," Taryn said, shifting the conversation back to the happy couple. "We need to celebrate! You must tell me all the details."

Evelyn's enormous grin returned.

"I will," she said. "But only if you promise to join us for a congratulatory drink first. And another to wish you well. I know we haven't known each other long, but, Becks, you're different.

"It's like you are the friend I've been searching for my whole life," Evelyn said, tightly grasping the other woman's hands with her own, looking tenderly into her eyes.

Taryn's stomach sank. And her heart felt like it was beginning to break.

Taryn's eyes moistened as she sniffled and looked up, wiping them away with her fingers. A sad smile grew on Evelyn's face as she wrapped her arms around Taryn again.

"I'm going to miss you, too, Evelyn," Taryn said, meaning every word. "You've really helped me heal from my divorce. I know I don't talk about it, but believe me, you have. Just being there, showing me things to do, welcoming a complete stranger ... I can't tell you how much that's meant to me."

Evelyn nodded as the two broke apart.

"I get off in fifteen," Evelyn said. "Let's head over to Red Rooster for our grand finale. Sound good to you both?"

Austin took the moment to rise from his barstool and slide a twenty across the bar to cover his tab.

"I'm going to have to bow out, ladies," he said. "I have some work to catch up on."

Evelyn rolled her eyes and sighed.

"Of course," Evelyn said. "We're going to celebrate our engagement without you. *That* makes sense. Party pooper."

"Someone's gotta bring home the bacon and pay for our second wedding," he jested, kissing her on the cheek before turning toward the door to leave.

"Uh, Austin," Evelyn said as he began walking toward the exit. "Becks is leaving tomorrow. You're not even going to say goodbye?"

His back to them, Austin sharply stopped in his tracks. His shoulders seemed to slump slightly, sickening Taryn. *He is repulsed by me,* she thought. *And ashamed, like me.* Austin slowly turned around and forced a smile, walking toward her in slow motion, it seemed.

"Rebecca," he said, closing in on her space, then pulling her in for the stiffest embrace she ever felt. Taryn went along with an obligatory farewell. "It's been a pleasure. I am so sorry about your sister. I wish you the best. Safe travels home."

Taryn pulled away from him and nodded.

"Thank you," she said, shifting her line of vision to the terracotta tiles. "Same to you. And congratulations again."

With that, Austin nodded back and began his journey back toward the exit. Taryn watched as he slipped out of the door—and her life. A twinge of gloominess seeped into Taryn's thoughts.

She felt like a jilted co-ed after a frat party hookup. Except now she was a real adult with real responsibilities. And being ghosted after a one-night fling felt just as shitty as it did in college.

Actually, a little worse.

Taryn refocused on the surroundings around her at the bar as Evelyn tended to her end-of-shift duties. By the time it hit five o'clock, she slid her tip money into the back right pocket of her jean shorts and lifted the bar top to slide to the customer side.

"Tonight's on me," she said, tapping the pocket with her day's partial earnings.

As the two grabbed their purses and headed toward the door, Taryn felt a sense of unease. Like she was being watched. Taryn felt relief wash over her as she walked out of the Wayside for the last time.

It was almost over.

CHAPTER
FORTY-FOUR

The plan was to stay for a couple of drinks. Taryn didn't want to be hung over when the alarm went off at four-thirty in the morning. The two girls were nestled atop their barstools when Evelyn spoke up.

"We need to have a special drink to commemorate this night," Evelyn said. "Something that packs a punch. Like a Long Island iced tea or dirty martini."

The thought of five different liquors in one glass made Taryn's head hurt.

"Let's go with something a little lighter," she said. "Like a beer or hard seltzer. I have to be up in a matter of hours for the airport."

Evelyn nodded in agreement.

"Understood," she said. "If you weren't leaving at the ass crack of dawn, I'd fight you. And I'm still getting a martini."

Evelyn turned to the female bartender, a busty blond woman in her twenties with a nametag that read "Julie" and asked, "Any chance you have blue-cheese-stuffed olives?"

Julie turned to her condiments and lifted a glass container of just that. Evelyn wooted at the sight.

Within two minutes, Evelyn's dirty martini and Taryn's hard seltzer were presented before them. Evelyn's face lit up at the sight of her drink, which sprouted a toothpick with four stuffed olives.

"You, my fellow bartender," she said, "will be getting a nice tip."

Julie smiled and turned to the next customer, leaving the girls to their own conversation.

Taryn knew she had to ask about the proposal. To not would tip off Evelyn something wasn't right.

"So," she said, sipping her seltzer and turning to face Evelyn, "tell me what happened. How'd he do it? And did you ever see it coming?"

Evelyn's smile grew wide as she peered down at the ring, waggling her fingers so the overhead bar lights reflected its brilliance. The ring itself was platinum, with a simple princess-cut center stone.

"Never in a million years," she said. "I mean, obviously, we've still had a thing for each other, despite the divorce. I guess he meant it when he said 'till death do us part' before. Even when we were technically apart, he's still been a part of me. He still takes care of me, in every sense of the word."

Taryn wanted to get to the meat of the story. How could Austin be intertwined in the sheets with her last night, only to turn around and ask his ex-wife to remarry him?

"So, how did he do it?" Taryn asked.

Evelyn's eyes lit up.

"I was completely blindsided," she went on. "After I got called back to work last night, I was dead tired when I closed. I didn't even have a nightcap. I just went straight to bed and fell asleep. It was about eleven thirty when I heard a knock at my front door. When I opened it, there was a trail of rose petals. I was a little confused but still followed the path. And it led me to the beach, where Austin was standing in the middle of a heart made from more rose petals. As soon as he saw me, he knelt on one knee, pulling my old ring from his back pocket. He said to me, 'I've figured out something. I am not me without you. Will you be my wife—again?'"

Taryn faked a delighted smile. She thought about how Austin pulled all this together, hours after he fucked her—and came on her goddamn face.

"Wow," was all she said, ignoring the bile building in the back of her throat.

"I KNOW," Evelyn exclaimed. "I really didn't realize until that exact moment that I felt the same. There is no me without him. And that includes all the good and bad we bring to the table."

Taryn's mind raced as she thought about the way most normal people would progress in such a conversation. She began going through the litany of questions. When would they remarry? Would it be a big to-do again or something simpler? She already knew Evelyn was banking on reusing her dress from Round One. Taryn did her best to feign interest in all the details, even though they were the last things she wanted to hear about. She just wanted to be back home and sweep this whole experience under the proverbial rug.

After a good twenty minutes of wedding talk, Evelyn turned to Taryn.

"Enough about me," she said. "Tell me what's next as you head back to Illinois. Are you going to live with your sister? Will you have to find a job?"

Taryn's mind began ricocheting around, trying to think of the best answers that would prompt the least number of questions.

"I really don't know yet," she stammered. "I just found out about my sister's cancer this morning, so all I can really focus on right now is getting home. Then, one step at a time."

The answer seemed to suffice, as Evelyn downed the rest of her martini and beckoned the bartender for another. Taryn followed in quick succession, and the two continued their conversation for another half hour. By the time the clock struck eight o'clock, they were both feeling on top of the world.

"Oh my God," Evelyn said, a seemingly bright idea coming to her. "I'm gonna ask Austin to swing by with our wedding album from before. Maybe we'll find some inspiration there."

Taryn's insides recoiled at the thought of seeing Austin again. But she knew objecting would only alarm Evelyn. Within twenty minutes of Evelyn's pleading phone call, begging Austin to bring the album to the bar, he emerged from the entrance, coming over to the girls and resting it on the countertop.

"Enjoy," he said, turning to leave.

"You're not getting away from us that easily," Evelyn said, motioning toward the empty seat to Taryn's right. A jolt of nerves shot through Taryn, but she tried her best to hide it. "You have to have at least one celebratory drink with us!"

Austin sighed and slid onto the empty seat. Taryn could sense him bristling at the discomfort. She felt it as well. He lingered for about fifteen minutes, not asking a thing, only curtly answering questions directed at him, before insisting to Evelyn that he had, in fact, been in the middle of work and really needed to get back to it.

"Bring your damn laptop next time," Evelyn yelled to Austin as he began to open the door to the exit.

Both women watched him leave. Evelyn's face grew perplexed, a look of sadness on her face as Austin zipped out the door.

"I'm gonna have to work on him," she said, her eyes scanning the crowd within her field of vision.

"Jesus," Evelyn suddenly said under her breath, breaking Taryn's focus on the Pinterest wedding hair feeds Evelyn had previously shoved into her face. "That weirdo in the ball cap is here. I wonder what her deal is. She seems to be popping up all over."

Taryn's buzzed mind began to wander. If Austin thought nothing of sleeping with her, was that his typical MO? Maybe this girl was someone he slighted after a one-nighter? After the night prior, Taryn considered it as a possibility, keeping her suspicions to herself. Regardless, her presence was creepy.

"Yeah, that's fucking crazy," Taryn said, suddenly realizing her bladder was about to burst.

"I have to go to the bathroom," she told Evelyn, steadying herself against the bar as she rose to her feet.

"I'll keep your seat warm," Evelyn said, patting the barstool as Taryn headed to the ladies' room.

With that, Taryn scrambled, as best she could in her mild stupor, throwing the single-person bathroom door open and running to the toilet. She felt as if she could spill her guts into the bowl but was able to settle her nerves. She stood in the bathroom, observing her reflection in the mirror. She looked awful. She sat on the toilet to pee, losing herself in the thoughts flooding her brain. Taryn flushed the commode, pulled up her pants, and dropped her bottom to the floor. She just needed a moment and leaned against the wall.

No more, she thought. *This is no way to live. Whatever this is. Things are going to change back home.*

Taryn wrapped her right hand around the grab bar affixed to the wall next to the toilet and pulled her thin frame upward.

Maybe I need to call Scoot and Get Sober with God myself, she mused.

Taryn needed to pay her bill, say goodbye to Evelyn and get her ass into bed for a few hours of sleep before heading to the airport. She felt a sense of impending relief this seemingly useless journey was almost over. She ran the faucet, bringing her face to the flow of water and gulping every ounce she could. Taryn was sickened by her reflection in the mirror. She saw nothing but a drunken, lost soul. A cheating cohort. And a goddamn stalker. She noted the irony that she'd blossomed into what surely was a problem drinker within such a fleeting time frame.

A problem drinker. Just like her dead rapist husband.

A furious knock reverberated through the door. Taryn groaned. It was probably another patron sick of waiting for her to get her shit together in a bathroom.

"Just a minute," she bellowed. "Almost done!"

This is almost over, Taryn thought. *In twenty-four hours, you'll be back home. And this will all be a distant memory.*

But the desire to vomit returned with vigor as soon as she opened the bathroom door.

Evelyn stood there. And she was furious. Evelyn thrust Taryn's iPhone, which had been left atop the bar, into Taryn's line of vision, her face seething with rage as her hands shook, trying to steady the phone.

"Something you need to *fucking tell me*?" Evelyn demanded. "*Taryn?*"

Taryn's face grew white as her eyes trailed over the phone. As she stepped forward to take it from Evelyn, Evelyn threw it forcefully onto the ground. Taryn could hear the screen shatter as soon as it hit the tiled floor. Taryn bent down to retrieve her phone before standing back upright, her mind scattered in a million places.

She'd been exposed. As a total fraud. And stalker.

Evelyn gritted her teeth, her fists rolling into balls, as if she was getting ready to throw a punch.

"I ... I ... I can explain," Taryn stammered. "Evelyn..."

But Evelyn wasn't having it. She glowered at Taryn, their eyes connecting as tears began to trickle down Taryn's face.

"*Fuck you!*" Evelyn huffed, turning and charging toward the front door.

Taryn stood in complete shock as a quiet hush mushroomed throughout the bar. Her hands trembled as she grasped her phone, turning it over to examine the cracked glass. She could barely see the screen. But she could see enough so to make out the last message that pinged her phone.

"Hello again, Taryn Sloan," it read. "Did you tell your new BFF that you're headed back to your dead rapist husband's grave? The one who assaulted her?

"And did you mention that you fucked her fiancé last night?"

CHAPTER FORTY-FIVE

As the shock of Evelyn's discovery sunk in, Taryn's jumbled mind started to straighten up some. And she knew she had two choices.

She could run like an escaped prisoner to get to the airport immediately and as far away from Gardenia Beach as she could. Or give Evelyn the answers and closure she needed.

Because Taryn knew. She owed Evelyn that.

If Taryn's mother taught her anything, it was to face her demons and be accountable. She thought about if the roles were reversed. *What would she want?*

Clarity, Taryn decided. *Closure. And peace.*

And the first step meant starting with Austin. He knew Evelyn better than anyone. And since he was bound to find out anyway, going straight to him seemed to be her best option. Whether he was appalled by Taryn's quest or not, he'd at least be a barometer for how to move forward.

Taryn was able to navigate her shattered phone enough to hail an Uber to bring her to Austin's house, nestled in a beachside subdivision, which she found through a quick internet search. She didn't know exactly what she was going to say. She just knew she needed to start somewhere. Very quickly.

As she exited the Uber, Taryn's heart beat so fast she feared she was in cardiac arrest. Or maybe having a panic attack.

Taryn hesitated as she stood at Austin's front door, wishing she could look through the peephole to see if Evelyn had beaten her there. She hadn't even considered that until this moment. She felt sick at the possibility that both might be there—and she'd be outnumbered.

When Austin opened the door, shock and fear washed over his face.

"Rebecca," he began. "What happened last night was a momentary lapse in judgment. For both of us. I don't think—"

"No," Taryn interrupted. "Forget that. It's irrelevant. I need to talk to you."

Austin's eyes scanned her face, recognizing the dread.

"Come in," he said, moving back to allow her to enter. "If you're looking for Evelyn, I think you can tell she's not here."

Taryn stood in the middle of Austin's living room. She felt lost. Sick. She was afraid to tell him who she really was. But she had to. If anyone could figure out how to work something out with Evelyn, it was Austin.

The two stood for a moment, looking at one another with unease. Austin remained silent.

"I fucked up," Taryn blurted out. "Like really, really fucked up. And I need your advice."

Austin stared at her as they settled into his living room, Taryn sitting on the brown leather couch that anchored it.

"Okay..." he said with hesitation. "You need a drink? Will *I* need a drink for this conversation?"

Taryn shook her head. "I think *you* might want a drink. A stiff one. But can you make some coffee? I don't think I'm going to sleep before my flight. I need to stay up."

Austin nodded and pointed toward the kitchen.

"I'll be right back," he said, leaving the room.

Taryn sat on the couch, her heart beating so fast she was sure it was about to explode. There was too much rattling around in her head. Her lie being exposed. The fact she slept with her pseudo-friend's now-fiancé just a matter of hours ago. And that fucking Text Tormentor, who somehow was immune when it came to blocking them.

The memory reminded her she needed to block the number again. It would hopefully give her enough time to avoid them until she could get a new anonymous number they hopefully couldn't trace to her. Taryn lifted her phone from her back pocket and pulled up the text, poised to block it. Again.

Maybe if she texted back that she'd been exposed, the person would give up. In her desperation, Taryn decided to at least try before she blocked the number for the temporary reprieve.

"It's over," she tapped into her phone. "She knows. Leave me the fuck alone."

She trembled as she went to file her phone back into her purse. But that's when she heard it.

Ping.

The sound came from beneath the couch. Right after she shot off the text.

There was no mistaking it. That was a text pushing through a phone.

Her message. Received by her Text Tormentor.

Right exactly beneath her.

CHAPTER FORTY-SIX

T hat single sound brought everything to a screeching halt. Taryn needed to get out of here. Immediately.

Taryn's heart raced, thumping in her chest, her jugular, her wrists. She felt the fear wash over her, paralyzing her body and mind as she sat petrified, the seconds ticking by.

It's a coincidence, she told herself.

But Taryn needed to make sure. She pulled her phone out again, quickly unblocking the Text Tormentor's number and tapping "fuck off" into the message. Anything to quickly verify she was, in fact, so wrong, perhaps even insane. There was no way the person digitally harassing her was one room away from where she sat, right at this exact moment.

Taryn's fingers shook as she hit send, holding her breath.

Ping, came the tone from beneath the couch.

Taryn's heart sank. There was no doubt.

Austin knew.

He knew who she was and what Graham had done. And he was undoubtedly bent on making her pay, even if it was the sheer mental torture he bestowed upon her.

Taryn needed to get the fuck out of here.

As her eyes lifted from the phone, she saw him. Austin was standing there, a hot mug of coffee, the scent and steam wafting into the room. All she knew was she had less than two minutes to get the hell out of there before the reminder ping came through. She didn't want to be in the same room with him when he realized she was on to him. If he'd gone to these lengths to torture the widow of Evelyn's assailant, she wasn't sure what his cutoff point was. And she didn't want to find out.

Taryn quickly shot up.

"I'm so sorry," she stammered. "I think I drank too much, and I feel like I'm about to be sick. I need to get back to the motel right now."

Austin's eyes grew puzzled with Taryn's sudden shift and insistence on leaving. Taryn knew he was moments away from the revelation that she had discovered he was her Text Tormentor. And the best place for her was to be as far away as possible. She was going straight to Tiki Torch, stuffing her belongings in her duffel bag, and ridesharing it straight to the airport. She didn't care if she sat in a stiff, non-cushioned chair in the terminal all night. There, she would be safe.

Austin trailed behind her as she hustled toward the door.

Just the threshold, she told herself. *Get past the threshold, and you can run.*

Taryn kept her vision glued to the door as her pace quickened. A few more steps and she was free.

"Rebecca!" Austin yelled in confusion from behind her as she swung upon the door.

Taryn could see the glow from the apartment's exterior lighting as she hurried toward the door.

Austin followed, asking "What are you—"

But that was the last thing Taryn heard before the crunch of a crushing blow struck her skull.

CHAPTER
FORTY-SEVEN

When Taryn came to, everything hurt. Her head pounded with piercing fury, and her wrists seared with pain.

She was afraid to open her eyes. It took her a moment to straighten out her mind. Taryn came into consciousness in complete confusion, taking several seconds to recall where she was.

Austin's house.

Or, at least, that's where she was when she got the lights knocked out of her.

Taryn's wrists felt like they were on fire, and she soon realized that she had been tied up. Her hands were bound together, and the ties felt like a steel cable. She finally opened her eyes, as slowly as she could, fearing what her vision would reveal. She knew she'd see Austin somewhere, likely gloating at her as she lay there, restrained.

As she lifted her lids to face whatever awaited her, she was surprised to see Austin.

But he wasn't perched over her in the bed she'd been laid in, sneering at her capture.

He was right next to her, his arms tethered together with a bike chain as well.

Terror overcame Taryn. *If it wasn't Austin who knocked her out and tied her up, who? Was he working in tandem with Evelyn? Or did Evelyn do this herself after finding out about Taryn sleeping with Austin? It didn't make sense.*

As Taryn lay frozen, terrified in the bed, her eyes scanned an equally bound Austin. She'd never felt so frightened or vulnerable in her life. Was Evelyn going to hurt her? Kill her? Her mind raced, considering the possibilities.

A cough on her right side startled her as Austin came to. His face was ashen as his eyes scanned the room. Taryn saw the fear spreading over his face as his eyes darted back and forth, looking for whoever lassoed them to the bed.

Their eyes locked, his fright evident. Austin opened his mouth, as if to speak. But before a sound could eek out, a higher-pitched voice came from the bedroom's doorframe.

"I'm sorry, my dear."

The woman's voice was directed at Taryn.

"I didn't intend to rope an innocent bystander into this, but you can thank your friend for it," the woman said.

The voice wasn't Evelyn's. As Taryn redirected her focus toward the door, she recognized the woman standing there. A blond bob peeked out from beneath the black ball cap. The light shone on the woman's face, which appeared heavily scarred with somewhat recent wounds. And the woman was sporting blue medical latex gloves.

That's when it clicked. It was Ballcap Girl from the Wayside. And the Red Rooster. And God knows where else, when Taryn hadn't been paying attention.

"What the fuck?" Austin sputtered. "Who the fuck ..."

Austin's voice trailed off. But his face gave it all away. Taryn could tell. He *knew* this woman. *But how?*

"Yep," she said with a sneer, walking over to the side of Austin's bed and gloating as he lay imprisoned below her. "You, Mr. Austin Witmer, owe me big time. We made a pact. And you broke it. So, I'm here to collect. Or at least make you learn a basic tenet of decency. That when you make a fucking promise to someone, you goddamn keep it."

Taryn's mind spun with tornadic ferocity. *This wasn't about her? Something completely different?*

She couldn't help herself, straining to turn toward Austin and look him directly in the eyes.

"What the hell?" Taryn asked in panic. "I thought ..."

Austin didn't speak a word. Tears began streaming down his face.

"Not gonna tell her, huh?" Ballcap Girl asked. "This is your chance to admit your wrongs and make amends."

The three remained in silence as Taryn felt the blood rushing through her ears. *What was this? What had he done?*

"Don't say I never gave you the chance," the woman said, jabbing her index finger at Austin's face as he flinched.

Then, she turned to look at Taryn.

"Your little fuck buddy here made a deal with me," she said. "I fulfilled my part. But he seemed to have forgotten his. Or he's just a piece of shit, which I suspect is the case anyway."

Taryn's heart continued to race as she looked at the woman. She didn't need to ask for an explanation. The woman was going to provide it, whether she wanted to hear it or not.

"Not sure if you know this, but fuck buddy's main squeeze experienced a trauma back in her college years," she went on. "Some drunken wedding guest and fellow undergrad helped himself to her vagina when she was as drunk as a skunk. And that can really fuck a girl up."

Taryn's eyes flitted between Austin, who kept his eyes shut as the tears continued to flow, and the erratic lunatic now perched at the foot of the bed.

"So how do I come in?" the woman continued, beginning to pace between the door and Taryn's side of the bed. "So glad you were thoughtful enough to ask.

"I know what it's like to have your innocence stolen from a fuckhead excuse of a man," she said. "My uncle, or really, someone I considered my uncle, was nice enough to ply me with enough alcohol to pass out. And then he took my virginity. Not that he asked first.

"I was fourteen," Ballcap Girl's voice creaked. "I was a kid. A teenage girl with her own big dreams. But one night changed it all. One man. One act. It ruined me in every way a person can be ruined. Physically. Emotionally. Everything."

Taryn's heart thumped in sick succession, watching Ballcap Girl as she began to pace back and forth at the footboard of the bed. She didn't appear to be finished with her verbal manifesto.

"It made me a shell of what I used to be, just trying to find a way to forget what he did to me," she continued. "But you can't. At least, I can't. Instead, I replay what he did to me, every damn day. And the nightmares. Those are fun, too."

The woman paused as she looked at the framed photo on Austin's nightstand. It was a picture of him and Evelyn, his lips pressed to her cheek as her head lifted in jubilation. The woman picked it up, reviewing it carefully, before she let it fall to the floor, shattering the glass. Taryn and Austin winced in thier discomfort.

"Unfortunately, most sexual assaults are never reported," she continued. "Did you know only twelve percent of sexual assault victims go to police to file a report? Which means eighty-eight percent of those fuckers are free to carry on, completely unaccountable for the lives they shattered. And let's not forget that those who do get charged usually turn their defense into a circus, putting the victim's personal life on public display. She's shamed and violated all over again. But this time, it's in front of whoever wants to watch it. So, whether you report it or not, your life as you'd known it is basically over. Your personal trauma is nothing but entertainment for courtroom fanatics. It's not fair.

"But life isn't fair," she continued, a venomous sneer spreading across her face. "That's why sometimes you have to seek an alternate form of justice. And that's where your buddy comes in. Except he didn't."

The pieces were starting to coalesce in Taryn's mind. Her nausea continued to intensify.

"Both of us, you see, had a right to wrong," she carried on, nervously picking at her cuticles as she patrolled the bed's perimeter. "And it doesn't make sense to do that yourself. Your rapist ends up dead? Guess who's the prime suspect?"

Taryn's eyes flitted from the woman to Austin, then the woman again.

"Bingo," the woman said, as if someone besides the silence had answered her, adjusting her ball cap. "You. So that's where a little creativity comes in. And the dark web.

"Mr. Witmer here portrayed himself as the perfect solution to my PTSD problem. Or, at least, in getting revenge. I needed a pervert uncle taken out. He needed a selfish prick to be eradicated. It was perfect. I'd kill his woman's rapist, and he'd take out mine.

"Except *I* did *my* part." She whirled and jabbed her right index finger into Austin's chest, her voice choking. "And *you* did *not.*"

Taryn's head spun. This woman, this Ballcap Girl, had been trailing Austin. And it was then that Taryn realized this woman was Adrienne Snyder—the same person who nearly plowed her car into Graham's motorcycle, sending his Harley into that massive tree, making Taryn a widow.

But now, Taryn knew it was no accident. This woman killed her husband. On purpose.

"*You* killed him?" she gasped. "*You're* the Adrienne Snyder who killed my husband?"

Adrienne immediately halted her back-and-forth stride. Taryn realized her grave misstep, and her complexion drained ghastly pale. Adrienne's head snapped to Taryn's face.

"Oh, this just gets better," Adrienne said, laughter bellowing from her belly. "*You* are The Rapist's *widow*? I *thought* you looked familiar. I just couldn't place you. But now.... nice dye job. And thank you for speaking up. I think *you* just solved the problem I was about to create."

Austin's head jerked toward Taryn, his eyes bulging as if to silence her. But the damage was already done.

"Stay put, you two lovebirds," Adrienne ordered, heading toward the bedroom door. "I have a surprise for you both."

A confident, brazen Adrienne briskly walked past the threshold, leaving the two alone again. In bed again. Just as they had been twenty-four hours ago.

"I thought it was *you* texting me," Taryn whispered to Austin. "I thought it was *you* harassing me."

Austin looked in front of him, refusing to look at Taryn.

"It was," he quietly confessed.

Taryn let the information seep into her mind.

"How?" she whispered. "*Why? I* never did *anything* to *you*."

Austin sighed, turning his head to the left to look toward her, though he refused to meet her eyes.

"As soon as you stepped into the Wayside, I immediately recognized you," Austin softly began. "I'd been following the news on Graham's death. The social media chatter about how devastating it was for the community. And, of course, there were plenty of pictures of you two with your friends before he died. All the tributes pouring in about him made me absolutely sick. And I wondered what kind of a woman would marry a rapist. Evelyn never went on social media. The possibility of Graham's face showing up on her Facebook feed was too much for her. She didn't want to know. She didn't want to see how he'd fared in life. Given he'd destroyed hers. *Ours*."

Taryn sniffled as her stomach continued flipping and flopping.

"I didn't know," she squeaked out. "Until after he died."

"That's irrelevant to me," he snapped back. "You clearly knew something. Because what are the chances, Taryn, that the widow of my ex-wife's sexual assailant would end up in the same *town*, the same *bar*, as her husband's *victim*? I knew it was no fucking coincidence. Just tell me, because our story looks like it's going to end here. Why? *Why* would you stalk her?"

Taryn sniffled and sucked in a breath of air.

"After Graham's death, I was looking for a file on his laptop," Taryn whispered, her voice cracking. "I found a confession letter to Evelyn in his laptop. And one for me."

"Wow," Austin said in a hushed tone. "I didn't think he'd do it."

"Do *what*?" Taryn panicked.

"I had been sending him anonymous emails," Austin confessed. "I described what he did, as a semi-witness had shared with me. I told him his secret didn't die that night. And if he didn't formally apologize to Evelyn, acknowledge what he did to her and beg for her forgiveness, my next email was to you. Because whether or not he told you he raped the love of my life, you were going to have to suffer through every explicit detail of his actions. Just like we have.

"Your husband destroyed our relationship," he continued. "So, it was only fair I returned the favor. Karma was knocking on his door, whether he liked it or not."

Taryn sniffled as her mind brought her back to earlier this year, up until Graham's death. His oddness, his jumpiness in the days and weeks leading up to the accident. The push to start a family. The moments of Graham just staring, as if he was mesmerized, in a trance.

It all made sense.

Graham knew he was about to be outed, Taryn thought. *He had been terrified of losing me. That's why he'd been pushing her for a baby so hard.*

Perhaps Graham saw it as marital insurance—by bringing a baby into the picture, it would anchor Taryn to him. He would forever be in her life, married or not. And the confession?

Perhaps, through his remorse, he thought I would stand by him, Taryn pondered. *And forgive him.*

Not that she could ask him now.

"Finding out what he did to Evelyn crushed me," Taryn wept. "I was sickened that I married a man who would sexually assault someone. I was devastated. I know what a sexual assault can do to someone. I've seen it myself. It happened to my best friend in high school. And I live with those feelings of guilt and remorse. That maybe I could have saved her, had I done something differently. So, I wanted to make sure. I wanted to make sure that Evelyn was okay.

"I wanted to see that my husband didn't ruin her life," Taryn whimpered.

"Well," Austin snickered, "I think you can see it didn't work out that way. He ruined her life. And mine.

"She trusted you," he chided. "The irony of that."

Despite the fear rising in her heart and throat, anger began to bubble to the front.

"I thought you *felt* something for me," she whispered in between angry tears. "Last night ... it didn't feel fake to me. It felt like something real. At first. Until you fucking *came on my face*."

Austin's chin sharply rose from his chest. He glowered at her.

"It sucks to be sexually denigrated, *doesn't it*?" Austin barked. "So now you *know* what it's *like*. I wanted you to get it. *Really* get it. The pain. To know what it feels like to be used. To be humiliated. To feel like a piece of trash. I wanted you to experience what it's like to be the end to the means of someone's sexual conquest. Just like your husband did to Evelyn.

"And I wanted you to leave," Austin added, his eyes as cold as his words. "I knew fucking you right before I proposed to Evelyn again would hurt. And I knew you'd be gone."

Taryn's mind raced as she let Austin's revelation sink in, but not for long. Adrienne swept in and centered herself at the foot of the bed.

"Okay, you two," Adrienne said, breaking up the conversation. "Your little soul-searching session has been great. So great, because it gives me some serious meat for this little setup."

Taryn widened her eyes in confusion.

"What are you going to do to us?" Taryn asked, fear squeaking from her voice.

"I wasn't sure what my plan was," she said. "Well, I knew one thing. I was going to kill *him*. Because if I can't have that peace he cheated me out of, he shouldn't have peace at all. Or anything. Not even his life."

Taryn shuddered. If Austin was destined for death, she knew she was, too. She was the witness. She'd seen enough crime shows and read enough books to know what that meant.

She'd have to be silenced as well.

Adrienne reached her right arm into the pocket of her hooded sweatshirt. When she pulled her hand from the fabric, a glint of metal sparkled from the overhead ceiling fan light. It was a revolver. Adrienne then used her left hand to fish something out of the left side of her shirt. She pulled the cylindrical chunk of metal, then twisted it until it resisted.

Of course, Taryn thought, her fright intensifying. *Not only did this psycho have a gun, but she brought a silencer, too. So much for concerned neighbors calling the cops.*

"Now that I have more bargaining chips, the plan is going to change a bit," Adrienne said. "Mr. Rapist's widow is going to end this miserable excuse of a man. Or really, I am, but you're going take full credit. Not that it'll matter. Because you're going to be dead, too. You know, since you just happened to jump in bed with my shitty justice-seeker pal. The news media is going to fucking love this. Especially after the ocean rescue. I can see the headlines now. 'Lifesaver killed in murder-suicide tryst.'

"Boy," Adrienne continued with a deep exhale. "This really is going to be quite a poetic ending. It'll be a great *Dateline* episode. Or Lifetime movie."

Taryn shivered at the realization. There was no going back to Illinois in the morning. No making amends with Evelyn. There was only darkness ahead. Soon, she would be dead, just like her husband. Except her legacy would be one of a crazed stalker-killer. Even though the killer part was a complete lie.

Her family, or what was left of it, would have to grapple with the notion that Taryn, a beloved former news journalist and recent widow, had married a rapist. And then stalked his victim before killing her fiancé and herself.

She'd be infamous. Just like the people Taryn used to cover on her crime beat. She could already see the story on the front page of *The Gazette* and the stories that were sure to go viral due to their sensationalism.

"So," Adrienne said, waggling the gun at Taryn's forehead. "Let's get this plan into play."

Taryn violently sobbed as she saw her life flash before her eyes, just like people say it does. She saw her wedding day. Her journalism awards. Her mom tending to her bloodied, bruised body the time she caught her pant leg in the chain of her bike, causing her to fall hard and break her arm. The Lucky Phoenix outing with Evelyn. Playing with Lucas at the park. Soaking in the beauty of the Atlantic Ocean. Seeing Sam's dead body wheeled out of her house in a stretcher as her mother's agonizing wails met her ears. The day Graham died.

Taryn saw it all.

Be done, she thought, wanting to end the torture. *Just be done.*

Taryn heard the gun retract and waited for the ka-boom that would end her thirty-three years on Earth.

And then she heard it. The click of the muzzled gunfire, milliseconds before everything would go black.

CHAPTER FORTY-EIGHT

Heaven felt the same as Earth to Taryn. There was no change. No glowing, brilliant light beckoning her to the other side. No late loved ones, like her mom or beloved grandmother, awaiting her arrival, welcoming her. There was just darkness. And the smell of gunpowder.

That's when Taryn realized she wasn't dead. She was very much alive, with the same terror running through her veins.

Her eyes opened. Adrienne stood before her, still holding the gun, now smoldering. Taryn whipped her head to the right.

Taryn wasn't dead.

Austin was.

Taryn shrieked, breaking down in tears as she saw his head loll to the side, a single bullet to his upper forehead. Austin's eyes were shut. The blood trickled down the side of his head, dripping onto his plain, gray comforter. Taryn wrestled to right herself in a sitting position, petrified and pushing herself as far away as she could from Austin.

Adrienne lowered the gun with a look of pride. Taryn expected her to raise it again and aim it directly at her. But she didn't. Instead, she brought the gun to her sweatshirt pocket and nestled it inside.

"Your job isn't done," Adrienne said matter-of-factly. "You, my dear, still have a suicide note left to write. It's not nice to leave your family with no explanation for the horrible things you've done."

Adrienne began scouring Austin's dresser and nightstands, looking for a pen and piece of paper to finish her mission. She sighed in aggravation, forcefully opening the closet and unearthing its contents in her search.

"Where does this fucker keep his work stuff?" she asked.

Taryn squeaked out, "I don't know. I've never been here before."

Adrienne huffed.

"Well, *think*," she demanded. "He's got to have something *somewhere*."

"I saw a computer on a desk in the family room," Taryn lied, even though she hadn't. But she needed time. Maybe she could wiggle out of the bike chain and be able to at least put up a fight. "Maybe he has a notebook there or even a printer with paper?"

Adrienne warily looked at the door, then shifted her eyes back to Taryn.

"Don't you dare try a fucking thing," she said as she headed toward the doorframe, then patted the gun resting in her pocket. "Remember, I'm the one packing heat. *Not you*."

Taryn nodded in agreement and watched as Adrienne briskly departed the bedroom. Taryn's eyes quickly scanned the room's contents. A half-empty, crinkled water bottle. A large Bose Bluetooth speaker. The picture shattered on the floor. None of these could be used as weapons. Maybe the speaker. But she'd have to squirm out of the lock and grab it in time to hide beyond the door and slam it onto Adrienne's head.

I just need to knock her out, Taryn thought. *Then, I can grab her gun and call 9-1-1.*

No sooner than she had the thought, Adrienne was back, a spiral notebook and pen in hand. She walked over to Taryn's side of the bed and callously dropped them on the bound woman's chest. Adrienne slipped her hand into her hoodie pocket, again retrieving her gun. She flashed it in front of Taryn's face.

"I," Adrienne began, "am going to untie you. And you are going to write every single word I say. And you will comply, because you're going to have this gun pressed to your head while you do it. If you pull anything, I'll pull the trigger."

Taryn's eyes pleaded with Adrienne's, bile building in her throat as her fright intensified.

"Please," she said, desperate for some kind of solution. "If you let me go, I promise I won't turn you in. I'll help you set it up like a suicide. I promise. I'm so sorry about what happened to you. I honestly never liked the bastard, either."

Adrienne paused, almost as if she was considering it. She momentarily took off her hat, and Taryn noted the scars that had begun to fade slightly on her forehead. Scars from when she purposely killed Graham.

"No," she said. "Nice try, but no. I'm not stupid. Now behave. Or your life will be even shorter than you just came to expect. A simple text message or email can deliver the same message, just not as convincingly. So don't try me."

As Adrienne held the gun in one hand and unraveled Taryn's arms with the other, Taryn's shoulders slumped. This was it. Twenty-four hours ago, she was having sex with the man now dead next to her in his own bed. And she was about to die, too. She took the paper and then pen as Adrienne shoved each to her in quick succession.

"To my loved ones," Adrienne began, gesturing toward the notebook. "Come on. If you don't cooperate, I'll be forced to use your phone and shoot off a suicide text to every contact in there. And that's not how you want people to find out, is it?"

Taryn's tears dripped onto the paper, causing the ink to bleed. She trembled as she began writing what was scripted to her. She used to think her mom and Graham's death were the worst moments of her life. Or finding out about Evelyn's assault.

But this. This scored top billing. And it was about to define her legacy. Would her family even challenge it? Or would Lynn, perhaps, see this note as the explanation for her sister's sudden departure to Florida? That Taryn had lost her mind after being widowed, became obsessed with finding the woman her husband had assaulted, trailed her and then took her and her fiancé out in a blaze of glory? A tale to share with the whole family, forever falsely scarring who they thought Taryn was?

As she neared the end, she lifted her head to look at Adrienne.

"Please," Taryn said between sobs. "I can't take it anymore. Just do it already."

Adrienne snickered.

"Oh, this is the best part," Adrienne said. "It's kind of profound, really. The prey becoming the predator. Now I'm in control."

And that was when Taryn saw the flicker of movement behind her captor. A silhouette appeared in the doorframe as someone crept forward. Evelyn.

Taryn immediately regretted begging for her death. Panic set in. Taryn knew if she gave any hint to Evelyn's emergence, it would be game over.

"I'm going to be sick," she blurted out, pointing to the small trash can next to the bed. "Please give me that, quickly. Or you'll have to contend with two dead bodies, blood and vomit."

As Adrienne leaned over to get the receptacle, Taryn darted her eyes to Evelyn, opening them as widely as she could to signal.

Evelyn received it. And as soon as Adrienne saw the expression in Taryn's eyes, she swung her head around.

Evelyn forcefully threw the boiling hot contents of the coffeepot into Adrienne's face. As the woman fell to the floor, screaming hysterically, Evelyn rushed to the gun on the floor next to her and picked it up, pointing it at Adrienne as the injured, wailing woman held her face in her palms.

"You're right," Evelyn said, pointing the gun at the still-screaming Adrienne. "The news media *is* going to love this."

Taryn trembled as her tears gushed. Her eyes lifted to meet Evelyn's. They conveyed a myriad of emotions. Gratitude. Relief. And a genuine plea for forgiveness.

Evelyn's eyes began to mist as she continued pointing the revolver at Adrienne.

"Evelyn," Taryn wept. "I am so, so sorry."

Evelyn surveyed the room, the shock written across her face. Austin, lying and tied up in the bed, a bullet hole in his head. His wounded attacker still screaming in agony on the floor. And the woman who brought them all together in this life-altering moment.

"So am I, Taryn," she said, sobbing heavily. "So am I."

Epilogue
Eighteen months later, Chicago

Taryn settled into the huge, ornate auditorium's seat, her nerves eating at the lining of her stomach. She wasn't even the one getting up to speak. But it was so deeply personal to her, she felt like she might as well be.

Dottie, seated to Taryn's right, grasped the younger woman's hand with a gentle squeeze, smiling and nodding at her. To her left sat Paul, who rubbed the nape of her neck with his right hand. It settled Taryn's nerves a bit as her hand instinctively rested on her belly, feeling the gentle flutters beneath her fingertips. Taryn was grateful Paul's mom agreed to take Lucas for a couple of days. That way, they could all be there for this incredibly big moment.

As soon as the applause started, Taryn's chest brimmed with pride. The spotlight shone on the speaker, clad in an off-the-shoulder black jumpsuit and dangling silver earrings, as she waved and walked to the microphone.

"Good afternoon, Chicago!" the dazzling woman greeted the audience, removing the microphone from the stand as she began to walk the stage. She took a few moments to close her eyes, dropping her head momentarily to pause before continuing.

"Resilience," the speaker began. "It's something we all hear about and even talk about, but really, what is it? And how can harnessing such a strength help you to rebuild your life? A life you thought was lost. Hopeless. Just one day strung to another, with nothing more than doing the bare minimum to get through each day.

"Sometimes, we have to sink to the depths of despair," she continued, making eye contact with various audience members, "because it's only from there that we can truly take inventory and determine the next chapter of our lives. Will it be one of gloom and indifference? Or will it be one of renewed purpose? A chance to rise like a phoenix from the proverbial ashes? An opportunity to recalibrate what's really important when it comes to our time here on Earth?"

A slideshow began to play on the large screen behind the speaker. Shots of Evelyn, her gregarious grin evidence she was loving life with Austin during their college courtship. Then, the photos grew dark. Photos of Evelyn inebriated, smiling but seemingly lost. Then came the crime scene images from Adrienne's attack. Screenshots of news stories about the incident—the headlines varying from "Botched Revenge Plot Ends in Arrest, Police Say" and "Cops: Local Hero Swapped Murders-for-Hire to Settle Sex Assault Score"—were interspersed with local news photographers' snapshots. Pictures of Taryn and Evelyn being led from the crime scene, escorted by police and paramedics, the distress and terror of the night still freshly strewn across their exhausted faces. Recorded footage of an emotional Evelyn brushing past a throng of reporters shoving their microphones and iPhones in her face as she exited the courthouse during Adrienne's trial.

The audience grew silent, except for a few gasps as some of the most emotional photos and video footage were splayed across the stage. Taryn and Evelyn embracing as they shook with sobs, the Gardenia Beach officers escorting them to the police car. The anguished looks on both women's faces as they testified on the stand, unsuccessfully fighting back tears as they recounted all that led up to Adrienne's attack.

"From our darkest moments come our greatest inspirations. That is, if you choose to travel that road," she continued. "We all have a choice when faced with adversity. We can crumple into a ball of anguish. We can give up.

"Or we can take back our lives—and rewrite our narratives. We can redefine who we are—not accept whatever label society decides to slap on us. We can embrace the bad to propel us forward. We can seize this opportunity as a rebirth. The opportunity to be who we really wanted to be, before we got lost. And take back who we are. Because we are more than what happened to us.

"My name is Evelyn Sanders." She beamed, her white teeth dazzling. Her sleek brunette locks shone under the lights. "I am the founder and president of Stand with Sam, a nonprofit named after Samantha Freedman. Sam was a teenage girl who was sexually assaulted. The trauma of the attack, and the bullying that ensued, was so agonizing, she felt her only way out was to end her life.

"We don't want another sexual assault survivor's story to end this way. And we're working feverishly to change the course of these survivors' narratives. But I'm more than a talking head. I know what I preach.

"Because I am a survivor. A survivor of sexual assault. A survivor of a system that scares us into being broken. A survivor of violence. A survivor of trusting the wrong person—but one who is rebuilding her strength to trust again.

"Because that's what life and love is," Evelyn said, locking eyes with Taryn, bringing a smile to the faces of both women. "Trust. Mutual healing. And leading the way for others who once felt like you.

"Together, we can build back our lives after assault," Evelyn said, "to something bigger and better. Because we can. There's no knocking us down. Together, we can rebuild—and rejoice in taking back what's ours. Our lives."

Taryn joined the audience in their thunderous applause and standing ovation, but the two women couldn't break their smiles or gaze.

They had both been broken. But those wounds had finally begun to heal. And become something more than nightmarish memory. It became their purpose.

Together.

***

Taryn, in a sleek empire-waist black dress, waited outside of the auditorium's hallway during the break, interlacing her fingers at the bottom of her belly. The attendees continued to flow from the doors, mingling with one another as Taryn's shoulders rested on the wall behind her, her auburn locks tucked behind her ears. She'd decided that moving forward, she'd be a redhead. The old Taryn no longer existed. And she liked who she'd become.

Taryn heard Evelyn's uproarious laughter coming from the doorframe before she caught a glimpse of her. Less than two years ago, it was a sound she only occasionally heard, usually when alcohol was involved. Now, it was almost infectious, following Evelyn wherever she went.

As Evelyn emerged from the auditorium, Taryn, standing just outside the exit to her right, said, "Any chance of an exclusive interview for my blog?"

Evelyn spun around, and her eyes sparkled at the sight of Taryn. She began walking toward her but couldn't resist quickening her pace, the closer the two women got to one another. Both opened their arms at the same time, wrapping them around each other as they cried happy tears. It felt like the best hug Taryn had ever received in her life, despite her huge belly forcing her to hunch over for the embrace.

"I," Evelyn said, leaning back and keeping her hands on the inside of Taryn's elbows, "would expect nothing less from my standwith-sam-dot-com Editor in Chief. But I can't promise exclusivity. The more press, the better," she added with a sly wink.

***

Evelyn and Taryn's relationship was a one-eighty from eighteen months ago, when the press coveted whatever interviews they could scrape from the two following Adrienne's arrest. The news coverage and media attention skyrocketed with the revelation of Adrienne and Austin's plans for vigilante justice.

At first, Taryn and Evelyn had done their best to stay out of the limelight. Evelyn ended her employment at the Wayside for a variety of reasons. The dive bar had become a tourist attraction of sorts, with true-crime enthusiasts filing in to see and question Evelyn and the rest of the staff about the chain of events that ended in Adrienne and Leanne's arrests, trials and sentencing. Adrienne would spend the rest of her life in prison. Leanne, thanks to her assistance in covering up Adrienne's actions and helping her sister plot her revenge, was destined for thirty years behind bars.

Finally. Things were good. Better than good. Life was a blessing. And both Taryn and Evelyn knew it.

Evelyn had shown she was a survivor. And one hell of one, too.

Uncle Coop also suddenly found his own notoriety. While the statute of limitations had run out for the assault of his goddaughter, the public scrutiny did him in. Excommunicated from his family, friends and the business world, a month after Adrienne's arrest, Coop put his revolver in his mouth and pulled the trigger. He left a three-word suicide note. "Forgive me, Adrienne."

***

While Evelyn and Taryn were bonded in their horrifying experience, forgiveness didn't come right away.

Initially, Evelyn was furious over Taryn's quest to tail her. Taryn begged for the chance to explain her side, from the bottom of her troubled heart.

When several texts, calls and even an email to Evelyn went unanswered for weeks, Taryn knew she needed another plan.

That's why Taryn had shown up on Paul's doorstep unannounced one Saturday morning. She didn't see Evelyn's car there and silently prayed she hadn't shifted her Sunday playdates with Lucas. Taryn needed to talk to Paul alone. If anyone could help Taryn get through to Evelyn, it was the husband of Evelyn's late best friend.

Paul opened the door to find Taryn standing there, a pleading look in her moistening eyes.

"Uh, hi," Paul said, wearing a blue T-shirt and black athletic joggers. "I thought you were an Amazon delivery."

Taryn took in his striking olive skin, peppered with sweat beads, as Paul wiped a runaway wisp of black hair. *He must have been working out,* she thought.

"I need your help," Taryn whispered, her voice croaking. "I need to make things right with Evelyn."

Luck was on Taryn's side. To her surprise, Paul invited her in. Lucas was napping, so it presented the perfect opportunity. And Taryn spilled it all, up until the very end—that very moment.

Instead of telling Taryn to get the hell out, Paul's hazel eyes began to shimmer. He hung his head after taking it all in, and as he lifted his gaze to meet Taryn's, his irises contracted a bit. Taryn thought she saw a flicker of vulnerability. The tears that began to trickle down his face confirmed it.

"I made a mistake," Taryn choked out.

"I'll do what I can," Paul said, his response prompting Taryn to break down in tears of gratitude.

Taryn was shocked when Paul pulled her into his arms. She shook with sobs as he tightened his grasp. The embrace lingered a bit longer than she'd expected. *What is this?* Taryn thought as her heart fluttered. There was a connection here. She felt it course through her veins.

"We all make mistakes," Paul began as he tenderly rubbed Taryn's back. "But sometimes, from our biggest mistakes and sorrows, we learn to go on. Especially when we seek—and get—forgiveness. I'll do all I can to get you that. Let me talk to Evelyn."

"Thank you." Taryn put her number into his phone. "I want to make things right. If I can."

As Paul opened the front door for Taryn to leave, she turned to pause.

"Please hug that little butter bean for me." Taryn sniffled. "I miss the little guy."

A large smile spread across Paul's face.

"I sure will," he said. "Maybe you can come visit sometime when he's not napping?"

Taryn's face heated. She prayed Paul couldn't tell.

"I would *love* that," Taryn said. "Lucas is an amazing little boy. And I miss him. And Evelyn, if that doesn't sound too fucked up."

"Sometimes," Paul said, "fucked up is the only way we can get through life. Since it doesn't always go according to plan.

"Oh, and Becks—I mean, Taryn," Paul corrected himself, adding a smile. "It was great to see you."

***

It wasn't until Evelyn had dived headfirst into her sobriety step work that she hesitantly agreed to meet with Taryn. She'd ignored Taryn's multiple pleas. But when Paul sat her down one Sunday afternoon after Evelyn's playdate with Lucas, something must have clicked.

Maybe it was the look in Paul's eyes as he spoke of Taryn's recent impromptu visit. How she'd told him the whole story and the guilt and devastation she felt after Adrienne's rampage. Evelyn even told Paul she was perplexed—why the hell would he care so much about helping the screwed-up widow of her assailant?

"Taryn has a good heart," Paul told her. "Just give her the courtesy to share her side with you. Just once. That's all I ask. Do it for me. Do it for Lucas."

That did it.

When the day came to meet at Cuppa Joe, Taryn brought an envelope containing Graham's confession to Evelyn, in addition to his letter to Taryn. Taryn nervously sat, sipping her latte. Her crossed legs jiggled under the bistro table as Evelyn unsealed the envelope, taking her time to read both.

Evelyn's face drained of all color as she read each letter, her face stoic. As she finished reading the second paper, she brought her eyes to meet Taryn's. As Taryn spoke of the whole tale from her viewpoint, Evelyn's eyes frequently welled up, a dribble or two slipping down her cheeks every so often. Some tears were from anger. Some from hurt. Some from relief.

And some from love.

That's when Evelyn broke. Into tears of gratitude, despite the other patrons' quizzical stares. Finally, she had discovered her long-sought answers. And for the first time in more than a decade, Evelyn felt peace. And a realization that she was someone who mattered. To Taryn. To others.

To herself.

Evelyn understood. Taryn's visit to Gardenia Beach wasn't out of spite. It was out of sincerely caring about a woman she didn't even know.

It was the most another human had genuinely been invested in her well-being—someone tied to her by one terrible bond. Taryn's acts weren't out of anger, spite or some kind of off-kilter vengeance. They were acts of love.

Love and genuine concern for a complete stranger.

With the skill sets that sobriety had taught her, Evelyn had a decision to make. She drew in a deep breath with her eyes closed, exhaled and opened her eyes to look Taryn directly in the eyes.

"I forgive you," she said, reaching her hands to interlock with Taryn's.

Relieved, Taryn trembled as she wept and Evelyn stood up, embracing her.

But Taryn didn't just want forgiveness. She wanted to do more.

After Evelyn and Taryn made amends, they continued to stay in touch, with Taryn eventually moving to Cordele Beach, a town five miles north of Gardenia Beach. She bought a two-bedroom condominium with a corner view, complete with a wraparound porch overlooking the ocean. Being there soothed her soul. Taryn felt triumphant, being able to create a new life for herself not too far from the place where hers had nearly ended—but a renewed sense of purpose had been born.

Three months after Adrienne's attack, Taryn chose to cut the booze out of her life. Maybe not permanently. But she felt it was what was best for her in this new chapter. After her ordeal, she knew life was a gift. And she wanted to embrace it. Taryn also quit smoking, knocking out both bad habits at once.

And Taryn and Lynn, who had stood by her sister's side after that horrible night, gradually began repairing their relationship. At first, Lynn had balked at her sister's decision to permanently relocate to Florida. But after her first visit, Lynn realized she liked having a sister with a beachside condo overlooking the Atlantic.

Without excessive alcohol in the picture, Taryn and Lynn began acting more like the siblings they once had been. Their childhood bond began to seep back into their sisterhood. When Lynn told Taryn one lazy Sunday during a FaceTime call that she was proud of her, they both broke down in sobs. Sadness for the time they lost, but grateful for a second chance to rebuild what they once had. Not just familial ties, but friendship.

As for Evelyn, she had decided the best way she could really make something of her life was to do so completely sober. She had just marked seventeen months of her alcohol-free lifestyle last week. Taryn had come, as had Paul, with little Lucas in tow. All had been so proud of Evelyn's accomplishments.

And Taryn, a maternal instinct seemingly starting to build in her, began spending even more time with Lucas. She loved being with the little boy and would stop by Paul's at least two nights a week to help with dinner and bedtime. Taryn also started having Lucas over for a sleepovers, where the two would wake early to see the sun rise, which mesmerized the little boy day after day. Sunrise never got old for either of them.

One night, after Taryn stopped by Paul's house to help with dinner, she read Lucas *Goodnight Moon*. After she tucked him beneath the sheets and planted a kiss on his tiny forehead, she began to turn the doorknob to exit. Then, Taryn heard his tiny voice.

"Good night, Auntie T," Lucas sleepily whispered. "I lub you."

Taryn's heart somersaulted. "I love you, too, my little butter bean," Taryn said, trying to hide the scratchiness building in her throat.

For a brief moment, Taryn imagined what a privilege it would have been to be Lucas's mom. A privilege Ashley never had the chance to savor. As she backed up to gently close Lucas's bedroom door, Taryn sensed a presence. As she turned around, she saw Paul, leaning against the hallway wall, his arms crossed and head down.

Is he upset? Taryn wondered. *What did I do?*

Paul was far from upset. As Taryn stood to face him, he lifted his face, their eyes uniting.

And that's when Paul uncrossed his arms, brought his hands to Taryn's face and began lovingly kissing her.

***

Things were good. So good.

Yet Taryn wanted to make them even better.

Taryn had felt sickened using the money from Graham's life insurance policy to facilitate her new life. It felt like blood money. It was during one of her afternoon lunches with Evelyn that Taryn had her epiphany.

The two women would grab a bite to eat at least once a week, where Evelyn eagerly soaked up all the details of Taryn's courtship with Paul. By then, the two had been dating for several months, much to Evelyn's delight. Falling for Paul was an unexpected, delightful surprise in this bizarre chain of life events. And playing an even bigger, regular part in Lucas's world was one hell of a bonus.

It was when Evelyn began telling Taryn how she wanted to stay out of the bar and restaurant scene for good—and actually use her bachelor's in social work—that the idea snapped into Taryn's mind.

"Maybe I'll look into grad school," Evelyn mused. "I could probably use a refresher in—"

"We should start a foundation," Taryn excitedly cut in. "Actually, *you* should do it."

Evelyn's immediate reaction was laughter. But when Taryn didn't join in the jubilance, Evelyn knew she was serious.

It took some convincing, but eventually, the two settled on it. Taryn would provide a gift to Evelyn, in the name of starting a nonprofit for sexual assault survivors. Stand with Sam would provide resources, a secure safe house, counseling, a twenty-four seven helpline and even financial support of sexual violence prevention research projects. Evelyn would be the president, with Taryn serving as chief operating officer—there, she'd be more behind the scenes, including taking the helm of the organization's blog. It made Taryn feel like a journalist again. She felt at home. She was herself again, finally. And a voice for the survivors who felt they had nowhere else to turn.

Stand with Sam took off immediately. Despite critics lambasting the nonprofit, arguing its success was due to the sensationalism of the case, Taryn and Evelyn ignored the haters—and considered it a blessing.

The rest was history. Finally.

***

"I have to go to the airport," Evelyn said, interrupting Taryn's thoughts as the two sat at a table outside the auditorium's doors. "I'm due back to Florida tonight. My talk in Jacksonville got bumped up a day. I gotta prepare."

Taryn nodded and sturdied herself to stand up and hug her friend. Paul watched from across the room as Evelyn hugged Taryn, then bent over to kiss her friend's blossoming belly.

"Oh my God!" Evelyn yelped. "She gave me a kick. Or an elbow. I can't tell."

Taryn smiled as she rubbed her six-months-pregnant belly. When she'd told Paul five months ago that she was expecting, he immediately jumped up with a fist pump before scooping her into his arms. A week later, he slipped a velvet navy box containing a stunning oval-cut diamond platinum ring on Lucas's pillow. As Taryn went to put the little boy to bed, Lucas scooped it up and ran toward her.

"Auntie T," Lucas whispered into Taryn's ear, "will you marry me and Daddy?"

Butterflies. So many butterflies. And pure elation.

"I would love nothing more than to be your bonus mommy." Taryn cried joyful tears. "And your daddy's wife."

When they married at the courthouse a month later, the two were joined by only Evelyn, Lucas and Lynn. And when Taryn and Paul learned they were having a baby girl, Taryn knew her name immediately.

Ashley Evelyn.

How perfect. It not only honored the woman who brought Lucas into the world but was a tribute to Evelyn, who loved her late friend, Ashley, so dearly. After all, this whole bizarre journey led to Taryn finding love.

Romantic love with Paul.

Motherly love for Lucas and the little girl she would be able to hold in her arms in a matter of months.

And love for someone who was genuinely now her friend.

Evelyn really was. Their mutual life experience had soldered them together. Even if they didn't spend every moment together, they were inseparable in their hearts.

That's how true friendships worked, after all.

***

"Austin is expecting my visit at Orlando Cognitive Care first thing tomorrow," Evelyn said as she broke apart from hugging Taryn and her pregnant belly. "If he even remembers."

"Tell him I said hello," said Taryn. "I hope he's getting better."

"He's not," Evelyn said, a hint of sadness in her voice. "He'll never be the same, losing his eyesight and dealing with brain damage. Honestly, his mental state is probably for the best, even though he thinks like an eight-year-old. He doesn't remember everything he did. And he's not psychologically fit for trial. But all he can do is move forward. Like the rest of us."

"Like the rest of us," Taryn repeated.

Taryn thought back to her conversation and walk on the beach with Austin before That Night. Given Evelyn's grace, Taryn had also chosen forgiveness for Austin. Not that Austin had any clue who she was and what had transpired. But it brought a sense of serenity to Taryn, lifting that burden.

I guess what you put out there really does come back to you, Taryn thought. *Some of it's good. Some of it's not. But it's what you make of it that matters.*

"Love ya, girl!" Taryn shouted as Evelyn walked closer to the curb to her Uber, tossing her briefcase and purse into the back seat before climbing in.

"See you on the sunny side, hot mama," Evelyn shouted, waving like a queen to Taryn.

"Bye," Taryn mouthed, watching as the car pulled away and swung a left to head toward the expressway.

Finally, it happened.

Taryn felt peace. A peace she hadn't felt in years. Decades, really. And a big part of that peace was Evelyn.

Evelyn was going to be okay. Scratch that.

Evelyn *was* okay. More than okay. She was thriving. And those vibes, Evelyn's good work, reverberated in everything she did.

That was all Taryn ever wanted to know.

And, finally, she did.

A Note from the Author

First off, I just want to say thank you. Thank you for taking a chance on me, a new author. The fact that you're even reading this now means the world to me.

While this is my debut novel, it's something that has ricocheted around in my mind for years. As an avid reader, writer, crime-show binger and newshound, I see reports and depictions of sexual assault all over—and it absolutely sickens me. The news stories throughout the years have flourished in intensity—from college kids assaulting their inebriated peers to the #MeToo movement. As a former journalist, I covered my share of such news stories myself.

I think about situations I put myself in in my younger years and shudder. The dangerous areas I would walk through to get to school, sometimes threading my keys through my fingers, ready to jab an eyeball should someone attempt to attack me. At nineteen, I remember walking past a man as I walked to my college campus in Chicago—who pulled out a pornographic magazine and gestured toward me. I immediately felt sickened. Violated. And that was just some random creepy guy with pictures of naked women. I've found myself cornered, propositioned, had my rear end smacked by a colleague (while off the job), to my complete shock.

Then there was the fellow journalist with some clout who raved about my writing—and offered me an opportunity to help co-write a fictional novel he was certain would get picked up. The catch? I'd have to agree to sleep with him on a regular basis. My reaction? Tears. And I said no. So, there went that shot. But at least not my dignity.

I could go on.

I would find my young self in situations that put me at risk. And most involved alcohol. But I'm proud to share that I am nearly four years into my own alcohol-free journey.

I was one of the lucky ones. So far. I know this danger isn't something that dissipates with age. So, I'm always on the alert for situations that don't sit right with me. I try to trust my gut when something seems off.

All the media around sexual violence buzzed in my brain, making me think even more about these survivors. The mental anguish that ensues after being violated. How selfless they are, putting themselves through absolute hell in their pursuit of justice. The police reports, invasive medical exams and documentation, the online hate that is often thrown their way. And the trial, should they choose to press charges. Just like their attacker, they're put under the microscope. And everything private is now put on public display.

The statistics alone are shocking. According to The Rape, Abuse & Incest National Network (RAINN), on average, someone in the U.S. is sexually assaulted *every sixty-eight seconds*.

That's simply unacceptable.

Which leads me to *Boomerang*. I've sat down many times to write the first few chapters, then thrown them away to start again. In the past year or so, I stopped making excuses. Through various ideations, and shifting scenes several times, it finally started to flow.

Please know this work is purely fiction. A fictional novel based on real-world problems. This is not something I have witnessed or experienced myself. And in no way am I trying to shoehorn a specific persona for any sexual assault survivor. This is a serious matter. I wrote with fierce intensity, trying to put myself in the shoes of each character—whether I liked the that person or not.

Which is why I want to step in here to say something.

The last thing I want is for anyone to feel minimized or traumatized by this novel. That is not my intent.

My intent is to not only tell a gripping story, but to make people really think. Think about how one selfless act can change the course of a person's life, no matter what stage of their journey they're in. The domino effect that follows, affecting their loved ones who ache to fix their pain. And more.

My heart goes out to each and every one of you who has experienced such a traumatic violation. I truly wish I could fix your pain.

My hope? That assault survivors have a voice and the support they need to heal.

If you are a survivor of sexual assault, I encourage you to reach out to someone who can assist, such as RAINN's National Sexual Assault Hotline. You can reach them at 800.656.HOPE or at https://www.rainn.org/.

Just know this. You are not defined by what happened to you. You are a survivor. You are not alone. And you don't need to be.

—S. Jennifer

ACKNOWLEDGEMENTS

Wow. Where do I even begin? After all, it took me a good ten years to mold *Boomerang* into its current format.

So, let's start here.

To my mom and dad, Karen and Ron Paulson: Mom, you have been the unwavering pillar of support in every chapter of my life. From the moment I picked up a pencil and scribbled illustrations of my first deranged story, you didn't bat an eye. You cheered me on instead. Your patience, encouragement, and belief in me never wavered, even during my darkest days. As a former English teacher, you not only nurtured my love of reading and writing, but also helped shape my creativity with each "book" project I dreamt up as a child. Thank you for being my biggest fan, and for supporting me through all the ups and downs in my life.

Dad, your tireless work ethic and your "no guts, no glory" catchphrase have been a big portion of the fuel propelling me forward. Your determination and resilience have shown me that success is earned through hard work, perseverance, and a willingness to take risks. Your example has been a constant reminder that with every obstacle comes an opportunity in disguise. And even when we stumble, it's our choice whether to wallow in self-pity—or trudge on to do something even better than before.

Together, you both have shaped not only my writing journey, but the person I am today. Thank you for being the kind of parents every human deserves. I sure lucked out. And I love you both more than I can ever express.

To my husband and soulmate, Kurt, who has tolerated me being teth-ered to my laptop for ten to twelve hours a day, seven days a week, with my don't-bother-me-headphones: Thank you, my love. You're also my biggest fan (yes, I'm claiming more than one), and I appreciate your patience as I toiled away at this story—the biggest passion project of my entire life. Thank you for handling groceries and dinner when I was too busy — or spinning off my frustrations of the day on my cycling bike. Your patience, kindness and support has helped keep me semi-sane. (And P.S., I love you more.)

To my children, Kristen and Jacob: You are the lights of my life. I can't imagine not being your mom. Thank you for being the generous, loving hearts you are. Thank you for your patience as I spent most of our last Christmas writing, writing and more writing. And thank you for inspiring me to go for my dreams. I've watched you both find your passion. Your thing. And go for it. You both inspired *me* to make the changes in my life I so desperately needed to. And you two have taught me to dream big and try, even when the odds are against me.

Another big shout out goes to the incredibly talented writer, editor, graphic designer and master-of-all-things in book publishing, Chris Kri-dler of Sky Diary Productions. Chris, from the moment I got serious about finally publishing *Boomerang*, you were kind enough to introduce me to the local author community. Without your eagle-eyed edits and brilliant suggestions, this book would have been a fraction of what it now is. Your insight and suggestions made it *so* much better. I thank you for the countless hours of advice, assistance and friendship you've generously given to me. And the cover? You nailed it. Thank you for everything you've done. (And sorry about all the vomiting scenes. Though Lucy Lakestone is free to use those that didn't make *Boomerang's* cut in her Bohemia Bartenders Mysteries book series if she wants.)

Thank you to my decades-long friend, Chuck McClung, for proofing this book and always encouraging me in my career. You're an incredible friend. And thank you to Bobby Ampezzan, who took my wonderful author photos. I am incredibly grateful to you both. Thank you for helping out a middle-aged gal with a decades-long dream.

Thank you also to Florida Star Fiction Writers, an incredible group of Central Florida authors who want nothing more than to see one another succeed. You are all so wonderful. Especially T.J. Logan and Jaimie Engle, for spending time with me, answering my slew of questions and showing me around the writing world. I have learned so much from so many of you. And I am beyond grateful. Having a group of supportive authors who are rooting for one another to succeed is a breath of fresh air. We need more that in this world. (And I am rooting for you all, too.)

To my family and friends who have been so excited for me, thank you. Again, I could cry. (And I have.) A special shout out to my journalism mentor and uncle, Ken Paulson. Uncle Ken, thank you for listening to me and giving me sage, fantastic advice. Our early conversations sparked my interest in journalism and the First Amendment. After one of our talks in my early twenties, I knew I wanted in on the Paulson journalism journey. I have simply been in awe of your incredible success, following your lead in a desire to inform and educate our local communities and, well, the nation. When I was a cub reporter at a biweekly newspaper, I had your journalism bio tacked onto the corkboard in my cubicle. I looked at it every single day, determined I would, too, one day follow your lead and work for a daily newspaper. You've inspired and encouraged me more than you'll ever know.

And, of course, my people. (I am afraid to list names, because I know I'll forget someone—given that always seems to happen when someone in our family submits something like an obituary.) But *you know who you are.* You have encouraged me along the way, whether it started when we met in fifth grade, crossed paths in the journalism world, work, a support group or elsewhere—and just *clicked.* Your kind words, your encouragement about my writing, your willingness to help spread the word about my book means so very much to me. I am forever grateful for your presence in my corner.

Thank you to Tyed's Teahouse in Cocoa, Florida, for letting me be a complete jerk and tap away at my keyboard with my headphones on for the last two years. You have offered people like me a safe space to socialize. You have no idea how much it's helped me. You're all like our second family.

Just know this. If you're mentioned above (or inferred to), I am eternally grateful. I wouldn't be where I am today without any of you. Thank you.

—S. Jennifer

About the Author

S. Jennifer Paulson is a former award-winning journalist for Gannett/The USA TODAY Network, where she wrote under her maiden name, Sara Paulson. A Chicago native and lover of all things storytelling, she earned her Bachelor of Arts in English (Writing) from The University of Illinois at Chicago. She is currently working on her Master of Arts in Mass Communications at the University of Florida. S. Jennifer lives in Rockledge, Florida, with her husband, two kids, rescue dog, Lolita, and an ill-tempered cat named Carole Baskin. *Boomerang* is her first novel.

Stay in the scoop with S. Jennifer! Sign up for exclusive updates, S. Jen's newsletter and other great stuff at sjenniferpaulson.com. Scan the code below for all of S. Jen's social media links.

Milton Keynes UK
Ingram Content Group UK Ltd.
UKHW012152270324
440282UK00013B/88/J

9 798990 172203